Maggie's Mountain Song

An Appalachian Love Story

Sheri Wiggins

Disclaimer

This is a work of fiction. While certain historical events, such as the flood and World War II, are real and the related facts are presented as accurately as possible, the majority of the characters and incidents are products of the author's imagination. Any resemblance to actual persons, living or dead, is purely coincidental.

Dedication

To my Momma, who was my greatest source of encouragement. Now at rest, but looking over my shoulder from heaven, still cheering me on.

Acknowledgment

I want to thank the Lord for His ever-present grace and patience in my life. For inspiration, and His faithful love.

Thank you to my daughter, Kristen, the English major, who gave me advice, and listened to my ideas without yawning.

Thank you to my daughter Kimberly, who gave me lots of encouragement and feedback. and also listened to me when I know I was boring.

Thank you to my friend Janet who was a great sounding board for ideas and helped me think my way through more than one plotline.

And thank you to my sister Rebekah, who has been my biggest fan and cheerleader, prodding me when needed and always encouraging me.

About the Author

Sheri Wiggins is a devoted mother of four and grandmother of seven. She has lived in Appalachia for over thirty years. Her love for the Appalachian region and its history, along with her desire to write, has been her inspiration for this book.

As a child and young teenager, she wrote short stories as gifts for family and friends and was encouraged by her eighth-grade English teacher to pursue writing.

For the last thirty-odd years, she has spent many days enjoying the North Carolina mountains around Boone and Blowing Rock, as well as driving the scenic Blue Ridge Parkway. Like Maggie, the mountains give her strength, rejuvenate her spirit, and inspire her creativity.

Chapter One

Lookin' out over my mountains from old Granddad Spencer's front porch, it's hard to believe that this was once a sparsely settled wilderness, with only a handful of cabins and farmhouses to clutter up the glorious view. Ski and cabin resorts, condos, and houses dot the mountainsides and valley floors where there used to be nothing but green mountains, with the occasional farm holdin' perched high on a ridge or cradled in a cove or valley below. Rich folks and people coming in from everywhere have changed my home place.

I'm not saying all the change has been for the bad. Folks were once a lot poorer than they are now, with tourists bringin' so much money into our town. One thing that has changed, that I don't think is for the good, is that we don't have that same feeling we once had when folks weren't so busy, and neighbors had time to drop in to pass the time of day on the porch. Now everybody's mind is on how they can pinch another dollar outta the tourists who pass through every summer and fall, or they're too interested in their favorite television shows to stop by and sit a spell like they did in times past. Folks just seem to be so busy doing nothing important at all.

I miss those slow-movin' times from my childhood, when our summer days were filled with catchin' crawdaddies and salamanders outta the crick, and makin' witches' brew in Granddad's old black cauldron, or climbin' way up high in the swayin' limbs of the poplar trees that grow thick on our crick bank. The young'uns I see nowadays are sittin' with a video game in their hands, or an iPhone, texting words I can't make out.

I reckon the ones comin' up now will never know the joys of ridin' their bicycles for hours around town and up and down country roads, or swimming in the many cricks and rivers that wind through my mountains. Times are just too dangerous for that now.

I was born and raised just outside of Deep Gap, North Carolina, in Watauga County, up in the northwest corner of the state. It's not a big place now, and it surely wasn't back when I was a young'un growin' up here in my mountains. It's more a collection of small farms and houses spread out around a small community that had a single store called Macpherson's, a schoolhouse, and a post office.

Twelve miles away is the city of Boone, North Carolina, named for Daniel Boone, who used to spend a lot of time in these here parts. It's changed a lot since the days when I was a young girl. We would make the trip with Mamma and Daddy into Boone about once a month or so. Boone used to be, and still is, the largest town in these parts, but it was a lot smaller and a lot different back in the thirties and forties. There were no paved roads back then; every road was a dirt road. Nowadays Boone's roads are all pavement, and it has more eatin' places than a body could imagine, with shops and one of them big schools called Appalachian State University.

The Appalachian Mountains: I call My Mountains, are practically blood in my soul. I couldn't live without them. They are granddaddy mountains, not new mountains like the Rockies or even those biggest mountains in the world over across the ocean. My mountains are old and wise, like Granddad Spencer. Seems like I was told by someone they might be the oldest mountains in the world. I believe that.

I would climb the old Indian trail the Cherokee made long before any of us white people came. Far above our house it winds in and out of coves and wanders over ridges and passes by my own personal spot. My spot is a slab of rock that juts out from the mountainside and hangs over the steep plunge to the valley far below. I would often sit and watch birds a flyin' beneath me and look into treetops far below my feet a-danglin' over the rocky edge of my perch. It looks to the east, where I could see mountains behind mountains, behind yet more mountains, all in various shades of blue and purple.

When I would climb to my spot in the spring of the year, I would feel like I'd been resurrected from a kind of death along with the trees and bushes. The Mountain Laurel is green all year, but it takes on a prettier, brighter green in the spring. Hard little knobs start forming at the ends of the branches, bursting into the most beautiful and delicate pink clusters of blushing blossoms humans ever clapped eyes on in June.

When I would climb to my spot in the summertime, I would soak up the soft breezes that blow the wondrous smells of summer over me while I lay on the slab of rock that overlooks the valleys below. The distant mountains would take on shades of blue and purple that somehow didn't look quite real, like a painting I once saw in a shop in town. The smells of little grass seeds bakin' in the sun, of warm dirt, and of all the different wildflowers combined made up the lazy, comfortin' smells of summer.

When I would go to my spot in the fall, it was glorious. I don't know any other word to tell you how it is. I know a lot of people don't care for fall, seein' as how it's a sure sign winter is comin'. A lot of folks dread winter so badly they can't seem to enjoy the most wondrous season of all. The smells of fall are truly a mixture of so many different things I don't think I could even list them all here, and you wouldn't want to hear it all. But the air smells different in the fall. It isn't as heavy as those humid scents of summer; it's crisp and sharp. There's the smell of leaves burnin', and leaves decayin' as they pile up.

Nowadays folks bag their leaves or rake them to the curb, and the town picks them up. But back then, everyone burned their leaves raked up from the yard. It gives the air another smell all its own, because it don't smell like wood smoke; it's leaves burnin'. It's different.

The mountainsides and valleys are ablaze with every shade of red, burgundy, gold, and green you could imagine. There are a lot of hardwood trees like Maple and Oak that seem to almost catch fire with color, one last colorful wild party before undressin' for winter. Intermingled with them are Hemlock, Fir, and Cedar trees that stay green year-round.

Granddad Spencer had a big wooden cider press, and nearly all of the families I knew had at least one apple tree, sometimes several. The womenfolk would make apple butter simmerin' over a fire, or apple sauce sometimes referred to as sas. But I especially loved it when neighbors would bring over their bruised or leftover apples, and Granddad would press their cider for them. Sometimes, if it was a lot of apples, folks would either pay him a little cash if they had it, but most often they just paid him in apples or let him have some of the fresh-squeezed apple cider. Granddad always set aside a little bit of the cider to let go to hard cider. It was sipped on by the adults in the family at Christmas, New Year's, or other special occasions.

Gardens and fields were harvested in the fall. It was a time of plenty, a time when the womenfolk were preservin' the abundance God had graced us with. My Mamma and Granny Spencer would work together, and sometimes aunts and cousins would come, and we would make a party out of the workload. My cousins, younger brothers Gerry and Charlie, and myself would pick our half-runner beans, string and snap them on Granny Spencer's front porch. Mamma and Granny Spencer would have two cookers goin' full speed, workin' for weeks on end canning jars upon jars of half-runner beans, tomatoes, pickled beets, and so many other homegrown vegetables.

Mamma made a couple hundred pints of relish called chow chow, to sell in the farm's produce stand out on the highway during the tourist season. Daddy kept bees, and over the years his hives grew to such a point that at the peak of his beekeeping years, he harvested nearly a hundred gallons of honey a year. Most of that was sold to local people and tourists in our produce stand we called Spencer Farms Produce. We sold all kinds of fresh vegetables: several varieties of tomatoes, pole beans, purple-hulled peas, sweet corn, potatoes, orangey-colored sweet potatoes, plump purple beets, and globe-shaped turnips. We also sometimes had mustard, turnip, and collard greens, and in the fall apples, pears, and even persimmons.

Mamma and Granny Spencer canned enough for our families and some for the Spencer Farms Produce stand. Tourists loved to take home a real bit of Appalachia. If Mamma's hens were layin' good and eggs were abundant, we even offered fresh farm eggs on the shelves at Spencer Farms Produce.

After the field corn was harvested for feed for the cattle and horses, we always had a corn shuckin' party and barn dance. This was always my favorite part of the harvest season. Contests were held amongst the fellas to see who could shuck the most corn in a certain amount of time. The winner always got first dibs on his partner for the opening dance.

Spencer Farm barn dances were always a local favorite, and Mamma and Granny always saw to it that the barn was decorated as festive as they could manage. The best fiddlers, banjo, and guitar pickers in the area made sure they penciled in the date on their calendar for the Spencer Farm barn dance. Our dances had the best and most lively music for miles around, and jigs, reels, waltzes, and cloggin' went on for the better part of the night.

Granddad Spencer had only one rule he enforced strictly at our barn dances: no moonshine, no likker at all. Not even the hard cider he made for Christmas was allowed. Too many fights had sprung up when the fellas would mix likker and parties.

I didn't go to my spot nearly as often in the winter months. I guess it don't take a real smart person to know why. Winter in my mountains can be really hard. Even on a sunny day, the wind can feel like my daddy's huntin' knife, cuttin' right through like it was tryin' to separate your body from your soul.

But once in a while, there would be days when the winter weather would break and the sun would warm the air and try to fool you into thinkin' maybe spring would be early this year. Usually that's all it was, a nice break from the cold that would creep through any crack it could find, and the wind that would nearly tear your clothes off.

It was still beautiful, and it was still my favorite spot, even though the trees looked exposed and embarrassed at their stark nakedness. But I knew winter would pass shortly, and the poor nude trees would soon be clothed in their beautiful dresses of every shade of green you could imagine. I've always heard Ireland is green, forty shades of green. I've never been there, but I can't imagine anything greener than my mountains in the spring.

Chapter Two

But I forgot to tell you who I am. My name is Margaret Faith Spencer Bruce, but my family and friends call me Maggie. I am now ninety-two years old. That sounds old, but the years have flown by so fast it's hard to take in that I am an old woman now. I wasn't always so old.

My Mamma was Dottie Nelms, and my Daddy was Edward Spencer. Mamma had a different heritage than a lot of us here in my mountains. Her daddy's people were originally English, which makes it funny to me that the English and the Scottish finally got together peaceably. Most of us here in my mountains were descended from Scottish folks who came to this country to escape persecution from the English.

Mamma was born to Presley and Geroline Nelms. Nelms is an English name that means one from the elms. I always have vague thoughts of some far-off English ancestors sittin' under their elm trees sippin' English tea.

My Poppy, Presley Nelms's people, had settled in the northern end of Virginia's Shenandoah Valley soon after the Revolution. I got to go there once, and it's a beautiful place to be sure. A wide, green, hilly valley with the Blue Ridge Mountains in the distance to the east and the Allegheny Mountains on its western side. It's a beautiful sight that I'll never forget.

Poppy left his home in the Shenandoah when he was nineteen and went west to work on a cattle ranch. I remember Poppy tellin' us young'uns cowboy stories when we were small. Those stories stretched from Texas to Montana, and after that clear out to California. Then he finally come to settle down to be foreman on a ranch in Oklahoma.

That's where he met Nana, in a little town called Shawnee. Nana's name was Geroline Carter, and she was what was back then known as a half-breed, meanin' she was half Cherokee. Nana's daddy's people were Cherokee and had come over the Trail of Tears from the mountains of North Carolina and had been put up on government land in Oklahoma called a reservation. Nana told us many stories that were mostly sad about how our government had treated the Cherokee.

I only saw Poppy and Nana twice in my life. Both times were when they traveled by train back to North Carolina to visit their only daughter and grandchildren. But the memories I have of them, and Nana and Poppy's stories, have lasted me a lifetime.

Poppy and Nana had one child, Dorothy LaVerne Nelms. A fancy name to hear, but she was just known to her family as Dottie. Mamma was one of the most beautiful women I have ever seen. She's gone on now of course, but I have an old picture taken of her just before she was married to Daddy, and she was a real beauty. No wonder Daddy lost his wits when he saw her. And here's how it happened.

While living in Shawnee, Oklahoma, Mamma had met Poppy's brother and his wife, her Uncle William and Aunt Esther Nelms, who still lived on the family farm just outside of Winchester, Virginia, in the Shenandoah Valley. They traveled by train out west to visit Poppy and Nana and stayed a month, forming a close bond with Dottie, their niece. When they went home, Mamma and Aunt Esther wrote letters to each other monthly, never missin' a time. Mamma said she was nine years old when she began her correspondence with Aunt Esther.

When Mamma turned eighteen, Poppy and Nana surprised her with a birthday gift she never expected: a train ticket to Winchester, Virginia, to spend a month with the aunt and uncle she had missed every day for ten years.

Aunt Esther and Uncle William had a large farm and did very well for themselves. They planned a large social in Mamma's honor, a barn dance. Mamma said she was so nervous she didn't know if she would be able to face all the strange faces of people she had never met. A lot of folks back in them days had a lot of prejudice toward anyone who had any noticeable Indian blood.

Mamma had beautiful creamy skin. It wasn't dark at all, but she had high Cherokee cheekbones and full lips under beautiful blue eyes. She needn't have worried. The fellas swarmed around her like they were bees, and she was a honey pot. Truth to tell, she wasn't used to that kind of attention.

That's how Daddy first saw her. Daddy was at the dance because, by chance, he was visitin' Spencer cousins who lived just outside of Winchester and was included in the invitation to the barn dance. Daddy loved to tell about how he first saw his little honey pot. That's what he called her sometimes, just to tease her about all the fellas he had to wade through just to get a dance with her.

Mamma had never seen hair like Daddy's before. Most Spencers have red hair, at least our line of Spencers do, and Daddy's hair was deep auburn red and wavy. Daddy actually walked up to Mamma and said, "Hey Honey Pot, my name is Ed Spencer. Can I take you for a spin around the floor?"

When I would hear that story, I always blushed for Mamma. I thought I would die if a strange boy came up and said that to me. But Mamma always smiled a little smile when Daddy told the story, so I knew it was a good memory for her.

Mamma and Daddy were married a year later, June 1, 1922. Mamma was nineteen, and Daddy was twenty-one. Daddy brought Mamma back home to begin a family of their own here on the Spencer Farm in my mountains. I was their firstborn and was born April 17, 1924.

My Daddy's daddy was the Granddad Spencer, or Alistair Spencer, you've already heard me tell of. Daddy's mamma was Martha Anne MacMann before she married Granddad, and we called her Granny. Nearly everyone around our parts called her Granny Spencer, even if she wasn't really their Granny. She was just the type of woman who would tuck a stranger up under her wing and be their Granny, even if it was just for the time they needed her.

Granddad and Granny's story isn't nearly as excitin' or interestin' I guess as Mamma and Daddy's, because they had grown up on the same mountain and had known each other since they were just babes. They had a bit of a bump during the First World War. Granddad was drafted for war, but when he went for his medical check, they sent him home.

Granddad was told he had a heart murmur, and the army decided he was a reject. Granny was so relieved. She had prayed and prayed that Granddad would be spared. He lived to be a ripe old age, and he did pass on with heart problems that he tried to ignore. But at least it wasn't a German bullet that took him, or else I wouldn't be here tellin' this here account of our lives.

Granddad and Granny were church-going people. Now I say this because Mamma and Daddy weren't, at least not in my younger childhood. They weren't bad people. Daddy didn't run around on his wife, and he didn't drink or beat any of us. In fact, my Daddy was a good husband and the best daddy there was. Mamma was a good wife and a loving mamma to us young'uns, but I wasn't raised on a church bench. We were taught it was wrong to lie, cheat, and steal, and pretty much the golden rule: do unto others as you would have them do unto you. But I wasn't taught about Jesus or the Bible from my parents. That came mostly from Granddad and Granny Spencer.

Granddad and Granny never gave up praying for Daddy and Mamma's souls, and they always believed they would one day surrender to Jesus and live for Him. Back then I didn't really understand what the big deal was. Mamma and Daddy were good people.

Granddad and Granny were what people refer to now as Old-Time Baptists. When I was a young'un, I used to go to brush arbor camp meetings with them. People came in cars, trucks, and wagons from miles around to have camp meetings. Sometimes there were about three arbors set up, and all three were going with preachin' off and on all day and half the night. Singin' would go on for hours, and the people would get so happy they would jump and shout and about beat their poor old tambourines near to death.

People set up camp all over the place in tents, in the back of trucks and wagons, even in cars. Back then I didn't appreciate what was going on. I mostly enjoyed the excitement of a large crowd of people, lots of other kids to play with, and picnics on the ground. There was one rich lady who brought in casks full of real fresh-squeezed lemonade. That was a treat I never forgot, and I've never had lemonade to this day that tasted better.

Granddad Spencer was the great-grandson of Scottish emigrants who came to this country from Ulster, Ireland. Actually, there would be several "greats" in there. I'm not real sure just how many, but the main thing is, our people were Scottish. A lot of folks call us Scotch-Irish, which isn't the right term. Scotch is a drink. Scots-Irish is the right way to say it, and here's how it happened that Scots who came to America came to be called Scots-Irish.

King James I of England was himself a Scot, so was very interested in Scottish affairs. As England had control over Ireland as well as Scotland, the English government had a hard time dealing with the unruly and disorderly Irish. In the early 1600s, with the hope of establishing a more loyal Protestant group of people in Ulster, which is a northern region of Ireland, King James founded what was called the Plantation.

The Plantations were settlements of lowland Scots who were loyal to the English crown. Those who lived there were not the rich noblemen, but tenant farmers and laborers. The Ulster Plantations were owned by landlords, their lowland Scottish lairds who lived in Scotland, but who recruited settlers to farm these plantations. Many of these lairds had been given large amounts of Ulster land by the English crown. The Scottish farmer-settlers went to Ulster looking for a better life but were disappointed by how things really were.

Most Irish were Catholic, and most of the Scots were strict Presbyterians, and they never did blend too well. There was a lot of bloody fighting and feuding going on between them. Catholics and Protestants did a heap of fighting in those days.

The Irish in Ulster felt that the English government was sendin' Scotland's lower-order riffraff and thieves, not the farmers they claimed they sent. In the 1640s, there began to be uprisings of the native Irish against the plantation Scots, which caused the English army to come into the area to make sure it was farmers, and not convicts being emptied into Ireland.

The last of the large emigrations from Scotland to Ulster was over by the end of the 1600s, when the lowlands of Scotland went through a major famine, forcing many Scots to join the Ulster Plantations or starve. The Scottish Ulster Plantations lasted into the early 1700s, with some families having been in Ulster for three or more generations.

Even though it was the English who sent the Scots to Ulster, those English folks never did think much of the Scottish or the Irish, and it seems like our history is full of one fight or another with them.

The Anglican Church was the ruling church in England, and the majority of the Ulster Scots were Presbyterian. There was resentment towards the Anglican Church because of penal laws made by the English government that protected the official church and punished those who were not a part of it. The laws kept everyone but Anglicans from having positions in the government.

Landlords also discovered there was more money to be made by raising sheep and cattle. Rack-renting was a trick used by some landlords to purposely force their tenant farmers off the land, makin' room for sheep and cattle grazing. Landlords would drive up their rents by renting the land to the highest bidders.

The hardship rack-renting caused was made even worse by the downturn in the Irish linen business. The chance for the suffering plantation farm families to earn extra money with spinnin' and weaving linen nearly came to an end.

The pull to find a land of freedom was strong. America had no emigration or religious hindrance. Most of the Ulster Scots were Protestants, Presbyterians, and it was the main religion of America at that time. Merchant ships sailed often, and emigrants were counted as westbound cargo. And so, they came to America's shores looking for freedom from unjust English laws, freedom of religion, and land. They were not Irish, not Scotch-Irish, but Scots who lived in and immigrated from Ireland.

I'm getting old now, the story of the people we came from and how we came to my mountains is getting lost to the younger folks. Seems like to me, with the influence of television and the internet, all folks have become so blended that what made us different from other people has melted away like spring snow. It used to be more common to hear the sound of the pipes floating out over my mountain ridges and valleys, and stories of Scotland used to be told to the children generation after generation.

Family groups were still called clans back in Granddad's childhood, and many of the phrases and words we use here in my mountains, some folks just think is bad English. But it's the leftovers of a way of speakin' my Scottish ancestors brought with them over the water when they came to this country, and I don't want to see it completely lost.

Some folks think that it's a good thing, all this blending, and maybe it is. I don't pretend to know everything. But I aim to make sure my children, and my grandbabies know who they are, where their people came from, and what made them leave the old countries and come to my mountains in America.

Chapter Three

I'm a going to start with me, Maggie, I was born Margaret Faith Spencer on April 17, 1924. This is the story, as I remember it, of my childhood and my sweetheart, the handsome lad Robert Alexander Bruce. Robbie was just about a week shy of two years older than I, born April 23, 1922.

Robbie's people were Scottish emigrants too, and I have heard him tell of his people comin' from Aberdeenshire in the northern parts of Scotland. John Bruce came with his wife Sarah about 1736 and settled in the northern end of the beautiful Shenandoah Valley.

There's a little settlement just north of Winchester, Virginia, called Brucetown. There's nothin' much there now, just a few buildin's and a church, but that is where Robbie's people first settled when they left Scotland and came to America. Down through the years, descendants from John Bruce migrated to North Carolina, Indiana, Kentucky, and beyond.

Robbie and I had known each other all our lives. Growin' up together here around Deep Gap, we played and fought all through our childhood. My Mamma and Daddy were close friends, best friends, with Robbie's mamma and daddy, Claire and Johnny Bruce.

Our daddies hunted and fished together since childhood and helped each other with farm chores too large for a man to handle on his own. Makin' hay, barn and house repairs, and advice on new farmin' ideas were shared between them, and their friendship was solid and secure.

Robbie's mamma, Claire, had reached out to my Mamma when she came to Spencer Farm as a new bride, and helped her adjust to a totally new way of life. Mamma was a westerner, and life in these mountains was new and different to her. She had lived on a cattle ranch, daughter to the ranch foreman and a half Cherokee. Life on an Appalachian Mountain farm couldn't have been more different. Claire and Granny Spencer taught Mamma all the traditions and passed down customs of our way of life here in my mountains.

Claire and Johnny already had two children, their firstborn, a daughter named Janet, and a newborn son named Robert, or Robbie. Mamma loved children, and she and Robbie's mamma, Claire, grew close as sisters in no time at all.

So, the friendship between both families' children, I guess, was just a predestined fact. Robbie was a two-year-old toddler when I was born in 1924, and I have heard all my life how Robbie appointed himself my protector and buddy, a brother without bein' blood kin. He was there when I learned to walk and taught me words my Mamma had to wash out with a bar of Ivory Soap. He picked flowers with me and taught me how to make flower chains, from which we fashioned necklaces and bracelets and even wrapped them around our heads and pretended to be fairies from the old stories we loved to hear told.

Robbie called his mamma Ma, and so I called her Ma too. He called his daddy Papa, so I called him Papa too. Robbie half lived at my house, and I half lived at his, and for the first ten years of my life we were nearly inseparable.

From Robbie I learned, at a young age, which tracks we would see in the dirt every mornin' belonged to which animals. The long slender print, fuller and rounder at the rear and curving into delicate points at the front, belonged to the shy White-Tailed Deer. The tiny, slender, almost human-lookin' paw prints belonged to the bandit of the mountains, the Ring-Tailed Raccoon. At six years of age, I could identify any animal's print that roamed in my mountains.

I knew every bird and its habits. I knew which ones were waterbirds living around the cricks, rivers, and lakes in my mountains, like the Great Blue Heron, Mallard, and Wood Ducks. In the spring, when the farmers were plowing the gardens and fields, Sea Gulls came all the way from the coast to gobble up the worms, grubs, and bug larvae brought to the surface by the plows.

I knew which birds were predators, like the Red-Tailed Hawk, the Northern Goshawk, Screech Owls, Barn Owls, the Great Horned Owl, and the Snowy Owl. There were also the majestic Golden and Bald Eagles, who were rare but occasionally seen soaring high above the mountain tops. Robbie and I once saw a pair of Bald Eagles perched high in the top of a huge Eastern Hemlock tree.

I knew which birds were good for eatin' and therefore hunted in our parts: Turkeys, Ruffed Grouse, and Doves. Woodpeckers were a treat to stalk and watch. Huge Pileated Woodpeckers and the smaller Red-Headed Woodpecker could be heard hammering away at trees, searching for invading insects.

Blue Jays, sportin' their bright blue crests, backs, and tails with white bellies trimmed in black, and bright red Cardinals were the bully boys of the bird world and often chased less aggressive birds away from their food. Red-Breasted Robins, Sparrows, Chickadees, Yellow Goldfinches, and Mockingbirds were familiar and welcomed.

But it is the songbirds I love the most: Golden-Winged Warblers, Chestnut-Sided Warblers, Bobwhites, and Whip-poor-wills, and of course the quiet cooing of Mourning Doves.

I was at home roaming the mountain trail, trotting along behind Robbie, learnin' which bird was makin' that noise, which animal belonged to that paw print, which plant was good to eat, and which ones were better off avoided and given a wide walk around.

I learned a skunk is a feared animal, but if you didn't bother him, most likely he wouldn't bother you. Robbie and I once saw a young black bear that hadn't learned that important lesson early enough. The bear had apparently badgered a skunk bad enough that he had received a blast of oily, odorous skunk spray right into his face. The poor bear's eyes were swollen nearly shut, and he was rubbing his face on the ground, on the sides of trees, and on bushes—just about anywhere he could think of to get rid of that skunk spray. He was makin' the most awful sounds. I didn't know a bear could moan and cry, but he sure was. It was a pitiful sight.

***

Granddad Spencer was the most wondrous storyteller I ever did hear spin out a tale. There are a lot of folks in my mountains who are pretty good at spinnin' tales, mostly just for the fun and amusement of others. But Granddad could tell a tale that left you unsure if it was the gospel truth or an amusin' yarn.

Some of the stories Granddad loved to tell were stories he had heard since his childhood, old Indian folk tales. I loved to hear Granddad tell Indian tales of Fox, Coyote, and Bear. Mamma, bein' a quarter Cherokee, loved to hear the stories handed down from generation to generation among her people. Her mother, my Nana, had told her the same stories as a young'un, and Nana's Cherokee mother had told them to her.

Christmas time, when the old Spencer farmhouse was overfilled with Spencer cousins, was when Granddad was at his best. I'm sure Granny, Mamma, and my aunts, busy with preparin' Christmas food, were more than happy for Granddad to take us rambunctious Spencer young'uns in hand and quiet us down a bit. Granddad tellin' a story was a sure-fire way to do that. The tale of *How Bear Lost His Tail* was my favorite, and I pestered Granddad into tellin' us young'uns the tale. Granddad gathered us around him beside the fireplace in the Spencer Farm living room and began.

"Back in the old days, Bear had a tail which was his proudest possession. It was long and black and glossy, and Bear used to wave it around just so that people would look at it. Fox saw this. Fox, as everyone knows, is a trickster and likes nothin' better than fooling others. So it was that he decided to play a trick on Bear."

"It was the time of year when Hatho, the Spirit of Frost, had swept across the land, covering the lakes with ice and pounding on the trees with his big hammer. Fox made a hole in the ice, right near a place where Bear liked to walk. By the time Bear came by, all around Fox, in a big circle, were big trout and fat perch. Just as Bear was about to ask Fox what he was doin', Fox twitched his tail, which he had stickin' through that hole in the ice, and pulled out a huge trout."

"Greetings, Brother," said Fox. "How are you this fine day?"

"Greetings," answered Bear, lookin' at the big circle of fat fish. "I am well, Brother. But what are you doin'?"

"I am fishin'," answered Fox. "Would you like to try?"

"Oh, yes," said Bear, as he started to lumber over to Fox's fishin' hole.

But Fox stopped him. "Wait, Brother," he said. "This place will not be good. As you can see, I have already caught all the fish. Let us make you a new fishin' spot where you can catch many big trout."

"Bear agreed, and so he followed Fox to the new place, a place where, as Fox knew very well, the lake was too shallow to catch the winter fish, which always stay in the deepest water when Hatho has covered their ponds. Bear watched as Fox made the hole in the ice, already tastin' the fine fish, he would soon catch."

"Now," Fox said, "you must do just as I tell you. Clear your mind of all thoughts of fish. Do not even think of a song, or the fish will hear you. Turn your back to the hole and place your tail inside it. Soon a fish will come and grab your tail and you can pull him out."

"But how will I know if a fish has grabbed my tail if my back is turned?" asked Bear.

"I will hide over here where the fish cannot see me," said Fox. "When a fish grabs your tail, I will shout. Then you must pull as hard as you can to catch your fish. But you must be very patient. Do not move at all until I tell you."

Bear nodded. "I will do exactly as you say." He sat down next to the hole, placed his long, beautiful black tail in the icy water, and turned his back.

Fox watched for a time to make sure that Bear was doin' as he was told and then, very quietly, sneaked back to his own house and went to bed. The next mornin' he woke up and thought of Bear. "I wonder if he is still there," Fox said to himself. "I'll just go and check."

So, Fox went back to the ice-covered pond, and what do you think he saw? He saw what looked like a little white hill in the middle of the ice. It had snowed during the night and covered Bear, who had fallen asleep while waitin' for Fox to tell him to pull his tail and catch a fish. And Bear was snorin'. His snores were so loud that the ice was shakin'. It was so funny that Fox rolled with laughter. But when he was through laughin', he decided the time had come to wake up poor Bear. He crept very close to Bear's ear, took a deep breath, and then shouted: "Now, Bear!"

Bear woke up with a start and pulled his long tail hard as he could. But his tail had been caught in the ice, which had frozen over during the night, and as he pulled, it broke off. Whack! Just like that. Bear turned around to look at the fish he had caught and instead saw his long, lovely tail caught in the ice.

"Ohhh," he moaned. "Ohhh, Fox. I will get you for this." But Fox, even though he was laughin' fit to kill, was still faster than Bear, and he leaped aside and was gone.

"So it is that even to this day Bears have short tails and no love at all for Fox. And if you ever hear a bear moanin', it is probably because he remembers the trick Fox played on him long ago, and he is mournin' for his lost tail."

Every Christmas Granddad would tell story after story, some crazy yarns that were silly and had us young'uns rollin' on the farmhouse floor with laughter. Some of his stories were old Indian folk tales, like *How Bear Lost His Tail*. Some were about when he was a young'un, in the years after the War Between the States. He would tell us stories about his daddy, Malcolm Spencer, and his Granddad that he was named for, my great-great-granddad Alistair Spencer, who was killed at Vicksburg, Mississippi, while it was under siege during the War Between the States. The stories that pulled on my soul were the true stories of loss and despair, stories of my ancestors who first left Scotland, then Ireland, so many years ago. And the wild stories about battles like Culloden and Bannockburn, and heroes of old back in Scotland

Chapter Four

In the fall of 1930, after I turned six in April, I started grammar school in Deep Gap. The schoolhouse was the newest building in the community; the state of North Carolina had provided the funds to build a two-level building. Grades one through five were on the first level, and grades six through twelve on the second. The outside was deep red brick, with a wide covered porch across the front. It was trimmed around the windows and doors in white, with white columns holdin' up the roof of the porch, and a white bell tower on top. It was without any doubt the most beautiful building I had ever seen.

Schooling was still seen as a privilege when I was a young'un, not especially a right, and I loved learning of any kind, so I loved going to school. Spencer Farm was almost a mile from the heart of Deep Gap where the schoolhouse sat, so it was a pleasant walk to and from school every day that the weather was good. When it wasn't, it was not so pleasant. Cold rain and wind could suck every scrap of warmth your body made right out of you and leave you feelin' frozen clear through, even when the temperature of the air wasn't that bad. And in the winter, storms could move in with a swiftness that could be dangerous and scary.

Miss Teague was the young and pretty new teacher for grades one through five at the Deep Gap School. She was smart as well as pretty, kindhearted, and especially friendly to the five newest members of the school, and I loved her. Miss Teague was impressed with my overflowing knowledge of anything concerning the birds, critters, and plant life in my mountains, and often called on me to spout off what I knew about birds that were a-callin' outside the schoolhouse window.

That first winter I was at the Deep Gap School, we had an uncommonly harsh winter. One late January afternoon, while us first-year students were huddled together writin' our alphabet, a sudden blast of wind hit the schoolhouse with a howl that brought everyone's heads up out of their books. Lookin' out the window on the side of the school, we could see dark gray clouds traveling at high speed across the sky.

Miss Teague asked Robbie and Johnny Bailey, who were third-year students, to step out on the porch to take a wider view of the sky and see how widespread the dark clouds were. Robbie and Johnny came back in pretty quick with wide eyes.

"Ma'am, I've never seen dark clouds move this fast," said Robbie, "and it's startin' to snow right now."

Robbie was an outdoorsman, and I knew if he was worried, there was something to worry about.

"Children, get your coats and hats on quick. We're going home before this storm gets bad," said Miss Teague, her eyebrows pulled down in the middle with an anxious frown.

All us young'uns responded immediately. This was an unexpected but welcome break from school. We sprang into action, haulin' on our coats and pulling caps down around our ears. Miss Teague moved quickly from child to child, making sure each one of us was properly bundled warmly into our winter outer clothing before sending us home.

Mr. Jenkins, a youngish man I thought to be old, but who was actually in his early thirties, taught the upper grades on the second level of the Deep Gap School. Mr. Jenkins had come to Deep Gap from Harrisburg, Pennsylvania, to teach school, and the young'uns would whisper to each other about his "funny talk." He had come down to confer with Miss Teague while she was inspecting our bundling-up job, and he had agreed that sending all students home right away was the proper course of action.

About half of the students lived right in Deep Gap: the Greene's, Roberts, Keiths, Tillie Macpherson, and the Mitchells, so their journey home should go without a hitch. But the other half of us lived varying distances out in all directions. Robbie's family lived about halfway between Deep Gap and the Spencer farm, and Spencer Farm, as I said, was almost a mile east from the schoolhouse. There were others, like Lonnie and Jenny McKemmy, who lived another mile further east beyond Spencer Farm. Others, like the five Bailey young'uns, the Shaws, and the Frasiers, all lived west and north of Deep Gap. There were not enough adults to escort all the young'uns home through the coming storm.

Just as Mr. Jenkins and Miss Teague were discussing their dilemma, the winter storm hit full force. The snow was not only falling too thick to see through, the howling wind was blowing it sideways. There was no going home now. Even the students who lived right in Deep Gap couldn't see their houses, not even the Post Office across the street, or the church right beside the school.

Fortunately, the coal bin at the back of the schoolhouse that fed the coal furnace in the basement had been filled to the brim by the state back in December. There was plenty of coal to keep us warm for weeks if needed. What we didn't have much of was food. The only food in the building was whatever students and teachers had brought for dinner that day and didn't eat, which wasn't much. I was always hungry, and so I always ate every scrap Mamma packed for me. Most everyone else did the same.

I wasn't usually the worrying sort, but I did start to fret over what would happen if Mamma or Daddy got worried and come a lookin' for me. It was too dangerous for anyone to try to get anywhere.

At home on Spencer Farm, there was Mamma's clothesline that ran from the back corner of the farmhouse to the back corner of Daddy's barn. It was very long for a clothesline. We sure didn't have enough clothes every week on wash day to fill the line, but Daddy had strung it that long to have a guide to the barn if and when necessary. There were stories we had all heard of men who started out for their barn to feed livestock, missed seeing their barn in the midst of a storm, and were lost and never seen again. At least that's how some of the stories went. At least I knew Daddy wouldn't get lost tryin' to feed our critters.

But here in the Deep Gap community, nobody had taken that precaution. I guess everyone figured the buildings were all close enough together and guidelines weren't necessary. Miss Teague and Mr. Jenkins had us all check our dinner bags or boxes to see how much food was present in the school. There was so little, mostly just a leftover bit of bread and butter, a few apples and pears, and Jimmy Johnston's piece of dried apple pie he was saving for his walk home.

We were going to starve. I figured the storm would last three weeks, and Mamma and Daddy would lie on the floor beside my shriveled-up skeleton and weep in anguish for me, their poor starved child. Or something like that. I had a pretty good imagination. But as I live and breathe, we were in a fix.

Miss Teague remembered there was a box of leftover Christmas candy in the bottom drawer of her desk, and there was enough for all fifty-two students to have two pieces of filled candy and one red and white striped candy cane apiece. Miss Teague said she did not care for any, and Mr. Jenkins said he did not really like candy, so that allowed for the even dispersal of every piece of candy. Those who had leftover crumbs or fragments from dinner ate them for supper, and Jimmy Johnston shared his generously sliced pie with as many as possible. That meant about ten different young'uns had a bite of that pie.

The water faucets in the restroom and the drinking fountain just inside the front door stopped working as soon as the sun's light, which had been faintly shining somewhere beyond the storm clouds, was extinguished. The faint light had offered just enough to make out daytime hours from night. As soon as total darkness fell, the outside temperature dropped to negative five degrees, and every water pipe bringin' fresh water to the schoolhouse froze up. It seemed like just knowin' the water was out made me thirstier than ever.

Mr. Jenkins scooped up two galvanized buckets, filled them with fresh fallen snow from the edge of the schoolhouse front porch, and set them to melt on the coal furnace in the basement. It did not take long to have drinking water again. Thank goodness for Mr. Jenkins' buckets. He kept two galvanized water buckets for toting water to the upstairs restroom, since at times the second-level toilet's water pipe did not have enough pressure to fill the tank above the toilet.

Since electric service was sometimes on and sometimes off depending on the weather, the school was equipped with several kerosene lamps for emergencies such as this. So, all fifty-two students and both teachers spread our coats on the lower-level floor of the schoolhouse and prepared to settle in and try to sleep for the night. As we settled in, there was a sniff or two from a couple of the younger students who were havin' a hard time holdin' in their tears. Everyone wanted their own mamma and daddy. I know I did.

The kerosene lamps cast a warm, low light over the room, and Mr. Jenkins stood to his feet, softly cleared his throat, and began to talk to all of us fixing to bed down for the night.

"Children, I know some of you are scared, and you're worried about your families at home." He let his eyes travel over each of us gathered in small groups on the floor. "I do not know how long we will have to stay here, and I don't know what we will eat for breakfast in the morning, but I do know who we can go to, to ask for help with our fears and our needs."

This was comforting talk, and it reminded me of Granddad Spencer and what he would always do when faced with worries and problems he couldn't fix.

"Let's pray. Our Heavenly Father loves us even more than our earthly fathers do, so I know He does not want us crying and scared, and He would want us to have breakfast in the morning."

Everyone nodded. Divine help from the Almighty sounded very good right now. We were warm and dry, and we were thankful for that, but we were all hungry. The crumbs and candy we ate four hours ago were long gone from our aching stomachs, and melted snow water wasn't very satisfying.

"Father, we come to You tonight with thanksgiving in our hearts for the safety of this sturdy schoolhouse for shelter. Thank You for plenty of coal, so we need not worry that we will freeze. Thank You for friends, so we need not be alone and scared, for we have each other. Most of all, we thank You for Your love. For since we know You love us, we know You are with us, and every fear we feel is just a fear, not a reality."

As Mr. Jenkins prayed, every sniff stopped, and every tear dried up. I felt comforted and safe. Nothing had changed, except fear was gone. It felt good. Mr. Jenkins was about to continue his prayer when we suddenly heard something. At first, I wasn't sure what it was, and then suddenly I knew. Someone in Deep Gap was outside their house playing the Highland bagpipes!

Mr. Jenkins stopped praying, and we all stood frozen in place for a bit. Then he ran to the door and yanked it open. The pipes were louder now. Someone was close by, very close it sounded like, and they were playin' loud and for all they were worth. It was a signal for us to follow the sound, to follow the pipes to someone's home in Deep Gap.

Miss Teague sprang into action, hurrying everyone back into their coats and caps, double-checking once again to make sure everyone was buttoned up tight. We were instructed to form a single line, holding tight to each other's hands, walk slowly and carefully, and for pity's sake whatever we did, not to let go of anyone's hand. Miss Teague would take the lead and follow the sound of the Highland pipes, while Mr. Jenkins would be at the very end to watch for anyone who might get disconnected from the line.

With a quick check to make sure we were all ready, Miss Teague stepped off the front porch of the schoolhouse clutching the hand of the young student behind her and inched toward the sound of pipes coming from somewhere across the street and down a bit. Miss Teague and Mr. Jenkins called back and forth to each other to make sure we were all still connected, and Miss Teague would call out to whoever was guiding us to safety with the sound of the pipes.

It was Mr. Mitchell's daddy, old Grandpappy Mitchell, who was well known in our parts. He was one of the few left who played the pipes, and he was called on often to play for burials and sometimes weddings. The four Mitchell young'uns' daddy was postmaster at the Deep Gap Post Office and lived in quarters built onto the back of the post office. Old Grandpappy Mitchell lived in a little one-room cabin to the rear of the post office yard.

Grandpappy Mitchell was on the front porch of the Post Office, playin' those pipes as loud as he could and guided us through that blowing snow that was so thick I couldn't even see Miss Teague, who was about four young'uns ahead of me. He piped until Mr. Jenkins entered the front door of the Post Office safe and sound.

We still bedded down on the floor, but we felt safer somehow with our bellies full of a meal of biscuits and gravy Mrs. Mitchell cooked up for us. She apologized for such a meager meal, but it was the best she could do for so many in such a short time. We were grateful, and the hot biscuits and gravy tasted as good as anything I ever ate.

It snowed and blowed solid for two full days. By the time it stopped snowin' completely, Deep Gap had a total of thirty-nine inches of pure white wonderland. Word had gotten to most of the families that their young'uns were safe, so there wasn't too much worry since we were safe, warm, and fed.

It was about four days before most of us got to go home, and it was sure a job diggin' out. Daddy had a wagon with runners he could bolt to the bottom instead of wheels, so he was able to give most of the students a lift home.

In years after that, those of us who stayed in Deep Gap would talk about that winter storm and remember how Mr. Jenkins calmed our fears. It was a lesson to me, and years later when I came to Christ, I always remembered to begin my praying with thanksgivin' for what the Lord had already blessed me with.

Chapter Five

Granddad told stories, as I have said before. One of those stories I remember so well was about one of our Spencer ancestors who was separated from his Comrades after a run-in they had with some English soldiers.

His name was Angus Spencer, and Granddad always liked to tell us young'uns this story on a cold winter night. Maybe it was to make us more thankful for the warmth and safety we had, or maybe he just wanted to keep alive the memory of the Spencer clan. But I can remember after our own experience with a winter storm, one cold day Granddad was tellin' stories for us young'uns, and he told us the story of Angus Spencer like this.

"It was a cold and bitter day, mid-December, and high in the middle of the Highlands of Scotland in 1746 following the English victory over the Scots at the Battle of Culloden. Angus Spencer, along with fifteen other Highlanders, had spotted a regiment of English soldiers marching along the road that ran from Fort William to Fort Augustus, then on to Inverness. It was too cold for the English to be out and about, yet here they were, marching towards Fort Augustus.

Further north, about thirty-five miles, lay the battlefield that had been stained dark with the blood of Scotsmen, Highlanders whose clans had gathered with the Bonny Prince Charles Edward Stewart in one last attempt to regain the throne for the deposed father of the Stewart prince, James Francis Edward Stewart, otherwise known by the English as The Old Pretender."

"Culloden had been the death of much more than just the Highlanders who died there. It was also the death of the dream of a free and independent Scotland. Scotland had fought many years of bitter warfare wantin' nothin' more than to be left alone to govern themselves as Scots, not English.

Centuries before, our friends Johnny and Clair Bruce's kinsman Robert the Bruce was king of Scotland. He was the greatest king Scotland ever had. He had defeated the English at the Battle of Bannockburn after many long years of fight-and-hide tactics."

"Nearly givin' up after years of bein' on the run and hiding in caves and out-of-the-way places, Robert Bruce lay watchin' a spider tryin' to cast its web across the ceiling of the cave he was sleeping in. For hours, Robert watched as the spider tried and failed, then tried and failed again. Over and over throughout the night the spider kept tryin' until finally succeeding and attached it's web across the ceiling.

This inspired the tired king and gave him the determination to keep tryin', to keep fightin' for what was worth having. He fought and retreated and fought again for eight long years before soundly defeatin' the English at Bannockburn. But it was another fourteen years before England signed a treaty and recognized Scotland as independent, and Robert Bruce as its king."

Granddad paused and grinned. He often got sidetracked from his main story if there was another story to tell. "Now, back to Angus Spencer," he laughed.

"Those redcoats had to be frozen. Those English weren't used to the freezing cold like they had in the Highlands of Scotland. It wasn't just the cold, the wind was fierce, blowing like a hurricane, drivin' cold and blowing snow like they was needles runnin' right through them red coats. Angus and his boys were cold too but used to it and knew how and when to shelter and take breaks from the cold.

After trailing the redcoats for a bit, they realized their commanding officers were marching without stopping. A thirty-two-mile march through a winter gale blowing snow and ice. Angus knew they were badly outnumbered. They were just a ragtag remnant, a handful of Jacobite soldiers hunted, on the run, hiding from capture by the ruthless English who never let up the search for Jacobite's."

"Angus turned to his companion closest to him and said, 'If we let them go, if they live, they willna stop hunting us. We canna defeat them in an open battle. There's at least fifty of them, maybe sixty, and only fifteen of us, and we are half starved.' His companion nodded in agreement. 'But we canna allow them to go without tryin'.' Again, his companion nodded, not sayin' a word."

"So, I propose that we divide ourselves. One half will try to draw at least some of them away in a chase. We won't try to fight, only make them think we will, and lead them awa from their companions, and hopefully the cold and the wind will do our work for us." Again, a silent nod of agreement.

"Soon after the first group is led to chase, our second half will appear in the distance to encourage the English to give chase and pray God that they don't have the sense to find their bearin's in this chankin blow!" Another nod.

"'You lead seven men, go around to the fore of the column but keep plenty distance so as not to be overcome and captured. Let them see you, and when they splinter as hoped and give chase, lead them off towards The Great Glen and lose them there. Mayhap they will become bogged down and freeze before they can regroup. I will do the same but try to lead them the opposite way deeper into the mountains, awa from any roads or help. Find shelter and we will meet tomorrow in the cave of Creag Meagaidh. Make sure you are not followed. They canna never know about that hide.' Another silent nod, then—"

"'Aye, Angus.' Pointing to seven other men of their company, he disappeared into the blowing snow and ice."

Angus reckoned it would take some time for his men to go around the redcoats and come out far enough ahead to encourage pursuit yet stay just ahead. He and his six men, staying far enough behind to stay unseen but able to hear the clanking and occasional shouts from the English soldiers, slipped silently from tree to rock and from rock to tree behind the marching men.

Soon he heard shouts far ahead and crept closer to see a group of soldiers veering off from the main body, perhaps thirty or so, forming a group that followed the small band of Highlanders off towards The Great Glen. Angus grinned in spite of the stinging, numbing cold wind. The first part of his plan had started as he had hoped. Half or nearly half of the soldiers were now separated from the main body, and hopefully also, as planned, wouldn't have the sense or know-how to survive a Highland winter storm.

Daddy had brought Granddad a big cup of coffee.

"Wet your whistle, Pa," Daddy said, grinning at his father.

Granddad paused and drank deep from his coffee cup.

"Granddad," I said, "I almost feel sorry for those soldiers. I was so cold and scared when we were walking through the storm from the schoolhouse to Mr. Mitchell's Post Office."

Granddad wiped his mustaches on his sleeve and said, "Compassion is always a good thing, Maggie, but difficult to have when your life is at stake."

Granddad continued.

"Angus trailed the group, waitin' and biding his time. He knew the terrain and the most dangerous place for the unknowin' traveler. After following for over two hours, Angus waved his six men to follow, and they veered off the road, headin' into the ravine to his right. He and his men could travel quicker this way, not havin' to be careful of sound or callin' attention to themselves. They would run, then walk, then run again, the ravine taking them between two mountains the redcoats would have to march around to stay on the road."

"It was late afternoon, and Angus feared he had waited too long to bait his trap and entice the redcoats to pursue his men and himself into the mountainous region. But upon hitting the road, he heard a shout and knew the commanding officer in the lead had spotted them. Feigning wounds, Angus and his men, supportin' and assistin' part of their little company down the road, slipped back into the ravine and hoped the redcoats would follow in pursuit."

"They did! The entire remainin' redcoats were in full pursuit, as much as they could, weighed down with their rucksacks and numb with cold. Angus and his men continued to pretend to be wounded or assistin' a wounded Comrade until the redcoats were nearly upon them. They quickened their pace ever so slightly, just enough to stay ahead, but well within sight. Blowin' wind and snow made visibility near impossible for the soldiers to use their muskets, so they were hopin' to capture the Jacobites with strength and swords.

"Makin' sure they had taken several turns and twists through one ravine leading into another, after about an hour of leading the redcoats deeper and deeper into the rugged mountains, Angus and his men dropped all pretenses and ran, doublin' back through crevasses and yet more ravines. Through the mountains they escaped, leavin' the soldiers to either find their way out or freeze in the storm."

"They met up with the other Comrades who also had managed to lead soldiers away into the boggy peatlands of the Great Glen and slip away to meet up with Angus and his men in the cave of Creag Meagaidh. There they rode out the storm, and a bit longer to make sure no English soldiers had managed to survive and follow them."

"Angus and his men were never sure if the English soldiers died pursuing them, or if they had somehow managed to find their way back to the road and each other, then makin' it to Fort Augustus. But they had survived that particular manhunt and lived for some time yet."

Gerry spoke up.

"What happened to Angus Spencer, Granddad? Did he come to America?"

"No, Gerry. Angus was eventually captured by the English soldiers, as so many Jacobites were. He was executed along with his father and an uncle. His widow came to America, though. She and her five children took offered passage and eventually married a widower with children, settling near Philadelphia, Pennsylvania."

Us young'uns sat quiet a moment, grateful for a warm fire that cracked and popped in the fireplace. I reflected for a moment on what good things I enjoyed. I had the warmth of a comfortable fire. I didn't have to fear my daddy bein' shot for a treason that wasn't treason to him. I had Mamma, brothers and cousins, aunts and uncles.

We didn't have extra things or fancy things, but we had each other, and we had good food and shelter. I was glad that some of our ancestors had braved the wide oceans and escaped the tyranny of the English. They had often paid a high price for that freedom, but here we were, their descendants, sittin' in our snug cabin in the Appalachian Mountains of North Carolina, snug, warm, and happy in each other's company.

***

Most of the games we played were invented ones. Other than baseball, kickball, tag, Mother May I, and Simon Says, which we played with other young'uns from school, we made up our own. We would come home from school, do the chores we couldn't put off 'til another time, and then would take off up the old Indian trail to play in the woods and rocks.

Robbie and I would play for hours, makin' up games where we were the famous outlaws and train robbers Frank and Jessie James, robbing trains and running from the law. We would pretend we were Civil War soldiers, fightin' in the famous Thomas's Legion that Robbie's ancestors had fought in during the American Civil War. Of course, we were fightin' imaginary Yankees, since neither one of us wanted to be a Yankee.

Sometimes I felt the need to prove I could do anything Robbie could do, even though he was older, bigger, and stronger. I had long, strong legs and could outrun many boys much older than myself, including Robbie. He knew it was pert near useless to try to catch me, unless I wanted to be caught. So, gettin' Robbie to chase me was becomin' a favorite pastime, just so I could remind him that even though he could beat me in just about any other activity, I was the fastest.

But nobody could throw a rock like Robbie. I know because when I was eight and he was ten, I took off runnin' on the old Indian trail up the mountain behind my house. The trail zigged and zagged back and forth like a snake, and because I could outrun Robbie, I laughed and screamed a taunt over my right shoulder: "Robbie is a slowpoke and runs like a girl!"

The next thing I knew, I came to, layin' on the trail with Robbie's face inches from mine, and white as paper, like all the blood had drained out of it. And, oh my, my head hurt like some mountain demon was pounding on it with a baseball bat. When I sat up, my head whirled like my little brother Charlie's whirly top toy. Nausea welled up inside me, and I thought I would throw up right there. I reached up to hold my achin' head in my hand to find thick, dark red blood pourin' down the right side of my head, ear and neck. I had never seen so much of my own blood before.

"What happened?" I croaked.

Robbie stammered and stuttered, then finally started to bawl. "I threw a rock at you," he sobbed brokenly when he realized he had hurt me pretty bad. "I don't know why. I just got so mad when you said I run like a girl."

"Oh," was all I could think to say. My buddy seemed to be hurting even more than I was, which was saying something. I reached up, patted his shoulder, and said, "It's okay. I know you weren't tryin' to really hurt me, but you still run like a girl."

Robbie suddenly stopped bawling, hiccupped, and started to laugh, then stopped suddenly, his eyes now blue pools of serious sorrow. "Your mamma won't ever let you come up here to play with me again, Maggie. She already doesn't like you runnin' the mountains with me like a boy. When she sees that gash, pump knot, and all that blood, she'll be madder than a rattler, and I wouldn't blame her."

"Help me get to the crick," I said. I was dizzy and thought it would serve him right to suffer a little, so I poured it on just a little worse than it actually was. "I don't think I can walk. My head is swimmy. You'll have to carry me."

Robbie's eyes nearly popped out of his head. "Carry you! I can't carry you all the way to the crick!" His voice came out at the same pitch as the steam whistle at the furniture factory, when it goes to shooting off at quittin' time.

"Well, then you'll have to go find my daddy and tell him what happened," I said. With a deep sigh and a defeated look, Robbie bent down, hauled me to my feet, gathered me up in his arms, and headed for the crick about a half mile from where we were.

Now, I wouldn't want you to think I was a mean girl, or spoiled, or anything like that, but I wasn't above having a little fun while makin' Robbie suffer for his impetuous, thoughtless rock throwin'. It wasn't long before Robbie started to puff a little. He was in good shape, and like most of us mountain people in the late 1930s, we walked pert near everywhere we went, unless it was a long journey, which most of us never took.

But even though I was a small girl and kinda on the skinny side, I was still a load. After about halfway to the crick, Robbie had to sit a spell and rest before taking me the rest of the way.

While we sat on a log from a storm-fallen tree, one of many from the wild storms that are part of life in my mountains, Robbie and I hatched a plan to pull the wool over my mamma's eyes. Robbie was, after all, pretty much officially my best friend. I had girlfriends, but most of them were scared of bugs, scared of mud, scared of—well, scared of pretty much everything, it seemed to me. I liked playin' with my one and only dolly once in a while, but it got boring after an hour or two.

The greatest fun to me was scrambling through the woods with Robbie, huntin' anything there was to be hunted. My favorite thing to look for was Indian arrowheads. Once we found a rock that we could tell was something more than just an old rock, though we weren't quite sure just what it was. Granddad Spencer said it was a tomahawk head from some long-ago Cherokee who had lived in these parts. I used to dream it belonged to some great chief who found me and made me his daughter, which in my eyes would have made me an Indian princess.

So, back to the plan Robbie and I hatched to fool my mamma. We would wash all the blood off in the crick and see just how bad the gash in my head was. Since it was in my hair, maybe it could be hidden in its thickness.

By the way, one of the things you will see a lot of in my mountains is red hair. My dark but bright copper-colored hair is a Spencer trademark. There are more Spencers with various shades of red than with any other hair color.

If the gash wasn't too bad, we'd spend some time soakin' it in the cold waters of Gap Crick. Hopefully, that would bring down the size of the goose egg pump knot on the side of my head. But my dress was hopelessly stained with lots of blood.

I had a shift on under my dress, which wasn't nothin' fancy a'tall. I only had two everyday dresses and one for church that fit me at the time. The lucky thing was I had on an old faded red calico print. If we could scrub out most of the blood, maybe Mamma wouldn't notice a wee bit of blood stain. So, we made a pact: clean the gash, cover it with my hair, scrub out as much blood from my dress as possible, and neither one of us would tell what had happened.

We made it to the crick and began the first job of cleaning the blood out of my hair, and off my face and neck.

"Oh man," Robbie groaned, "I'm so sorry, Maggie. I really busted your head bad."

The thought of my badly busted head made my head swim for real. "How bad?" I whispered.

Robbie looked at me, his blue eyes fillin' with tears again. "Bad enough I think we should go see Doc Braden."

First off, I knew my mamma and daddy couldn't actually afford Doc Braden's services. He was a good man who didn't charge nearly what his work was worth, and he made house calls all hours of the day or night, weekends too. But no matter—my mamma and daddy couldn't afford it.

"Nope," I said. "If we do that, you'll get a hidin' like you never had before. Your papa will smoke your britches good for throwin' rocks at a girl."

"That may be so, but it looks deeper now that it's cleaned than it did with blood all over it," Robbie said, worry and conflicted thoughts written all over his face. He was in for it if we went to Doc's, and he was runnin' the risk of his friend not bein' okay if we didn't.

In the end, we did as planned. We went swimming, so comin' home soakin' wet was no big deal. Mamma didn't really like me swimming without a grown-up around, but I never seemed to come to any real harm, so she quit fussin' about it about the time I turned eight.

Robbie gently washed the blood from my thick red hair, made a compress out of his handkerchief, and applied pressure to the gash. That and the cold, cold waters of Gap Crick finally slowed the bleeding, and after about an hour, it stopped. With the blood gone and my thick hair pulled over the gash, the somewhat smaller pump knot barely showed. Unless Mamma had cause to get suspicious, she would never know.

Good thing my dress was a faded red calico. The splotchy, faint bloodstains that wouldn't rinse out in the cold waters just sort of blended in, more or less with the print pattern of my dress. It didn't appear to be noticeable unless you knew what you were lookin' at.

I went home about supper time, wet and tired from all I'd been through, and my head throbbing like Satan himself was poundin' out some awful song from hell inside my skull.

I never did tell Mamma what happened. She thought I'd come down with some virus or something. I ran a fever and didn't feel good for about a week, so Mamma made me stay in bed, which was probably just what I needed. By the time I was eight years old, I combed my own hair, so Mamma never saw the spot on the right side of my head where the hair no longer grew.

In later years Robbie would rub that little scar on my head and we would laugh about that long-ago day. I would always kid him about tryin' to brain me when I was eight.

Chapter Six

Granddad Spencer had a huge black iron cauldron. I never did see him use it for anything; it just sat over in a corner of his barn. Granny Spencer made her apple butter in a copper kettle that was used mostly just for makin' apple butter, but Granddad's cauldron seemed to have no purpose.

But I had plenty of use for the cauldron, and bein' the understandin' soul my granddad was, he moved it to a level place beside the crick that ran behind our house.

The crick wasn't Gap Crick, where Robbie and I washed away the evidence of his rock throwin'. This was a smaller crick that ran into Gap Crick further down. I don't ever recall hearin' it called anything other than "The Crick." It was full of interestin' creepy crawlies, teemin' with crawdaddies, salamanders, brown brook trout, and frogs of many sizes and colors. All these were ingredients for witch's brew in Granddad Spencer's cauldron, along with anything else disgusting to thicken it with, such as cow patties or horse biscuits, various fungi such as toadstools, and mold.

Robbie and I made many a fine cauldron full of witch's brew in all the years of our childhood. Often, if the mountain trails were slick with rain and too wet to climb on, Robbie and I—and sometimes

Gerry, my younger brother, or Jamie, my closest cousin, or other cousins who were over at the farm—would pretend to be a secret coven of witches and warlocks.

Many a day was spent seein' who could concoct the most horrible, the most evil, the nastiest-smellin' witch's brew ever. Nothin' was off limits unless it was human flesh. We would build a fire under the cauldron and cook our vile potions, chanting anything we had ever read or thought of: "Eye of newt, toe of frog, fang of bat and hair of dog. Dung of cow, feather of fowl, tail of cat, spit of owl." We were inventive, creative young'uns to be sure, and it was often a large group effort.

As time passed, I came to realize that Robbie was a handsome lad, and I also began to notice that when groups of us came together to play, many of the other girls seemed to think so too.

It first happened one day when I was ten and Robbie was twelve. We were brewing up an especially fine and smelly witch's brew when Tillie Macpherson, who was also twelve and my sometimes friend, asked to join us. She wanted to be the one to stir our concoction. That was just fine with me, as I would rather be findin' disgusting ingredients for our brew. But I soon noticed that Robbie was spendin' more time hangin' around the cauldron, stirrin' the brew, and laughin' with Tillie than he was gatherin' the necessary ingredients.

That was when I also noticed Tillie was actin' different. She hung onto every word my Robbie uttered, batted her extra-long eyelashes at him, and looked at him with a sick-cow look, cuttin' her eyes up at him through those extra-long lashes. Then it dawned on me—he was MY Robbie! At ten years old I knew he was mine, and Tillie Macpherson, with her extra-long eyelashes, was trespassin' on my land.

Here in my mountains, we are very familiar with trespassing and what it means to violate the claims and rights of ownership. Many a feud has sprung up lasting for years, even generations, over one person not respecting the rights of another. Deciding it was time I filed my claim, I stomped over and planted myself smack between MY Robbie and Tillie Macpherson.

Tillie was about three inches taller than me in those days, so she was lookin' down on me—literally as well as socially—makin' her own claim on Robert Alexander Bruce. Tillie was a year and a half older than me. She used that, as well as her superior height, long golden curls, and extra-long eyelashes, to wage her war for ownership. The fact that her daddy was James Macpherson, who owned the largest store in the whole area, made Tillie an adversary with a definite advantage over me.

It was a store of unbelievable magnificence, at least to most of us poor children who lived in my mountains. It was a store that had everything, from candy—which most of us couldn't afford—to kitchen pots and horse feed. It had one gasoline pump out front, the only one for miles around.

There was a soda machine on the front porch of Macpherson's, and sometimes Granddad would give us young'uns a nickel. We knew the only way to spend that nickel was to buy an ice cold soda from that machine. We would sit on the porch of Macpherson's, suckin' away at that bottle of ice-cold soda. It was so cold, about one third of the glass bottle was soft, slushy ice floatin' on top of the cold soda below. Not much came close to beatin' that.

I have a tendency to get caught up in rememberin' and talkin' about how things used to be. My great-granddaughter Chloe bought me a Dr Pepper out of a soda machine not long ago in Boone, and she paid a dollar and a half for it. It wasn't nearly as cold as those sodas of long ago, and not nearly as good. I feel sorry for young'uns who will never know the small joys of childhood in the same way I did. Times are just too different.

So now you know Tillie had quite a bit of advantage over me. She was tall and older, almost a woman in my ten-year-old eyes. She had long golden curls that hung to her waist. I had bright copper hair that, while thick, was straight as a board and fell to the middle of my back. I didn't bother curlin' it very often. No matter how long curlin' rags were in my hair, the curls fell out within minutes. There was no point.

Tillie had the longest dark eyelashes I have ever seen, and she knew how to use them like a tool. I had never before given any thought about my own eyelashes. They weren't bad as eyelashes go, but they were nothin' like Tillie's.

Tillie had beautiful clothes, made in the same styles I saw in ladies' magazines in Macpherson's store, and she wore shiny black shoes. My dresses were few, and even my good ones were made of the cheapest cloth Mamma could get. My everyday dresses were made from flour sacks Mamma had dyed usin' herbs and wildflowers for color. I had never thought much about my dresses, since most of the girls I knew didn't dress any different than I did. Most everyone was just as poor as we were. The only time most of us wore shoes was when it got cold enough for the frost and cold to bite our toes, but Tillie's family was one of the few exceptions.

So, as I said, I planted myself between MY Robbie Bruce and Tillie Macpherson and said, "Tillie, it's time for you to go home. I'm pretty sure I heard your mamma callin' your name."

"My house is too far away to hear my mamma callin' me," said Tillie with a superior smile. "Mamma said I could come play, but to be home by five o'clock; it's only three thirty." She held out her watch, dangling from a golden chain around her neck.

"Well Robbie and I are tired of playin' with you now; we were havin' more fun before you came. Besides, you won't help catch any crawdaddies or cow patties for the witch's brew, so just go home," I screeched.

That's when the unbelievable happened. Robbie rounded on me like a duck on a June bug.

"Why are you so mad at Tillie?" he asked angrily. "What's she done to make you so mad? Besides, I like her here playin' with us, and if you don't like it, she can come to my house. We can find plenty to do if you don't want her here."

Robbie's blue eyes shot sparks of anger that startled me. For the first time I knew what jealousy was, deep down, mean, pea green jealousy. Robbie had been my best friend ever since I could remember. I had few memories that didn't include Robbie.

Now, because I was younger, shorter, less pretty, and poor, he was going to pick her over me. Well, that's how I saw it at the time. Never mind that I was acting like a baby and not bein' reasonable; all I could think of was he's picking her over me, his best friend.

"Go ahead and pick her!" I screamed and ran up the hill from the crick into my daddy's barn. I climbed the ladder to the haymow, threw myself down onto a hay bale, and sobbed. My heart was broken, and the dam burst, flooding my eyes with tears and my heart with jealousy and bitterness.

Five minutes later I heard a tapping on the barn door; it was Robbie.

"Maggie, you in there?" Robbie asked.

"Git on outta here, go on back there and play with HER!" I screamed.

"I don't know why you're so mad, Maggie," Robbie said. "What made you so mad?"

What did make me so mad? I hardly knew the answer to that myself. All I knew was he was MY Robbie, and Tillie Macpherson was acting in a way I only vaguely understood. But it affected the way my Robbie acted, whether he knew that or not.

I was afraid. I was afraid I would lose my friend, my buddy I had played with and conspired with. I was afraid Tillie Macpherson, with her golden curls and long eyelashes, would come between my Robbie and me.

And she did, for a time.

Chapter Seven

The Bible says jealousy is as cruel as the grave. I know that's true; I nearly dug my own grave with it. Robbie left the barn that awful afternoon, and nothin' was the same between us after that. Any time we were together I kept rememberin' how he had looked laughin' with Tillie while I gathered crud for our witch's brew. I kept rememberin' how he grinned at her when she batted her long eyelashes at him.

I didn't treat him the same after that. I would remember, and the jealousy would rise up in me, and somethin' hateful or hurtful would come spewing out of my mouth. Oh, I would regret it and often would apologize for sayin' mean things, but they were said and couldn't be stuffed back into my mouth once they had left it. That's the hard thing about words spoken with no bridle on your tongue. Words spoken in anger with no self-control can be the hardest things to take back. Because no matter how much you didn't really mean them, they still cut like a knife and wound the person they are thrown at.

Granddad tried to talk to me several times, tried to tell me my hateful words and spiteful actions would hurt Robbie, and hurt me too. He tried to tell me my attitude, and my actions weren't pleasin' to the Lord. Now, I'll just have to tell you the truth. I really wasn't too caring about whether I was pleasin' to the Lord or not at that time. My feelin's and my pride smarted too badly with Robbie choosing Tillie over me. I was too uncaring of the truth. Robbie hadn't stopped bein' my friend at all, but Tillie was obvious competition, and I didn't feel I should have to compete for him or share him. He was supposed to be mine, and I wanted him all to myself.

Robbie still came around off and on for a while, and I would even stop by his house sometimes if I were going to go for a climb through my mountains. But it seemed like nearly every time we saw each other there would be an argument over something, and then awkwardness followed. After about a year, it seemed we began to really drift apart.

I began spendin' more time either alone, preferably at or around my personal spot, or at home with Mamma when I wasn't at school. I had developed a sharp tongue that most people avoided. The only person who seemed to want to be around me, to really be my friend, was shy Betty Holder.

Betty's family was new to our area. They had moved to Deep Gap from Tennessee to be close to Mr. Holder's people and were much poorer than we were. Her daddy was a drinkin' man who would be gone for weeks at a time. Rumors had it that he and his brothers had a moonshine still back farther into the mountains. If he did, he didn't spend much of the money he made moonshinin' on his family. I've seen Betty and her little sister and three brothers barefoot all winter, with little more than rags to cover their bodies.

Betty's mamma was a thin, worn-out lookin' woman who was always kind and very quiet. I heard her tell some of the womenfolk she missed her family in Tennessee. The happiest I ever saw her was when I was in church with Granddad and Granny Spencer at Easter. The preacher was talkin' about the resurrection of Christ and how Jesus was God in flesh, who died for us sinners to take on the penalty for our sins. How he died on a cross and took our sins to the grave with him and rose victorious over sin and death. I always thought she glowed like one of the angels who were in Jesus' tomb on Easter mornin' when she was in church.

Betty was more scared of bein' lonely than she was of my sharp tongue, I guess. For a period of time, my misery over my broken friendship with Robbie infected my whole bein' like a festered sore. I snapped at everyone, including Betty. I don't know why she put up with it really. I guess it's just sad evidence of how lonely she was after leavin' all she knew behind in Tennessee.

After a time, Betty's patience and sweet nature caused me to soften towards her, and I realized no matter how things were with me and Robbie, it wasn't Betty's fault. I began to spend more time with her, and she began to spend more time at the Spencer Farm. Poor as we were, we were rich to Betty. While at our farm at least she got a decent meal, and many a day Mamma would send our leftovers home with her, sayin', "Betty, would you be a sweetie and take this here leftovers to your mamma? They's gonna ruin if they stay here."

It was during the summer when I was eleven that Mamma told me I would be a big sister again. Gerry and Charlie were off with Granddad Spencer, suppos'd to be shovin' up the spring where we drew our drinkin' water from. One of the cows had gotten in it and knocked down the rock walls that lined the spring. But I suspected they were all actually fishin'.

Mamma and I sat on the porch while we were shellin' peas when she said, "Maggie honey, how would you like another baby brother? Or sister?"

I stared at her, uncomprehending for a minute. Was this a game? A "what if" or "would you like" game we played sometimes while doin' this sort of sittin' work? What if...toads had tails? What if...you had a million dollars?

Mamma's eyes danced, 'cause she knew I was gearing up to participate in our "game".

"I'm not foolin' ya," she laughed. "Your daddy and I will be welcomin' another Spencer baby come December."

I was struck dumb with the joy of it!

"Can it be a baby sister? Can I name her? Can she sleep with me? Can I take care of her?"

Mamma threw back her head laughin' as she said, "Whoa Maggie, whoa! Babies don't come from the Sears and Roebuck catalog! I can't fill out an order form and expect to get what I checked in the boxes for."

She smiled, pleased that I was excited and happy to welcome a new baby.

"You know we take what the good Lord sends us. Does it really matter that much if it's a brother or sister? We can't send him back to where he came from if it's a baby brother," she said with a twinkle in her pretty blue eyes.

"I guess not," I said, thinkin' about it for a bit. "Baby brothers are cute and sweet, even if they grow up to be boys."

Mamma laughed again. "Boys are more feelin' and tender inside than they like to show on the outside, Maggie. Remember that when dealin' with them."

"Well, I'm gonna ask the Lord to give me a baby sister anyway. We got enough boys hangin' round here!" This was said as a joke, but a joke I meant, nonetheless.

Summer was long and fruitful. With the news of the comin' baby, I was eager to show Mamma and Daddy that I was a big girl and more than able to be responsible enough to take care of my comin' baby sister. I had put my order in with the Lord one Sunday when I had attended church with Granddad and Granny Spencer and felt sure that I had done everything proper and He understood that I had a clear preference for a baby sister.

I tried to make the garden work easier for Mamma by taking over the heavier chores, like bending over for long periods to pick beans and haulin' them to the porch for snappin'. School would start the second week of September, so I had to shake a leg to help all I could before then. I hauled basket after basket of tomatoes into the kitchen and helped with the process of skinning off the peels and helpin' Mamma turn them into jars of tomatoes, juice, and tomato preserves.

We canned cooker load after cooker load of green beans, butter beans, chowchow, and pickled beets. Then we started on the apples and pears that were beginning to ripen. Time was workin' against me, because I had a lot to prove to Mamma and Daddy before school started.

I was hopin' to convince Mamma that when I turned fourteen, I would be old enough to be through with schoolin' and stay home to help her. This was less than two years away, and I wanted to show her how grown up I was already. Most of the youn'uns I knew were finished with schoolin' by the time they were fourteen and dropped out to help provide income for their families. Many of the girls in our parts were married by fifteen and mothers by sixteen.

September came, and I went off to school with Gerry and Charlie, though I longed to stay behind to help Mamma. It seemed to me she looked awful tired, and her feet were swelling sometimes, making it hard for her to wear any shoes. She would get these queer looks sometimes, and thinkin' I didn't notice, would give a little jerk. Her hand would fly to her rounding belly and clutch at it for a moment. Then she would straighten up and say, "Lands sake, but this young'un is makin' hisself known!"

"Herself, Mamma," I would say. "It's a her."

Mamma would always laugh it off and say, "I hope for your sake you're right, Maggie girl. But remember, little boys are mighty sweet too. Sweet as sugar pie!"

I'd always agree but I'd stick to my guns.

Two weeks into the school year, I came home from school one day to find Grandad and Granny Spencer on the porch, sittin' in the rockers where Mamma was usually sittin' this time of day. As I came closer to the house, I could hear moans and little cries comin' from inside.

I ran the last several feet across the yard, headin' up the porch steps, and Grandad rose from his chair and stopped me from chargin' through the front door.

"Maggie girl, sit down a minute. Granny and I want to talk to you."

"No!" I panted. "Mamma needs me. What's wrong? Mamma said the baby wasn't gonna come until the first part of December. Why's she cryin'? What's wrong? What's happenin'?"

Granddad Spencer tucked me under his arm and pulled me around to sit on the stool by his and Granny's rockers. Gerry and Charlie had reached the porch by this time and could tell somethin' was terrible wrong. Their eyes were scared, and their mouths puckered, tryin' not to cry. We could all tell somethin' was wrong with Mamma.

Granny motioned the boys to sit on the porch beside me on the stool and said, "Mamma's baby is comin' early. We don't know what happened, but somethin' ain't been right with her the last month or more. Doc and your daddy are with her, and we need to stay out and let them help her best they can. And we can pray."

The afternoon wore on into evenin', and the moans and pitiful cries kept comin' at intervals. My nerves were wracked, and I felt jumpy like a cat walkin' on hot metal. Charlie put his head down on his arms and cried quietly. Gerry would inch closer to me when Mamma's cries got the best of him. I could tell he wanted to cry too, but he felt he was too close to bein' a man to give over to cryin'.

Once in a while Daddy would step out of the room for fresh water, and Granny would take his place while he fetched water from the spring or hunted up fresh cloths for Doc. It was close to dark when he quietly told Granddad to take us young'uns over to his and Granny's place for the night. It was lookin' like a long, hard night, and his eyes told Granddad he feared the worst and wanted to spare us best he could.

We didn't want to leave Mamma, but Daddy said there wasn't anything we could do, and it was best for all concerned if we went with Granddad. So, we did. Gerry slept with Granddad, and Charlie slept with me in the one spare room they had, since their own young'uns were grown and gone. It was a long, hard night. Once alone, while Charlie slept, worn out from cryin', I finally gave myself over to my own tears and fought the fears of losin' my Mamma.

I had heard many stories of women in my mountains a dyin' in childbirth. It wasn't all that uncommon. Even in the modern times of the 1930s, poor women back in the mountains sometimes died. Lots of babies died too. Most of us just didn't have the money to go to the hospital in Boone. Women nowadays see a doctor throughout their pregnancy, and doctors keep a close eye on the baby and mamma the whole while. But it wasn't so then.

I finally slept, but fitful like. We rose early, and Grandad made us breakfast as best he could. He could actually make good flapjacks, and tryin' to cheer us a bit, he set about makin' flapjacks with honey and maple syrup. We hadn't had much the evenin' before and didn't want much either. This mornin' we were hungry, and Granddad's flapjacks were so good.

We finished up and headed across the holler to our place. Everything was quiet. As we came close to the house, Granddad picked up his volume a bit with the squirrel story he was tellin' Gerry and Charlie. I knew he was alerting Daddy and Granny that we were approachin' the house.

Granny came through the front door. She was dressed in the same rumpled clothes she had worn the evenin' before, and her eyes were sad and full of exhausted compassion when she looked into my own anxious eyes.

"How's Mamma?" I asked, feelin' the words sounded breathy and not at all like the direct and boisterous Maggie I usually was.

"Your mamma is tired. No, she's completely done in. Exhausted. But she will be fine, eventually. Your mamma and daddy are sleeping now. Come, sit here on the porch and I'll tell you all about it."

We plunked down, feelin' like our legs wouldn't hold up under the weight of relief. Our Mamma was alive, and would be alright, even if the word *eventually* sounded scary.

"Your mamma was delivered of a baby girl about two o'clock this mornin'," Granny said tiredly. "It was a long and difficult birth."

"A girl?" I stammered. "It really was a girl? Why did I doubt that the Lord would give me the baby sister I had dreamed of, had asked Him for?"

Somethin' in Granny's eyes made me stop in the middle of my excited questions. Somethin' that made my heart stop and drop into the pit of my stomach, heavy and cold as a rock.

"What's wrong?" I asked. "What happened?" Surely somethin' terrible had happened, judging by Granny's sorrowful eyes.

"Your baby sister was stillborn," Granny said simply. "She's flown away and is in the arms of Jesus now."

I stared at her blankly. How could this baby sister I had hoped for and prayed for be gone? But then, weren't our mountain graveyards full of baby sisters and baby brothers? And mammas too, for that matter.

"You mean she's dead?" I asked bluntly.

"Yes, Maggie girl, she is," Granny said gently, tryin' to wrap me in soft words in response to my stark, blunt ones.

I sat quietly, letting the harshness of my loss seep into my very bones. Gerry hunched his thin shoulders and stared at the porch floor, and Charlie began to cry gulping sobs. Granddad picked him up, even though he was a big boy of five, and held him close to his chest, cradling him in his tough, old, comfortin' arms.

"I wanted to be a big brother," Charlie sobbed. "I wanted a baby sister so I could be her big brother. I, I, I didn't want to be the baby anymore. I, I, I wanted to let her be the baby."

Gerry sniffed, and I saw a big tear roll down his cheek and drop onto the knee of his overalls from his bent head. He stayed silent, but I could feel his sorrow.

"Why would God let our baby sister die?" I asked, with an angry flash of temper and sorrow all rolled together. "Why would He let that happen? She didn't even get the chance to live or nothin'. God isn't fair. It isn't fair that a baby don't even get a chance at all."

I jumped up and ran towards the crick behind our barn. Passing the barn, I suddenly veered off and ran through the door and up the ladder to the haymow above. Panting from my run, I clawed and climbed over the top of the loose hay, slid down the backside, and burrowed in the corner. I clutched my sides, achin' from my sprint and climb, and fought to quiet my breath. I didn't want to be found. I wanted to be alone with my sorrow.

I could hear Granny and Granddad on the porch, talkin' about whether to go after me or not. Granny wanted Granddad to follow, but I peeped out a crack in the boards and saw him shake his head. I couldn't hear everything they were sayin', but they stayed on the porch for a long time, talkin' with Gerry and Charlie and waitin' for me to be ready.

Mornin' was turnin' into noontime when Daddy came onto the porch. He and Mamma had just woke, and he told Granny that Mamma probably needed to eat somethin' now. I heard my name and peeked through the boards of the barn. Granddad shook his head, wavin' his hand toward where I lay hidden. Granny heaved herself out of the rocker like she was old and very heavy. I knew it was just tiredness and sorrow weighin' her down. Granny probably weighed just over a hundred pounds soakin' wet.

Daddy stepped off the porch and started walkin' toward the barn. I didn't know if he was comin' to see to the animals below or if he was lookin' for me. I stayed quiet as a dust mote and barely breathed when he came through the barn door. I could hear him movin' around a bit, like he was lookin' for somethin'… or someone. Or maybe he was huntin' hen's eggs and seein' to our cow Abigale and our horse Bob.

"Maggie girl?" Daddy said quietly.

I kept quiet.

"Maggie, I know you're in here. Up in the mow, I suspect."

Still, I kept quiet.

"Come down, hon. You gonna make your tired old Daddy climb those stairs so he can talk to you?"

No. I didn't care how bad off I was, I wouldn't make my sweet Daddy, who had been through a terrible night climb those stairs unnecessarily.

"No sir," I said. "Comin'."

I was stiff from bein' rolled up in a wad in the haymow for hours in the cool mountain mornin'. I climbed down the ladder and stood before my Daddy, refusin' to meet his eyes.

Daddy held his arms out to me and said, "Maggie girl, your Daddy needs a hug."

I broke, and with a sob threw myself into my Daddy's arms. He held me for a long while, sayin' nothin', lettin' me cry until I was finally empty of tears. He sat on a wood crate that was set against the wall separating the barn and the chicken house and drew me down to sit beside him.

"Maggie hon," Daddy said after a minute, "I know you're sad. I know your heart is broke and hurts. We're all sad, and we all hurt right now. That's why it's best if we all stick together and help each other. Charlie needs you and Gerry, and you need him. Gerry needs you and Charlie, and you both need him. I need you, and you need me. Granddad and Granny need you, and you need them. Most of all, your Mamma needs you, and I know for a fact that you need her. She's your very best friend in the world, and you can each help the other through this."

He was quiet a minute and let his words seep into my heart. Fresh tears started rollin' down my cheeks as I listened to his soft words pourin' love into my achin' heart.

"I know," I sobbed. "I just couldn't stand it and took off."

"I know," Daddy said, and I knew he really did know. "Are you ready to come back to the house? Granny has some soup ready. Mamma's havin' some right now, and I know for a fact she wants to see her girl."

"Yes sir," I said as I hiccupped. I dreaded facin' my family after up and runnin' off, but I needn't have. Charlie wrapped his chubby arms around my waist, and Gerry slipped an arm around my back. Nothin' was said; we just held on to each other.

Granny was in the kitchen dishin' up bowls of chicken and vegetable soup and sliced up a loaf of homemade bread. She sat a crock of butter on the table and some apple butter along with a pitcher of milk. On her way back to see to Mamma, Granny came around the end of the table and dropped a light kiss on the top of my head.

"Maggie, go ahead and eat, and when you're finished, come on back to see your Mamma."

And she was off with fresh water in a bowl for Mamma to wash in.

We ate the good soup quietly while Daddy and Granddad talked about how to manage the farm, garden, produce stand, and young'uns without Mamma while she recuperated. When Granny came out of Mamma's bedroom, she told the men that she would stay and take care of the house and garden with the help of the young'uns. The men could see to both farms and the produce stand and help with the garden, and Granddad would take his meals here with us but sleep over at their holdin' to keep an eye on things as best he could. Granny was a decision maker.

I finished up my soup and had a thick slice of bread and butter with a big spoonful of apple butter spread over it. I stood a bit uncertain about goin' in to see Mamma. I was a little nervous. How should I act? I had lost a baby sister, but Mamma... Mamma had lost her baby.

I slipped through the bedroom door silently. Mamma was layin' in bed and looked nearly as pale and white as the sheet pulled up over her chest. A kerosene lamp was lit to give more light to the darkening room and cast shadows on Mamma's face, and for one scared moment I thought Mamma too had flown away, restin' in the arms of Jesus.

Sensing my presence, Mamma opened her still beautiful blue eyes and smiled a small little smile. She held out a hand to me. I sidled up to the bed, not knowin' if I should sit or lay beside her or just stand awkwardly holdin' her hand.

She patted the bed beside her and said, "Maggie girl, lay here and cuddle with Mamma for a minute."

My eyes again filled with tears, and I said, "I won't hurt you?"

"No, I need to hold my girl."

I softly crept into the bed and snuggled into my Mamma's arms. She held me, and we both cried quietly. After a long time, I asked, "Mamma, are you really going to be okay? You're not going to die too?"

Mamma's arms tightened around me just a little. "No, Maggie girl. Doc said that even though it was a rough birth and all, I should be alright, but I will be weak and need several weeks, maybe even months, to regain my strength. But I will be fine."

Mamma was fine, and as Doc had said, it was Christmas before she began to have color in her cheeks again. We rarely talked about the baby girl we lost. After a small private family funeral, she was buried in the Spencer family cemetery with a headstone that read:

Baby Girl

Daughter of Edward and Dorothy Spencer

Still Born September 20, 1935

It has always grieved me that my baby sister never had a name. In my heart, I had called her Hope.

Chapter Eight

Robbie was now fourteen and was really startin' to look like a man. He was tall; at least to me he was tall. Spencers aren't known for any great height. Most of the Spencer men are about five foot seven or eight, and I myself am five foot two; at least I was before age shrunk me down a bit. Robbie wound up topping out at an even six foot. He had wavy golden-brown hair, blue eyes, and the prettiest lopsided smile I ever saw on a man.

A lot of men in my mountains chew tobaccy or smoke, women too, but not Robbie. So his teeth didn't have the rotten spots so many did, even at a young age, and they were white and beautiful.

By the time Robbie was fifteen and I was twelve, we hardly spoke at all. I was so eaten up with bitter feelin's because he had started spendin' most of his spare time with Tillie. It was so bad that even when I did come face to face with him, I would either ignore him or throw dark looks his way. That time of our lives still saddens my heart, too much wasted time that could have been better spent. But enough on regrets; they only make you sadder still.

When he was fourteen, Robbie had taken a job workin' for Tillie's daddy, Mr. Macpherson, in his store. Sometimes, when passing by the store on my way to Betty's or our produce stand, I would see him pumping gasoline or sweeping off the porch. I hardly ever went into the store; it hurt too much to see him face to face. My hurt didn't show itself very well, and always looked, and sounded like anger. Sometimes Mamma would ask me to run to the store and get some eggs when our hens weren't layin' or some other item, but I would always say, "Let Gerry do it, he likes going to the store."

Gerry's my younger brother; I have two younger brothers. Gerry Stewart is just a year younger than I am, and Charlie is the baby. His given name is Charles Presley, and he is six years younger than me. Gerry's greatest desire is to grow up and be a man. He loves to read anything he can about the army, and the heroes of the World War. Charlie is following in my footsteps, runnin' the mountains like a wild Indian and brewin' another generation of witch's brew in Granddad's cauldron with his hoard of cousins and buddies.

Robbie bought an old 1926 Ford Model T pickup truck when he was sixteen from his uncle who lived in Asheville, North Carolina, and owned a used car lot. It wasn't very pretty, but the mountain roads were going to be rough on it anyway, so I guess pretty wasn't one of the things he was lookin' for.

Everyone congratulated him... everyone except me. It was a big thing for a sixteen-year-old lad to save his money and buy his own truck. I was proud of him, so proud of him, but it had been so long since we had spoken, I couldn't bring myself to tell him so. I just couldn't humble myself and be the first to break our silence.

Somethin' new had crept up and stole away in my heart: pride. Jealousy and pride. Now I had two demons on my back. I hated that I was that way, miserable in fact, but I couldn't seem to break away from the fierce pride that wouldn't allow me let go of my hurt and just be nice to my old friend like I used to. Now that he had a truck, I would see him sometimes bouncing down the dirt road in it with Tillie sittin' happily at his side.

A year later Robbie and Tillie were only sixteen and seventeen, but things seemed to be gettin' real serious with them. That sounds young to folks these days, and it is. But in my mountains back in those days, folks didn't see it as too young to marry. A lot of people did. Robbie was well set with his foot in the door at Macpherson's store. Mr. Macpherson really liked Robbie and was always braggin' to anyone who would listen that he was raisin' himself up a fine future son-in-law.

Tillie was an only child and was set to inherit the store when her daddy either retired or passed on. Tillie seemed mighty flighty to me, and lazy. I couldn't see her buckling down to work no store, but whoever married up with her was set, if they could stand to pay the price.

I never could quite understand why the fellas all seemed to like Tillie so much. No, actually like isn't the word. They chased after her in droves, even though she was goin' steady with Robbie. Come to think of it, even goin' steady with Robbie, she flirted with all the fellas.

It didn't seem to faze Robbie at all. She was pretty, beautiful actually, there was no way for even me to deny that. By sixteen she had blossomed into a tall, slender but shapely young woman. I always figured the fellas were so caught up with that glorious golden hair, extra-long eyelashes, and blue eyes that they couldn't think straight enough to pay attention to how she treated her daddy, and how she didn't seem to have a constant or faithful bone in her body.

Course, I always figured it was Mr. and Mrs. Macpherson's fault for raising Tillie so spoiled. Maybe if she hadn't been given everything she cried for, or maybe if she had been popped on the mouth like I was for sassin' my parents, maybe... just maybe she would have turned out different.

Actually, Tillie and Mrs. Macpherson both talked to Mr. Macpherson like he was some kind of mentally retarded young'un. He always had the look of a whipped huntin' hound to me, and I always felt kinda sorry for him. I couldn't for the life of me imagine talkin' to my daddy the way Tillie talked to hers. Mr. Macpherson was a nice man but didn't have much gumption to stand up for himself. Maybe that's why he liked Robbie so much. Robbie called him sir and was always respectful like he'd been taught to be. He worked hard, and by workin' hard made Mr. Macpherson's work easier. Little by little, Mr. Macpherson began relying on Robbie to take on more and more of the runnin' of Macpherson's store.

***

It was 1940, and there had been talk about the possibility of another war comin'. But this place called Europe was so far away I never did think it would have the least bit of effect on those of us in my mountains. I never gave it much thought until I started hearin' about somethin' called a draft that the government was tryin' to get made into law, and that young men over the age of twenty-one would be obliged to sign up for military service. I knew a lot of young men that was like Robbie, eighteen, too young to be drafted if it came, but gettin' uncomfortably close to it.

Now it would sound like from my ramblin's here that Robbie was the only fella I knew. That's not true; I knew all the boys I had gone to school with. There was Johnny Bailey, he was almost exactly Robbie's age, and so was George Hamil. Douglas Frasier, who most of us fondly called Doogie Fir, was sixteen, the same as me. Arthel Watson, who was blind but could play any instrument you put in his hands, was seventeen. Michael Shaw and Leonard McKemmy, whose nickname was Lemmy, were seventeen, nearly eighteen, and were on the same grade level in school as Robbie. They were just about finished with grammar school. Then there was Hooper Greene. He was nineteen and the oldest of the bunch of fellas.

There were lots of others. These were just the ones I guess I knew the best, the ones who would cause the war to have the most effect on me when it came. I had countless cousins too, loads of them in fact. Some of my cousins were near to bein' a brother to me.

Jamie Spencer was nearly as close to a twin to me as real twins are. We were born the same day practically beside each other. Daddy's brother, Uncle James, and his wife, Aunt Eunice, had the farm on the west side of the mountain we lived on. The fastest way to Jamie's was up over the mountain on foot on the old Indian trail.

Then there was my brother Gerry. Gerry was only a year younger than I was, and I was fifteen, going on sixteen. Gerry was close to bein' obsessed with war. I was young and still had no real understandin' of what kind of effect somethin' happening so far from my mountains would have on us. Mr. Macpherson had a radio in his store, and we often would sit on the porch of Macpherson's, drinkin' an ice-cold soda and listenin' to the radio.

The newscasts about what was going on in Europe seemed to trouble some folks quite a bit. Daddy didn't think we would get involved in this war. He said it was too soon since the last World War, and President Roosevelt wouldn't get us into another.

I heard Robbie, Lemmy, and Hooper Greene, and some of the other fellas talkin' about how Hitler had gobbled up one country after another, and Britain, France, Australia, New Zealand, and Canada had already gone to war against Hitler and his Nazis.

By his talk, I knew Robbie felt like the United States wouldn't be able to stay out of the war entirely. I felt like a traitor to Daddy, but I figured Robbie probably paid more attention to what was going on over there. Daddy was busy tryin' to support his family and make the farm pay. And it was doin' pretty good.

That summer of 1940, Mamma had agreed to let me try a small business experiment. Four of Mamma's Rhode Island Red hens had decided to set their eggs, and I asked Mamma if I could have the new pullets to raise and try to sell eggs over to the larger grocery store in Boone. Some of the fellas I knew had jobs at the furniture factory and had agreed to carry my eggs over for me to sell when my pullets began layin'.

Mamma was proud and happy that I was at last branching out and gettin' out of her skirt tail to find an interest in somethin' besides Robbie. I liked chickens and was happily counting my chickens before they hatched, literally. Each hen had a dozen eggs under her, so I was wholeheartedly counting on four dozen eggs a day when the hens began layin'.

If I got thirty-five cents a dozen for four dozen eggs a day, I would be earnin' a whoppin' nine dollars and eighty cents every week. I was extremely optimistic, or over-optimistic, whichever way you would want to look at it. I brooded over my mother's hens with almost as much motherly dedication as they brooded over their eggs.

By late June I wound up with a total of thirty-two Rhode Island Red pullets and ten roosters. We decided we would raise up the roosters to fry, and I would be left with thirty-two layin' hens if they all survived. Rhode Island Reds are good layers, and at the end of their layin' careers they make the finest pot of chicken and dumplings you ever tasted.

I was disappointed there were only thirty-two hens, but Mamma said I was very lucky that the ratio of pullets to roosters had been very high. Somebody had charmed the eggs in my favor. Now I was calculating thirty-two eggs a day, two hundred twenty-four eggs a week, eighteen and a half dozen at thirty-five cents a dozen, which would earn me about six dollars and fifty cents a week. Mamma still warned me that I was counting on too much.

July saw me spendin' a lot of time makin' sure that my pullets had the very best of care. I cleaned their coop every day and dumped the droppin's on Mamma's compost heap. Every other week I painted their roost with lime whitewash to kill mites and other pests that would affect the health and layin' of my new industry. Betty came over often too and offered her help. She was fascinated by the thought of me havin' my own property to take care of, and the idea of ownership of anything made me practically a millionairess already in her eyes.

It rained more often than was normal all summer, which sounds like a good thing, but it seemed nothin' ever had the chance to dry out good, that included the ground. Everywhere I stepped it seemed I stepped into a hole filled with sticky red clay mud, deep enough to suck Daddy's boots I would wear right off my feet. In fact, I quit tryin' to wear boots and just learned to not mind the mud, sometimes reachin' halfway up my shin when I stepped into a mud hole by accident.

August 5th, it began to rain and continued to rain off and on for a week. On August 11th a hurricane struck the coast of South Carolina and Georgia and then moved inland toward us, and on August 13th it began to rain hard. That's when the unthinkable nightmare began, and it seemed to me the very mouth of Hell opened up and swallowed so much of my home place, my community.

The cricks and rivers began to rise even higher than they already were, and the hillsides and mountainsides couldn't hold any more water. Great chunks of saturated soil and rocks broke away and began slidin' downwards, causin' mudslides everywhere.

Late in the afternoon, Granddad and Granny Spencer took refuge at our place on Spencer Farm. Their little cabin house was so close to the crick that the fast-rising water was swirling under the front porch and eroding the soil the porch posts were set into. Granddad said the porch was listing in the direction of the current when he and Granny left, throwin' a few clothes and their wedding picture into the space behind the seats in Granddad's pickup truck.

I was scared. The rain was like nothin' I had ever seen in my mountains. I was used to wild storms. There were times I thought it sounded like great giants were crashing through my mountains, heavin' rocks at each other and causin' the great booming thunder. But this was different. The rain was solid sheets of water falling out of the dark sky. Lightning split the sky and trees all around us, and when it thundered, it felt as though our house was bein' shaken by some huge unseen force.

Suddenly, just as it was gettin' dark, we heard a rumble. It sounded like a great thunder that didn't have an end, but rumbled and shook continuously, growin' louder and louder. There was a mudslide comin' from the mountain behind the house. We didn't have time to run away or do one thing about it.

Granddad Spencer had called us all to come together in the living room, which was in the front part of our house. We huddled together while Granddad called on the Almighty for protection. Daddy had his arms around Mamma and me. I had one arm around Daddy and one around Gerry. Mamma had Daddy and Charlie, and Granddad and Granny completed the circle, arms around each other and us young'uns at their sides. My mind was taken back to when the winter storm had trapped all us schoolchildren at the schoolhouse, and Mr. Jenkins prayed, and God answered.

As Granddad prayed, again a great calm came over me. There was no change in anything, except I was no longer terrified, even though the house was shakin' like I had always imagined an earthquake would feel. I looked up and out the side porch window, lookin' toward our barn that I couldn't see for the great sheets of rain pourin' down. I could hardly believe what I was seein'.

A massive river of mud was tearin' down the mountain. It was so close I could see it in spite of the rain. Rocks, trees, and boulders tumbled and mixed with the rollin' mud that almost looked like a living thing in its movements. The noise was so loud by now we could hardly hear Granddad praying, and it had taken on a sort of hissing or whizzing sound mixed with the thunderous bangs and cracks.

Mamma looked about the same time I did and screamed somethin' awful, turnin' her face into Daddy's chest. I know she thought, like I did, it was over for the Spencer family of Spencer Farm.

Granddad never even paused in his prayin', and I kept waitin' for the house with all us Spencers in it to be gobbled up by the mudslide. But we weren't, and after what seemed like several minutes the shakin' and continuous thunder slowed, then finally stopped.

We all just stood there in the middle of the living room with our arms around each other, holdin' on for all we were worth. Mamma was cryin' and shakin' so bad she was havin' a hard time just standin'. Had it not been for Daddy's arm around her, I don't think she could have stood. Charlie held tight to Mamma's legs, scared both by what had just happened and by our Mamma's scream and tears. Gerry and I were silent, as though sayin' anything might start the mudslide again. Granddad continued to pray out loud, with Granny praying silently. I could see her lips movin' as she prayed for our protection.

By now it was dark, and the rain was still pourin' down in sheets, like someone was dumping water out of thousand-gallon buckets from the sky. Lightning zapped, popped, and banged all around us, lighting up everything in scary blue flashes. The thunder was still crashing with booms that shook our house, but at least they had an end, unlike the thunderous sounds of the mudslide.

Granddad continued to pray, but his prayer had become a prayer of thanksgivin'.

"Lord, we thank you for protecting our family from this evil. Thank you for sparing our lives and keepin' us safe. We know not how others in our parts have fared, but we ask you, Lord, to be with our family James and Eunice and their children. Keep them safe. We pray for our neighbors and friends and ask for their protection. Hide them under your mighty wings, Oh God. Keep them safe through this storm. Protect the stranger or travelers who may have been passing through; may they find safety and refuge. We are grateful for your strong hand that delivered us from destruction. May we ever thank you and serve you. Amen."

Chapter Nine

August 14th dawned gray and dismal, but at least the torrential rain had stopped. We went out onto the front porch to see how much damage had been done. We all stood frozen on the front porch of Spencer Farmhouse, hardly able to believe what our eyes were seein'. The mudslide had passed between the house and barn and missed the back corner of the house by only seven or eight feet, but it had hit the side of our barn facing the house. It was hard to tell from the porch just how much of the barn was still standin', but I could hear our Jersey milk cow Abigail lowing from somewhere inside, needing to be milked since it hadn't been done the night before. It was good to know she had survived.

Between the barn and the house was a wasteland of mud, rocks, and broken trees where there had been green grass and flowers the day before. The crick at the bottom of the hill below the barn had almost, but not quite, reached the barn. That was a good thing for Abigail and any other critters that had survived. We could see how high the waters had reached by the pieces of trees, debris from the crick, and what looked like wooden boards and such strewn along the high-water mark.

Daddy and Granddad Spencer decided to try to wade across the mud to feed Abigail and our old horse Bob that Daddy used for plowing. It was about seventy-five feet from the house to the barn, so it was going to be a tiring trip across.

"Stay on the porch," Daddy said. "Aint' no use ya'll gettin' muddy and wet. Granddad and I will see to the critters and check how much damage there is."

It was only after Daddy had made his way across the mud to the barn that he was able to see what had saved us. The house was built on a vertical upcropping that ran up and down the mountain at a slight angle. It wasn't all that high, but just high enough to cause the mud to shift course enough to miss the house. Without knowin' it, Daddy had chosen the site of our house well, with natural protection from the mudslide.

Granddad said it was Providence that had caused Daddy to build the house in that precise spot. He said God knew that almost twenty years later we would need that protection. Daddy didn't argue the fact. It seemed like he was more open to believing the Almighty might have had a hand in it.

After Daddy and Granddad had fed Abigail and Bob, he skirted around the mudslide to pick up the old Indian trail up and over the mountain to check on Uncle James and Aunt Eunice. Granny Spencer had fretted herself near sick over how they had fared, and Daddy, bein' concerned about his brother and his family, promised to hike over the mountain on foot to check on them. He was back home within a couple of hours to report that the other side of the mountain had weathered the storm very well, and there were no mudslides. Flooding was bad everywhere, and all the cricks and rivers had overflowed their banks, but Uncle James and Aunt Eunice, Jamie, and the girls were all fine and dandy. The worst problem they had to contend with was a couple of shingles blown off Uncle James's barn roof during the storm, which had caused a leak. Uncle James promised to help Daddy with his barn repair as soon as Daddy wanted to get started.

Robbie came by Spencer Farm later that day to check on us. He said he was goin' around the Deep Gap community to check on folks. He had parked his truck up the road, as it was blocked by one of the nearly eight hundred landslides that marred the mountainsides of Watauga County. His family's home had survived unharmed except for some roof damage from the heavy rain and high winds. But Macpherson's store was another story.

A massive mudslide nearly two hundred feet across had engulfed Mr. Macpherson's store, bustin' it loose from its foundation, then rollin' it over and over until it was finally crushed to pieces. The only good thing was Mr. and Mrs. Macpherson and Tillie were in Boone at the time, havin' gone to the theater to see a picture show. The massive slide had hit the store after Robbie had decided to close up early because of the storm and go home.

I wasn't going to say so, but I sure was glad Robbie hadn't been workin' in the store when it was ground to pieces by that mudslide. Mighty glad.

Other folks, like Robbie, were out helpin' with the attempts to find people who were still missin'. Searches and rescues were havin' to be carried out mostly on horseback or on foot. Just about every single road had at least one mudslide blocking the way. Later we heard that on Highway 421 there were twenty-one places where mudslides had blocked the road. It would take a lot of work to get the roads passable.

***

In all the aftermath of the great flood, something happened that was barely noticed at the time. On September 16, the government put into law the Selective Training and Service Act of 1940. This law required all men between the ages of twenty-one and forty-five to register for the draft.

There had never been a peacetime draft before, and a lot of folks hardly knew what to make of it. The President had been insisting we were keepin' our noses out of the fighting that had broken out in Europe. We had been supplying Britain with weapons and supplies, but not men. Most of the older people of Granddad's generation remembered the previous war, The World War, and they didn't want to see their grandsons fightin' in no war.

Numerous young men from our area were lost to that horrible time, and many weren't even brought home for their families to mourn over and bury. They were buried in countries none of the people from my mountains had ever been to and had barely heard of. Granddad lost cousins and friends in that war, and it always bothered him, seein' as how he had been rejected by the government on account of his heart murmur. I never could understand why Granddad seemed to feel guilty, or like he was somehow at fault for the deaths of his cousins and friends.

The more I heard about how that Hitler fella was taking huge bites out of Europe and swallowing them up like a monstrous dragon into his somethin' or another called a Third Reich, the more I was afraid we wouldn't be able to keep out of this fight for long. No matter what President Roosevelt said.

A lot of folks everywhere were against getting involved. They just didn't feel like it was our war, and none of our business. I sure wasn't a politician, and I never did claim to know anything about how the affairs of this old world work. But one man taking over Europe one country at a time like some big bully just didn't seem right to me. The way I saw it, if nothin' stood in his way and he got Europe like he seemed to be wanting to, what was going to keep his sights off our shores?

Cleanup from the great flood was going on, and that was the main thing that occupied most folks' minds. The cricks and rivers had to be cleaned; they were clogged with everything from broken-up trees, mud, and dead animals to pieces of the busted-up houses and buildings that had been destroyed. The smell from all the rotting dead animals trapped in the flood debris was so overpowering in some areas that the men workin' the cleanup often vomited and had to tie handkerchiefs over their noses just to be able to stand it.

The body of a woman from the area was found in a river clear over in Wilkes County. A dam had busted on the Watauga River and had sent a twenty-seven-foot wall of water crashing down the already flooded river through several communities and towns, reachin' clear into Tennessee. Every day there was news of this loss or that tragedy. The already poor people were now dealin' with so much more than they already had been. Trying to put food on their tables and make frazzled ends meet somehow.

I was grieving over so many things. The losses were mind-boggling to me. Fifteen folks dead in Watauga County alone. Among those dead were my friend Betty Holder, her mamma, little sister, and two of her three brothers. All dead, their little cabin shack buried under one of the many mudslides that devastated my mountains. It was a couple of days before I heard of the tragedy. There was so much destruction, death, and loss of property that it left me feelin' numb, like some Doc had stuck me with a needle and numbed my mind and body.

About half of the Greene family had been killed too. Out of Mr. and Mrs. Greene and five young'uns, the only ones to survive were Mrs. Greene, the youngest child, and the oldest son, Hooper. Mr. Greene and three daughters, all dead. The same massive mudslide in Deep Gap that had destroyed Macpherson's store had traveled a mile down the mountain before smashing into their house. I reckon it was a miracle any of them lived at all.

Railroad tracks were washed away, scores of homes either smashed by mudslides or buried. Nine bridges over New River and many farms were laid in ruin from almost every corner of the county to the other. Railroad service to the area was out for a month, and some areas never did get it back. The cost of rebuilding a rail bed and layin' new track was too great. In the days and weeks following the flood, the papers told of the enormity of the flood's destruction. They estimated that thirty homes and fifty barns were completely washed away, not counting the severe damage to seventy-five more homes. Then there were the damaged crops and gardens of almost a thousand farmers. I was one of those farmers, or at least a prospective farmer.

I realize my loss was nothing compared to the loss so many of my friends and neighbors faced. Some had lost entire farms that slid down mountainsides and came to rest in smaller mountains of a grotesque mixture of mud, wood, dead animals, and anything else that got caught in its path. But my dream of being a businesswoman with my own income hurt when it died.

My daddy's barn was badly damaged, but salvageable. It would take a lot of time and lumber to fix it though. My poor pullets had been in the destroyed section of daddy's barn. It was a mess, and my egg-selling enterprise was gone with it.

Walking across the mudslide was next to impossible, so daddy pulled some wood planks out of the debris along the crick and laid them on top of the mud to have a path to walk on to the barn. It only took a time or two across, and the planks were sinking out of sight and had to be replaced every couple of days. Wood became more and more scarce. The same rain and mud that had wiped out farms and houses had also wiped out many of the area's lumber mills. That made lumber near impossible to get and very expensive if you did.

Daddy worried over how he was going to be able to fix the barn that was propped up on one side with poles cut from trees. In the end, he and Uncle James went far into the surrounding area to find spots that weren't so hard hit by the devastating mud and cut trees to rebuild the missing section of barn out of small logs. The barn always had a queer pieced-together look after that. I guess it was a reminder to us afterward that it could have been worse. It could have been the whole barn with Abigail and Bob in it, or the house too with us in it.

As with just about any disaster, folks start lookin' for the cause. Over a week of heavy rain is a lot of rain, but why did the mountainsides just give way and take off? The landslide that took out Macpherson's store and the Greene's was reported to be two hundred feet wide and slid several miles, wiping out two service stations, any many houses on its way down.

The cause of the whole awful mess was, of course, the fact that huge areas of the mountains had been stripped of their trees, leavin' no roots to hold the ground, and not enough thirsty trees to drink up the hundreds of thousands of gallons of water poured out on the mountains in a matter of a few days. Spencer Farm had been logged years before, back before the turn of the century, by Granddad's daddy. They just didn't consider back then what would happen to the land when they stripped it of so many trees.

As I have said before, most of the folks here in my mountains are poor, very poor. It takes every bit of imagination a body has to find ways to make enough cash to buy the things folks can't raise up here. Like wheat flour, and other things like medical care beyond the care we gave ourselves through herbs, and other mountain medicine.

That's one reason why some folks, who really are good people, would convert the corn they raised into corn likker, or moonshine. It brought more cash than corn did and was easier to carry out of the mountains. I don't hold to moonshinin'. I'm just sayin' things aren't always as cut and dry as outsiders might think. Sometimes, poor people feel they have to get the most cash they can out of their farmin' efforts.

Sellin' the timber off their land to the lumber companies was another cash crop a lot of folks made use of. The lumber companies promised big dollars to anyone who would sell them their trees. The problem was, when they sold their timber off the land, it was left naked with nothin' to hold the soil in place on those steep mountainsides. Instead of selecting certain trees to be harvested, they just took them all out.

Nowadays lumber companies replant the trees they take out. True, it will take hundreds of years to restore the old forests that used to be here, but at least it's better than not planting anything at all. There used to be chestnut trees that were so big it would take six or seven grown men circling them with their hands clasped to go around them. It was a blight that took those glorious giants, and over time they just died out. The old pictures I see of those trees make my heart so sad. They were still around when I was a young'un, and that should tell you how quickly things we take for granted can change.

Chapter Ten

The young men of twenty-one and over had to find time, in all the hard work of tryin' to restore and clean up after the flood and mudslides, to register for the draft that President Roosevelt had put into law in September. I had second cousins in Virginia who fell in the age range of twenty-one to thirty-five who were called up. We weren't at war yet, although a lot of folks, including Robbie, didn't think it would be long before we would be in the middle of it.

The young men bein' called up at this point were right jolly about it, and eager for the chance to teach that Hitler fella a good lesson. The United States didn't seem to be in too much danger. Actually, if it weren't for the fact that we were allies with so many of the countries involved, I wouldn't have given the war in Europe very much thought. It was so far away.

My second cousins, Marvin and Kenny, thought the whole thing was an exciting adventure that would last a few months, then they would be back home to carry on with life and work. They were off to Army trainin' camp before we knew it, and their mamma and girlfriends enjoyed readin' their letters and tellin' about the great time Marvin and Kenny was a havin'. They were big, strong, hardworkin' men, so the trainin', though tough, seemed like one big outdoors adventure to them.

Lookin' back, I guess it was a good thing I didn't know Christmas that year, 1940, was the last Christmas we had together with the Spencer family intact. I was sixteen years old, and it was an especially happy time. Christmas had always been a time the whole clan came together. Spencer's from all around, even as far away as Virginia, came to enjoy a week of family togetherness and lots of good food. None of us were what you would call rich, but we always had plenty to eat, what with the gardens and meat-producin' critters Daddy, Granddad, and Uncle James raised. So, Christmas was a time of indulgence as far as food was concerned.

Granny Spencer was famous for her pies. Flakier, tenderer crust has never been turned out by any cook, anywhere. And she passed her pie-makin' legacy to her daughter-in-law, my mamma, and myself. Christmas was a time we made many pies, so delicious it almost hurts to think of them. Apple, huckleberry, peach, pumpkin, and mince pies were so numerous you could almost hear the old dining room sideboard cryin' for mercy.

Smoked hams cured by Daddy and Granddad had a place of honor in the middle of the table. And there were always other meats too: roasted chicken, venison roast, and Aunt Eunice's spaghetti that all the young'uns loved so well. Bowls and bowls of vegetables lined the kitchen counter: creamed corn, lima beans seasoned with bits of ham, green beans, also seasoned with bits of bacon, mashed potatoes, and sweet potatoes swimming in candied sauce, fried cabbage, mashed turnips, turnip greens. And Mamma's sourdough rolls to sop gravy were so good I sometimes chose one more roll instead of dessert.

Mamma always made sure the house was decorated real festive for Christmas too. The woods were full of all we needed. Boughs of Eastern Hemlock with its tiny cones clingin' to the branches were my favorite and filled the air with a wonderful smell. Branches of Mountain Laurel, always green, looked so beautiful when Mamma would string the branches together to make a garland to lay over the fireplace mantel. Tucked in here and there would be large pinecones and red berries to make everything beautiful, warm, and festive. Simmering on the back of the wood cookstove was a small pot of orange peel and cloves, or bayberry or wintergreen leaves gathered from the woods, to make the house smell like Christmas as well as lookin' like Christmas.

This year, Granddad's youngest sibling, Uncle Albert, and his wife, Auntie Mae, were comin' for Christmas from Virginia along with their son Uncle Albert Jr., who was my Daddy's cousin, and his wife Aunt Ellie, and their teenage sons William, Carter, and David. With all of us North Carolina Spencer's and the visitin' Virginia Spencer's, we were in for a full house and a good time.

Granddad had promised to tell the story of how our ancestors came to be in Scotland, bein' as how the name Spencer is originally

English. So, with all the young'uns gathered around after dark on Christmas Eve, Granddad began his story.

***

"Liam Padraig Spencer was my great-grandad seven times removed. He was a medium-tall redheaded man like most of our Spencer men are. He lived in Ulster, Ireland, and he and his wife Fiona inherited a large store from his parents James and Bridget in Belfast."

Grandad Spencer sat back in his rockin' chair and stared up at the ceiling for a minute like he was tryin' to read the story from the rafters of the old farmhouse. He was at his best when he had all his grandkids gathered around, hangin' on his every word.

"Liam was the first Spencer to cross the water to America and settle in this new land. He was the son of James and Bridget Spencer. Bridget was a Catholic Irish girl who had black hair and blue eyes so blue they would startle a body who looked into them for the first time. She was a bonny lass, make no mistake about that! It's no wonder my great-grandaddy fell head over heels in love with her. Her family were not rich, but not poor either. Her daddy owned a store in Belfast, and it did a right good business."

"James was the son of John Robert and Margaret Spencer, who were Lowland Scots and strict Calvinist Presbyterians. They agreed to go to Ulster, Ireland, and settle with other Lowland Scots to farm and help populate the area with Protestants. Ireland had been mostly

99

Catholic before English kings decided to send Protestant landowners and farmers to farm the Ulster Plantations."

"John Robert had been loyal to the hope of a Scotland that was free from English tyranny. He knew all the stories of the atrocities and horrors the English government had hammered Scotland with for centuries. There had been famines in the Lowlands for several years in a row. Crop failure and looming starvation caused much despair, and finally, in desperation, John Robert decided to declare loyalty to the English government. He agreed to take his newly pregnant wife and work for a new Laird in Ireland in hopes that the promised better life would happen. They arrived in Ireland in the fall of 1661."

"Over the next few years, John Robert and Margaret became skilled linen weavers. The linen industry had once been a huge success in Ireland, but government regulations had nearly destroyed it completely. On a few Plantations, though, there was enough flax grown to keep some weavers in business. John Robert and Margaret were two of the few remaining linen weavers, workin' twelve to fourteen hours, six days a week."

"Life was still hard. The promised 'good life' had not been a reality, and starvation never seemed far away, even with John Robert and Margaret both workin' hard. Life as a tenant Plantation worker had not been as promised. Besides the terrible living conditions in rat-infested hovels and long workdays, there was the constant tension between the Irish Catholics and the Protestant

Plantation workers. Fightin' was a daily happening, expected. Each side bitterly hated the other."

Grandad Spencer paused to look down at his audience of us grandkids and frowned thoughtfully. He seemed to think hard about what he was fixin' to say, pushed his spectacles higher up his nose, and went on.

"Fightin' and hatin' lead to sorrow and death no matter where it's goin' on, kids. Don't ever forget that. There's a reason the Good Book tells us to love our neighbor. Proverbs says, 'Hatred stirreth up strifes: but love covereth all sins.' If folks all over the world would read and obey the Book, we wouldn't have all this talk of war and fightin'."

"John Robert and Margaret had six children born to them, and a set of stillborn twins. James Robert was their firstborn. He was handsome and smart and had a twin brother, William Alexander. He saw the hard life his parents had, despite their long hours of hard work, and determined in his heart that someday, somehow, he would break free of this world of servitude—not only to a Laird who only got richer by the hard work of his tenants, but also to a government he despised."

"Children began work at an early age, helpin' their parents with what work they could. By the time James was sixteen, he too was a skilled weaver and worked as hard as his parents before him. His mother Margaret, worn out from hard work and bearin' children, had died when James was only ten years old during the birth of her youngest child, his baby sister Marjorie.

Not long after Margaret's death, James's twin brother William was accidentally killed when caught in the middle of fightin' between a bunch of Catholics and Protestants while playin' in the street. The little cottage became such a lonely place, even with people living in it. James would often wander around the streets of Lisburn because he couldn't bear to be in the cottage without his mother and his brother."

When James was sixteen, he asked his Da if he could go to Belfast to find work. John Robert hated to see his eldest child leave but knew that it was the best way for James to find a better life than he had. James promised to come home as often as he could, bein' that Belfast was only ten miles away.

"John Robert had remarried a widow lady named Sara Dougall, who was also a Lowland Scott. Her husband had died two years before. She had two young daughters, so the little cottage was bursting at the seams with children, leavin' no room for him anyway."

"So, in the summer of 1668, James walked to Belfast after havin' only been there once before in his life. He didn't have a plan or a place to live, only the clothes on his back and a poke with some bread and sausages to eat, enough for a couple of days."

"He was in awe of the city and all the comin's and goin's. Horses and carts clattered up and down the streets haulin' this and that, makin' deliveries, and transporting goods to and from the wharves and docks. He decided that the best place to find a job in a place like Belfast was at the docks."

"When he got there, he saw a man overseein' the loading of boxes onto a large wagon pulled by four stout horses. The man looked prosperous, but he looked around him kindly and smiled big at James when he approached."

"'Are you lookin' for a job, Laddie?' asked the man.

'I sure am, sir. Do you know of anyone who needs a good strong back?'

"The man threw back his head and laughed a big jolly laugh.

'Well, as it happens, I sure do! And it's me. When can you start?' he asked."

Grandad looked us young'uns over again and said, "Never be afraid of good honest hard work, kids! There's joy to be found in the satisfaction of standin' back and lookin' at all you've accomplished."

"Speakin' of hard work, Maggie, ask your Granny how much time I have to finish this here story before the food's ready. The smells are about to kill me!"

I jumped up and ran to the kitchen, scared to death I would miss some of Grandad's story, and was back in a flash. Granny had shooed me away, pink-cheeked with damp bits of hair around her heat-flushed and pleasantly wrinkled face, with an impatient hand tellin' me it would be ready when it was ready. Then she quickly added, "'Bout thirty minutes."

"'Bout thirty minutes, Grandad," I said when I slid back into my spot on the floor.

"Shoot," he said, "I'll have to hurry, and I still won't get finished!

"So, James went to work for Mr. Devon Kilpatrick, owner of Kilpatrick's of Belfast, a mercantile store in the middle of Belfast that sold a little bit of just about everything. James's first job for Mr. Kilpatrick was loading the boxes of goods that arrived on the docks onto Kilpatrick wagons headin' for the store's warehouse. He would then unload the wagon, then ride the wagon back to the dock for another load."

"It was hard work, but James was happy. He got plenty to eat, he had a warm bed in a small room in the warehouse, and he had every Sunday and a half day on Saturday off. After his room and board, he had a little money left over and began to save every pence that he could spare."

"After workin' for Mr. Kilpatrick for a month, he decided to walk home for a visit to his family in Lisburn. He figured it would be an easy thing to leave Belfast after his half Saturday and be back Sunday night, ready to work again on Monday. He had been so busy workin' hard during the day, and so tired from the hours of heavy lifting, he crashed into his bed, sleepin' like he had been knocked in the head until daybreak the next mornin'. He had hardly even thought about his family in Lisburn and felt like a heel for it."

"Saturday after workin' his half day, he informed the warehouse manager that he would be away to visit his family and wouldn't be around until Sunday evenin' late. Folding a bit of bread and roasted mutton into a cloth, he set out for Lisburn. The weather was good, only a brief bit of misty rain, and the rest of the way was a pleasant walk."

"It took James about half the afternoon, but he didn't mind and soon arrived at his family's cottage long before it was gettin' dark. But the small cottage didn't show any signs of life, and now that James thought of it, neither did the little town of Lisburn. He ran the last bit toward his Da's cottage, only to be stopped by the sight of his father, thin, bent over, and limping slowly through the open doorway of the little cottage."

"Da!" James cried out. "What is wrong? What has happened?"

John Robert turned to see James runnin' toward him, and slowly held out his hand to stop James from comin' closer.

"No, Laddie, don't come any closer. There's sickness in the house. Bad sickness that is catchin'."

James obeyed his father and stopped short of him, but longed to gather his sick Da into his arms. Da had always been a big man, a strong man. This thin, bent, gaunt-faced stranger could hardly be his strong handsome Da!

"What is the sickness, Da? Who all is sick? Is there anyone to care for you all? What can I do?" James felt like he could hardly breathe for the fear that rose in him.

"It's the bloody flux, lad," said John Robert. "You canna come any closer. You canna help except to pray. Sara and both her daughters, your sisters Marjorie and Agnes, are all gone. They're dead," he replied, as though he could hardly believe what he was sayin'. "I believe I will live, although I am terrible weak. Your brothers Malcome and Charlie are very sick. I don't know if they will live."

John Robert leaned on the walkin' stick he gripped in both hands and fought to keep his composure as he went on.

"The bloody flux came to Lisburn not long after you left for Belfast. It's been the worst I've ever seen. Some say it's caused from warmer than normal weather, but I don't know. Our neighbors have been bringin' food as they can and leavin' it by the door, but all are afraid to come in to help, and rightly so. They have families to protect too. Go back to Belfast, lad. Pray for us, but go back. You canna help us here, and I want at least one of us to survive this terrible thing."

James stood fast, feelin' helpless. Then he remembered the few coins he had in his pocket. He had brought them just in case he needed them. He took his poke off his back that had the bread and mutton in it and laid it on a wooden box in the front garden of the little cottage. He placed two small handfuls of coins on top of the poke.

"This isn't much, Da, but maybe it will help some. Maybe with the coins you can get a doctor for Malcome and Charlie. I'll wait a few weeks and come back, Da, I promise I will!"

James gulped air, tryin' to keep from cryin' out when he saw the tears shinin' in his father's dull, sunken eyes.

"Send word if you can, Da. I'm workin' for Mr. Devon Kilpatrick in Belfast. He owns Kilpatrick's Mercantile."

"I will, son, if I can," said John Robert. "I need to get Malcome and Charlie some water now. They are awful hot with fever. You take good care of yourself, James, and pray for us."

"I will, Da! I promise I will!"

James whirled and ran as hard as he could, retracin' his earlier joyful steps back to Belfast. Only this time, it was fear for what remained of his family that drove him onward. He had promised his Da that he would pray for him, Malcome, and Charlie.

Pray. He hadn't prayed since he had left Lisburn over a month ago. Truth to tell, he hadn't prayed much since the death of his mother and brother William six years earlier. He hadn't really thought about it a lot, but felt a sudden jolt of anger and realized he hadn't prayed because he was mad. Mad that God had let his mother and brother die.

Now that same God had let his younger sisters, stepsisters, and stepmother die. How much good, he wondered, did the prayin' actually do? He thought of his baby sister Marjorie, only six years old and as pretty as a little wildflower that grew by the riverside.

James stumbled into Belfast in the early mornin' hours of Sunday. The city was mostly asleep, and the warehouse manager was certainly asleep. James slumped onto the ground beside the main door and slept fitfully for a few hours. At dawn, he was awakened by the warehouse manager shakin' him awake.

"Boy, what are you doin' out here? I thought you were goin' to visit your family in Lisburn," he said shortly.

"I did," said James, avoidin' the man's eyes. "They were sick, some of them dead. My Da wouldn't let me come near. He told me to come back, to stay away until the sickness passed."

The warehouse manager's abrupt manner changed, and he looked at James with sympathy.

"You say you weren't around them? Do you know what the sickness was?"

"No," replied James. "My Da wouldn't let me come near him. Da said it was the bloody flux."

"Go to bed, boy, get some sleep. I'll let Mr. Kilpatrick know what happened."

James stumbled off to bed, achin' in body as well as spirit. Fallin' into bed without takin' off his clothes, he finally allowed himself to let the tears fall.

"Why God?" he cried. "Why little Marjorie? Why Agnes, Sara, and her little girls? Why my Ma and William? Why did they all have to die?"

He had been fond of Sara and her little girls. Sara was kind and motherly without tryin' to be a replacement for his own mother. He had loved her like an Auntie.

Grandad Spencer paused long in his story, and us young'uns sat quiet while the fire snapped and popped in the fireplace. It seemed he was completely overcome by the emotion of his story of long-ago ancestors.

Grandad began his story again but felt the need to explain somethin'.

"Each generation is shaped and molded by the events that affected our ancestors. One traumatic experience or a string of traumatic experiences can sometimes wound a person's spirit, causin' a deep hurt that turns into bitterness, that turns into anger, that lashes out at everyone around them. It doesn't mean they are evil, but they can sometimes let the Evil One have control over them for a season, not even knowin' that is what is guidin' their actions.

"James did just that. He woke up, went back to work for Mr. Kilpatrick, but he was wounded and different. Instead of turnin' to his Maker for comfort, he dwelled on his loss and his hurt. He didn't seek God or realize that bein' a mortal man, he wasn't able to know the end as though it were the beginning. He didn't seek or find comfort in the words in The Book:

And we know that all things work together for good to them that love God, to them who are the called according to his purpose.

"After all, what good comes from such loss? Mortal man doesn't have the answers to that question, and it doesn't help a body to demand to know. That's where faith and trust has to be your solace. That's where a body has to be able to let go of the hurt and anger and allow the Almighty to be the Almighty. Only He knows from eternity to eternity."

Grandad let his eyes land on me. Ever so briefly, not to draw attention, but I knew. I knew his loving heart was concerned for me, was reachin' out to speak to the bitter anger that festered and was like acid eatin' away everything good in my heart.

Granny Spencer stepped through the door and with a wave of her hand said,

"Come on and get it or I'll throw it out!"

Laughin' her rollin', good-natured laugh that made her pink cheeks even pinker.

All us young'uns jumped up and headed for the big room that was both kitchen and dining room. There, on the dining table and the big oak sideboard Grandad had made, was a feast that made all other feasts look like humble pickins!

Chapter Eleven

After dinner, everyone was so stuffed full of all the abundant goodness that Granny Spencer, Mamma, and all the aunts had provided that things settled down to a comfortable quiet. I was of an age, caught between bein' one of the young'uns and a full-grown adult, and was expected to help clear the table. I was the eldest of the girl cousins, Uncle James and Aunt Eunice's twin girls, Maude and Lilly Anne, were four years younger than me. So, it was also my job to scrape what little scraps were left on plates onto one plate to take out to the barn and feed to the hogs and chickens.

Granddad, Daddy, and all the uncles, moaning over their full stomachs, went to the big living room before the fireplace to sit and either stare into the fire or quietly discuss the ever-present war news. Granddad seemed tired and nodded off from time to time, while the low drone of male voices lulled him to doze. Daddy wanted to talk about the ongoing flood cleanup efforts and stock prices with the uncles, but I could hear the teenage male cousins, along with my brother Gerry, sittin' separate in a corner talkin' about the draft and the possibility of war.

I didn't like hearin' the talk of war. It made me feel uneasy, and somethin' inside of me wanted to dig a deep hole out in the garden, crawl in, and pull the dirt over the top of me. As though I wanted to hide from what I knew deep down was a comin'. It hadn't been all that many years since the Great War had stolen many a young man from my mountains and left gapin' holes in the hearts of mothers and sweethearts. Many a family farm suffered too, because strong young sons had not come back home to help bear the burden of raising crops to sustain the family.

My own sweet Daddy had narrowly escaped bein' sent to Europe to fight in that war. He turned 18 the month before the war ended. Granddad had been branded an F-4 unfit for service, and it had gnawed at his pride since. Granddad was forty years old and told for the first time in his life that he had a heart murmur bad enough to keep him home. He worked the fields as hard as the mules he used before gettin' a tractor and had never known about the heart murmur until the Army doctors examined him. Granny always held that it was the hand of the Almighty that had culled him out and kept him home. He still would get steamed up about it.

Later, after I had fed the scraps of food to Granny's flock of Rhode Island Reds, I went back into the warmth of Granny and Granddad's house and wandered from room to room, listenin' a bit to the older men's talk of farmin' and the younger boys' talk of war.

In the kitchen, the women were talkin' about the year's harvest and the many quarts and pint jars of everything from a host of different vegetables to canned meats, jams, jellies, chutneys, and relishes. They talked about how much had been set aside for family use and how much was to be sent to our family produce stand that was such a hit with the annual summer tourist crowd. There was Auntie Mae's newsy chatter about all the cousins in Virginia who were either engaged to be married or expectin' a whole new crop of little Virginia Spencers.

Aunt Eunice and Granny were debating whether the rich cane sugar the farm produced every year from a patch of sugar cane Daddy grew was better for sweetening the scrumptious pies they had made than the maple syrup collected from the big sugar maples in the back woods and cooked down to a thick amber syrup. They were both equally good in my book.

I grew restless and went from room to room lookin' for somewhere to fit in and feel comfortable. About that time, Granddad snorted awake, looked up at me, and said, "I wasn't asleep, girlie, I was just restin' my eyes."

We all grinned silently at each other because we had all heard him snoring, but we didn't say so, and I plopped down on the hassock sittin' beside his rocker.

"Granddad, what happened to James? The James who lived in Ireland?"

Granddad rubbed his eyes and looked up at the old grandfather clock that held a place of honor in the middle of the biggest wall in the room. "I guess there's time left in the evenin' to finish tellin'

James's story. Gather up the other young'uns that want to hear and I'll finish."

I jumped up and ran upstairs where I knew Lilly Anne and Maude were sharin' secrets and gigglin' with some of the younger girls and said, "Quick, girls, Granddad is going to finish James's story!"

I jerked open the back door and hollered out to the boys who had been sleddin' on the hill beside the house long enough to be half frozen and ready to come inside to warm up and hear the rest of James's story.

Granny smiled from her rest at the kitchen table and said, "How about some hot cocoa to go with Granddad's story?"

"Yay!" A cheer went up from all the young'uns who were blowing through the kitchen to hang snowy coats, hats, and scarves on pegs that lined the kitchen wall beside the back door, and a jumble of boots was tossed into a pile beneath the drippin' coats.

Soon everyone was settled back into the living room, sittin' in a semicircle in front of Granddad Spencer as he rocked and smiled at the jostlin' and settlin' in. Even the adults were pulling up chairs to hear Granddad tell of our long-ago ancestors who lived across the water in Scotland and Ireland.

I don't know why. I've never really understood why I always feel such a tug on my heart when I listen to the stories of our ancestors and the strange and glorious places they came from. I felt such a kinship when I heard about their struggles and their overcoming them. I was especially lookin' forward to hearin' the rest of James's story, because I knew in my heart that somewhere down the family strain had trickled down to me the tendency to hold a grudge in my heart and bear the unwillingness to forgive and let bygones be bygones.

After all us young'uns and most of the adults were settled down, cradlin' steamy cups of Granny's wonderful, sweet cocoa, Granddad smiled at his own little clan that looked up at him from their places on the floor with expectant looks on every single face. He rocked quietly for a minute and began James's story where he had left off.

"I want to say here before I finish up James's story that the Almighty never loses control of those who are called according to His purpose. It may look like it for a season, and wayward children often think they are completely on their own while away from Him, but that's just not how it works. The Lord never loses sight of His own young'uns."

"Just as James had a Heavenly Father who loved him and cared for him through his rebellious years, he also had an earthly father, John Robert, who faithfully prayed for his son daily."

"John Robert managed to care for his sons Malcolm and Charlie even though he was desperately ill himself. They all survived, and their convalescence was long and difficult."

"Malcolm remained sickly the rest of his life and died in his twenties because of the damage the illness had done to him."

"Charlie recovered and continued to live and work with his father John Robert as a linen weaver. He married a Scottish girl from the area and had a family. He was the great granddad of Angus, the highlander who escaped from the British. They lived in the little cottage with John Robert and cared for him until his death as an old man."

"James continued to go back to Lisburn to visit his family every month and at Christmas. But his job became his solace, and he worked long hours, pushing himself as he loaded wagons like a madman, pushin' back the memories of all he had lost."

"After six months, the warehouse manager approached James with an offer. He needed an assistant to help him with managing the wagons and drivers that brought goods from the docks to the warehouse."

"Mr. Kilpatrick had expanded his store to become the largest and finest mercantile in Belfast. Goods were comin' into Belfast harbor on a daily basis, and the warehouse manager, Mr. Feeney, was feeling more frazzled tryin' to manage both the warves and the stocking of the warehouse."

"James began his new role as assistant warehouse manager after six months of workin' for Mr. Devon Kilpatrick at the ripe old age of seventeen. He had impressed Mr. Feeney with his honesty and his dedication to his job. James had found an error in Mr. Feeney's accounting of the wagons of merchandise."

"A ledger was kept of each day's deliveries made from the docks to the warehouse, and James saw that Mr. Feeney had failed to list a wagon of farm equipment that he had unloaded in the warehouse. With no record of it bein' delivered, James could have quietly stowed the equipment and sold it privately for a tidy profit. Many unscrupulous workers would have done just that and felt justified in doin' it. The work was hard and the pay not great. But James had better raisin' than that. He went to Mr. Feeney privately and told him about the error in a manner that wouldn't make Mr. Feeney embarrassed by his oversight."

"Mr. Feeney went to Mr. Kilpatrick and convinced him to let James have the opportunity to be his assistant even though he had no management experience and he was so very young."

"When Mr. Feeney relayed the story of James's honesty and hard work, Mr. Kilpatrick was willin' to give him a chance to prove himself."

"James became the youngest worker to have such a position of responsibility in the history of Kilpatrick's Mercantile. He worked hard and was able to save even more money to help his Da, Malcolm, and Charlie."

"He was given a small suite of rooms over the warehouse that included a small sittin' room with a tiny peat-burning stove as well as a bedroom. He also had access to Mr. Feeney's private water closet. Not havin' to go to the outside privy on a cold winter night was the change James appreciated most! For a boy raised in a tiny cottage crammed full of people, this was a big luxury."

"James's life fell into a pattern. He went to visit his Da and brothers the first Sunday of every month. Mr. Feeney gave him permission to use a company horse, which made his trip much easier and quicker. He worked for Mr. Feeney and made himself available to take on more and more responsibilities, makin' Mr. Feeney's life much easier and his burdens lighter."

"Mr. Feeney had grown children, and his brood of grandchildren was growin' rapidly, so he appreciated bein' able to spend more time with his family. His own dear wife had passed away five years prior to James comin' to work with him, so he understood the bouts of melancholy that plagued James often."

"Sometime after James's nineteenth birthday, during one of his bouts of depression, he stopped in one of the many pubs that were close to the docks. They were frequented by rough dock workers and often lawless men who were always lookin' for young gullible men to fleece or recruit to their seedy way of life."

"James had often had a pint or half pint of bitter once in a while but had never sampled the poteen that was often referred to as Irish moonshine, made from potatoes instead of corn. It packs a wallop like the corn likker moonshiners here in our mountains make. Strong stuff, better left alone."

"James had ordered a pint of bitter ale and took it to a corner table, wanting to be alone with his internal misery. He noticed a couple of disreputable toughs sitting at another table. They were sizin' up each man who came and went. They would look a man up and down, watch him a few minutes, then disregard him."

"James had nearly finished his second pint and was about to toss back the last inch or so left in his tankard when one of them left his companion, went to the counter, and ordered two cups of poteen. He brought his two cups with him over to James's table and said—"

'Are you waitin' on someone, lad?' The man's shifty-lookin' eyes slid from James to glance at the door.

'No,' James said, not desirin' to make conversation, especially with someone who didn't look very reputable.

'I just thought you looked like you were a bit lonely, maybe waitin' for a friend or someone?'

The man looked back at James, tryin' to make his face look innocent-like.

'Thought I'd share a drop of the Water of Life wit ye. Ever had poteen before, laddie?'

Everything in James told him to have nothin' to do with this man. He looked seedy, smelled seedy, acted seedy. But James had let down his defenses with the second pint of ale.

'Why not,' he said, shoving down the warning clangin' inside his head.

He was tired of bein' the "good lad," always strivin' to do the right thing and never takin' time to have any fun. Always the dutiful son, brother, and employee.

The man grinned at James as he sat down in the chair across from him, scootin' the cup of tater moonshine under James's nose.

'Thanks,' James said shortly as he picked up the cup and took a swift swallow. James gasped as the fiery poteen scalded his throat.

The man grinned knowingly at James. 'Never had it before, I see,' he laughed as James wiped his streaming eyes on his shirt sleeve.

'If I'd a known that, I'da warned ye, lad.' The man slapped his leg as he laughed at James's reaction to the strong drink.

James smiled weakly and said, 'If I'da known it was like drinkin' fire, I'da said no thank you,' he sputtered.

"Ah lad, that first drop of potcheen is like blazin' fire for everyone." The man laughed harder, amused by James's coughing. "Drink up lad, potcheen is the drink of men and kings!"

"The drink of men and kings." James liked the sound of that. So, James took another gulp of the liquid fire, and the second mouthful went down a little easier than the first.

Granddad paused for a minute to sip on his cooling cocoa. "Ah, so good, so good. And not nearly as damning as James's poteen."

Granddad's direct look at his grand-young'uns told me we were about to get another life lesson, Granddad style.

"That's exactly how Satan the Evil One works in your life. He doesn't hit you with a big one all at once. He reels you in little by little. Startin' out with what seems like a small sin and works his way up.

James had never even had ale before he started stopping at the pub for a little companionship. John Robert didn't drink, bein' a staunch Calvinist, and had taught his sons the evil of it. But James started with what seemed mild, and once his senses were a bit fuddled, he was more easily convinced to try somethin' stronger that had a much more devastating effect."

"James drank three rounds of poteen with the stranger and failed to notice that the man was not drinkin', only pretending to. The strong drink on top of the ale was more than James's body could handle, and he was soon so drunk he left the pub willingly with the two strange men, convinced they were his new friends who were more fun than anyone he had ever known."

"James had little memory of all that happened, but once in the alley behind the pub, he was plied with even more drink, participating in what he was told was a drinkin' game that real men enjoyed."

"When James woke up, he had a ragin' headache, vomiting up what he later swore had to be his very innards, so violent was his heavin'. He was in his own bed, tho he had no idea how he got there."

Mr. Feeney knocked and came in during one of James's vomiting spells, lookin' at James with a mixture of pity and anger.

When James stopped throwin' up at last, Mr. Feeney dipped a towel in James's wash basin and gently patted his face with the cool, wet towel. It was so soothing and helped to quell James's rollin' stomach. After a few minutes of redippin' the towel and wiping James's flushed face, he draped the towel over the washstand towel bar and sat on the chair in the corner.

"Now lad, tell me how you came to be in this sorry state."

It wasn't a request but a quiet command.

James began with admitting that he had started droppin' in to a pub a couple evenin's a week and partaking in a pint or two. "Nothin' horrible, just a pint, sometimes two." He told about meetin' the man in the pub but then realized he didn't have a name or anything to connect to the man.

Mr. Feeney broke in and said, "I'm assumin' that you had your money pouch on your person at the time?"

James nodded while his hand flew to his pocket where he kept it.

"It's not there," said Mr. Feeney tersely. "When you did not come back to your rooms at your accustomed time, I went looking for you. I feared that something had happened, as you had always been very reliable and not prone to the vices that so many young men indulge in." He cut his eyes over James's disheveled appearance with a raised eyebrow.

"I found you lying in the alleyway behind the pub, passed out drunk. I don't mind saying I was shocked and extremely disappointed in you. I checked your pockets, and not finding your pouch I was hoping that you had left it at home. It would seem you were robbed. How much were you carrying?"

James answered, "I had six shillings, more than my last month's wages. I was plannin' on leavin' for Lisburn today to visit Da and give him a few shillings as I do the first of every month."

"We need to let the Constable know. Apparently, your 'new friends'" Mr. Feeney smiled tightly "knew just how to time their attack to avoid being detected by the night watchmen."

James dropped his head into his hands, partly from feelin' sick and partly in despair that through his own stupidity he would not be able to help Da, Malcolm, and Charlie this month. He sat that way for several moments, and Mr. Feeney thankfully sat quietly as well, sensing that James was punishing himself quite enough without him heaping coals of fire on his head.

"Well James, I suggest that you rest. Get some sleep and drink as much water as you can for the rest of the day. This evening I'll bring you a light supper. You will be able to tolerate it by then. I'll post a letter to your Da to let him know you are well but will be unable to come this week. Maybe you can go next week, but you need to rest the remainder of this day so you will be fit for work tomorrow."

James just stared at him. He had assumed that he would be dismissed for his behavior. He fully expected to be told there was no place in this fine company for a drunkard.

"You mean I still have a job?" he said, unbelieving.

"My dear lad," said Mr. Feeney patiently, "you are not the first young man to be swindled, nor the first to get slobbering drunk, nor the first to need a second chance to prove himself. Up until now you have been dependable, honest, and hardworking. This, however, puts you back to proving yourself. I'm willing to give you a second chance if you are willing to re-earn my trust."

"I once stood in your shoes and needed grace and the opportunity to prove that I could do better than I had done. I made some drastic changes and proved to my employer that I was changed. I spent a year on probation before my employer cleared the air and let me know I was forgiven and off probation.

I made some of the same mistakes you have made, lad. I am not saying it will take a year. I don't know how long it will take before I feel confident there will be no more incidents like this. But are you willing to lay aside drinking altogether? No more innocent stops at the pub? As you well know now, it wasn't so innocent after all."

James couldn't believe that stern, tho kind, Mr. Feeney had ever gotten himself into a similar situation, and although he would have liked to know details, he didn't want to press his luck by askin' for them.

"Yes sir! I sure am grateful you are willin' to give me a chance."

James was close to tears and still feelin' as though his stomach would start heavin' again any second.

Mr. Feeney stood up. "Good lad," he said quietly. "I'll see you around six or so this evening with a light soup. Nothing heavy on the stomach." He picked up his hat that he had hung on a wall peg and turned toward the door to leave.

James spoke up before Mr. Feeney had reached the door.

"Mr. Feeney, I want to thank you for bein' a real friend. There was nobody else to wonder where I was or if I was in trouble. You took the time and bother to find me, get me home and into bed. Then you came back to check on me again. You gave me a chance to do better and gave me counsel as my father would have done had he been here. I appreciate it more than I can say."

"You're welcome, lad. Now try to sleep, and I will see you later."

Chapter Twelve

Granddad paused in his story and swigged down the last of his cocoa, now cold in his cup.

The young'uns stayed quiet, knowin' that Granddad wasn't quite finished with James's story. There was more. I knew there had to be more. Who had James married? Did he have children of his own? Had James found a way out of his bitterness at God for all the loss he had endured?

I had to admit, I had not come close to the loss that James had experienced. And much of my loss I knew was of my own makin'. Robbie hadn't forsaken me as a friend. I had shoved him out of my life. If I couldn't have all of Robbie, I didn't want any of him. I knew it wasn't right, but I seemed unable to beat down my stiff pride and admit it out loud.

Granny Spencer brought Granddad a cup of hot tea to "wet his whistle," and after a couple sips he carried on with James's story.

"James did earn Mr. Feeney's trust again. By sheer will he kept himself out of the pubs and focused on his work. He went to see his Da and brothers the first of every month, and he never put himself in the position to lose everything he had again.

"But James sensed that a part of him was not content with things as they were. He didn't know why, but he would feel a restless longing. For what, he didn't know.

"Time went by, and after he had been Mr. Feeney's faithful assistant for two years, Mr. Feeney suffered a heart attack. He survived, but it left him nearly an invalid and unable to work more than an hour or two a day.

"Without bein' asked to, James stepped up into the role of Warehouse Manager with the intent of lightening Mr. Feeney's load. He had grown to love the dear man like a second father and would forever be grateful for what he had done for him.

"After about six months of tryin' to recoup his strength and reassume his role, Mr. Feeney asked James to come to his office one evenin' after he finished his day's work. When James knocked on the office door, Mr. Feeney said, 'Come in, James.'

"James pushed the door open and was surprised to see that Mr. Feeney was not alone. Mr. Kilpatrick was also there, seated in a chair behind Mr. Feeney's large oak desk. It was evenin', so Mr. Feeney had lit an oil lamp, givin' the room a warm, comfortable glow.

"'You wanted to see me, sir?' James asked.

"'Yes lad, come in. You know Mr. Kilpatrick?' Mr. Feeney put it as a question.

"James usually saw Mr. Kilpatrick from afar. He was often in and out of Mr. Feeney's office while James was workin'. He knew that Mr. Kilpatrick knew everything about his store and warehouse. He had made it his business to employ good managers who gave him weekly reports on their domains. He knew his employees by reputation if not personally through his excellent managers.

"'Yes sir,' James replied. He took Mr. Kilpatrick's extended hand and found his handshake firm and confident.

"'Good evening, James,' said Mr. Kilpatrick. 'I hear you have come a long way from that ragged hungry little boy I employed on my wagon that day years ago.'

"'Yes sir,' said James. 'That was nearly four years ago now.'

"'Mr. Feeney has had high praise for you, James. How old are you now?' Mr. Kilpatrick smiled at him as he stroked his well-kept beard thoughtfully.

"'I will be twenty next month, sir,' said James.

"'Young. Mighty young,' said Mr. Kilpatrick, mostly to himself.

"'Young, yes. But mature for his age and dependable,' said Mr. Feeney quietly.

"James was a bit confused and was wonderin' where in the world this strange conversation was going.

"Mr. Kilpatrick paused a moment, lookin' into the warm glow from the oil lamp still stroking his beard, deep in thought.

"'James, Mr. Feeney is desiring to retire. His health isn't improving as much as he had hoped, and the stress of his position has become more than he would like to deal with. He has recommended that I hire you into his position as Warehouse Manager for Kilpatrick's of Belfast.'

"James sat in stunned silence. He had hoped that someday he might assume the role but thought it would be years down the road, when he was older, more mature, more experienced.

"'What do you say, James? Are you willing?' asked Mr. Kilpatrick.

"'I...I...I don't know what to say, sir,' stammered James. He looked to Mr. Feeney, feelin' some confusion. Was he ready for so much responsibility? It was a stressful job with a heavy responsibility. In offerin' him this position, Mr. Kilpatrick was extending him an enormous amount of trust.

"'Who would take over my job as wagon master?' he asked to cover his confusion.

"Mr. Feeney said, 'I have been grooming Davey Allen for the last year. I've been doing it quietly and without him even knowing that was my purpose in his training. I have always anticipated you taking the reins. It just so happens that my health has pushed my plans up a couple years.'

"The room fell silent. James still sat stunned, tryin' to pull jumbled thoughts together and form an answer that didn't sound as unintelligent as he felt.

"Mr. Feeney looked at James with kind eyes. He finally spoke.

"'I've known since I dragged you home drunk and your actions afterward that I would hand this job over to you someday. James, every man makes mistakes. Every man will fall. It's how and if he gets back up that tells the world what he's made of. You proved to me that yes, you were a human prone to mistakes, but you also proved that deep down inside you were made to be a leader. You have integrity and loyalty. Those are traits that can't be bought. Either a man has them, or he doesn't.'

"Again, the room fell silent for a time. Then Mr. Kilpatrick straightened in his chair, slapped both palms against his knees, and said in his jolly way, 'So is it agreein' you are to take the job, my boy? Because I'd rather not beg!'

"'Yes sir!' James cried. 'I'm honored and will do my very best to follow Mr. Feeney's example."

"The three men rose, shook hands, and Mr. Kilpatrick said, 'I'm off! Mrs. Kilpatrick will have a thing or two to say about me being late for our dinner party if I don't hurry. My daughter Bridget is of age now, and Mrs. Kilpatrick is wanting to launch her into society. It begins tonight with a big dinner party. Thank you, James. Mr. Feeney will settle the details with you, best wishes, my boy!' And he swept out the door.

Granddad grinned at his captive audience as he gulped his cooling tea.

"James did well at Kilpatrick's of Belfast. He worked as warehouse manager for many years and acquired a small fortune and lived happily ever after. The end."

I gaped at him. "You can't do that, Granddad!" I cried. "You can't stop with that. Did James marry? Did he have children? Well, he must have or we wouldn't be here, would we?"

Granddad chuckled. He sure did love teasin' us young'uns and gettin' a rise out of us!

"Yes, Maggie girl, James did marry and have children. So let me finish."

Bein' warehouse manager, James was in and out of Kilpatrick's store often. He had been given a huge raise in wages and Mr. Feeney's much finer rooms over the warehouse. James lived frugally. He didn't have to spend much money since he had his accommodation supplied.

 He had access to the company's horses and didn't have to own and maintain a horse of his own. He dressed finer since he had a higher position and was required to look the part, and he still gave his Da help, though Malcolm had since passed away, and Charlie had married and moved back to Scotland where his wife was from.

Mr. Kilpatrick had started inviting James to dine with the family about once a week, sensing that James was lonely and would enjoy bein' with a family. Little did he know that his only child, his daughter Bridget, would fall in love with the steady, quiet Scotsman.

The Kilpatricks were Catholic and faithfully went to Mass every Sunday. James had been raised Calvinist Presbyterian. He had not been to church in years. While his burning anger had abated, he had simply fallen out of the habit of going to church, although at times he felt a tug in his heart to go.

Mr. Kilpatrick was not happy with his daughter's infatuation with James. He liked James, trusted him, and had a great fondness for him. But the Kilpatricks were Catholic and James was Protestant. Moreover, he was a Calvinist Presbyterian, albeit a lax one.

But Bridget managed to sweet-talk her father, much as girls do today.

Granddad grinned at me. He knew I could sweet-talk my daddy into 'bout anything.

After courtin' Bridget for about three years, Mr. Kilpatrick gave his consent to the marriage, even though James would not become Catholic. The parish priest threatened to excommunicate the Kilpatricks if they allowed Bridget to marry outside the Catholic faith. But in the end, he didn't, because Mr. Kilpatrick gave too much money to the church to cast him out.

Granddad threw back his head and laughed heartily. "Money talks louder than most people most of the time," he chuckled.

Granny stuck her head through the door and scolded Granddad.

"That's not nice, Alistair!"

"No, but so true!" Again, he howled with laughter, and Granny huffed back to the kitchen.

"So, James married Bridget Kilpatrick?" I asked hopefully.

"He did," Granddad smiled. "Indeed, he did."

Mr. Kilpatrick sent them on a wedding trip to Dublin. There they experienced dining in a fine Inn, went to the theater and a new type of entertainment called opera.

One evenin' they were drivin' in an open carriage from the opera to their hotel when they saw and heard a big commotion in the street ahead.

Some rough-lookin' young men were shouting and waving torches above their heads, chanting, "Hang the heretic! Kill the heretic!"

Bridget was frightened and cringed back into the seat of the carriage. But James called out to one of the youths chanting the phrase.

"What's going on here? Why the mob?"

"There's a heretic preacher we're hopin' to catch and hang," the excited youth said breathlessly.

"Who is it?" asked James.

"A preacher named Michael Bruce!" shouted the young man as he surged on with the mob.

James sat back in the seat as Bridget clung to his arm in fear.

Michael Bruce. He had heard that name before, but where?

Bridget spoke softly from under his arm where she sought refuge. "Isn't Michael Bruce the preacher Papa was angry about a few weeks ago? Seems like I remember him saying that Father Bannon wanted to have him brought to trial for heresy and have him killed or banished from Ireland."

"But what in the world is all the fuss about?" James mused. "What is he sayin' that is causing such a riot?"

James was soon to find out, because after turnin' off the main street the coachman slowed the carriage to give the horses a rest. Out of the darkness two men stepped out with arms outstretched like they were pleading with them.

"Please, sir, would you please give this gentleman a ride to safety? He is in danger and is fleeing for his life."

"Who is it?" asked James, not willin' to put them at risk without more information.

The taller, thinner of the two stepped forward and spoke quietly.

"My name is Michael Bruce. I am a minister of the Gospel of Christ. I am branded a heretic because I preach a gospel of God's love and forgiveness without the need for buying indulgences or confessing to a priest. For that, I am condemned and hated. If they catch me, I may be hanged without the benefit of a trial, for it is a mob that is chasing me."

"Where are you going? Or where do you need to be taken?" James asked.

Bridget spoke from beside James. "James dear, we are supposed to do this. I know it in my heart! Somethin' just spoke to me and said, 'Take him to safety. Take him to Howth Castle.' I don't understand, dearest, but I believe that is where we are supposed to take him."

Michael Bruce spoke slowly. "I believe the Baron would be sympathetic to my plight, but I cannot say for sure. But Howth is close to the sea, and I need to get back to Scotland."

James spoke to the carriage driver. "Coachman, can you drive us to Howth Castle tonight? And does the top of this carriage go up easily?"

"Yes sir, to both," the man answered quickly. "But it will cost you, dear sir. To Howth and back will be an all-night trip."

"We won't be returnin' to Dublin but will catch a coach to Belfast from the closest station to Howth Castle. Can you take us first to our Inn to collect our trunks? We were leaving in the mornin' and are already packed. We need only to collect them."

"I can, sir, if someone will help me get this top up. It appears it might rain." This was said with a twinkle in his eyes. For once the Irish skies were clear and the half crescent moon glowed beautiful in the dark sky. But the man perceived that the top was needed to shield Michael Bruce from bein' seen.

Michael Bruce sprang forward and helped the coachman to pull the top forward and fasten the latch into place.

"God go with you, Brother Michael," said his companion. "I will be praying for your safe return to Scotland until I hear from you that it is done."

Michael Bruce turned to him and said, "And God bless you for putting yourself in harm's way for me this night, Brother Colin. Lay low for a bit and don't be as outspoken as I am wont to be." He smiled at the irony of his request.

Michael Bruce sprang into the carriage beside James and settled back into the shadows, not wantin' to be seen and cause trouble for his rescuers.

The coachman snapped his whip over the horses' heads, and they were off toward the Inn, where they were able to have their trunks loaded into the carriage, check out of the Inn, and be on their way quickly.

They were able to outmaneuver the mob that was still searching for Michael Bruce, skirting around the area through back roads and streets. When it appeared that they were safe and that arrival at Howth Castle would take hours, James decided to learn more about this man and what made him so different from the angry mob that sought him.

He asked Michael what it was that he preached that made the Catholics so angry. He was conscious of the fact that his lovely wife beside him considered herself to be Catholic, although she had just married outside the faith and aligned herself with a "heretic."

Michael sighed and said, "Because I teach that ministers should not only preach God's Word but also live it out in their daily lives. I emphasize the importance of a holy life as a demonstration of the power of the gospel. I don't make the Bible fit into a predetermined theological framework. Instead, I let the written Word speak for itself and let the Word of God be its own interpreter. The hierarchy of the Catholic Church hates me for this. The Catholic Church has preyed upon people and their fears for centuries. I simply introduce them to Christ, not a creed or a dogma, but to Christ alone."

James felt that old somethin' stir in him, a long-repressed longing for that somethin' he couldn't quite put his finger on.

Beside him, Bridget said softly, "Why would the priests be angry with that? It sounds like nothing but good to me."

Michael Bruce smiled over James in her direction. "Sister Bridget, that is true, and it's God's Word, not a church creed. Man slowly got away from the pure Word of God. Satan found an avenue into the church through men who were unconverted and impure, seeking to create kingdoms for themselves. They created positions our Lord or even His disciples, never mentioned; like Popes and Cardinals.

"They introduced damnable doctrines, making our Lord's lovely mother Mary into an object of worship, when Jesus never taught that. In fact, Jesus rebuked Mary for her error in calling Joseph his father when she said to a young Jesus after finding Him in the temple preaching at the age of twelve: 'Son, why hast thou thus dealt with us? Behold, thy father and I have sought thee sorrowing.' And Jesus replied to her, 'How is it that ye sought me? Wist ye not that I must be about my Father's business?' God was His Father, not Joseph."

"First Timothy, chapter two, verses one through six, says: 'I exhort therefore, that, first of all, supplications, prayers, intercessions, and giving' of thanks be made for all men; For kings, and for all that are in authority; that we may lead a quiet and peaceable life in all godliness and honesty. For this is good and acceptable in the sight of God our Saviour; Who will have all men to be saved, and to come unto the knowledge of the truth. For there is one God, and one mediator between God and men, the man Christ Jesus; Who gave himself a ransom for all, to be testified in due time.'"

"The apostle Paul taught that we should pray for leaders, people in authority, that they would lead godly lives and be an example to the people they lead. I've known too many in the hierarchy of the Catholic Church to believe they fit this description.

But it isn't just Catholics in need of learning God's Word. Even in my own ranks there is hypocrisy and corruption among the leadership of the churches. And because I preach it, I point it out, because God has called me, even commanded me, to preach His Word exactly as the Bible teaches it, without the corruption of man's ideas and creeds.

"His Word also clearly states that there is one God and one mediator between God and men, the man Christ Jesus. Tell me then, how can they justify teaching people to access God through His mother Mary? It's damnable! It will take them to hellfire, and those who believe it!"

Michael Bruce spoke with thundering conviction, and his words startled Bridget. She had never heard the likes of this before.

The Blessed Virgin, Mary the Mother of God, had always been revered, even prayed to, in her home. After all, God was so big, so great, and so vast that He seemed unapproachable. It seemed safer to go through the gentle Blessed Mother to appeal to God on her behalf.

But according to the apostle Paul, that was wrong. There was no mediator between her and God except Christ Jesus. If this was true, and of course the Bible is truth, why did the Holy Father the Pope and all the priests and church leaders pray not only to Mary but to St. Michael the Archangel for protection, St. Jude for hopeless causes, St. Joseph for household matters, and St. Christopher, seeking his intercession for safe journeys and protection during travel, and countless others?

Bridget sat stunned, yet somethin' inside her knew it was truth. Men had always rejected truth and persecuted God's messengers. All the disciples save John were put to death for standin' for God's Word. She knew this too was truth.

She looked up at James with tears shining in her beautiful dark eyes. "Oh James! This man is speakin' truth, I know it! I want what he has. I want to know the Living God he speaks of; a God who speaks to my heart and guides me into truth!"

Michael Bruce reached over James and took Bridget's hand. "My dear sister in Christ! The Lord Jesus has spoken to your heart and called you by name tonight. He wants to draw you into a relationship with Him that is like nothing you have ever known before. As much as your husband James loves you, Jesus loves you more! He died for you that you might have eternal life.

He longs for you to know Him personally and to communicate with Him, and serve Him with love and devotion, not out of fear. Not out of fear of being lost or cast out. In return, you will know peace like you never thought possible.

Even in the middle of life's storms, loss, and sorrow, as all men must face, you can have peace. Philippians, chapter four, verse seven, says: 'And the peace of God, which passeth all understanding, shall keep your hearts and minds through Christ Jesus.'

"No more paying for indulgences for forgiveness of sin, no more hoping that someone else will be successful in accessing the throne of God for your needs. You simply go to your Heavenly Father and petition Him yourself."

Bridget was weeping and trembling with the force of her emotion. God had called her to come out of her "Egypt" and to follow Him in the light and understanding of His Word.

James suddenly had a blindin' revelation. This was it! This was what had called to him deep inside so often over the years: a personal relationship with God Himself.

While he had not been bound by the creeds of Catholicism, he had been bound by anger and bitterness. If he had let himself trust God like his father John Robert, bitterness and anger at God would never have taken root.

"James could almost hear his father praying in their little cottage, suffering because he had loved James's mother, his wife Margaret, his sweet Maggie. The loss had nearly broken him, but James could recall hearing his father as he sobbed the same words of surrender that Jesus had prayed in the Garden of Gethsemane: 'Not my will but thine be done.'

God had given peace to his father John Robert; he had found healing from life's pains over and over again, praying the same prayer: 'Not my will but thine be done.'

Was it truly that simple? Surrendering your will? Yielding yourself to accept God's will even when you neither understood it nor wanted it?

James found himself kneeling on the floor of the carriage with his brother in Christ, Michael Bruce, praying and calling on heaven to accept his wayward son James back into the sheepfold of Christ. James repented of all his sins, not just the sin of anger and bitterness, but for rebellion against God's Word, against His laws He had put in place for mankind's protection against the evil forces of the world.

After some time, he realized that the three of them had been kneeling on the floor of the carriage as it rocked along toward Howth Castle.

'What now?' he asked Michael after they had found their seats again and were all three wiping tears of joy from their faces.

Michael laughed softly. 'The same question was asked of our brother Peter when he was preaching after the Day of Pentecost. Acts two, verses thirty-seven and thirty-eight, says: Now when they heard this, they were pricked in their heart, and said unto Peter and to the rest of the apostles, Men and brethren, what shall we do? Then Peter said unto them, Repent, and be baptized every one of you in the name of Jesus Christ for the remission of sins, and ye shall receive the gift of the Holy Ghost.'

'I was baptized as a baby,' Bridget said.

'But under the Catholic tradition of "in the name of the Father, the Son, and the Holy Ghost,"' Michael said. 'That's not what was given by the apostles in the New Testament. For an example, I am a father. I am also a son. I am also a husband, but those are not my name. They are my titles. Three different identifications, if you like, but not my name.

The same applies to our Lord. Deuteronomy chapter six, verse four, states, Hear, O Israel: The Lord our God, the Lord is one. And the first commandment given to Moses in Exodus chapter twenty, verse three, says, Thou shalt have no other gods before me. God is a triune being; He plays a different role, you might say. Just as I am father to my son, I am also a son to my father, and I am a husband to my wife. Each is a different role, although I am the same person. I behave differently in each different role.'

'God in His first role was Father, God the Father who created the heavens and earth. He then changed roles and played the part of

God the Son. God the Father created a human body in Mary; that body was Jesus the Christ, in whom God was pleased to dwell. After His crucifixion and His ascension back to heaven, God sent Himself back to earth in Spirit form to dwell in the hearts of men. First on the Day of Pentecost, and since then whenever a Believer follows His Word and obeys the guidelines He laid out.

'You repented of your sins tonight and asked Him to come be with you and live out His Word through you. Next you go to water in baptism, not in titles, but in HIS NAME, which He gave inspiration to Peter to give. The name of Jesus Christ. For the remission of sins, and THEN ye shall receive the gift of the Holy Ghost. And what a gift! The very Spirit of the Living God, living in human flesh once again! Hallelujah!'

'Yes!' James and Bridget cried in unison. 'We want to be baptized in His name! How do we do that? Where do we go?'

Michael smiled and waved his hand to the right-hand side of the carriage toward the open water of Dublin Bay and began to quote Acts chapter eight, verse thirty-six: 'And as they went on their way, they came unto a certain water: and the eunuch said, See, here is water; what doth hinder me to be baptized?' He smiled at James and Bridget. 'If you want to be baptized, we can do it now, right here in Dublin Bay!'

'We don't have to wait?' cried Bridget.

'No, dear sister. If you are willing to get in the water in your fine gown, there's nothing to hinder you either.'

Granddad was winding down his story; I could tell. He sure was a fine storyteller! He brought a body right into the story like they were there watchin' it happen in real life.

James and Bridget were both baptized that night in the cold Irish Sea waters of Dublin Bay. They and Michael Bruce rejoiced and praised God for His love and mercy, and Michael declared that he had a magnificent haul that night fishin' for the Lord.

James and Bridget corresponded with Michael Bruce for years, although they never saw him again in this life. He mentored them like Paul did, writin' to Timothy from his prison cell—guiding, encouragin', and teachin' through the power of letters.

Michael later wrote to James and Bridget that an undergardener at Howth Castle had heard him preach and was a disciple of sorts. He hid Michael in an old hunting cottage not far from the coast and made arrangements for Michael's return to Scotland on a fishin' boat that belonged to a local fisherman and friend of the undergardener.

Michael continued to preach God's Word and continued to make enemies of church leaders both in the Catholic ranks and in the Protestant church as well. But he stood a firm defender of the Word of God until the end of his days. Michael died in sixteen ninety-three at the age of fifty-nine and was buried in the churchyard of Anwoth, Wigtownshire, Scotland.

James and Bridget returned to Belfast. James continued to work for his father-in-law, Mr. Kilpatrick, and when Mr. Kilpatrick passed away, he left the whole of his business, Kilpatrick's of Belfast, to Bridget and James with the understandin' that Bridget's mother would live out her life with them in the big house on Malone Road not far from the city center.

James and Bridget continued to serve the Lord and attended First Presbyterian Church of Belfast, pastored by William Gilchrist, whose daughter Fiona would later marry James and Bridget's eldest son Liam. James served on the presbytery for many years.

James and Bridget had five children: Liam Padraig, Sarah Elizabeth, John Alexander, Owen Ross, and Elisabeth Ann. Liam inherited the store and warehouses, still called Kilpatrick's of Belfast, and in later years married his childhood sweetheart, Fiona Gilchrist. He sold it all to his brother Owen Ross when I decided to leave Ireland for America.

Liam Padraig Spencer emigrated to America with his wife Fiona and family, and became friends with John Bruce of the Shenandoah and is the ancestor of all our line of Spencers, both here in the Carolinas and in Virginia. John Bruce of the Shenandoah is the ancestor of our dear friends and neighbors Johnny and Claire Bruce—Robbie's Ma and Pa.

Why did Granddad feel the need to clarify who they were? We all knew Claire and Johnny were Robbie's Ma and Pa. Well, truth to tell, it didn't bother me so much anymore to hear Robbie mentioned. Funny, but time seemed to have healed some of my pain and anger. Or was Granddad's account of James and his life journey partly responsible for that? That's somethin' I'd have to think about.

Chapter Thirteen

Life in my mountains moves slower than it does in some places. We just don't feel the need to run like chickens with their heads chopped off. We enjoy porch sittin' on a summer evenin', but we make use of that time. Womenfolk usually have some sort of handwork to do, whether it is mendin' the menfolk's overalls or stitchin' new dresses or shirts for the young'uns.

Most of the flour companies had been sackin' up their fifty-pound bags of flour in cotton flour sacks with pretty prints on them. Ever since the Great Depression, there almost seemed to be a competition between the companies as to who could produce the prettiest prints. Poor people would have been nearly naked if it hadn't been for flour and feed sacks.

I have such memories of my mamma sittin' on the porch in the evenin', stitchin' away. With me growin' like a polkweed, and Gerry and Charlie growin' fast too, somebody was always needin' a shirt or a dress.

If Mamma wasn't sewin', she was snappin' beans, shellin' peas, or shuckin' corn. Sometimes Granny and Granddad Spencer, Aunt Eunice and Uncle James, and all their young'uns would bring their porch work over on an evenin' and we'd make a party out of our workload.

Daddy was a fair hand with a mouth harp, and often neighbors drivin' past the house would see our party and stop in and join us. The Watson family was the most musical family in these parts, and they often stopped in with their fiddles, banjos, and guitars. General Dixon Watson was the best banjo picker around and had taught all his children to play and sing. They all did—even their son Arthel, who had been blind since he was a little fella.

That's how things were done back then around here. A body didn't wait for an invitation to drop by to porch sit and jaw wag, as we called it. It wasn't uncommon to wind up with a yard and house full of folks, and the porch would ring with music and laughter 'til after dark.

One such early July evenin' began with Mamma sendin' out word to Granny and Granddad and Uncle James and Aunt Eunice to bring their beans and such over, and we'd have a porch party. Mamma and Daddy had splurged and bought some sweet corn from a vegetable peddler who had brought up a truckload from the Carolina lowlands.

Our corn was a lot later since we lived up so high, and it was a treat to get ahold of sweet corn so early. Mamma was cookin' up a big pot of green beans with potatoes and bacon cooked in them, and she had a big plate of sliced garden tomatoes and another big pot of turnip greens cooked down and seasoned with bacon grease. It was a meatless garden supper except for the bacon in the beans, and it was so good!

We were all stuffed to the gills and sittin' on the porch to start on our porch work while we talked and the men played music. As usual, neighbors started droppin' in when they saw the goin's-on. I didn't pay much mind when I heard another truck pull into the driveway and cut off the engine. Just another neighbor stopping by.

All of a sudden, I heard Gerry send up a whoop from out in the yard.

"Rooooobbbbieeeee!"

My head nearly jerked off my neck from turnin' to see the latest arrival. It was Robbie Bruce. I couldn't hardly believe my eyes. It had been a long time since Robbie had stopped by. My anger and hateful behavior had run him off, and I thought it was for good. But there he was, walkin' up to the porch with his hands stuck in his back pockets like he didn't know what else to do with them.

Robbie was eighteen now and had gotten so tall and lanky. He wasn't skinny, but he worked hard and was slim and well-muscled. I couldn't help noticing that his arms were no longer those of a boy but of a man.

I wondered where Tillie Macpherson was. I knew they were considered a couple by folks around. I was always hearin' someone sayin' somethin' like, "I saw Robbie and Tillie at the Appalachian Theater in Boone on Saturday night." Or "Me and Larry went on a double date with Robbie and Tillie last week." I had sort of gotten used to hearin' about it, though it still chapped my hide, so to speak.

"I just came from work at the store," said Robbie. "The Macphersons are vacationing at Myrtle Beach. I was able to finish up quick-like and leave as soon as the store closed. Saw ya'll a sittin' on the porch and thought I'd stop by for a spell."

Granddad hollered out to Robbie. "How's your daddy doin'? Ain't seen ol' Johnny in a fair bit."

"And Claire, how's Claire? I guess she's keepin' just as busy as we are with her garden and all," said Mamma.

Robbie quick cut his eyes over to me for just a split second before answering Granddad and Mamma.

"Papa's doin' just fine. The new sawmill he's tryin' to get set up is keepin' him mighty busy." Then, "Yes ma'am, Ma is doin' what you're doin' probably right now," said Robbie, grinnin'. "But I reckon she's not havin' quite as much fun."

"Where did Johnny get his sawmill from?" asked Daddy. "Was it ready-made and rarin' to go, or did he have to set it up?"

"He got it piece by piece from here and there," said Robbie. "He shopped around for the best deal, gettin' a big old band saw from a feller over near Hickory, and a circular saw from another feller over in Elizabethton, Tennessee. Doin' it that way, he was able to save quite a bit of money. He's settin' up the mill over on the edge of our west field."

"Well, he orta do real good," said Granddad. "Lumber is fetchin' a lot of money with the big demand for it. Here we are comin' up on one year since that dang flood, and people are still tryin' to patch up or rebuild. Just not been enough lumber to go around."

"Yes sir," said Robbie. "That's exactly what he's hoppin' for."

"Come sit, son," said Daddy. "Take a seat over there on the steps. Plenty of room."

"Don't mind if I do," said Robbie as he sat down beside Charlie, who was taking a rest from the kids' game of tag out in the yard.

I didn't say nothin', which, since I usually always had plenty to say, spoke louder than if I'da spoke up and said somethin'. Granddad kept glancing over my way, and I knew he was tryin' to decide if Robbie's drop-in visit had ruffled my feathers or not. Secretly, I was thrilled, but that old hateful pride just wouldn't let me show it.

I wondered if Mamma and Daddy were concerned about how I was going to react to Robbie's droppin' by. I was wishin' there was some way I could let them know that I was fine. Actually, I was feelin' better than fine.

Granddad must have decided to grab the bull by the horns, because he asked Robbie questions about his work.

"You still workin' at Macpherson's Store?" asked Granddad slyly. Which irritated me inside. Granddad knew full well that Robbie still worked for Mr. Macpherson.

"Yes sir," said Robbie, looking just a tad bit nervous. "Mr. Macpherson ordered a big load of lumber from Johnson City right after the flood and even brought in carpenters from out of the area to get his new store up fast. I worked during that time as a carpenter's helper and now am back to runnin' the store for him."

"Smart move, smart move," said Granddad. "It don't help to sit around and wish somethin' hadn't happened. Best to jump in with both feet and swim."

Talk went on like that for some time, and my tension slowly released. It was startin' to feel more like old times, and I was mighty glad of it. I was talkin' with Mamma quietly about how many quarts of green beans she was hopin' to can this year when I noticed that the men's talk had turned to the war in Europe. Robbie had more up-to-date news because they had a radio at Macpherson's store, and he was talkin' about what had come over the news that day.

"Hitler has invaded Russia now. It's only a matter of time before more countries get dragged into it. I don't see things goin' any differently than it did during the Great War."

The adults, and those of us old enough to understand the impact of what Robbie was sayin', were quiet. It was sobering to think all the young men who had been drafted from the ages of twenty-one to thirty-five might be among the first Americans to be sent to Europe if America became involved.

There had been anti-war rallies held in faraway cities like New York and Chicago, but nothin' like that here in our mountains. We had a way of tryin' to ignore what was goin' on as best as we could. Nobody wanted war except a few of the fellas who were too young and foolish to understand the finality of death.

War was so much more than patriotic music with flags waving and pretty girls sendin' shiploads of young men off to fight overseas. It was family members and neighbors not comin' home, but lyin' in a grave across the sea. It was young men with arms and legs blown off comin' home broken, then tryin' to rebuild their shattered minds and lives. It had only been seventy-six years since the American Civil War, many of our Old Timers had been young children then. And the Great War had ended only twenty-three years ago and there were many folks who could remember the horror of that war.

Granddad steered the talk to other subjects, thankfully, and the rest of the evenin' passed with good-natured teasin' and plannin' for harvest that would be comin' up in a couple of months. Granddad was tellin' folks that the annual campground-style meetin' would be startin' the following week, and we womenfolk finished up our porch work, with our baskets of snapped green beans ready to start canning tomorrow. At last, we were sittin' with our hands free of work.

I helped Mamma carry our two-bushel baskets full of snapped beans into the kitchen to be ready for a long day of canning tomorrow.

Night had fallen, and still folks was a lingerin' on the porch, reluctant to leave while everyone was enjoyin' each other's company and the cooler night breezes. Whip-poor-wills were callin' to each other down near the creek while tree frogs sang their steady nightly songs. Once in a while an owl would hoot, and it was a soft and pleasant night.

Finally, folks began gatherin' up their young'uns and porch work and headin' home. Calls of "Good night all, and thanks for the evenin'" rang out as the porch and driveway cleared. Yet Robbie showed no signs of leavin'. Mamma would look at him a little funny now and again, like she was wonderin' why he didn't head home too.

Every now and then Robbie would glance over at me, and I was able to finally meet his eyes and give a small smile that said I was okay.

Granddad and Granny Spencer had left before dark-fall because they didn't want to be gropin' around in the dark to get into their house and risk a fall. So it eventually came down to Daddy, Mamma, Gerry, Charlie, me, and Robbie. Charlie's head was noddin', so Daddy told him go get on off to bed."

Robbie got to his feet. "Reckon I'd best head on home."

"Gittin' late," Daddy said with a grin at Robbie. "I'm headin' on in. Dottie, I'll help you get the canners set out for tomorrow. Gerry, off to bed, son."

And just like that, my Daddy had cleared the porch except for me and Robbie. Was that done on purpose, I wondered?

I started to get up too when Robbie said, "Maggie, can we talk a minute?"

My heart hammered inside my chest so hard I thought sure anyone standin' on the porch could not only hear it but see it too. "Why, I reckon so," I replied, and sat back in the rocker I had been sittin' in.

Robbie sat down in the rocker beside me, the one Mamma had been sittin' in, and sat quiet for a minute before he started.

"How have you been doin', Maggie?" Robbie asked quietly.

"Fine," I replied. "I've been busy helpin' Mamma and haven't been around much."

Robbie nodded in understandin', then spoke again. "I mean how are you doin' since the flood? I hated to hear that Betty and her family were among those who were lost. That must be hard to bear, losin' a close friend like that."

"Yes." I dropped my eyes, not willin' to let him see the pain there—pain but guilt too. I hadn't always been the best of friends to Betty when I was younger, and I regretted it bitterly. "I miss Betty somethin' terrible. I wish I had been a better friend to her."

Robbie looked at me astounded. "Why, Maggs, you were a good friend to Betty. Why would you think differently?"

I knew Robbie hadn't been around to see and hear the times I had bullied Betty. I was not the nicest of friends to her, at least for a time.

"Well, I wasn't, and that's a fact. But I don't really want to talk about that right now."

Robbie dropped the subject immediately. I guess he didn't want to risk makin' me mad again.

"Well, I've thought about you a lot, worried about you a lot, and prayed for you a lot," Robbie said quietly.

Tears started to well up in my eyes, and I tried to hold them back. I didn't want to bawl. Bawlin' was weak, and while I was prepared to offer my forgiveness and even ask for forgiveness, I didn't want to bawl doin' it.

"I thank you, Robbie," I said. "That means a lot to me." I sniffed. "I want to say I'm sorry I've been so hateful to you and ruined our friendship. I don't know what got into me—just pure Satan, I reckon—but I truly am sorry I let bitterness take over me and let hurt turn to pure mean anger."

Robbie looked at me puzzled, and I could see he didn't get somethin'. Finally, he asked, "Why was you hurt?"

I looked at him with surprise. Did he truly not know? I may have only been a little kid at the time, but I really did feel that he had chosen Tillie over me. As I got older, I realized how irrational I was, but really! Could a nearly grown man not see through someone like Tillie Macpherson?

I didn't want to appear jealous, even though, as a young woman, I had to admit to myself at least that yes, I was jealous of Tillie Macpherson.

Robbie had been all mine up until that day she started battin' her eyelashes at him. And as of yet I could tell that her pretty face, beautiful hair, and striking figure stood in the way of Robbie bein' able to really see the shallow person she was. But he'd have to learn that on his own. It wasn't my job to educate him about it.

"Let's just say I was much younger then, and now that I'm older," I grinned to lighten the mood, "I have grown up a little bit since then and am willin' to let old bygones be bygones."

Robbie's relief was so great that I thought he would dance a jig right there on our porch. "I'm so glad!" he said. "So happy and so relieved! I've missed you and missed our tramps through the woods and teachin' you to read signs and—"

I laughed at his exuberance. He was like a happy puppy thumpin' his tail on the porch floor. But I knew—I could tell he didn't feel like I did. I saw him as grown now. He looked and sounded like a man, but I was sixteen, a bit of a late bloomer, and still had a straight, twiglike figure. He sure didn't see me as he saw the curvy, golden Tillie Macpherson. But I could wait. For now, we were friends again, and that was good.

Chapter Fourteen

After Robbie's visit and us gettin' the air cleared between us, he dropped in often to visit with the family. Sometimes he was with his mamma and daddy, and sometimes he was with Tillie. Tillie Macpherson continued to send little jabbin' insults in her honeysuckle syrup voice that coated her true meaning. In the South we have a way of makin' our insults less offensive with a "bless her heart" or "Lord love him."

But sometimes he dropped in by himself. One evening early in August we were sittin' on the porch. Mamma and I were peelin' peaches for making peach preserves the following day, and the menfolk were shuckin' field corn for the animals' fodder. Granddad and Granny Spencer had joined us for supper and were relaxin' on the porch, helpin' with the porch work as well.

Robbie joined in with his hands, helpin' shuck corn, and conversation would come and go. I decided to run an idea by the family that I had been thinkin' on for a few weeks.

"What would you think of me givin' chickens another try?" I asked to no one in particular.

"Why, Maggie hun, I've been thinkin' of it too." Daddy smiled over at me. "I didn't know if you would want to try again after losin' all your hard work in the flood, but I believe it would be a good thing for you."

Mamma nodded her approval while pickin' up another peach to peel, sweet, sticky peach juice drippin' off her hands onto the towel layin' across her lap.

"I've got a little bit of money saved that I was going to buy a new dress with, but I'd rather buy some chicks and get started as soon as I can," I said quickly. "I heard Mr. Macpherson tellin' Old Man Harvey that the feed store in Boone was plannin' on gettin' a late shipment of chicks, and most of them are supposed to be Rhode Island Reds, just what I was wantin'."

"Leghorns are better layers," said Mamma quietly.

"Maybe," I said, "but there's no meat on them. Once a Rhode Island Red is finished layin', they sure are good eatin'."

"True," Mamma said.

Robbie jumped into the conversation. "Maggs, I can come help you with gettin' your space ready for your chicks. Where you puttin' them?"

"Since it's plenty warm yet, I think they'll be just fine in the barn. But I need to get some fine chicken wire to make the stall secure from critters. And then I'll need to get a good-sized run fenced outside. It won't take them long to need outside space."

"You know," Robbie was speakin' somber like, "with it lookin' like we're headin' into the war in Europe, things like eggs will be mighty hard to come by in the cities and towns. Might be a good idea to plan bigger than you was thinkin'. How many chicks was you thinkin' of gettin'?"

"I was thinkin' fifty, knowin' some of them will be roosters."

"I'd get more if you can," Robbie said quickly. "I have a feelin' that you will be able to sell any amount of eggs you can produce."

I just stared at him. I hadn't thought of it from that angle. I was just hopin' to sell a few eggs in Boone and have eggs and meat for our family.

Daddy looked over at me with a serious, thoughtful look in his eyes and said, "Maggie girl, Robbie is right. The military especially will be combin' the countrysides lookin' for supplies to feed the troops they are trainin'. How much money do you have to spend?"

"I only have twenty-five dollars, which is partly why I was gettin' fifty chicks," I said. "Fifty chicks would be twenty dollars, and I have to buy starter feed for them too."

We all sat quiet for about thirty seconds, which felt like minutes, when Granddad, who had been very quiet throughout the conversation, suddenly sat up, his eyes dancin' with excitement.

"Granny and I will help you get started, Maggie girl!"

Granny smiled brightly and chirped, "Oh yes! Yes, Alistair! What an idea! We've talked about givin' the grandkids a little hand up, gettin' a start at somethin'. This is it for our Maggie!"

I sat stunned. I had not expected such enthusiasm for my dream and sure didn't expect money to help get my egg business up and runnin'. I was shocked into gapin' silence. My mind was racin' in a dozen different directions and I couldn't seem to gather up my thoughts. Everyone was excited and talkin' at once, addin' to my confusion. This went on for several minutes before Daddy said loudly,

"Okay, everyone simmer down! Maggie girl can't think or get a word in sideways!"

Everyone looked at me, and I took a deep breath and stammered.

"Granddad, Granny, I…I…I don't know what to say! Are you sure? Are you able to do this without hurtin' yourself?"

"Now Maggie girl, would we offer if it would?" Granddad laughed.

"Yes!" I said. "Yes, I think you would!"

Granddad looked at me with twinklin' eyes that shone with so much love. So much love and excitement. He reached over and took Granny's hand in his, and they were both smilin' at somethin'— some secret that they held between them.

"We didn't realize the time had come already, but we have been plannin' on this sort of thing ever since you were born, Maggie girl." Granddad rubbed Granny's work-worn hand gently and continued. "We started savin' a bit here and there since you was a wee little thing. Then Gerry came along, and the other grandkids, and it became the one thing we felt we could do to help our grand-young'uns.

"We put by a bit every time we had extra. Every time we had change left in our pockets at the end of the day, we dropped it into a big crock Granny had accidentally cracked, makin' it no good for usin' for food. But it holds a heap of coin! Over the years it became too heavy to even pick up, so we would scoop out and bag up the coin and take them to the bank and convert it to bills. At the end of the month, if we had extra, we would put part of it with those bills. We've been doin' this for sixteen years, and you'd be surprised that when you make it important, you can save more than you think you might, just by savin' your coins left at the end of the day or week."

Robbie jumped in the conversation, the excitement gettin' him too. "Hey, Pa would let me use his sawmill to cut wood to build you a chicken house, Maggs! I know he wouldn't mind, and I could get your cousin Jamie and some of the fellas to help cut logs, and we could build you a chicken house that wouldn't cost you hardly nothin'!"

"I'll help!" yelled Gerry. "I can help Robbie and the other fellas. Wow, this is gonna be fun! The cat's pajamas!"

Everyone laughed. Gerry loved usin' popular slang to sound big and grown up. Mamma wouldn't let him use foul language, but she turned her head to the silly slang. "Young'uns talk," she would say, shakin' her head and laughin'.

I couldn't believe how my small dream had turned into somethin' so much bigger than I ever dreamed. I certainly didn't know at the time that it was the beginning of what would be a life's work and income for Robbie and me and the family we would eventually raise. But I'm jumpin' the gun here. I need to woah up and get back to my story.

Everyone was offerin' some kind of help. Eventually word got out among our Deep Gap community, and many friends were offerin' to help get my new business goin'. Soon Robbie and the fellas had a growin' pile of sawmill lumber pilin' up.

My old schoolteacher, Mr. Jenkins, had a cousin in Georgia who had a huge egg business and offered to share plans they had drawn up for a modern, well-ventilated commercial chicken house. Mine would be scaled down and built out of sawmill lumber, but it was designed by someone who understood the needs of chickens and egg production.

I ordered one thousand Rhode Island Red chicks the end of July. Most were supposed to be pullets, but it was understood that mistakes were inevitable, and a certain percentage could be counted on to be roosters. That was fine. We were lookin' forward to canning a fair amount of them and keepin' several for an experiment with hatchin' our own chicks in a used commercial incubator Daddy had located and picked up near Hickory.

I felt a little panicky when I thought about what all I was takin' on. Here I was, sixteen years old and goin' into business on a much larger scale than I ever dreamed of. But I was mature for my age and used to hard work, so I just put my head down and plowed on. Family and friends helped me as much as their work and obligations allowed, but often it was mostly me workin' around the growin' chicken house, dreamin' of the day I would be runnin' my own business.

Robbie, Gerry, and several of the fellas who lived in our community worked as many hours as they could spare away from their jobs and obligations, and soon my new chicken house was up and ready for my little Rhode Island Red chicks, who would arrive any day now.

Bless Granddad and Granny Spencer! This would never have been possible had I not had self-sacrificing grandparents who loved their grandchildren like they did. I took great pains to write up an account of how they had made my new business possible through so many different ways.

First of all, I always knew I had their unconditional love and support. I knew that I would always get honest counsel from Granddad, whether I liked the advice or not. It was sound, and if I stayed smart, I would always listen and be willin' to take advice.

Secondly, Granddad and Granny could have spent more money on themselves. They could have maybe traveled a bit or bought finer things for their home. Maybe they could have driven a fancier car like the MacPhersons. But they had chosen a simpler life. They didn't live in poverty, didn't go around with big holes in their clothes, but most of the time Granddad just wore denim overalls that Granny had often patched and repatched.

Granny wore flour sack dresses she sewed from flour and sugar sacks, like most of us did, covered by a well-worn apron to protect the dress, makin' it last for years. Granny didn't wear fine jewelry. She wore a wedding ring that had belonged to Granddad's grandmother, and it was worn thin by years and generations of Spencer brides wearin' it. She had a few strings of beads that, while pretty, were inexpensive, and some of them had been gifts and hand-me-downs.

Lookin' back, I know Granddad and Granny considered themselves to be very well off. Not necessarily with things and possessions, but they were wealthy in family, love, and the respect they earned in their family, church, and community. They were wealthy in peace, contentment, and the love they held for each other.

It was hard boilin' down all their qualities onto a one-page tribute that still hangs in the office of Deep Gap Chicken and Egg Enterprises.

Chapter Fifteen

August 13, 1941, one year to the day after the horrific flood that changed the whole landscape of My Mountains. I thought there should at least be some sort of speech day in Boone or somethin', but there was nothin' planned. Cleanup and rebuildin' was still going on. It would take many years to fully recover, and some things never did, like the Linville River Railway, permanently ending train service to Boone.

The flood's devastation had resulted in over two thousand landslides and many folks dead. It had washed away parts of the railway, including bridges, between Boone and Elk Park. The East Tennessee and Western North Carolina Railroad, also known as "The Tweetsie," which connected Boone to Johnson City, Tennessee, was also permanently shut down. We were a bit isolated.

Goods to be sold in stores in Boone now had to be brought in by truck, but our mountain roads were not made to bear the weight or size of large trucks, and one rail car could bring in three to four times the amount of a large truck.

That night at the dinner table, Granddad Spencer gave thanks over our evenin' meal and took the time to thank the Lord for His protection and mercy that night a year ago.

"Lord, we thank You from our hearts again for shelterin' our family from the evils of the storm one year ago. So many lost so much, and life has been hard for many since, but we thank You for keepin' us safe and for providin' help when we needed it and for givin' us the strength to in turn give help to others. Thank You for the courage You give to keep going, to keep tryin', and to never give up on ourselves, our neighbors, or on You. We are tested but not broken, burdened but not in despair, concerned but not afraid, for we know You hold us in the palms of Your hands.

Your Word says, 'He shall cover thee with his feathers, and under his wings shalt thou trust: his truth shall be thy shield and buckler.' Thank You, Lord, for the protection of those mighty feathers. We are grateful and want to return with thanks on this one-year anniversary of that tryin' time."

We all raised our heads and murmured a heartfelt amen, but what surprised us all was that with tears in his eyes, my daddy said, "Amen. Amen."

***

My baby chicks arrived the very next day. Fred Berry's Hatchery out of Ohio had mailed one thousand Rhode Island Red chicks. Normally the mailman was responsible for delivering live animals shipped through the post office, but our mailman, Marvin Malcome, didn't have the space for them. There were ten boxes with airholes, one hundred chicks in each box. Daddy and I drove into

Boone the mornin' of August fifteenth, and by that afternoon we had released the chicks into the broodin' nursery of the chicken house.

Carefully counting and examinin' the chicks as we emptied each box, there was a total of one thousand twenty-two live chicks and thirteen that didn't survive the journey. All in all, it was better than expected. Fred Berry's Hatchery and the United States Postal Service had done a good job.

I had carefully spread the sawdust Robbie had brought from his Papa's sawmill and was promised an unending supply for as long as the sawmill produced lumber. A total of ten heat lamps, suspended low enough to keep the chicks warm and healthy, would remain for about six weeks until the chicks were fully feathered and able to maintain body temperature on their own.

Every few days their space would be expanded by a few feet, and after about two weeks I started turnin' down the temperature on the heat lamps by a couple of degrees every day. By the time cold weather arrived, my chicks would be fully feathered and well on their way to bein' adults.

While the chicks were little, I didn't have to clean out the dirty sawdust and replace it with new but about once a week. I knew that would change once they were older, and it would be a two- to three-times-a-week job. The good thing about all this was good fertilizer for the garden and fields. There isn't a better fertilizer than rotted chicken droppin's.

I was now so busy that I paid no attention to anything but my chicks and gettin' our summer and fall harvest canned and preserved. Next thing I knew, fall had come, and we were plannin' our big Thanksgivin' dinner that Spencer Farm hosted every year for any relations that could make it. Uncle Albert and his wife, Auntie Mae from Virginia, had come for Christmas last year, but they would not be comin' down this year. Uncle Albert was having health problems, and they were spendin' the holidays at home with their own children and grandchildren in the Shenandoah Valley.

Two days before Thanksgivin', we were baking and preparin' for our mountain feast with Granddad, Granny, Uncle James and Aunt Eunice, Jamie, Maude, and Lily. It would be a strangely small crowd of us on Thanksgivin' this year. But I was also lookin' forward to it bein' just us North Carolina Mountain Spencers for a change.

We were so used to makin' about twenty pies to feed a horde of Spencers over a couple of days, so plannin' on makin' only six pies made me feel panicky, like we wouldn't have enough. But there would only be twelve of us, and six pies would be more than enough; that was a half a pie apiece! I knew I wouldn't eat half a pie even over two days of feasting. But Mamma had insisted we make two pecan, two apple, and two pumpkin pies.

Then there were smaller amounts of turkey, ham, mashed potatoes, candied sweet potatoes, green beans, sweet corn, turnip greens, and hot buttery yeast rolls, not to mention bowls of cranberry relish and other delicious relishes Mamma sold in our produce market every summer.

November nineteenth we had our first snowfall of 1941. Thanksgivin', November twentieth, was beautiful and so cozy. It will live in my memory for as long as I live. It was a long day of feasting, sharin' what we were most thankful for, playin' games, drinkin' spiced apple cider, and Granny Spencer's famous hot cocoa.

About four in the afternoon, we heard a truck pull into the drive, and Jamie ran to the window and then yelled out, "It's Robbie!"

I wondered, but didn't ask, why he wasn't at the Macphersons, spendin' the holiday with Tillie and her family. I was just glad he would be spendin' the evenin' with his other family, we Spencers. Robbie came through the door lookin' handsome, his face red from the cold and his eyes a-dancin' with happiness.

"Ma and Papa will be along in a few minutes. With Janet married and livin' in Knoxville, we thought we would just come join you all since you are missin' family this year."

"And rightly so, Robbie! Rightly so!" Granddad called out from his rockin' chair by the fireplace. I knew that Granddad was so glad the feud I had dragged out with Robbie was over and that he was enjoyin' the old closeness with Robbie and his family once again. Johnny Bruce was, after all, like a second son to him.

It wasn't until this moment that I fully realized what my uncalled-for anger and hard feelin's had cost not only me but my whole family. We had enjoyed a family relationship with Claire and Johnny Bruce and their children up until the time I banished Robbie's friendship from my life. Robbie stayed away for four years or better because of me. Oh, he still dropped by to chat with Gerry, Jamie, or Daddy occasionally, but he never came in or sat on the porch with us like he did now. And I felt a great sorrow sweep over me for what I could never give back to my family—four years of loving friendship dampened because I chose anger over forgiveness.

Granddad must have seen it on my face because he followed me into the kitchen when I offered Robbie some of Granny's delicious hot cocoa.

"What's the matter, Maggie girl?" Granddad asked softly.

I couldn't help it. Tears threatened to come, and my throat was so tight with regret I could hardly get words out of it. "Oh Granddad! Look at what I caused. Look at what the years of holdin' onto stupid anger has cost Daddy and Gerry, and even Mamma and Charlie. Everyone loves Robbie, Johnny, and Claire like family, and I never saw how far reachin' my anger was until now. How do I make up for it now?" I sobbed.

Granddad put one of his comfortin' arms around me and with the other hand firmly propped up my face so I couldn't hide and had to look at him.

"Maggie, you have done what you can to set things right. It's true that everyone felt the weight of your anger and missed the Bruces mightily. But your family and your friends, the Bruces, have gladly forgiven you. The only one who has not is you. In order for you to fully put this behind you, you must forgive yourself. I know you have spoken with Robbie and made things right between you?"

It was a statement but put as a question. I nodded yes to let Granddad know he was right.

"Have you asked the Lord to forgive you for hangin' onto anger? Have you asked Him to change your heart, so it doesn't happen again?"

"Nooooo," I said slowly. I had not. The simple act of makin' things right between Robbie and me had made me feel so much better, I hadn't thought that I owed the Lord anything over it.

Granddad just looked into my eyes for a bit, sighed, and spoke softly.

"Maggie girl, it's good that you made things right with Robbie. A good start. The right start. But it shouldn't end there. You must have a complete change of heart. A rebirth. A total surrender of yourself, your thoughts, and feelin's to God, and ask, then allow Him to change your heart. If you don't, it's only a matter of time before somethin' makes you angry again, and it will happen again and again until you surrender to God."

We stood silent for a moment while I got myself under control and stopped sobbin'. I hate it that I bawl so easily anymore. Makes my eyes all puffy and red, then everyone knows I've been a bawlin'. I wiped my eyes and blew my nose on the handkerchief that Granddad pulled out of his pocket for me.

"You understand what I'm sayin', Maggie?" Granddad asked. "It's just not an option because you are human and have flaws and tendencies toward evil like everyone else. The only way to overcome this is through our Lord and Savior Jesus. That's why He went to the cross and suffered, Maggie, because He wanted you to live an overcomin' life, but you can't because you are an imperfect, flawed human bein'. He took upon Himself all the hurt, shame, and consequences of your anger, then died to pay the penalty for it just so you could be free of it. And the only way you will be truly free of it, and the guilt it brings you, is to surrender it to God. Ask Him to not only forgive you but clean it out of your heart, change your heart, and fill it with Himself."

Granddad and I had had this conversation before. I know it's so and don't understand the stubborn reluctance I felt inside. Why was surrender so hard for me?

"Think on it, Maggie, and pray. Ask the Lord to help you. I know that you have a fear of surrenderin'. I think you feel it's givin' in, or bein' weak. I know you resent your tears. You feel it's a weakness. But it's not. It's tenderness."

"Now let's get everyone another round of Granny's cocoa. We haven't quite foundered ourselves on it yet."

I laughed. I always could count on Granddad to tell me straight truth and love me at the same time, then give me assurance that all is well between us.

***

173

With Thanksgivin' over, we were preparin' to face winter. My new responsibilities with my growin' chicks got me up earlier than I used to get up. I still milked Abigale in the mornin' and evenin', and Mamma still needed my help too. Life was busy, and I didn't have time to pay any heed to talk of the war in Europe or anything else really.

I was proud of how well my chicks were doin', and I was constantly readin' poultry farmers' magazines and books I checked out from the library in Boone. I was givin' my girls the best care I was physically able to give, and it showed. They were beautiful, deep, dark red pullets with glossy feathers that shined in the sunlight. I loved them, and they seemed to know it and loved me back.

Sometimes I would go out to the chicken house just to be with them. I would sing little ditties, and they would sing along in their little chicken voices. We were in the first week of December, and I was expectin' my hens to start layin' in another month or so.

Daddy and Granddad had built rows upon rows of layin' boxes that we had installed about a week ago. We had cushioned the insides with a layer of sawdust, and I had started checkin' them a couple of times a day now.

***

Sunday mornin' December seventh we got up early to do chores like we did every Sunday mornin'. Church service started at ten and Granddad and Granny would stop by so those of us who wanted to

174

go could hitch a ride with them. So, we had to get up early and work quickly in order to clean up, eat breakfast, get dinner in the oven for later, and get to church before the church bells rang out over the countryside.

Daddy never said a word or got angry over the rest of us leavin' him to go to church. He even drove us some Sundays and would sit in the truck nappin' or sometimes would drive into Boone if the weather allowed and sit and pass the time with other men who didn't attend church with their families. Mamma had started goin' nearly every service since the flood last year. It had seemed to have an effect on her. Since she was goin', she prodded Gerry and Charlie and took them too.

The snow from Thanksgivin' had melted and the temperature was just a bit above freezing with bright sunshine. The weather was good, and I could tell that Daddy was plannin' on drivin' us to church because he had put on his coat and was waitin' by the door for a signal from Mamma to start the truck and get it warm before we piled in.

We only lived about a mile from the center of our Deep Gap community. The little Non-Denominational Church and schoolhouse were nearly side by side. Since it wasn't far, Gerry and Charlie rode in the back of the truck like so many of the mountain young'uns did.

Most of the time I didn't mind ridin' in the back either but goin' to church was different. I had on my best dress and usually spent a rough Saturday night with my hair rolled up in rag curlers, so I didn't want to blow out my curls in the back of the truck.

The church bells began to ring just as we pulled into the parking lot, and down the road about a half mile or so I could hear the bells of Deep Gap Baptist Church pealin' out. It was a beautiful sound and a gentle reminder to everyone that it was the Lord's Day and time for church.

After church was over, everyone stood in the churchyard for a few minutes and visited with each other. The weather wasn't too cold and there was no wind to cut through us. Church usually dismissed right at noon, so Daddy was in the parking lot waitin' for us when we walked out.

We chatted with everyone a few minutes and Robbie told Mamma he would likely be over later after dinner to beat Gerry in a game of chess. I would play checkers, but not chess. It made no sense to me, and I didn't like the slowness of the game. More than likely I just didn't have the patience for it.

Granddad and Granny Spencer always spent Sunday dinner with us, so there was no need to invite them. They were always there.

Mamma had splurged and had bought a beef roast for our Sunday dinner. Now I'm a tellin' you I might not be a big woman, but I always could pack away more than my share of beef roast. Mamma slow cooked it in her Dutch oven along with carrots, celery, and onions, and made a rich beefy gravy with the drippin's. We always had mashed potatoes to pour that wonderful gravy over.

Couldn't nobody serve up a beef roast dinner like my Mamma Dottie Spencer!

Dinner was over, dishes washed, and we were lazin' in the living room around the fireplace expectin' Robbie, Claire, and Johnny to come soon. They usually came after their own Sunday dinner and around four in the afternoon. But at nearly three thirty Robbie's truck came tearin' up our driveway. He was alone and didn't even have his coat or hat on. He jumped out of his truck and ran up the walk onto the porch. I could tell somethin' was wrong.

By the time he had reached the door I had yanked it open, and Robbie ran straight into the room. He was pale and his eyes were more somber than I had ever seen them. We all stared at him, waitin' for him to tell us what he had come to say.

"I was at the Macphersons for Sunday dinner," he said. "And Mr. Macpherson always has his radio on. About two thirty a special announcement came over the radio. Early this mornin' the Japanese attacked our naval base at Pearl Harbor in Hawaii. They don't know the full extent of the damage and loss of life, but some are sayin' it was catastrophic. Some said it was a loss unlike anything our country has ever witnessed. At any rate one thing is for sure. For certain we will be at war."

I sank down onto the bench along the wall opposite the fireplace. My mind was spinnin', tryin' to take it all in, tryin' to make sure I was awake and not havin' a nightmare. We were all stunned, silent for a bit, then Robbie spoke again.

"I'm sorry to be a bringin' such bad news, but I knew you would want to know as soon as possible. Ma and Papa will be here soon, but I had to hurry over to let you know what has happened."

Again, there was no sound in the room except the snap and crackle of the flames in the fireplace. Usually a comfortin' sound, now it sounded loud and intrusive.

"God help us," Granddad said quietly. "God have mercy."

Mamma began to cry softly. She knew that if the war lasted but two and a half years Gerry would be eighteen and would be going to Europe to fight too. Gerry was only eleven months younger than I was, and I would be seventeen in April. Charlie was five years younger, so Mamma wasn't as worried about Charlie as of yet. But Gerry…

I looked at Robbie. He was already eighteen, had already registered for the draft. No doubt he would be among the first to be snatched away. In a little over a year Jamie would go. There were all the cousins in Virginia, many of them over eighteen as well.

I felt fear wash over me like a cold flood. Surely someone had opened a lid on top of my head and slowly poured in icy water. I felt it trickle down through and over my body. I looked at my arms, surprised that they were dry. They were dry, but my eyes were not. Normally I didn't want anyone to see me cry. Couldn't stand it, but not today. The icy shock had dulled my caring and silent tears poured down my face. I couldn't even sob, but my eyes did. And I couldn't stop them.

Daddy sat beside Mamma and put his arms around her. He didn't say anything to comfort her. I could tell he had nothin' to say, couldn't say anything. A few years later, after he was saved and had given his heart over to the Lord, he was able to comfort Mamma. But as of yet he was too empty himself to say anything she could hold onto.

Granddad and Granny suddenly looked so old. So very tired and old. But I knew Granddad. I knew he would wrestle the demons of fear and would win and recover his spark. He'd put that old whisperin' tormenter in his place. But that would be tomorrow. Tonight, he looked tired.

We weren't to know at the time that America would be at war for nearly four years. We weren't to know how many young men in our Deep Gap community would be lost to us, how many family members we would mourn the rest of our lives.

Johnny and Claire arrived soon after and we spent a very quiet and subdued evenin' with our friends, tryin' to form a plan of support and help not only among ourselves but with and for our neighbors. For we knew that in a matter of hours, days at the most, we would be a nation at war.

Chapter Sixteen

Monday evenin', Robbie stopped by after he closed up Macpherson's store to tell us that even though he wasn't required to join up with the military just yet, he had decided to go into the recruitment station in Boone and sign up with the Army. The draft was amended to include all men between the ages of twenty to forty-four, expanding the age range for mandatory military service, and requiring men aged eighteen to sixty-four to register for the draft. It was only a matter of time before he would have to go anyhow, and like hundreds of thousands of young men across the nation, he was angry about the horrific attack on Pearl Harbor.

The age requirements of the new draft amendment were sobering. Granddad Spencer was sixty-four, the outer limit of the age requirement. If it weren't for his old heart ailment that had disqualified him from the Great War, he would be expected to at least sign up. Daddy was forty and would have to register, although him bein' a farmer might keep him home.

President Roosevelt announced a declaration of war with Japan earlier that afternoon, and that was the final straw that made up Robbie's mind for him.

In the comin' days and weeks, recruitment stations all across the United States were swamped with young men who were chompin' at the bit and ready to give those Japs and Germans what was comin' to them. England had been at war with Germany since September of nineteen thirty-nine, and we were about to join them as part of the Allied Forces.

I couldn't hardly stand to think about Robbie bein' across the ocean and fightin' in this war so far away. It had never felt close or connected to me in any way until the mornin' of December seventh. Japan had brought the war into my peaceful, quiet world and dropped it squarely on us.

Robbie had given Mr. Macpherson his notice and let him know he would likely be leavin' for Fort Jackson in South Carolina sometime between Christmas and New Year. That would give him a little time to settle his personal business and say goodbye to family and friends.

***

Christmas was sober this year. Like Thanksgivin', it was just we Mountain Spencer's gathered to celebrate the Lord's birth. And our friends Johnny, Claire, and Robbie would be joining us for Christmas dinner. I thought it odd that Robbie wasn't spendin' the day with Tillie and her family, but I kept my mouth shut and was content to be happy he would be with us.

Granddad had a huge smoked ham he had been savin' for Christmas, and Claire and Johnny were bringin' a traditional roast goose with apple stuffing. The Bruce family had carried traditions from Scotland, and a roast goose for Christmas dinner was a must for the Bruces. Mamma and I had made six pies again: two apple, two mince, and two pumpkin pies. There was Mamma's creamy mashed potatoes, candied sweet potatoes swimmin' in a buttery candied sauce, cranberry relish that glowed in Mamma's antique cut glass bowl makin' it look like a table centerpiece, several vegetable dishes, and a big basket filled with homemade yeast rolls. It was a Christmas table fit for a king.

Christmas fell on a Thursday this year, and after our Christmas feast, and dishes were washed up and put away in Mamma's hutch, we all gathered in the big family room with a warm fire cracklin' in the fireplace. Robbie and I sat on the long bench that sat along the wall opposite the fireplace, while Granddad and Granny Spencer sat in the cane-bottom rockin' chairs. Mamma, Daddy, Claire, Johnny, Uncle James, and Aunt Eunice sat on the two couches. The young'uns were either sprawled on the floor or occupied upstairs.

There was more than one conversation goin'. Daddy, Johnny, Granddad, and Uncle James were talkin' about the war and speculatin' on the course it would take. Granny was chattin' with Gerry and Jamie, while Mamma and Claire talked about the goin's on in the community. Some of the women had put together a food drive to gather donations and had made boxes of Christmas dinner for families who had suffered most, and were still affected by last year's August flood. The drive had been a huge success, and they were rememberin' the joy it had brought to the families they had delivered boxes to on Monday.

Robbie and I sat for a time just a listenin' to the conversation and soakin' up the warmth from the fireplace. It took me a minute to realize that Johnny was talkin' about two new Army trainin' camps that were bein' established in North Carolina: Camp Butner and Camp Sutton. Both would be operational next year.

Robbie turned to me and said, "Maggie, I'm a leavin' Monday mornin' early. I'm supposed to report to Fort Jackson in South Carolina by three o'clock Monday afternoon."

I sat quiet for a moment, a bit stunned. I had known this was a comin'. It shouldn't have been a shock, but now it was actually here, I was shocked into silence. A creeping feelin' of terror was seepin' around me and clenchin' at my heart. I was fearful of breakin' into tears and bawlin' in front of everyone. So, I swallowed hard, took a deep breath, and said, "So soon? Why so soon?"

"Now Magg's, I told everyone I would be goin' by the New Year. New Year's Day is one week from today, so I expected it to be real soon."

"When did you hear? How long have you known?" I asked in a whisper.

"I got a telegram yesterday mornin'," said Robbie. "I didn't think it would make any difference if I just waited until today to tell everyone. Course, Ma and Papa know."

Robbie seemed uncomfortable with my silence, but I didn't know what to say. I sure as everything couldn't say what was achin' inside my heart!

I was just about to suggest that we have a send-off party or somethin' here at the farm to give everyone the chance to say goodbye to Robbie, and a couple more of the fella's in the community who were also going when Robbie slapped his hands on his knees and said brightly, "Mr. Macpherson wants to give us fella's a big sendoff from his store Sunday evenin', and everyone is invited to come!"

My heart sank. *Oh well,* I thought. *Just as well. He belongs to Tillie anyways. Guess I'll have to make myself get used to the idea that Robbie will only ever be my friend. But my very best friend in the world.* So, I smiled and said, "Why, that's very nice of him, Robbie. What can we bring?"

"He said he is going to provide hamburgers and drinks, and to put word out that the ladies in the community could bring things to go with it, and dessert. I hope it's not too cold, snowin', or rainin' cause George Hamil and Bob Harkin are going to be grillin' hamburgers outside the store. I sure don't want no one gettin' sick on my account!"

I then realized that the others in the room were listenin', so I put on a bright and happy smile that I just wasn't feelin' and repeated Robbie's news, and Mr. Macpherson's invitation to the Deep Gap community.

"We will miss you, young man," Granddad said in his kind and serious voice. "We sure will miss you, but we will pray for you. Every day." He said it with emphasis on *every day.*

"Thank you, sir," Robbie said. "It's a comfort to be able to count on the prayers of friends and family, and to know that you all will be thinkin' about us fella's that's joinin' up."

I was tryin' to focus on what we should bring to the sendoff. If I didn't, I would start bawlin' again, and I was determined to save that until I was alone.

Mamma and I settled on our family bringin' a big bowl of baked beans chucked full of bacon, seasonings, and brown sugar, and a big bubblin' apple crisp with lots of cinnamon, knowin' these were among Robbie's favorite foods and would also go well with hamburgers.

I dreaded the gatherin' at Macpherson's store. Not only would most of the community be there, but Tillie would be there, no doubt on Robbie's arm and throwin' her overly sweet false compliments and subtle insults not only at me, but other girls as well. But it was for our Robbie, so I would buck up, put on my own false smile, and endure Tillie with as much grace as I could scrape up. The thought hit me when I was puttin' the finishin' touches on my hair-do that maybe I should call on the help of the Almighty to help me put a bridle on my own mouth and muster up a cheerfulness I didn't feel.

I had curled my shoulder-length hair and pinned the sides back with the new jeweled barrettes Mamma had given me for Christmas, and was satisfied that I looked very grown up. With sellin' eggs to the stores all around our area, I had a bit more money and had also bought myself a new store-bought dress from Hunt's Department Store in Boone. After-Christmas sales and summer markdowns made the dress more affordable, as well as bein' the prettiest and most grown-up dress I had ever owned. It was made from a tiny navy-blue checked material with tiny red flowers sprinkled around it and had the popular midriff bodice and a cute little short navy-blue bolero jacket with red trim around it. Even though it was technically a summer dress, I felt stylish and very grown up.

I paused before leavin' my room and bowed my head. "Lord," I said under my breath, "Lord, please help me to keep a civil tongue in my head when it comes to Tillie Macpherson, and help me to not say anything I'd be regrettin' later. Amen."

We entered the crowded store bearing our contribution of steamin' baked beans and apple crisp. Mr. Macpherson was smilin' and invitin' folks into the warm store, takin' coats and hats to be laid away in his office. Even Mrs. Macpherson, who was normally too stuffy and high and mighty to mix with us country folks, was there receivin' people as though she were Lady of the manor welcoming high society into a palace. I knew it wasn't sincere, so did Mamma and Granny, but we didn't let on and thanked her for her hospitality and asked where she wanted us to put our baked beans and apple crisp.

The store's big checkout counter had been cleared to make way for food, as well as extra tables set up for food and seating. I was surprised at how much room was made by movin' shelves back against the wall. We set down our food and turned to Mr. Macpherson to give him our coats and hats we had removed. At that moment Robbie and Tillie emerged from the office. Robbie's face had a strained look, and I could tell that he and Tillie had been havin' words. But upon seein' the Spencer family, he straightened his face, and a genuine smile replaced the frown that had been there.

"I'm so glad you came, so glad you're here," he said with what sounded like relief to me.

I handed my coat to Mr. Macpherson with a smile and "thank you," then turned to say hello to Robbie and Tillie. When I looked up, I saw two things: admiration on Robbie's handsome face, and anger on Tillie's as she glared up at him. Robbie grinned, his eyes lightin' up, and he said, "Well look at who's lookin' so fine and pretty to—"

About that time Tillie snatched his arm, cuttin' short his words, and said, "New markdowns at the store, Maggie? Summer clearance isn't the thing to wear in the middle of winter."

It was the first time I had witnessed Tillie bein' openly rude and hateful in front of Robbie, and he looked genuinely shocked by her condescendin' words.

"Tillie!" Robbie said in a stunned reprimand. But Tillie just looked me up and down and had neither an apology nor an answer to Robbie's rebuke.

I decided to act as though she wasn't there. I knew the dress was out of season, but those of us who weren't born with a silver spoon in our mouths shifted and made do with what we had, when we had it. "It's okay," I said. "Don't worry about it."

But I knew it bothered him. Robbie saw me as one of his very best friends, and his girlfriend, the one he thought he was in love with, had been unforgivably rude to me. Robbie had never really *seen* this in Tillie, bein' a man and a bit blind to her nature.

Robbie turned slightly to Tillie, laid his hand over hers that clutched at his arm, and said quietly but firmly, "That wasn't kind, Tillie, wasn't nice at all."

Tillie shook off his hand and said with a pout, "It wasn't intended to be kind or nice, it was instructive. She obviously doesn't know she is wearin' a summer dress in the dead of winter. I was showing her a kindness by instructing her."

I felt my face flush, and before I responded, my mind flashed back to the request I had made of the Lord before comin' here. I took a breath and said, "It's okay, Robbie, really it is." Then I turned to Tillie and said quietly, "Tillie, you are right. This is a clearance summer dress I bought for seventy-five percent off at Hunt's Department Store. Yes, it's not as warm as a new wool suit would have been, but then I couldn't afford a new wool suit. But I'm happy with it." And I turned and walked to where Mamma was sittin' at one of the tables chattin' with women from our community, pulled out the chair beside her, and sat down.

That's when I realized my hands were shakin' and my legs felt wobbly. *Good Lord,* I thought. *Why did that upset me so?* Then I realized I had been the recipient of answered prayer! I had answered Tillie but had done so in a civil manner. Exactly what I had asked the Lord for. Had to have been the Lord, because normally I would have torn into Tillie with cuttin' words and hostility.

I stuck close to Mamma the rest of the evenin'. Since losin' my friend Betty in the August flood last year, I realized I didn't have another girlfriend that I was especially close to. I had socialized mostly with Betty, family, and Robbie. With Betty gone, I felt the lack of havin' girlfriends deeply. I'd have to try to be more social and make friends with some of the girls in our community. Hard to do when your life is centered around work.

As the evenin' came to an end, and we had gathered up our dishes that had been scraped clean of every single bit of baked beans and apple crisp, Daddy asked for our coats and we said our goodbyes and headed toward our truck. We were puttin' our dishes in the back while Gerry and Charlie climbed in, pullin' blankets around them for the short trip home, when Robbie came runnin' down the store's steps, pullin' his coat on while he ran.

"I wanted to come out and say thank you for comin'," Robbie panted from his run. "Thank you for bringin' baked beans. I know you did it for me." Robbie grinned at Mamma.

"We did," Mamma smiled back at him. The whole family loved Robbie like he was family. "And you are very welcome, Robbie. You know you will be in our prayers and our thoughts while you're away from us. Let us know how you are doin'. I know your Mamma will no doubt keep us up to date with how you are, and you won't have time to write everyone, but a letter once in a while would be welcomed by the whole family."

It was hardly noticeable, but Mamma cut her eyes over at me for a fraction of a second when she said this. She gave Robbie a big hug, held him close for just a second, then stepped back to let the rest of the family tell Robbie goodbye and give him a hug. We aren't usually so huggy in these parts, but then we aren't usually sendin' one of our own off to war.

Mamma and Daddy climbed into the cab of our truck, and Gerry and Charlie huddled in their blankets in the back, and I just stood there. How did I say goodbye and God bless to Robbie Bruce? I loved him. I may have only been sixteen, but I knew in my heart that I loved him, and only him.

Robbie reached for my hand and held it tenderly in his larger, rougher hands. "Goodbye, Maggie," Robbie said softly. "Think of me sometimes?"

I nodded my head. My throat was closed up and so tight I couldn't get any words out, so I just nodded.

"I'm sorry Tillie was so rude earlier, Mag's. I was proud of you, how you responded to her rudeness. I…"

I didn't want to waste precious time discussin' how rude Tillie had been.

"It's okay, Robbie," I said, "really it is. Tillie always has somethin' mean or rude to say. I'm just gettin' better at handlin' it."

Robbie's forehead wrinkled slightly with a frown, and with a still puzzled sound he said, "I hadn't ever noticed before."

I felt like rollin' my eyes, but I didn't.

"I know everyone is tellin' you goodbye, be careful, take care and all that, but…" I dropped my eyes that had started fillin' up with tears, and my voice had taken on a husky, quivery sound that made it clear full throttle bawlin' was next. So, I just gripped his hands with both of mine as tight as I could. I wanted to hang on forever and not let him ship off to Europe and fight in this war.

"Magg's, when the weather is better, after we are sent over there, will you go up to your favorite spot up off the old Indian trail where we used to traipse and track critters? Think of me so hard I'll feel it all the way to Europe and can imagine you there and pretend I'm there too? Hopefully I'll be able to come home on leave before we go after trainin', but just in case I don't, I would like to know that you will think of me from up there and pray for me from up there."

I was cryin' now, tears flowin' down my face. I threw my arms around him. This friend who my very soul loved. This friend who had been my childhood buddy, who had been everything to me. Who I now loved but couldn't say so. Robbie's arms slid around me, and he held me close while I sobbed against his chest. I didn't care who saw me. Mamma and Daddy, Gerry and Charlie, they surely saw me cryin' in Robbie's arms, but I just didn't care. Robbie was holdin' his friend in comfort, but I was holdin' my world, my only love in mine.

We eventually stepped back from each other, and Robbie reached out and wiped tears off my cheeks. He laughed quietly.

"We may be all sad for nothin'. I may be in trainin' so long the Japs and Germans whipped, and the war wrapped up before I go anywhere."

I knew that wasn't likely but played along.

"You wish!" I croaked.

He stepped back and saluted me as though I was a five-star general and said, "Write me, Maggie?"

I nodded, and Robbie turned and ran back to the warmth of the store.

Chapter Seventeen

Monday mornin' I was up early, like every other mornin', and went out to feed, water, and check on my hens. I always checked the bottom of the chicken house first thing because I had once caught a fox tryin' to dig under it. I nearly caught the red devil red-handed, so to speak, and after that we had to dig down around the perimeter of the chicken house and bury about two feet of fencing and barbed wire to keep the varmints out. It's always somethin'.

I walked around the chicken house, makin' sure there was no new evidence of diggin', then went in to feed my girls. They were singin' up a storm, and the twenty or so roosters we had kept so our eggs would be fertile were crowin'. It was a noisy place.

I filled all the feeders and water tanks and, by habit, went to check through the egg boxes, not really expectin' anything. To my surprise, in the fourth layin' box I saw two small, light brown eggs! They weren't much bigger than a bird's egg, but they were chicken eggs! I whooped and danced, picked up a couple of my girls, and gave them a big kiss.

After a close look in every layin' box, I counted my treasure. Twenty-eight eggs on the first day of findin' eggs. Normally I went straight from the chicken house to the barn to milk Abigail, but not this mornin'! I trotted as quick as I could without jostlin' the eggs too badly, back to the house with my surprise.

Mamma was in the kitchen preparin' breakfast when I busted through the back door with my haul and set the basket on the table with a huge grin plastered across my face without sayin' one word. I didn't need to. Mamma knew.

We had scrambled eggs that mornin' from the very first eggs my hens produced. They were so tiny it took most of them to satisfy five hungry people, but they were my eggs. And they represented the beginning of my dream of havin' my very own business.

***

A month later I received a letter from one Robert Bruce, Pvt., Fort Jackson, South Carolina, dated January 28, 1942. Robbie had arrived on time after a small delay in bus service due to a flat tire. He was well and had sent me a three-page letter detailing his new life as a Private in the United States Army. His basic training had begun.

He described his barracks, his uncomfortable cot, and the camaraderie among the young men there. He was unimpressed with the food, mostly because he was used to good mountain fare that had plenty of seasoning and bacon grease added for flavor.

His Drill Instructor, Sergeant Tucker, he was pretty sure hated everyone's guts, and his sole mission in life was to make their lives as miserable as he could possibly manage.

"Our first week," Robbie wrote, "in the middle of the night Sergeant Tucker threw open the door of our barracks, screaming at the top of his lungs, 'ALRIGHT YOU MISERABLE PANSIES, COME TO ATTENTION!' I will tell you right here, Magg's, that I did not quote the Sarge word for word. Ma would kill me for the language if I even wrote it. He screamed at us for failing to run our daily five-mile run in his required time limit. Screamed at us to dress and fall out, giving us three minutes to comply. It was two AM. We ran the five miles, collapsed into our cots, only to wake up to his screaming at us for being lazy so-and-so's at quarter till six. And, my dear, here is a summary of our days here at Fort Jackson: wake, eat, endure screaming, drill, run, eat, run, puke, endure screaming, drill, march, eat, and fall into bed. If we are lucky, we sleep through the night. Many nights we do not but are screamed out of our cots to be run through our five-mile run, sometimes twice in a night.

"But we are getting stronger, and some who were carrying extra weight are getting leaner and faster. We are beginning to march as one and pull together as a unit. So, I guess ol' Tucker is getting us somewhere after all.

"How are your chickens doing, Magg's? I guess by now you are gathering eggs. You have a good head, and you aren't afraid to work hard. I know you will do well with your egg business. Have you considered contracting with the military to supply them with eggs? It might be a good idea. I know a guy here from Charlotte whose uncle has a pig farm, and he has a contract to supply the Army and

Marine Corps with pork here in South Carolina. Check with the Quartermaster in North Carolina and see if that's a possibility. Might be a good thing for you.

"Don't forget to write and give me all the news. Sometimes I feel so homesick for news, and even little things have become so interesting.

"Your devoted friend,

Robbie."

***

February 4, 1942,

Deep Gap, North Carolina

Dear Robbie,

Fort Jackson sounds divine. Cookies and tea on the veranda every evening and stimulating conversation with Sergeant Tucker. My! I'm jealous. Sorry, but I couldn't resist. Don't tell me too much about your dear sweet Sergeant Tucker, or I might send him a box of rotten eggs! Why is he so mean, and couldn't a higher-ranking officer put a stop to his abuse? It made me and Mamma both so mad reading about how he was treating you and the others under him. Surely, he should be reported.

My hens are doing terrific, and their egg production is keeping me very busy. I collect eggs several times a day now to keep so many from being broken. I know modern poultry farms don't allow the hens to roam in an enclosure like I do, and hens are kept in small cages that allow the eggs to roll out of the way so they don't get broken as much. But I can't stand to do that with my girls! I feel bad enough that they can't roam the property like our chickens used to, and I cannot condemn them to a miserable life cooped up in a small wire cage. It makes more work for us, but so be it.

Yes, I said us! Daddy has thrown his lot in with me, and we are combining our efforts into one business. Daddy will still farm and has turned toward growin' as much of our chickens' food as possible. He has converted some of his hay fields to oats and corn, and since the hens can't roam and eat bugs, we have started raising our own grasshoppers to feed them. I found out that while man can't live on bread alone, neither can chickens! They must have protein, and grasshoppers seem to be the best way to give it to them.

There has been so much to learn, and it's a good thing I didn't know how ignorant I was, or I may have thought twice about starting out as big as I did. But it seems to be working out, and we find the help we need when something comes up. So, all's well that ends well.

Gerry and Charlie will also work with me, making it a family business. We plan to build another chicken house as soon as we can assemble the lumber, and as soon as it is nearly finished, we will be ordering another thousand chicks! Can you believe it?

Thank you for your suggestion. Daddy had mentioned that possibility when we joined together, and we will be talking with the Quartermaster in North Carolina when our new chicken house is ready and we have our new chicks. I don't want to count our chickens before they hatch. Ha ha!

It's been a pretty cold and snowy winter so far here in the mountains. I know they don't get so much weather in South Carolina. Mr. Jenkins was rememberin' the blizzard we got trapped in years ago at church Sunday. Remember how cold it was and how scared we were that we would never see our families again? Charlie and his friends have had a blast, though, skating on the pond. Some winters it doesn't get cold enough to make skating safe, but this year has been a good skating year. Sleddin' too. We have all been taking a little time for a sleddin' party or two.

Jamie said to tell you hello. He's here to hang out with Gerry and has been pestering me to say hello for him. So, hello from Jamie the pest.

I know you probably already know that President Roosevelt has ordered the nation to go onto a year-round Daylight Savings Time until the end of the war. Personally, I prefer the extra hour of daylight at the end of the day instead of the beginning. It will begin on February 9.

I guess you have also heard that the government is rationing tires now. That's going to make it harder to travel and take care of business. Hopefully, if we're careful and take care of our tires, we will last out this war. Your Papa told Daddy he is thinking about tryin' to start up a tire recapping business as well as his sawmill. With tires rationed and new ones harder and harder to get, it sounds like a good thing to consider. He has the space for it and can mill his own lumber and build it on the side of his sawmill. The dirt and gravel roads don't help us none, though.

I heard someone say the other day that automobiles will be added to the rationing list by the end of the month. I guess all the automobile factories that once built cars and trucks have been retooled and will now produce tanks, military trucks, airplanes, Jeeps, torpedoes, and even helmets. Daddy's old truck had better last until the end of this war! It's liable to be held together with wire and bubble gum by the end.

We are all well and healthy, my dear friend. We pray for you every day when we come together for meals. Even Daddy adds a fervent "Amen" when your name is brought before the Lord at our table.

Your friend,

Maggie

***

February 28, 1942,

Fort Jackson, South Carolina

Dear Maggie,

Thank you for the laughs. Pass the cookies, I'll serve the tea. I am halfway through basic training and will no doubt ship out to one of the other training camps for extended training. I can't seem to find out anything about when we can expect to be sent to Europe. So, I guess what that actually means is we have a lot of training ahead of us, and I'm just fine with that. From what I've been hearing of the war, the more training we can get the better off we will be. Sargent Tucker might just do us in first, and we won't even have to worry about it!

Kidding aside, Sargent Tucker may have let something slip yesterday in his screaming at us. He said, "You think I'm bad? You think I was sent from Hell to make your life Hell? You don't know what Hell is until you have laid in a trench soaked to your innards in filth of every kind crying for your mamma."

I don't mind telling you it kind of scared us all. Not so much the layin' in a trench full of filth, but for things to be so bad that a grown man might lay there and cry for his mamma. I found out Old Tucker is a veteran of the Great War, so I'm thinking he knows what he's talking about.

Running five miles is easy now, so the Sarge has extended the run to seven miles. I don't know where we will end up, but at least it isn't as hard as the five-mile runs were when we first arrived. Oh, we also have started running with a full pack of gear on our backs that weighs sixty pounds. I overheard a bunch of NCOs laughing the other day when they heard some of the fellas grumbling about running with the packs. They were saying, "Wait until those packs weigh eighty pounds, they will cry for the sixty-pound packs."

We also began rifle practice, which is about as close to fun as it gets here. We were all issued an M1 Garand, also known as the M1 rifle. Sargent Tucker can't help but be just a little bit impressed with the shooting ability of our group of mountain boys. When he asked us about it, Johnny Bailey spoke up and said, "Oh man, Sarge, all of us mountain men can shoot. We were born with a rifle in our hand and was bringing home squirrels for the table by time we were two." Sarge didn't laugh, but I could tell he was amused. I told him part of Johnny's lie was true. We were actually handed the rifle at birth, then brought home squirrels for the table at two. Sarge just snorted, but he was impressed all the same.

I loved hearing about the boys sledding, and pond skating. Sometimes I can nearly imagine I'm there with you all, like old times when we were carefree kids. We sure had some good times growing up. Funny how at the time it felt like those days would go on forever and time seemed to go so slow, especially when we were sitting in class all day! It feels strange to be nearly nineteen and wishing you could roll back time. I would love to be ten and you eight once again, taking a lunch in a poke off into the mountains all day, climbing rocks, laying in the sun, or playing in a creek. We had the most idyllic childhood, Maggie girl.

Remember the time I accidentally clobbered you in the head with a rock? Lord, but that scared me to death! First, I thought I had killed you, then I thought your Daddy would kill me! Did anyone ever know the truth about what happened? I feel bad now that we are older that I didn't confess.

Yes, I had heard that the government had started rationing new tires, and now new automobiles. Before this war is over, I wonder just how lean times may become. In England it has really gotten bad, and people are actually hungry. Thank God that will never be the case for our people in the mountains. There are so many who are poor, but nearly everyone has a garden and chickens. It's the folks in the cities who will suffer the most if we see a shortage of food in this country.

I think Papa is on to something great with opening a tire recapping shop. Since folks won't be able to buy new tires, they will need to make theirs last longer. I'm glad he and Ma will have something else to help them get through these times. I just hope that they don't start requiring forty-five-year-old men to serve active duty in this war. It would kill my Ma for him to be taken.

Well, Maggs, it's nearly time for Lights Out and I'm ready for it. One thing about all this running is when it's time for bed nobody complains! We are all happy to lay ourselves down, and we are so tired we don't even notice how uncomfortable the cot is anymore.

Take care, my dear friend, and keep the letters coming. Sometimes I read parts with news from home to Johnny Bailey and George Hamil. They don't get as much mail as I do, so I like to share mine with them. Poor old George especially gets awfully homesick sometimes.

God bless and keep you.

Robbie

Chapter Eighteen

Winter soon passed and it was the first of April. Our new chicken house was finished, and the second batch of chicks ordered. I was just a little bit nervous about our bein' able to handle the workload. It was going to be a huge amount of work, and most of it was hard work. Gerry was nearly seventeen and Charlie was twelve, and they did most of the shovelin' and cleaning out the chicken houses, but they were both still in school.

I had gone until I was past sixteen as the law required, but Mamma agreed that I had done well learnin' my three R's and had plenty of learnin' to give me the life I wanted. I knew I would never leave my mountains unless I was to visit somewhere. I never had the urge to leave the shelter and beauty of this place. It was more than enough for me.

I thought about Robbie's request that I go to my favorite spot in the world up off the old Indian Trail, my rocky slab that jutted out over the valley below and think of him. Now that winter was over, I would do that soon. I was so busy last year I never made it there one time. I would do better this year, if for no other reason but to be able to take paper and pencil with me and write Robbie a letter from my bird's-eye perch.

But that would have to wait until next week. Today we were gettin' the heat lamps ready and sawdust down in the broodin' nursery. I was worried that it was too cold yet, even with the heat lamps, so Daddy had rigged a homemade water boiler that would pump hot water through pipes laid on the floor under the sawdust. This way there was no danger of a wood stove inside the chicken house causin' a fire. The wood stove, water tank, and pump were in a small shed not far from the chicken house, but far enough to not be a danger. The hot water circulated through the pipes and warmed the broodin' nursery. There was a thick layer of sawdust over the pipes, but since heat rises, it worked just fine. We were ready for the new chicks.

I was hopin' to have the same good fortune we had with our first delivery. I don't mind tellin' you I was nervous. Though it was April and spring had definitely sprung, it was chilly for newly hatched chicks. I just prayed that the United States Postal Service had looked after my treasures and kept them warm. All it takes is for one person to fail to do their job.

Mamma and Daddy had telephone service put in our house in March. It was a big expense, and if it wasn't for the growin' egg and poultry business it would have been considered an unnecessary luxury. But with Daddy havin' to "borrow" the phone at Macpherson's store so much, and for longer periods of time while talkin' with the Quarter Master and his staff, and different local stores about egg deliveries, we decided that it was necessary for the business. So, Spencer Farm became one of the first residents to have a telephone in the whole area. That was only possible because we lived on a main road through the mountains, but we had to pay for telephone wire to be run all the way from Macpherson's store, which was the closest point of connection.

I was stationed in the house by myself waitin' for a call from the Quarter Master over at Fort Butner to set up an egg delivery schedule. Until the incomin' chicks were grown and producin' eggs, every egg we could spare was goin' to Fort Butner. Daddy, Gerry, and Charlie were haulin' fresh sawdust from Johnny Bruce's sawmill, and Mamma was at Granddad and Granny Spencer's today. Granny had been feelin' poorly lately, havin' had influenza, and Mamma was helpin' her with housework. So, I was alone in the house, sittin' on the front porch mendin' one of Daddy's work shirts he had torn while workin' on the new heat system for the chicken house.

I heard a vehicle turn off the main thoroughfare that runs north and south, onto our road that ran east and west. We usually didn't pay much mind to traffic. We were used to it, and unless a friendly neighbor tooted their horn in passin', we didn't even look. But this vehicle had a different sound to it. I could tell it wasn't a pickup truck, which was what the majority of our local vehicles were. It had a powerful sound to it.

I looked up to catch a look at what I knew was somethin' different, when a car like nothin' I had ever seen before came roarin' by. It was the sleekest, most stylish vehicle I'd ever seen in these parts, and it was bright red with an open top. I heard a woman's laugh comin' from it, and that's when I saw that the woman was Tillie Macpherson. She was sitting in the passenger seat, laughin' over at somethin' the driver, who was a stranger, had said. She never looked up, and in a flash, they had passed by.

I sat still in shock for a moment. What in the world had I just seen? I may not have liked Tillie because of our history, but I sure didn't want to automatically think the worst of her. Maybe the man drivin' the snappy car was a cousin or relative from elsewhere. He sure wasn't from here!

I tried to put the incident out of my mind. First of all, I thought, it was none of my business. Second of all, I had an extreme dislike for nosiness and some people's habits of assumin' things. Best to forget what I had seen because more than likely there was a reasonable explanation for Tillie's behavior. But I couldn't help it; it niggled at my mind for days.

***

My chicks arrived, and the Post Master in Boone called on our new telephone this time as soon as they came in. Daddy and I drove to Boone again to pick them up. Granddad came along for the ride since he insisted on helpin' us with unboxin' and examinin' the chicks and gettin' them settled into their new home. We were all excited to see our business grow by double! Robbie had certainly been right when he said he believed the military could use any amount of eggs we could produce. Eggs were right healthy and a good source of protein for the soldiers in trainin'.

This time more chicks had died on the journey. There had been a total of one thousand thirty-two chicks, and forty-four of them were dead in the boxes. We worked fast to get them unboxed, examinin' each one before releasin' them under the heat lamps, where they could get to the warm mash and water we had set out for them.

With the hot water heat Daddy had put in and the heat lamps, I no longer feared that the nights would get too cold for the new chicks. The broodin' nursery was toasty warm, with plenty of space and kept as clean as possible. I had mixed plenty of black pepper and garlic powder in the mash to prevent Coccidiosis. We were set, and with hard work and a watchful eye we would double our egg production by fall.

***

April 17, 1942,

Deep Gap, North Carolina

Dear Robbie,

Well, here I am on my eighteenth birthday. I gathered pen and paper and climbed the old Indian Trail, and I am now sitting on the big rock that juts out over the valley. It is a beautiful day. It has rained quite a bit this spring, which is normal and what we need. But I am happy that today, on my eighteenth birthday, I have sunshine to enjoy this time alone with my thoughts of you. This is what you asked of me, and I am here not only to think of you, because I do that often, but to write and catch you up on all the going's on.

Later this evening the family is coming to help me celebrate, and it will be wonderful. Mamma said eighteen is a special birthday and we needed to make it special. She and Granny will be making all my favorite foods for dinner and are making homemade ice cream for later on the porch. It would be absolutely perfect if only you were here to help us celebrate, my dear friend.

Gerry is seventeen now. Can you believe it? In just one more year he will be drafted, and no doubt will follow you to Fort Jackson to begin his own training to be a soldier. I pray that the war is over before then.

Your Papa's tire recapping business started off with a bang! Granddad had a tire that kept going flat because it was so worn, so he stopped by Johnny's Recapping a couple of days ago and said there were several people waiting their turn, and Johnny had several to get to. I know you will be pleased to hear it's doing so well. Between tires and the sawmill, he might have to hire on some help.

My chickens are doing very well, and the new chicks we received two weeks ago are feathering out nicely and growing fast. There is something so satisfying about watching living things grow, especially when they are your livelihood. There's not much that is cuter than baby chicks, and I love spending time with them. You should see how they flock around me when I sit on a low stool in the brooding nursery. They will jump up on my lap and look me square in the eye, cocking their little heads from side to side as though they were looking for something.

The hens are doing well too. I am amazed at how well they are laying, and now that they are older, they are producing the finest eggs you ever saw! I'm glad we made the decision to let them free-run in an enclosed area. There is a risk of losing some to hawks and other varmints, but all in all I believe it is still best. We put ground oyster shells out for them, and Granddad is doing a wonderful job raising grasshoppers to feed them. Did I tell you Granddad was in charge of grasshoppers now? It has truly become a family business, giving him more purpose. It's also much easier on his aching knees and his heart than field work. He never complains, but I see him rubbing his knees a lot.

With the government contract and the hens producing so well, everyone is earning a wage now, which is good. Charlie is so funny. You can tell he feels very grown up when Daddy pays him every Friday now. But he earns it and works about an hour before school and about three hours afterwards every day. Charlie has surprised us all with his hard work. I feel bad for being so surprised, but he is a little bit spoiled, being Mamma's baby and all. Still, he's a good, hard worker and doesn't complain at all.

We started using egg crates we order from Texas for transporting the eggs bound for Fort Butner. The wood crates hold thirty dozen eggs each, stored in twelve trays holding three hundred and sixty eggs each. Each egg has its own compartment with a horizontal separator between each tier, from the bottom to the top of the case. The wooden crates are then filled with sawdust to create a cushion.

We have contracted a delivery of five hundred twenty-five dozen eggs every Friday to Fort Butner. It's quite a drive for Daddy, because he has to drive slow and careful. What would normally be a three-hour drive is an all-day trip there and back for him. We are allowed extra tire rations to be able to keep up the deliveries. Every week Daddy delivers seventeen and a half crates to the Quarter Masters Warehouse and brings back the empty crates from the week before. So far everything has worked smoothly.

Speaking of rationing, we were told that gasoline and sugar would also be rationed as of next month. Heavens! Sugar is one thing. We can make do with the cane sugar Daddy and Granddad make every year and the honey. But gasoline? Surely, they will grant us extra gasoline for our egg deliveries to Fort Butner. Otherwise, I don't know what we will do.

Granddad has decided that there isn't enough fun going on around here, and I have to agree with him! He told me yesterday that a young lady eighteen years old should have more things in her life besides taking care of chickens and old folks. Ha-ha. So, he is arranging a few parties to be held in his old barn like we used to for harvest barn dancing and such. He is holding a party the first Saturday of every month through the rest of summer and fall. People are so happy to have something besides the drudgery of work, flood cleanup, and war that he has had a lot of offers of help. The first party is the first Saturday in May, and I am looking forward to it.

When is your basic training finished? It seems like you had said about four months, so I'm thinking soon. Is there any possibility that you might come home for a visit before you go elsewhere? It would be wonderful to see you again.

Well, the afternoon is waning, and I shouldn't be late for my own birthday supper. So, I will bring this letter to a close by describing how beautiful our mountains are on this late afternoon. There's not much haze in the sky, so I can see clear out over the Piedmont. Mountain ridge after mountain ridge standing south and east of me, and the light of the sun that is getting lower in the sky to my west is beginning to cast a golden glow over them. As they progress to the east, each ridgeline gets bluer, and finally in the farthest distance, purple. Birds are singing, and I can hear a cricket or two chirping in the grasses behind me. It's so peaceful here that it is very hard to imagine something as terrible as war going on elsewhere.

Take care and God bless you, Robbie.

Maggie

***

The first Saturday of May was beautiful. Everyone was lookin' forward to the party that afternoon. Granddad didn't want it to be an all-night party, so it was to begin at three. Every Spencer was bathed and spruced up and ready to head around the corner to Granddad and Granny's.

Donations had been collected ahead of time, and Granddad had bought a yearling pig to barbecue over a spit beside the barn. He had been at it since early this mornin', and we could smell the yummy roasting pork stokin' our hunger at our house.

Mamma had surprised me for my eighteenth birthday with one of the prettiest dresses I had ever seen. She had bought fabric instead of usin' flour sacks. It was a beautiful dark, bright red with tiny raised white dots. She said it was dotted swiss, and it looked and felt luxurious. She had used a pattern that gave the dress a very full skirt but nipped in with princess seams at the waist. It had a square neck that I loved, and the sleeves were flutter sleeves that came about halfway between my shoulder and elbow. It was pretty and flattering, and I was wearin' it to the party. I didn't want to scuff up my new white pumps, so I wore my old pair from last year that I had cleaned and polished with white shoe polish.

Girls were wearin' a new hairdo called victory rolls, inspired by the rollin' maneuvers fighter pilots would make in their planes, and I knew we would be seein' a lot of it at the party. I had tried it a time or two but hadn't taken the time to master it. So, I decided to keep my shoulder-length curls pinned back on the sides with the pretty jeweled barrettes I had received at Christmas.

Mamma had sent Daddy and the two boys over to Granddad and Granny's earlier with two big pails of her wonderful baked beans.

Everyone was bringin' somethin' to go with the barbecue pork. Clair had told Mamma she was bringin' scalloped potatoes, which were so good and loaded with melted cheesy goodness. I was sure that there would be lots to eat and drink.

Granddad told Daddy that Mr. Macpherson was bringin' two hundred paper plates and a big washtub filled with iced bottles of Coca-Cola, Root Beer, and Grapette. I didn't know who, but someone else was makin' homemade lemonade.

People were pullin' in regularly, and Granddad and Granny's yard was fillin' up fast. Some folks were bein' directed to park at our farm and walk over. I was helpin' Granny arrange food bein' brought in by everyone when I noticed a pretty dark-headed girl in a bright pink shirtwaist dress standin' beside a newer Ford Standard car. I had never seen her before and wondered if she was visitin' family or friends in our area. I caught her eye, and she smiled a small, shy smile. I flashed her a friendly one but was too busy to stop and introduce myself at the moment.

By three-thirty Granddad whistled for quiet so the blessin' could be said over the food. We all gathered in closer while the men took off their hats and women shushed the kiddos.

"Dear Lord," Granddad began his prayer, "thank you for this glorious spring afternoon to gather with friends and family to share thy bounty and each other's company. We thank you for this good food and thank you for the beautiful hands who have prepared it all. Most of all, we thank you for the gift of your love and forgiveness you have given to us all. Be with us, and may all we say and do be pleasin' to you, Lord. Amen."

Granddad didn't believe in long, drawn-out fanciful prayers over food that hungry people were waitin' on! Thank God!

I was standin' in the long line for food, listenin' to the sounds of conversation and laughter all around me with a little smile. Granddad had known what we all needed. Then suddenly I heard a well-known and well-loved voice beside me.

"Hey Magg's, how you doin'?"

It was Robbie!

I spun around so fast I nearly lost my balance. Robbie, laughin', put out his hand to steady me.

"Whoa! I didn't mean to startle you! Only surprise you."

Robbie stood lookin' down at me with laughter dancin' in his blue-grey eyes. He was wearin' the khaki uniform that was seen everywhere these days and looked so very handsome.

I was just about to throw my arms around my friend when it suddenly registered in my head that he was not alone. There was Tillie Macpherson smilin' at me with a nasty little smile that told me she was up to no good.

I decided to ignore her, try to pretend she wasn't there gloatin' and tryin' to goad me with her smugness. I tuned her out and smiled up at Robbie so he could see only how pleased I was that he was here, and not how annoyed I was with Tillie.

"When did you get home?" I asked in surprise. "Why didn't you let us know?"

"I got home late last night," Robbie said, still smilin' his big, happy smile. "And it was last minute. I didn't know I was bein' given leave until two hours before I left. Ol' Tucker went to bat for us fellas, and since we weren't bein' deployed or sent anywhere else right away, they let us have a four-day leave."

"Sargent Tucker did this for you?" I asked, shocked. "I thought he hated you fellas."

Robbie laughed out loud. "Actually, I've come to realize Ol' Tucker was just toughenin' us fellas up. He's really a fine man. He was just tryin' to get us tough for the fight ahead. He likes us as much as an NCO can and convinced our commander to let us have leave. It might be the only one before we are sent to Europe."

"Bless him!" I said fervently, meanin' it.

"Who's Tucker?" Tillie asked with a pout. She didn't like me knowin' somethin' she didn't seem to know. But if she were writin' Robbie and gettin' letters from him, why wouldn't she know who Tucker was?

Robbie had a small pucker between his brows as he answered her. "Tucker is Sargent Tucker. He was our drill Sargent in charge of our basic trainin'. I told you about him in my letters."

Tillie waved her hand airily, dismissin' Robbie's explanation. "Robbie, you know I don't do letters," Tillie said with a pretty little pout of her bright red lips. "I find writin' them too time consumin', and I don't like wrackin' my brain tryin' to think what to say. And I don't like readin' them. They are too tedious and full of boring details."

She pouted prettily up at him, and I knew she was just tryin' to distract him from her words with the enticement of her lips.

Robbie smiled a small, tight smile at her, and I decided to ignore Tillie again.

"Well," I said brightly, "I'm so glad you are home, if only for a few days. Will you be over sometime to visit before goin' back? I'm sure Gerry and Jamie would love to hear about your trainin'."

Robbie nodded. "I'm sure I'll be over sometime. Not sure exactly when just yet."

I smiled, nodded, and watched as Tillie tugged him away, headin' toward a group of young people who had been sittin' at a table enjoyin' the barbecue pork.

I looked up to see Granddad lookin' at me with a questionin' look. I knew that Granddad knew more than he said about my feelin's for Robbie. But I just shook my head and smiled at him to fend off any questions at the moment.

I filled my plate with barbecue pork, baked beans, scalloped potatoes, green beans, and Granny's spicy pickled beets and went to find a spot at one of the tables covered with red-and-white checkered tablecloths. That's when I saw the pretty dark-headed girl sittin' with what I supposed was her mother and little brother, and I made one of the best decisions I had made in a very long time.

I paused in front of her on the opposite side of her table and smiled. "Do you mind if I sit here?" I asked.

"Oh no, please do!" she said, smilin' happily at me.

I set my plate down and reached across the table with my hand. "My name is Margaret Spencer, but everyone calls me Maggie. This is my Granddad's place, and he and Granny Spencer are hostin' this party."

Her eyes sparkled as she took my hand in a small but firm shake. "And my name is Rachel Potts. We just moved here from Arkansas about a week and a half ago. Mr. Jenkins, the schoolteacher, is my uncle, and we are stayin' with him until we are settled. My daddy is the new preacher at Deep Gap Baptist Church, and the old preacher needed an extra week to vacate the parsonage."

"Oh yes, I heard they were gettin' a new preacher over at the Baptist church. Well, welcome to Deep Gap! We don't get a lot of new faces around here, so it's a refreshin' treat." I grinned at her. I liked her immediately and had a hunch that Rachel and I would become good friends. The friend I had been lookin' for.

We spent the rest of the afternoon and evenin' talkin', laughin', and gettin' to know each other. By the end of the party we were makin' plans to visit each other. I only danced a couple of dances all evenin', and not at all with Robbie. Tillie had kept him strapped to her side, and he didn't seem to be makin' much of a protest about it. But I couldn't help but wonder what she was up to.

Who was the man I saw her with a month ago? I wasn't about to ask any questions, and since I wasn't one to gossip and didn't go to school any longer, I didn't hear gossip. But that didn't mean I didn't wonder. I did. For all I knew, the man was a relative, and she was sure clingin' to Robbie like a band-aid this evenin'.

Chapter Nineteen

Robbie was at church Sunday mornin' with Johnny and Claire. He grinned at me from across the aisle, and I grinned back. It was a rainy day, so folks didn't hang around outside to talk, but Robbie told Mamma and me that he and his parents would be over like old times around four that afternoon if that was okay.

Mamma smiled and gave a little wave to Claire, who was across the vestibule puttin' on her jacket. The rain had brought cooler temperatures, and we were back to wearin' jackets. "We would love that, Robbie," Mamma said. "We will see you later."

Sunday dinner was a nice, comfortin' beef stew and warm homemade bread—just the sort of thing that made comin' home to Sunday dinner a marvelous treat.

At almost exactly four o'clock the Bruces pulled into our yard and made a run for it to our front porch. Laughter filled the air, and Mamma had a hand towel ready for them to pat their rainy faces and heads dry of the drippin' rain.

It was wonderful, like old times. It was cool enough to make a fire in the fireplace, and it filled the room with its cracklin' sounds and flickerin' light. Conversation, like always, hummed around with several conversations goin' at once. Robbie and I sat on the bench chattin' about nothin' in particular when Robbie suddenly said, "Maggie, take me to see your chickens. I've been dyin' to see them."

"In the pourin' rain?" I asked.

"Why not?" Robbie laughed. "We aren't made of sugar, so we won't melt!"

We put on our jackets and hats and made a run for the chicken house, sendin' up a loud chorus of squawkin' from the startled hens when we busted through the door. Robbie clamped both hands over his ears and, tryin' to talk over the racket, yelled, "How in the world do you stand this?"

"They'll settle down in just a minute," I yelled back, then laughin' I said, "Watch this." And I started singin':

Down in the valley, valley so low

Hang your head over, hear the wind blow

Hear the wind blow, love, hear the wind blow

Hang your head over, hear the wind blow.

By the time I reached the last line, the hens had quieted down and were singin' softly in their little chicken voices, and Robbie had a look of pure amazement on his face.

"How did you do that?" he asked, eyes wide and lookin' at me strangely.

"I've always sung to them," I said a little shyly. I had never been one to just sing in front of anyone, so his reaction kinda set me back a second.

"Maggie, that was beautiful. No wonder they got quiet, but... I never knew chickens would sing along!"

I laughed and said, "Most people don't know how nice chickens are, and they do seem to like music. At least they have always liked me singin' to them."

"Sing the rest. Please, Maggie. I know there are more verses. I just never heard you sing before, and it's just beautiful!"

I didn't really want to, but how could I say no to Robbie?

"Roses love sunshine, violets love dew

Angels in heaven know I love you

Know I love you, dear, know I love you

Angels in heaven know I love you.

If you don't love me, love whom you please

Throw your arms 'round me, give my heart ease

Give my heart ease, love, give my heart ease

Throw your arms 'round me, give my heart ease."

I stopped suddenly, embarrassed, realizin' the words I was singin' and who I was singin' them for. The hens were very content though and had continued to sing softly on their own. Robbie and I just stood there for a second before he shook his head, still seemin' amazed.

"Maggie, you have the luckiest chickens on earth if they get to hear that all the time. You have a beautiful voice. Just beautiful."

I hadn't thought to put on an exhibition; I had just wanted to demonstrate how singin' would calm the hens and make them happy. Chickens sing when they are happy like any other bird.

"Thank you," I said, shy now, lookin' into his admirin' eyes. Then wantin' to free myself of the strange and funny feelin's I was havin', I said, "Let me give you a tour. They're calm now and it won't be such a racket." He just nodded but clearly had been affected by the song. Why I didn't really know.

I showed him the large main chicken house he had helped build—much like a low barn that measured thirty-five feet wide and sixty feet long—with the broodin' nursery at the front of the buildin' beside the workroom we had set up that housed tools and equipment and had a large industrial sink for washin' feeders and water tanks in. Cleanliness was key to keepin' disease and parasites from the hens. I also took him into the heater shed and showed him the system Daddy had more or less invented to warm the broodin' nursery, explained how it worked, and bragged on Daddy for his ingenuity. Daddy had built it for next to nothin'.

All shyness had disappeared, and Robbie was my childhood friend again. We sat in the workroom, and I told him all about our future plans and how we were going to try to hatch our own chicks next year. I didn't see why it wouldn't work, and you never knew until you tried.

"You are somethin' else, Maggs!" Robbie said with admiration.

"Well, I've had lots of help. I didn't do it alone, you know. Far from alone." Robbie nodded, and I said, "It's turned out to be a real blessin' to the whole family. It's going to bring in more money than the produce stand ever could and with about the same effort. And it gives Gerry and even Charlie a job and a chance to earn money, and has given Granddad somethin' to do that isn't as hard as field work, and he loves it."

"So, the produce stand is going by the wayside?" Robbie asked.

"I think Mamma is reluctant to let it go completely," I said. "She said she would like to see if she and Granny could try to keep it goin'."

We sat quiet for a moment, then I said, "Robbie, tell me about your trainin'. With basic trainin' over, what's next? Have they said where they will be sendin' you now?"

"Not really." Robbie spoke slowly and hesitated, like he wasn't sure he should say anything. "I gather their plan is to keep us at Fort Jackson for the time bein' and just give more advanced trainin' on top of what we have already had." He looked at me and said, "Magg's, don't tell anyone what I'm about to tell you. Partly because I don't know if there's any truth in it; it might be a pack of rumors. But somethin' deep inside believes there might be at least a little truth in it."

I nodded. "Of course," I said, a little scared at what he would tell me.

"There is a rumor I've heard from more than one source that a large-scale invasion of Europe is bein' planned. How true it is I don't know. But it would make sense. In the past we would have finished basic and been deployed right away. But I think the large amount of casualties in Europe has them wantin' to get more organized and make a large invasion. I'm thinkin' huge, involvin' all the Allied Forces."

I just sat, feelin' a little scared by it all. "When do you think? Will it be soon?"

Robbie shook his head. "I doubt it. It wouldn't make sense to go half-cocked and do a halfway job. Sergeant Tucker hinted that we would continue trainin' at Fort Jackson and then possibly be sent to Florida for more intensive trainin'. And that makes sense. The swamps would be the perfect trainin' grounds for the possibility of fightin' in marshy terrain."

Again, we were quiet. After a few heartbeats I asked quietly, "Are you afraid? Knowin' you will likely be sent into battle if the war doesn't end." I hated myself for askin' him but thought maybe he needed to talk about it.

"I don't know if it's bein' afraid, or the feelin' that I'm not yet prepared. I'm glad we aren't goin' right now. Glad we are going to be gettin' more trainin'."

I nodded and sent him a small quavery smile. Robbie smiled back and continued, "I think everyone is scared in battle, and if they aren't somethin' isn't quite right with them. But you know what encouraged me?"

I shook my head. "What?"

"General Stonewall Jackson. Whether you agree with the South or the North, there's no mistakin' that he was one of the greatest generals ever. One of his most famous quotes was, 'Never take counsel of your fears.' So simple, but it's powerful. He was a devout Christian who had an unshakable belief that God was with him, and that nothin' could happen to him unless it was the will of God.

"Another famous quote from him was when he was asked about how he could be so brave in the heat of battle, and his response was, 'My religious belief teaches me to feel as safe in battle as in bed. God has fixed the time for my death. I do not concern myself about that, but to be always ready, no matter when it may overtake me. That is the way all men should live, and then all would be equally brave.'"

"I want to have that same confidence, and like Stonewall Jackson I believe that I am safe in God's hands. Whatever that means. If it is his plan for me to pass through the war and come home safely, then I am safe. If I fall in battle and lose my life, then I believe that is also God's plan, and if it is I am still safe because I will be with Him. Fightin' an enemy in a bloody war scares me, yes. But meetin' God does not."

We sat in companionable silence, listenin' to the sounds around us. I thought maybe we should go back in the house, but I loved havin' Robbie to myself for a change and was reluctant to give him up. Talkin' with him like this was like sharin' our souls with each other. Knowin' a person's most inner thoughts on death and if it scared them felt so intimate somehow.

"Maggie, I loved your last letter you sent me. When I do ship out will you keep writin'?"

"Of course I will!" I said, surprised that he would think I wouldn't.

"Only, I know that when soldiers are actually deployed and fightin', letter writin' isn't always possible, so you might go longer periods of time without hearin' from me. But will you write anyway? Keep sendin' me word from home even if I can't respond?"

I looked at him helplessly. Tears formed in my eyes, and I said, "Oh Robbie, why would you think I wouldn't? I… I…"

I very nearly said *I love you*. Of course I would write you. But I caught myself just in time.

"I promise, Robbie. I will write you every week. At least I will write somethin' every week. Maybe like a journal, write a little every day, then send it off once a week."

I decided to bite the bullet, so to speak, and ask him about Tillie. "Robbie, doesn't Tillie write to you? Surely she was teasin' yesterday. She writes… Surely?" I trailed off when I saw his face.

Robbie grinned weakly and said, "You heard her, she doesn't read or write letters. I sent her a few and I got one brief note about a month after I went into Basic, but no. Tillie just isn't the sort to put much effort into a letter." And he laughed a short little laugh.

Again, all I could do was nod. How could she wrap him around her little painted fingers and then treat him like this? And why would he not see that it wasn't even normal for a girl to treat someone she was supposed to have feelin's for this way? It bamboozled me. How in the world was he so wise and perceptive in some ways but blind when it came to Tillie?

He grinned brightly at me and said, "But hey! That's why I have you! You are my friend that sticks closer than a brother. Since I don't have a brother…" and we both laughed.

It had stopped rainin', so we gathered our jackets and hats and walked back to the house in the wanin' light. Standin' on the porch, Robbie stopped me from goin' straight inside, and with a hand on my shoulder he said, "Maggie, this might be my last leave before deployment. George, Johnny and I were really lucky to get this one. A lot of units have shipped out immediately after Basic, but Tucker pulled strings to get his fellas leave. It might not happen again, especially if the rumors are right about a big invasion.

"Tonight might be goodbye for a long time. There's no knowin' how long this war will last. Germany spent years buildin' up their war machine, and well… they're puttin' up a real fight. So, let's say goodbye to each other here. I'm horribly afraid of everyone seein' a grown man cry. But I don't mind if my very best friend does."

With a cry I threw myself into Robbie's arms. We dropped the jackets and hats and stood on the porch holdin' each other tightly. I couldn't say anything for the sobs that tore at my heart and all my defenses. I don't know how long we stood on the porch cryin' and holdin' each other, but it wasn't nearly long enough.

Eventually my cryin' eased, and Robbie just rocked me gently back and forth for a time, then slowly let his arms loosen and slide from around me. That's when I saw I wasn't the only one cryin'. Robbie's cheeks were wet with tears, and he pulled a handkerchief from his pocket to blow his nose.

"Take very good care of yourself, Robbie," I pleaded. "Please take care."

It sounded so foolish. It's not like he was a reckless person, but what else could I say if I couldn't say *please come back to me, I would be lost without you because I love you*?

"I promise. I will, and God willin' I won't be gone long, and will come home in one piece. Goodbye, Maggie girl, and may God bless and keep you safe as well."

I fought down fresh tears, gripped both of his hands in mine and said, "Goodbye, Robbie Bruce." Then Granddad's prayer of thanksgivin' on the year anniversary of the flood came to mind and I repeated it to Robbie.

"May He cover thee with His feathers, and under his wings shalt thou trust: his truth shall be thy shield and buckler."

***

That summer was a whirl! Granddad's plans for a series of parties to liven up our lives were just what was needed. It not only gave the young people the chance to come together for a wholesome social event, but it was also good for Mamma and Granny and the other women of the community, givin' them a chance to rest and visit during the heavy workload of summer.

Women started bringin' their sewin' projects to work on after dinner in the shade of the big oak and poplar trees. Granny had been workin' on an intricate version of a double wedding ring quilt, and it was going to be beautiful. Every bit of it was hand stitched in Granny's tiny, precise stitches.

I never could master the tiny stitches that made Granny's quilts so strong, and they held together for many years. But Granny usually made quilts that, while beautiful, were less fussy and the piecin' less time consumin'. When I asked her why she was botherin' with such a fussy pattern, she just smiled and said, "It gives me a chance to use up the tiny scraps we've been a savin'. Lookit here, do you recognize any of this?"

I looked closer and saw bits and pieces of fabrics used for dresses and shirts she and Mamma had made for the family. Most of it was scraps left over from the flour sack dresses and shirts she and Mamma had stitched for us over the years. But there were bits and pieces from the occasional fabrics bought from the dry goods store in Boone as well. It was going to be a pretty work of art for sure.

The first Saturday in July fell on the Fourth, so Granddad had a really special treat planned. He had started a fireworks fund at the June party and had managed to find a few boxes of fireworks that the peddler Mr. James had left from last year. Granddad hoped they wouldn't be duds and would fire off okay. He found out after collectin' the money that fireworks would be in short supply due to the war effort. He kept shakin' his head and mutterin' to himself, "I shoulda known that. Shoulda known."

Granddad had rigged up a large grill by stretchin' heavy-duty chicken wire over a fire contained inside layered concrete blocks. It was pretty rustic, but it worked for puttin' out a large amount of hamburgers and hotdogs in a short amount of time. Besides the juicy hamburgers and hotdogs, there were bowls upon bowls of dishes brought by the women of the community: coleslaw, potato and macaroni salads, baked beans, green beans. And there were lots of jars of pickled things like dill and sweet pickles, chowchow, relishes, pickled beets, and onions.

Mr. Macpherson had taken a cleaned-out whiskey barrel and filled it full of homemade lemonade with fresh crushed strawberries in it. I had never tasted anything so delicious, and it was such a treat on a hot July day!

As it was gettin' dark, that time of the evenin' we call *the glomin'*, the flashy red sports car I had seen back in April pulled in. And once again, there sat Tillie in the passenger seat while a strange man I didn't know was the driver. I had a feelin' I was fixin' to have my questions answered.

Tillie never had been one to care about what anyone thought, as long as she got what she wanted. I looked over at Mr. Macpherson, who was mannin' the lemonade and had been busy fillin' cups from the spigot of the barrel. He had glanced up like everyone else when he heard a car door slamin' shut and did a double take when he saw his daughter with her arm looped through the stranger's arm, laughin' up at him. Mr. Macpherson looked anything but pleased. He looked embarrassed and even angry.

Tillie was dressed to the nines in a patriotic dress that was stylish and beautiful. Half the bodice was navy blue with white stars on it, and the other half and the skirt were red and white striped. She had on red high-heeled pumps (impractical for an outside party, I thought cattily) and bright red lipstick, with her honey-blond hair perfectly styled in an elaborate victory roll hairdo. There was no denyin', she was stunningly beautiful. I made up my mind to counter my petty thoughts and tell her how pretty she looked.

Her companion was dressed in a way that suggested he could afford the sleek sports car. He wore white linen trousers, a blue and white button-down shirt, and a red cotton pullover sweater vest. His shoes were black and white oxfords, and the whole ensemble gave the impression of sporty wealth. As they approached the table occupied by most of Tillie's friends, the young man swept the blue fedora off his head to reveal very dark hair that was parted on the side and combed back, slicked down with pomade. He and Tillie made a handsome pair.

Tillie tightened her grip on his arm and announced, "This is Harold Duff from Raleigh. Say hello everyone."

Everyone stared in surprise, then remembered their manners and said in a chorus, "Hello!" A few of the fellas went forward politely to give their names and shake Harold's hand, makin' him welcome.

"My name is Harold, but friends call me Harry," he said in a friendly manner, flashin' a million-dollar smile at everyone.

I smiled too, thinkin' Tillie would soon say, *He's my cousin twice removed on my Mamma's side*, or somethin' similar. But she didn't. After a few introductions and a few more minutes, I heard one of Tillie's friends, Mable, say, "Say Tillie, who is Harry? You've never even mentioned him before."

"Harry," Tillie said smugly, cuttin' her eyes over at me as she dropped the rest of her sentence like a bomb, "is my new beau."

Everyone gaped at her, and I'm sure I did too. Even though I had seen her with him three months ago, I didn't seriously think it was a romantic involvement. Especially after how she had acted while Robbie was home on leave!

I was saved from havin' to respond by some of the ladies callin' for cleanup help. We needed to get the food put away and tables cleaned off before it got too dark to see, and before the fireworks show Granddad was plannin'.

I turned to the table behind me and began gatherin' up paper plates and cups to toss onto the fire. My mind felt like it was caught in a fan! Could Robbie possibly know this? Surely if Tillie was courtin' someone else, especially if it were serious, she would have told Robbie? But Robbie hadn't seemed to know when he was last here in May. And he hadn't said a word about Tillie one way or another in the two letters I had received since he had gone back to

Fort Jackson. But then, we didn't usually discuss Tillie one way or another.

I kept myself busy but also kept one eye on Tillie to see where she was and what she was up to, but all the while my mind was a buzzin' tryin' to take it all in. I was finishin' up clearin' the tables and was about to join the others near the field to watch the fireworks when I heard some of the girls with Tillie gigglin', and one of them said, "But what about Robbie? We thought you and Robbie were nearly married."

"Yeah," the other girl jumped in, "you were all over him back in May. What happened?"

"Pshaw!" Tillie flipped her hand in a dismissive manner. "Robbie Bruce was just a local bumpkin boy that I kept company with until a bigger fish came swimming by. Surely you never thought I would settle for someone like Robbie Bruce?"

The girls laughed nervously. Everyone liked Robbie, and no one wanted to see him treated badly. But they were too cowed by Tillie to answer back. I wasn't. I completely ditched my plan to force myself to be cordial and Christian to Tillie.

"Someone like Robbie Bruce?" I spat through clenched teeth after I had marched over to Tillie and her little group. "What do you mean by someone like Robbie Bruce?"

Tillie seemed taken aback by my attack, and it was clear she hadn't intended for me to hear her condescendin' and belittlin' remark.

"Why, I meant that I never intended to marry Robbie, just have a little fun until I met someone else. Besides"—Tillie recovered from her surprise and began her attack on me—"besides, it's none of your business, Maggie. You aren't Robbie's keeper, and you certainly aren't mine."

"No, I'm not," I agreed. "But I am Robbie's friend, and that means I have his interest at heart. I might not say anything about you two timin' Robbie, that is between you and him, but I can sure stick up for his character. How dare you say somethin' against him as though he wasn't worthy of you. He's worth you a million times over and you know it."

"Oh, he's a decent sort, I agree," Tillie smirked, "but he will never have much money and would never be able to give me the things in life that I want."

I nearly shook with the anger that washed over me, and it came out of my mouth in a heated rush. "You aren't fit to wipe his boots, Tillie Macpherson! Robbie may not know it yet, but you are doin' him a favor. You would have made his life a misery anyway, you with your selfish and self-centered ways. Always lordin' over everyone around you, makin' fun of anyone who doesn't have the things you do. I'll bet these girls here don't even know the things you say about them behind their backs. You're a two-timer in every way, Tillie. I feel sorry for Harry Duff. He seems like a decent sort, as you like to say. I'd bet money you're only after his money, and I'd also bet he doesn't even know it."

Tillie's mouth popped open. She had never had anyone oppose or confront her before. I sure hadn't intended to, nor to do it so publicly. I turned to the girls beside Tillie, who just stood there in shocked silence. "I'm sorry. I should not have involved you. Please forgive me."

And I turned and walked over to where Mamma was headin' toward the house with Granny to watch the fireworks show from the rockers on the porch.

I was still shakin' when I went up the steps behind Mamma and Granny, and I was glad they were preoccupied with settlin' in their chairs and findin' a spot for their glasses of lemonade. About that time my new friend Rachel came over to the porch and said, "Room for me?"

"Yes, of course!" Just what I needed to pull my mind off Tillie and the very public dressin' down I had given her, and I was grateful to have Rachel's company.

Rachel looked over at me and grinned, whispering so that Mamma and Granny wouldn't hear her, "Whoooooeeee! Girl!"

"Oh no! You heard?" I whispered back.

"Honey, everyone is talkin' about it!" Rachel whispered gleefully.

I put my head down briefly and groaned. Why hadn't I held on to my temper a little better? I could have stuck up for Robbie without losin' my temper.

Rachel quickly put her hand on my arm and said, "No! Everyone is makin' you the heroine! I only met Robbie for a few seconds when he was home, but I can tell by the things everyone says that they all think the world of him, and NOBODY is impressed with how Tillie has behaved. You're the only one that has the guts to tell her how it really is. The awful thing is, that Harry guy seems like a nice fella. Do you think he knows she was stringin' him and Robbie along at the same time? And Lord only knows if they were the only two!"

Lordy. I hadn't even thought of that.

Chapter Twenty

The rest of the summer passed so quickly, it felt like a blur. It was September now, and things had settled into a routine with the expanded chicken houses and growin' pullets. I was expectin' to start findin' tiny eggs from the younger pullets by the time October arrived, if not sooner.

I had been readin' as much as I could on hatchin' chicks on a commercial scale. We were plannin' to expand our flock by a thousand hens every spring until we reached five thousand. At that time, we would then have to start replenishing the older hens since egg production would be startin' to fall off. Our plan at that point was to sell butchered hens for eatin'. Nothin' makes better soups and chicken and dumplins than an old hen.

Daddy and I had been thinkin' that we would need to hire some help. Gerry was in his last year of school and come April would be drafted if the war continued. It would be a huge loss, not only for the family but for the business too. Most of the able-bodied young men were away now if they were eighteen or older, so I was going to ask two of the young women I knew if they would like a job workin' for us at Deep Gap Egg and Poultry, one of them bein' Rachel.

Talk had been circulatin' in the community ever since Tillie brought Harry Duff to the July party at Granddad and Granny Spencer's. Since it was no longer a secret, Harry was around quite a bit. Rachel told me he was makin' the trip from Raleigh about every other weekend to see Tillie. Rachel also told me that Harry's father, Harold Duff Sr., was the owner of the biggest tobacco warehouse in North Carolina, and Harry was heir to this tobacco kingdom.

It would be easy to be catty and believe that Tillie was only after money, except Harry really seemed to be a nice fella and handsome to boot. Everyone liked his easy and friendly personality. Even Daddy and Granddad said he was likeable and not all high and mighty like so many rich men were. So how well could he actually know Tillie? Of course, lookit how blind Robbie had been! I kept wonderin' how Robbie had taken the news of Tillie's new boyfriend when Tillie told him, as surely she had. But as of yet, he had not mentioned her or her new beau in his letters.

Rachel was comin' over this afternoon and would stay the night. It would be the first of our many cozy sleepovers. We were in charge of plannin' the last of the parties Granddad was hostin' this year. It bein' October, and at the end of a busy harvest season for everyone, we would of course be plannin' on a harvest-themed party.

Uncle James had experimented with growin' a wide variety of pumpkins and gourds this year. Some were good for eatin', and some only good for settin' on the porch to look pretty. He had piles of them at the produce stand, and it occurred to me that they looked right pretty piled up as they were and would add to our party's harvest theme. I volunteered to ask him if the pumpkins could be hauled over to Granddad's barn for the party, and Rachel suggested that if we made cute signs with the prices on them, he might be more willin' to haul them for us if he would get sales out of it.

We had games and dancin' planned but hadn't secured anyone to provide the music. Sometimes people just showed up with their fiddles, guitars, mandolins, and banjos, and it just happened. But we didn't want to chance no one showin' up. We had checked into a few local bands, and it seemed that it just wasn't workin' out.

Rachel and I had our notebooks out, layin' across my bed wrackin' our brains on what to do when she said, "There's a young man who's been makin' a name for himself that I think you know, Maggie. Arthel Watson. What about askin' him and his family if they would supply the music? They all play somethin', don't they?"

I smacked my forehead, feelin' pretty stupid. Of course! Why hadn't I thought of askin' the Watson family? They had played alongside friends and neighbors on our porch many a summer evenin', as well as at local church singin's.

"Yes! But I'll have to see if they can. Some of them at least are always at the parties; they just live down the road a piece."

"What happened to Arthel's sight?" Rachel asked. Not bein' from the area, she only knew he was blind.

"I'm not completely sure," I said, "but it seems like he had some sort of eye infection when he was really little. He's one year older than me, so I was just a baby when it happened. But I can tell you it doesn't slow him down much. He might be blind, but he can build and make things. Daddy was braggin' on him last year, sayin' how Arthel was right handy with his tools and even had built some sheds. Don't ask me how he does it, but he did."

"Well, I hope they can do it," Rachel said admiringly. "Arthel has even been on a radio show in Lenoir. He might be too busy to come to our little party."

"I hope not," I sighed. "We'll see. Maybe we can get Daddy to run us over to their place tomorrow. I need to get Daddy to teach me how to drive. I hate havin' to pull him away from his work every time I need to go somewhere. I think I'll talk with him about that too."

***

The October party was a huge success. Lookin' back, I'm so glad it was, because it was the last party we had for quite a while. Wartime rationin' of gasoline and tires, loss of young men in the area, and overall hard times made havin' a big party impractical.

We still had our visits on the porch with family, friends, and neighbors, but it was mostly those close enough to walk. There were a few gatherin's in Deep Gap itself at the schoolhouse, because it was more central for everyone in the community. For the most part, though, the big parties with music and dancin' were put on hold until after the war and rationin' was lifted.

Arthel Watson and his family said they were happy to play music for Granddad's party. Granddad Spencer and Arthel's own granddad had been friends for years. Music rang out from the old barn, and Granddad allowed the party to go on longer than he normally would have. We danced, clogged, and sang until midnight to tunes like *Fish in the Millpond, How Many Biscuits Can You Eat, Give the Fiddler a Dram, Shady Grove, Old Groundhog,* and *Marthy Won't You Have Some Good Old Cider.*

Instead of barbecue or such, every family brought a big pot of soup or stew and some sort of bread to go with it. We had spiced apple cider, and Granny had made a version of her usual hot cocoa usin' powdered milk, which was surprisingly good! Cakes, pies, cookies, and tarts filled the dessert table, and there was plenty to go back to between dances.

Around eleven o'clock, the music changed, and instead of dancin' and whoopin', everyone gathered around a big fire. The Watson family began to sing old hymns *Will the Circle Be Unbroken, When the Roll Is Called Up Yonder,* and *Angel Band.* The singin' went on for about an hour before everyone said goodnight and went home.

It wasn't too long before Arthel Watson became very famous in the Bluegrass world and was better known as Doc Watson, the blind boy from Deep Gap, North Carolina.

***

November 1, 1942,

Camp Blanding, Florida

Dear Maggie,

Well, here we are already in November and it's still sweltering hot in Florida! When the heat gets to be more than I can stand, I close my eyes and think about the crisp mountain air of home, and I swear it makes me feel cooler. I know that by now the nights are cool even if the days are warm. I know that harvest is taking place, and all the fields are being emptied of the summer's bounty. I get all weepy-eyed just thinking about it. Enjoy it enough for both of us, my friend. I sure do miss it!

Well, here we are at our next assignment, Camp Blanding, Florida. I am proud to say I have been assigned to the 30th Infantry Division of the United States Army, nicknamed Old Hickory after President Andrew Jackson. It was formed during the Great War and reactivated last year. They have combined us with some new fellas who are fresh out of basic. Not sure yet what their aim is beyond that. But Sergeant Tucker had told us they will likely be expanding the training we have already received. I'm going to miss ol' Tucker. He was hard and crunchy on the outside but a softie inside. I'll never forget all he did for us fellas.

I had never been to Florida, so I'm eager to see new places. Camp Blanding is about forty miles southwest of Jacksonville, and not far from the Atlantic coast. I know it's not too far from the

Okefenokee Swamp, and if we can get passes out of camp to go see it, I just might see my first alligator!

The war in the Pacific is really heating up. There have been some pretty big naval battles and a big campaign for an island called Guadalcanal. It's been a real fight, but the last I heard we finally had a decisive victory against the Japs towards the end of August. I think if they were sending us to the Pacific, we would have gone by now. I'm starting to feel more and more that we are being trained for something really big possibly mainland Europe.

About our training here at Camp Blanding: it's tough! If we wanted to complain about ol' Tucker at Fort Jackson, we should be bawling' our eyes out here at Blanding. It's Fort Jackson but doubled, at least doubled.

And if we thought mosquitoes, gnats, and other creepy crawlies were bad at Fort Jackson, they were nothing absolutely nothing compared to the flying and creeping monsters they have here! Those tame little pests we have at home aren't even the same species, I don't think. These Florida mosquitoes surround you and one will chuckle to the others and say, "I've got him cornered, boys, get him!" Then two get you under each elbow and carry you back to their lair in the swamp. True story.

We're going to start training with heavy artillery now mortars, bazookas, and anti-tank guns. I suppose we will be given jobs based on our ability; right now, I'm not sure what that will be.

Marching through the swamps with an eighty-pound pack on my back isn't the most fun I've ever had. With a pack on my back and a rifle in one hand I'm constantly taking a swing at the flying demons tormenting us and all I can think is, "People actually live here year-round!"

Would you mind asking your Mamma if she makes a concoction for keeping these devils at bay? I don't care what it smells like! I know she makes salves and other things; if she could do this for me, I would be grateful forever.

Maggie, I need to ask you something. I hate putting you in this position because I know you have made it your business to mind your own business. George Hamil and Johnny Bailey both have received letters from home hinting that Tillie is seeing someone else. I write to her every two weeks and, as usual, she never replies, but I didn't think much of that because she never does. My last letter was returned unopened with no explanation. I hope you don't mind a friend asking, not for gossip's sake, but if George and Johnny's letters from home are correct, I need to know, and I'd rather ask you than Mamma. Do you know what is going on?

I know you like a good joke, and I heard this one in the mess hall the other day. Two Irishmen had landed in America and taken a room at a seaside hotel. To their surprise, they were attacked by a couple of mosquitoes, an insect new to them. They quickly turned out the light, jumped into bed, and dove under the covers.

One of them looked out from under the covers just as a firefly flitted through the window.

"It's no use, Mickey," he said, "they've come back with lanterns looking for us!"

Once again, I'm pushed for time, and there's already been one call for lights out. Take very good care of yourself and I promise to do the same, unless the skeeters carry me off before I can write again.

Your itchy friend,

Robbie

***

November 22, 1942,

Deep Gap, North Carolina

Dearest Robbie,

I was so glad to finally hear from you. I guess the relocation to Florida no doubt left little time for letter writing. I'm also glad to know that you are happy with your placement. No doubt the 30th Infantry Division will live up to their reputation for bravery. (Daddy told me a bit about their exploits during the Great War.)

I wish I could explore the Okefenokee Swamp with you! Reading about it makes it sound very exciting, and even dangerous, and I know we would have a time; maybe someday. I would love to see a real live alligator, but at a distance! When you mentioned the Okefenokee Swamp in your letter, I checked out a book in the library that had pictures, and it sure looks and sounds interesting. But like you, I wouldn't like to put up with those mosquitoes either, ours are bad enough. Mamma is going to mail you some salve she has put together for you, George, and Johnny. She makes it with beeswax and the oils from things she knows bugs and mosquitoes don't like. You should get it soon, and she would like to know how it works. It helps with our mosquitoes and gnats here, but yours sound like especially evil beasts.

And you know how fond I am of snakes. I don't mind the little garter snakes and king snakes, and I even tolerate the black snakes that live in the rafters and corners of the chicken houses because they eat the rats and mice. But I draw the line at those rattlers and copperheads, they scare the tarnation out of me! I read in the book I checked out about cottonmouths, or water moccasins. No thank you!

Training sounds as though it's tough. I don't think I would be able to carry an eighty-pound pack very far! I hate it for you, but I understand why they demand so much from you all. You must be prepared to face whatever is coming. What in the world is a bazooka and a mortar?

My pullets I got back in April are laying full speed ahead now, and we have doubled our military contract for eggs! Fortunately, we deliver them all to the Quartermaster at Camp Butner, and they distribute them to other military installations from there. Thank God, because we would have to apply for more gasoline ration stamps otherwise. We are allowed more than most people anyway (and tires too) because of our military deliveries, but if we had to deliver to Camps Sutton, Mackall, and Fort Bragg, we wouldn't be able to do it.

I wish you could have been at Granddad's last party! We had a time, and Arthel Watson and the Watson family did a great job with the music. You would have clogged your shoes clear through the soles! Parties will likely be scarce until after the war. The average family with A ration stickers is only allowed two to four gallons of gasoline a week. That sure won't get you far, so folks are either combining their stamps and cramming too many folks into a vehicle or staying at home if it's too far to walk.

I saved the hard part for last. All of us had assumed that Tillie surely had the courtesy to tell you about Harry Duff. I haven't mentioned him because I figured she had told you about him and you just didn't want to discuss it. So here goes.

Back in May I saw them together for the first time. Tillie was with him in a fancy red sports car. I've since learned it is a 1940 Jaguar Roadster. You can imagine the attention it got; I had never seen a car like it. I never mentioned it to a soul because I thought it might be a relative, a cousin from somewhere else. But Tillie brought him to the July party at Granddad's and introduced him as her new beau, and it caused quite a stir, I can tell you.

I'm so sorry, Robbie. Tillie and I have been like two cats in a poke with our tails tied together all our lives, but I never thought she would string you both along like she did. I don't know if Harry knew she spent time with you when you were home on leave or not.

Please don't blame Harry. Believe it or not, he seems to be a really nice fella and has been well liked. I kind of lost my temper with Tillie at the July party and told her off for how she had treated you.

I don't like to say this part, but if you really want the whole story, and I believe that is what you were asking of me, I have to tell you all that was said. When I reproached Tillie for two-timing you, she said she was only going with you for fun, and that she had never intended to marry you. I believe the words she used were "waiting for a bigger fish to come along." She said she was waiting for someone with money to come along that would give her the things she wanted. I'm truly sorry for you, Robbie. It breaks my heart to think of how hurt you must be.

Just a bit about Harry. His name is Harold Duff Jr. His daddy is Harold Duff Sr., and he owns a big tobacco warehouse in Raleigh. They must be pretty wealthy, judging by the car he drives, and he just plain looks wealthy. But he really is a likable fella. It also seems likely that an engagement will be announced soon. I heard Tillie tell someone she actually met Harry when they were vacationing at Myrtle Beach the summer of 1941. His family spent the summer there, and apparently they have been writing' to each other ever since. And the little trips into Raleigh weren't just for shopping.

At the risk of sounding like a spiteful cat, I don't know what he sees in Tillie. But in all honesty, I didn't know what you saw in her. She is mean, a bully, and self-centered. I honestly tried to just keep my mouth shut after we mended our fences, which is partly why I didn't mention her at all. You know the old saying' "If you can't say anything nice, don't say anything at all." So, I didn't.

I'd like to end this letter with something more positive. You know how much I like puns and corny jokes, so here goes. I heard this one the other day and it tickled my funny bone.

What did Tennessee? Whatever Arkansas.

Your devoted friend,

Maggie

Chapter Twenty One

December 12, 1942,

Camp Blanding, Florida

Dear Maggie,

You made me laugh. What a punny joke! Now I'll have to try to best it, but I'll have to think about it a bit.

Here it is mid-December, and I can't believe how warm it is here in Florida. Tell Mamma Dottie that the bug salve she sent me has been a gift from above. If I had a mind to, I could sell it like it was black-market merchandise! It works better than anything the fellas and I have tried, and we are eternally grateful. Give her the biggest hugs and kisses you can from me, Johnny, and George.

George, Johnny, and I had made plans to go to Okefenokee Swamp last week. We had passes for a day leave and everything, and guess what happened? George came down with some sort of stomach bug the kind that puts you out of commission for a time. So Johnny and I decided to wait until George could make it. I haven't seen a water moccasin yet, but everyone tells me to beware. I don't hope to see one of those!

How was Thanksgiving? Holidays must seem a bit lonely these days with family not able to come in from Virginia. I was pleasantly surprised by what they served us for Thanksgiving dinner: roast turkey and stuffing, mashed potatoes and gravy, cranberry relish, corn, green beans, and yeast rolls. While it wasn't as good as home, it was a real feast! We were also given most of the day to rest or have fun. Some of us fellas got up a softball game and had a relaxing afternoon playing ball.

I am so glad that your egg and poultry business is doing so well! I'm sure you would have made a success of it no matter what, but wartime is a funny thing; it will make or break a business. In your case, war has created an opportunity for you. I'm so glad you were able to get those government contracts they will carry you all through the hard times to come.

Thanks for bearing with me, Maggs, concerning Tillie. You have always been such a good friend, and a good friend will always tell you the truth. Funny thing is, I'm not nearly as sad or affected by Tillie's desertion as you might think. The truth is, the more I've thought about it, the more I've come to realize that she was more of a habit than anything else. Now that I've been looking at the whole picture through hindsight, I'm seeing that you weren't being judgmental of Tillie, merely observant. Chalk it up to male stupidity, my dear friend. But like most stupid beasts, we can learn some things! I wish her and Harry well and sincerely pray they are happy together. If the opportunity ever comes up, would you tell her that for me? Don't put yourself out or anything, but if it ever comes up you can tell her I'm happy for her. God bless them.

Now about our training. Every time we get used to the level of training, they crank things up. Some of the fellas have had a hard time with it, and some have not been able to get used to the brutal training. And it is brutal! At this point, I am one hundred percent convinced we are being prepared for something big.

Besides the running, which God knows I believe might be the death of every one of us, there are the obstacle courses: jumping over hurdles, vaulting fences, running through a maze, climbing over walls, crawling under obstacles, jumping ditches, and crossing high beams. It wears me out even writing about it!

We have also started tactical training, which begins in a classroom. Then we go out to the training grounds to practice what we have learned. They have mock villages where we train in battle techniques for urban warfare, and we practice with grenades, bazookas, and mortars. Bazookas are anti-tank rocket launchers fired from the shoulder, and mortars are for close-range firing. They have a tripod attached and can be quickly set down and fired. They are used to support infantry and clear areas that are being entered by infantry.

Rifle training is probably where we have the most fun. The standard issue is an M1 Garand, which is a fine rifle. I'm hoping at the end of this war I can bring one home to Papa, he would sure love it! And guess what? That crazy outfit Johnny Bailey is so good at rifle practice they are training him as a sniper. He's got the big head over that. His sniper rifle is his baby, a M1903 Springfield bolt action. He loves his rifle! I told him he loved his rifle better than he loved Mable Jessup, so he named his rifle Mable. The jokester will hold it, croon over it, and kiss it, saying, "I love you, Mable girl." He sure is a nut.

George told me that your cousin Jamie has been assigned to a tank division. I can see him fitting in there! What do you all know about his assignment? George doesn't know anything other than that. I'm sure you all must know something more. Us fellas like to keep track of each other if we can.

Well, once again they have been calling lights out for the third time. Right before bed seems to be about the only time I have to write, or on the occasional day off. I may try on a Sunday after church service next time.

Take very good care of my dear friend!

Robbie

***

Christmas 1942 blew in on the wings of a ferocious winter storm. Lord have mercy, but it was a fierce one! It was nearly as bad as the storm we had back when I was a young'un, and we were rescued by old Mr. Mitchell's bagpipes.

But Mamma was bound and determined to make Christmas as festive as possible. This year Jamie was also missin' from around our table. Jamie and I shared a birthday, and like me, he had turned eighteen back in April. Since he was so close to graduatin' from high school, the draft board allowed him to complete his schoolin' before going off to basic trainin'. When he completed basic trainin' and was tested for his aptitude, he was placed in the 745th Tank Battalion at Camp Bowie, Texas, and had been trainin' as a driver there ever since.

Granddad was really proud of him and said, "You've got to be smart to be placed there. A driver has to be able to think fast and react instantly."

Jamie? I could hardly think of him that way. Jamie was such a goofy guy who seemed to thrive on silliness. But according to Uncle James, he had scored really high on his aptitude test. They tested the recruits' drivin' ability in a pickup truck out in the desert around Camp Bowie. They were impressed with his ability to maneuver through and around the terrain and obstacles placed there. Funny how people you are so close to can have talents and hidden parts of themselves that you never saw before.

Speakin' of drivin', around this time Daddy had taught me how to drive the old farm truck, and I was thrilled. I loved the freedom of drivin' by myself on farm errands and for the Deep Gap Egg and Poultry business. Back in the forties, there were few women who drove automobiles in our area. I'm not sure why, but while it wasn't exactly frowned on, there was a funny attitude about women drivin. As though they weren't quite up to it, or such. I have to confess, even though I'm an old woman and ought to be immune to it, I still get annoyed with jokes about women drivers. I'll grant you there are some awful ones out there to be sure. But some of the worst drivers I've encountered in all my born days are some of the men I've known. It's tit for tat, really. I don't think a body's sex has one thing to do with how good or how bad of a driver you are.

We have to conserve, though, and drive only when necessary. I'm grateful we do get extra gasoline and tire rations because of our military contracts. Without them we wouldn't be able to operate at all. But no joyridin' at all, and I take great care to avoid the many potholes and rocks that sometimes stick up out of the ground. As I've said before, all of our roads back then were dirt.

Back to Christmas, we were missing both Jamie and Robbie this year, and we were really feelin' it. Aunt Eunice and Claire were havin' a difficult time stayin' cheerful and keepin' their chins up. So was Mamma, knowin' that unless the war was over by next Christmas, Gerry would be goin' away too. So, Granddad decided it was time for a story after Christmas Dinner. We women put away the leftovers for later and washed dishes as quick as we could. We were all lookin' forward to seein' what story, or yarn Granddad would spin for us this year.

When we all got settled, Granddad said, "Well now. The story I'm about to relate to you is called *The Gift from the Magi,* and it came out in the *New York Sunday World Magazine,* December 10, 1905. I can remember readin' it as a young man, and I read it to my sweet Martha." Granddad smiled at Granny Spencer, who smiled back at him with loving eyes. "I have always loved the story, for it is a story of self-sacrificin' love. It goes like this."

One dollar and eighty-seven cents; that was all. She had put it aside, one cent and then another and then another, in her careful buying of meat and other food. Della counted it three times. One dollar and eighty-seven cents. And the next day would be Christmas. There was nothing to do but fall on the bed and cry; so, Della did it.

While the lady of the home is slowly growing quieter, we can look at the home. Furnished rooms at the cost of eight dollars a week. There is little more to say about it.

There was a name beside the door: "Mr. James Dillingham Young." When the name was placed there, Mr. James Dillingham Young was paid thirty dollars a week. Now, when he was being paid only twenty dollars a week, the name seemed too long and important. It should perhaps have been "Mr. James D. Young." But when Mr. James Dillingham Young entered the furnished rooms, his name became very short indeed.

Mrs. James Dillingham Young put her arms warmly about him and called him "Jim." You have already met her; she is Della. Della finished her crying and wiped her face. She stood by the window and looked out with no interest. Tomorrow would be Christmas Day, and she had only one dollar and eighty-seven cents with which to buy Jim a gift. She had put aside as much as she could for months. Twenty dollars a week is not much. Everything had cost more than she had expected. She had spent many happy hours planning something nice for him. Something almost good enough, something almost worth the honor of belonging to Jim.

There was a looking glass between the windows of the room. It was very narrow. A person could see only a little of himself at a time. However, if he was very thin and moved very quickly, he might be able to get a good view of himself. Della, being quite thin, had mastered this art. Suddenly she turned from the window and stood before the glass. Her eyes were shining brightly, but her face had lost its color. Quickly she pulled down her hair and let it fall to its complete length.

The James Dillingham Youngs were very proud of two things which they owned. One thing was Jim's gold watch. It had once belonged to his father. And, long ago, it had belonged to his father's father. It was as fine as any gold watch owned by a king. The other thing was Della's hair. James loved and was proud of Della's beautiful, flowing hair. No queen ever had hair more fair than Della's.

So now Della's beautiful hair fell about her, shining like a falling stream of brown water. It reached below her knees. It almost made itself into a dress for her. And then she put it up on her head again, nervously and quickly. Once she stopped for a moment and stood still while a tear or two ran down her face. She put on her old brown coat. She put on her old brown hat. With the bright light still in her eyes, she moved quickly out the door and down to the street.

Where she stopped, the sign on the storefront said: "Mrs. Sofronie. Hair Articles of All Kinds." Up to the second floor Della ran and stopped to get her breath. Mrs. Sofronie, large, too white, cold-eyed, looked at her.

"Will you buy my hair?" asked Della.

"Take your hat off and let me look at it," said Mrs. Sofronie.

Down fell the brown waterfall.

"Twenty dollars," said Mrs. Sofronie, lifting the hair to feel its weight.

"Give it to me quick," said Della, and the next two hours seemed to fly.

She was going from one shop to another, trying to find a gift for Jim. She found it at last. It surely had been made for Jim and no one else. There was no other like it in any of the shops, and she had looked in every shop in the city. It was a gold watch chain, very simply made. Its value was in its rich and pure material. Because it was so plain and simple, you knew that it was very valuable.

As soon as she saw it, she knew that Jim must have it. It was like him. Quietness and value, Jim and the chain both had quietness and value. She paid twenty-one dollars for it. And she hurried home with the chain and eighty-seven cents. With that chain on his watch, Jim could look at his watch and learn the time anywhere he might be. Though the watch was so fine, it had never had a fine chain. He sometimes took it out and looked at it only when no one could see him do it.

When Della arrived home, her mind quieted a little. She began to think more reasonably. She started to try to cover the sad evidence of what she had done. Love and large-hearted giving, when added together, can leave deep marks. It is never easy to cover these marks, dear friends, never easy.

Within forty minutes her head looked a little better. With her short hair, she looked like a schoolboy. She stood at the looking glass for a long time.

"If Jim doesn't kill me," she said to herself, "before he looks at me a second time, he'll say I look like a girl who sings and dances for money. But what could I do? Oh, what could I do?"

At seven, Jim's dinner was ready for him. Jim was never late. Della held the watch chain in her hand and sat near the door where he always entered. Then she heard his step in the hall and her face lost color for a moment.

She often said little prayers quietly, about simple, everyday things. And now she said: "Please God, make him think I'm still pretty."

The door opened and Jim stepped in. He looked very thin, and he was not smiling. Poor fellow, he was only twenty-two, and with a family to take care of. He needed a new coat, and he had nothing to cover his cold hands.

Jim stopped inside the door. He was as quiet as a hunting dog when it is near a bird. His eyes looked strangely at Della, and there was an expression in them that she could not understand. It filled her with fear. It was not anger, nor surprise, nor anything she had been ready for. He simply looked at her with that strange expression on his face.

Della went to him.

"Jim, dear," she cried, "don't look at me like that. I had my hair cut off and sold it. I couldn't live through Christmas without giving you a gift. My hair will grow again. You won't care, will you? My hair grows very fast. It's Christmas, Jim. Let's be happy. You don't know what a nice, what a beautiful gift I got for you."

"You've cut off your hair?" asked Jim slowly. He seemed to labor to understand what had happened.

"Cut it off and sold it," said Della. "Don't you like me now? I'm me, Jim. I'm the same without my hair."

Jim looked around the room.

"You say your hair is gone?" he said.

"You don't have to look for it," said Della. "It's sold, I tell you, it's sold and gone too. It's the night before Christmas. Be good to me, because I sold it for you. Maybe the hairs of my head could be counted," she said, "but no one could ever count my love for you. Shall we eat dinner, Jim?"

Jim put his arms around his Della. From inside the coat, Jim took something tied in paper. He threw it upon the table.

"I want you to understand me, Dell," he said. "Nothing like a haircut could make me love you any less. But if you'll open that, you may know what I felt when I came in."

White fingers pulled off the paper. And then a cry of joy, and then a change to tears. For there lay the hair combs that Della had seen in a shop window and loved for a long time. Beautiful combs, with jewels, perfect for her beautiful hair. She had known they cost too much for her to buy them. She had looked at them without the least hope of owning them. And now they were hers, but her hair was gone.

She held them to her heart, and at last was able to look up and say: "Don't worry, Jim, my hair grows so fast." Then she jumped up. Jim had not yet seen his beautiful gift. She held it out to him in her open hand. The gold seemed to shine softly as if with her own warm and loving spirit.

"Isn't it perfect, Jim? I hunted all over town to find it. You'll have to look at your watch a hundred times a day now. Give me your watch. I want to see how they look together."

Jim sat down, pulling Della down with him, and smiled.

"Della," said he, "let's put our Christmas gifts away and keep them a while. They're too nice to use now. I sold the watch to get the money to buy the combs. And now I think we should have our dinner."

The magi, as you know, were wise men who brought gifts to the newborn Christ-child. They were the first to give Christmas gifts. Being wise, their gifts were doubtless wise ones. And here I have told you the story of two who were not wise. Each sold the most valuable thing he owned in order to buy a gift for the other. But let me say a last word to the wise: Of all who give gifts, these two were the most wise.

The fireplace snapped and popped, and the old grandfather clock struck the hour. Mamma leaned against Daddy's shoulder, Johnny had his arm around Claire, and Uncle James and Aunt Eunice smiled tenderly at each other from their places on the couch. We all just sat quiet for some time, enjoin' the feelin's of love that bound us all together.

Then Granny Spencer spoke up quietly and said, "Mind the time, Alistair, when you sold your Civil War musket to buy flour and shoes for our young'uns back durin' the hard times following the Panic of 1893? You weren't but twenty years old and we had two young'uns by then."

Granddad squirmed just a bit in his chair.

"My Marthy, why bring that up?" Granddad said uncomfortably.

"Because," Granny smiled at him, "you gave us the same unselfish love then that Jim and Della had for each other in your story. That rifle meant a lot to you. It had belonged to your Great-Granddad, who was killed at Vicksburg durin' the Civil War. But it was the only thing of worth you could sell to buy our babies' food and shoes for the winter. And I know it had to hurt your heart, but you never showed it. You sacrificed yourself for your family, and I never forgot, Alistair."

I had never heard this amazin' bit of family history! My Granddad was one of the finest men I have ever known.

Granddad harrumphed, cleared his throat, and said gruffly, "Yes, well. I did what needed to be done. Did what was needed."

That was Granddad. That was love. And if it ever came to it, I knew my daddy would do the same. Mamma, Granny, Uncle James and Aunt Eunice, Johnny and Claire… I knew every one of them wouldn't think twice, wouldn't even hesitate to give themselves for their families. That's just what love does.

I sat in thought for a bit and thought of Robbie. I loved him and missed him so badly that I would have gladly sold every tooth in my head, as well as all my hair, just to have him home again. I grinned to myself, just imaginin' the sight. What good would that do? He wouldn't even look my way, lookin' like that!

Chapter Twenty Two

January 1, 1943,

Deep Gap, North Carolina

Dear Robbie,

Here we are in the new year. The past year has been strange to me, both flying by in a blur and dragging so slowly. All at the same time! How in the world can that be?

The blur comes from all the busy work! My goodness, the chickens and eggs, the farm work both to feed the chickens and raise food for the family, *and* the produce stand (yes, Mamma and Granny both insist on keeping it going) keep us all busy, busy, busy! But I would rather be overly busy than not busy at all.

What makes it feel like time is dragging is missing you and Jamie. You wouldn't believe how often your names come up in everyday conversations. The wondering what will happen, and when it will happen, it just wears a body out sometimes. I know you would say, *"Don't worry about me, Maggie, I'm fine."* But I do worry. I worry about when and where you will go next, and how long you will be there. I worry that you will be sent to Europe or the Pacific, and we won't even know until after you're already gone.

I keep making myself think about what you told me about General Stonewall Jackson and his belief that he was just as safe on the battlefield as he was at home, all snug in his bed. It's like I believe that in my heart… but my head, it just seems to do what it wants. And it wants to worry, I guess!

Christmas was very much a winter wonderland this year. We don't often get that much snow before the first of the year, but it blew in on a Nor'easter and it was fierce! Still, it was so beautiful when it stopped, and the roads were cleared off enough by Christmas morning for your Ma and Papa to make the drive over for dinner. The sunshine seemed much more brilliant than usual. I guess it was just from reflecting off the snow, but it actually hurt our eyes. Your Papa said he had a hard time keeping his eyes open for the drive over. But my, how the snow sparkled! It looked like the angels had thrown diamonds out everywhere, and they sparkled and shimmered in the sunshine. And the snow caught in the hemlocks and pines you can imagine how it looked!

I'm glad to know that you aren't suffering overmuch about Tillie. As of yet, I've not seen her and Harry since the October party. The Macphersons go to the Baptist church, and we go to the Non-Denominational church now, and there haven't been any parties or gathering's since October. So I'm not sure when or if I'll have the opportunity to pass on your blessings. I've not heard anything about an engagement yet. By the way, you weren't stupid, just a bit blind to her ways.

My goodness! Training sounds really tough! I hate knowing you are being run ragged, but then again, I'm glad to know they are preparing you for the hardships of whatever you will be facing. Have they run you down to a skeleton?

Thanks for explaining the difference between a bazooka and a mortar. I didn't know one from another. And it's good to hear that Johnny Bailey has some skills! But then we all knew he was a good shot. He won the turkey at many a turkey shoot the last few years! I'd be willing to bet that all of the mountain boys are good shots. You never brag about what you are doing or mention any recognition you have been given, but I have no doubt that you are noticed too. I know how all the fellas here at home always looked to you, so I wouldn't think things are any different there at Camp Blanding.

I didn't know Johnny Bailey had an interest in Mable Jessup. What next? Or was he just being silly? She's a sweet person, but so serious. I would never have put them together. George maybe, but not Johnny!

About Jamie yes, you heard right. Jamie went into the 745th Tank Battalion at Camp Bowie in Texas right after his basic training and assessment. Granddad was right proud of him. Apparently, you have to be fairly smart to be placed there and almost immediately assigned as a driver. Funny, did you see that coming? Because I sure didn't. Jamie has always been such a goofy, silly clown, never seemed to have a serious bone in his entire body. I love him, of course I love him. I just never saw him as especially bright or capable. Obviously, he hid his better qualities well. Ha ha. Like you, he has no idea where they will be sent.

Daddy and I have been making plans for our first incubation of chicks. Exciting! We have been reading everything we can get our hands on. Daddy subscribed to the *Poultry Tribune* magazine to keep us up to date with the latest on chicken farming of all kinds. But since our incubator isn't huge, we will be hatching chicks in multiple batches well up into the end of summer.

The incubator holds about two hundred and fifty eggs, and we will have to manually turn them every day. Some of the big nurseries have incubators that turn the eggs for them. We will begin in April and hatch out two hundred and fifty chicks every twenty-one to twenty-three days. Sterilize the incubator, reload it, and begin it all again. We are planning to do five hatchings this April through August in case something goes wrong, and we don't have a full thousand pullets for layers. Fingers crossed it goes as planned.

Well, I will close for now. But I wanted to wish you a Happy New Year. Wouldn't it be great if Hitler surrendered or dropped dead and brought the war to an end before you have to leave? I would like him much better if he did either.

Take care,

Love, Maggie

***

Winter passed in a sort of monotony, each day almost exactly like the day before it. We had so many heavy snows, it seemed like we stayed snowed in! We would get a snow, dig out, and no sooner had we finished digging out, it would snow again.

The intense sun would help melt the snowy, icy roads a bit on sunny days, but the north and east sides of the mountains didn't get so much direct sun. So the soft, half-melted slush would refreeze into ice when the sun went down. Then it would snow again, and the whole thing would just start over. This went on and on through March.

Rachel had been workin' with us since before Thanksgiving, but most days she couldn't get through the fresh snow and ice. So for the majority of the time from Christmas clear through March, it was Daddy, me, Charlie, sometimes Granddad, and even Mamma workin' to keep the chicken houses goin' and the eggs going out. More often than not, we were workin' ten to twelve hours a day at least Daddy and I did.

Finally, it was April, and though a bit chilly at times, it seemed that the snowstorms had at least stopped. We were sure hopin' so! It's been known to snow in April sometimes. Come April first, Daddy and I loaded our first batch of eggs gingerly into the incubator, carefully inspectin' each egg and markin' a big X on one side with a pencil. That way we could keep track of the eggs, makin' sure we were turnin' each egg every day.

Daddy had picked up the old kerosene egg incubator for nearly nothin' from a farmer down near Hickory. The farmer had bought a new electric incubator that looked a lot like a refrigerator with a window in it and was just wanting the old kerosene one gone. Since it was run off kerosene, and had a flame goin' nonstop, we put it in the same building as the boiler that was for heating the brooding nursery and chicken house. There were any number of things that could go wrong, causin' the incubator to topple, or some freak accident that could start a fire in the chicken house. It was a risk none of us wanted to take.

With the incubator set, and our first batch of chicks in the oven so to speak, we started makin' plans to build chicken house number three. The first to be built was the largest, at sixty feet long and thirty-five feet wide. The second didn't need to be that big since we only needed the one nursery and equipment room. It measured thirty-five feet wide by forty-five feet long. It was just right for housing the one thousand or so hens, give or take a few, so chicken house number three would be built exactly the same. Daddy was headin' over to Johnny Bruce's sawmill to put in a big lumber order for chicken house number three.

This mornin', I stood in the doorway that led from the equipment room filled with buckets, extra chicken feeders, watering cans, rakes, shovels, and other tools, lookin' into the big open hen run. I marveled at how quickly things had changed! In two years, we had gone from nothin' to runnin' an egg business that housed about two thousand hens, and startin' on our third chicken house that would house another thousand by the end of summer. My, how life can change and move from one phase to another.

Every day I spent some time just lookin' and watchin' to make sure everything was workin' well, and just observin' the hens. There were things to watch for, and with this many hens all in together, it did make it harder to see that one hen who might need attention. Coccidiosis, Fowl Cholera, Bacillary White Diarrhea, among others, were concerns for poultry farmers, and the biggest deterrent was cleanliness. We were very diligent to keep the chicken houses as clean as possible and didn't let the sawdust become too dirty and wet with the chickens' droppings before shovelin' it out and replacin' it with fresh sawdust from Johnny Bruce's sawmill.

It was nice to have my dear friend Rachel workin' with me three days a week. We worked so well together, and best of all, Rachel didn't have to be told every single thing to do. She could see what needed to be done and would just set to doin' it. I liked havin' someone around like that. It made my day easier not havin' to supervise someone all the time. And it was plain nice to have someone to hand that I could talk to, easy girl chat that made the days so much nicer.

On one such day, the first part of May, I was tellin' Rachel about my anxiety over Gerry just turnin' eighteen at the beginnin' of April and how he would soon be goin' to basic trainin' at Fort Jackson like Robbie had. Then I moved on to tellin' her the latest news I had heard from Robbie about George and Johnny, who were stationed at Camp Blanding with him. Robbie had mentioned that George didn't get as much mail and news from home as he and Johnny did. Johnny's Ma and sisters wrote to him as often as I wrote Robbie, and I found out he and Mable Jessup had been correspondin' too. George's Ma had passed away not long before he was drafted, and his Pa wasn't much to write, and neither were his sisters.

"How about I write to George sometimes," Rachel offered. "I feel bad for him, and it would be something I can do for at least one of our soldiers."

"He'd like that!" I smiled, pleased that my caring friend would take the time to write a letter to a boy she had only briefly met, just out of the kindness of her heart.

"Don't let me forget," I said over my shoulder as I washed my hands, "I'll write that address down for you before you leave today. I am expectin' a letter from Robbie soon. Seems like we have fallen into a habit of writin' each other about every two weeks or so. I'm due a letter from him any time now."

I smiled happily at the thought.

Rachel was watchin' me with a slow smile.

"What?" I asked her, puzzled.

"You are in love with Robbie." My friend grinned at me.

I blushed from my hair roots to my toenails. I could feel it.

"Does it really show that easily?" I asked.

"Judgin' by the way your voice changes and you sound happy, your eyes light up, and you talk faster, I'd say yes. It shows. But is that a bad thing? Surely you aren't tryin' to hide it, are you? Cause if you are, you're not doin' a very good job of it."

I put my head down and sighed. "Well, not tryin' to hide it really, just not advertisin' it. Robbie just sees me as his childhood friend, and after the whole nasty ordeal with Tillie, I don't know that he would be interested in a girl right now. Besides, he's no doubt goin' to be shipped overseas any time. But I have a suspicion that my Mamma and Daddy, Granddad and Granny at least know."

I was rememberin' the sidelong glances I had seen from Granddad and Daddy in Robbie's presence, and the soft, understandin' look in Mamma's eyes at times. I looked up at Rachel and said,

"I don't know that I'm the type of girl Robbie is attracted to."

Rachel looked at me blankly. "Whyever not?" she asked, surprised.

"Well, I may not like Tillie because of her nature and how she treats people, but there's no denyin' that she's very beautiful, has a beautiful figure, and… well… a certain way about her that men seem to find attractive. I am none of these things."

Rachel just looked at me for what seemed like a full minute. Then she said,

"Really? What do you think Tillie has that you don't have? Besides a connivin', deceitful, self-centered…"

I waved my hand to shut Rachel up with a little laugh.

"Now, now," I started to say.

"No, let me have my say," Rachel said firmly. "I agree, Tillie has a beautiful face and figure, but it ends there. Maggie, that is ALL she is. It's all she has to offer. And other than that, she is like a pretty Christmas package that is all shiny gilded paper and shiny bows, that is opened only to find nothin' inside the box. A package that Harry is going to open, if he has the misfortune of not seeing through her, and findin' nothin' of substance inside. Think of how sad that is…"

Rachel paused for a moment to let her words sink in.

"You, on the other hand, Maggie, are a young woman of real worth! You're carin', you're loyal and love fiercely, you're a hard worker, and you treat people fairly and with great consideration. And while you might not be beautiful in the same way that Tillie is, you are just as beautiful. Your hair is glorious, and I know many girls would love to have your dark copper-red hair. It shines, and when you curl it and fix it up, you look stunnin'. And your figure is pretty and womanly. You are always sayin' you are a late bloomer, and maybe you were, but you have certainly caught up! There's nothin' wrong with your figure. You are slim, but well-muscled, because unlike Tillie, you work, and you're fit."

Rachel paused for breath in her rant.

"I hope you're believe'n me, Maggie, because I'm not flatterin' you. I'm speakin' truth."

My family has always been a lovin' family. We supported and helped each other but have never been big on dishin' out compliments. It might stem from the belief that an overly complimented child would come to think too highly of themselves, you know, get the big head and all. At any rate, I had never had anyone say so many nice things about me all at once, and I hardly knew how to take it, or what to say to my friend. So, I didn't say anything for a bit.

Rachel sighed as though defeated.

"Again, Maggie, I'm not just bumpin' my gums together or talkin' just to hear myself. Robbie would be a very lucky man to win your heart. And you know what? I think he will grow to see that he loves you. He may have been blind for a long time where Tillie is concerned, but didn't you tell me yourself that he wasn't torn up about her switchin' beau's?"

I nodded.

"Well. There you are."

I just looked at her questioningly. "There you are what?" I asked.

"He wasn't in love with her, silly." Rachel laughed. "He wasn't in love, or it would have been hard for him. As it was, didn't he want you to wish her well?"

Robbie hadn't been in love with Tillie? I had never thought that idea was a possibility.

***

May 14, 1943,

Camp Forrest, Tennessee

Dear Maggie,

As you can see by my postmark, we have been relocated. We had a one-day warning that we were going to be packing up and moving out. Camp Forrest is located on the outskirts of Tullahoma, Tennessee, about seventy miles south of Nashville. And I will tell you right now, it isn't any better than Florida when it comes to mosquitoes, snakes, and other pests! But the countryside has a beauty to it that is very different from the beauty of our mountains. This is the beauty of farmland. There are a lot of trees, but the terrain is mostly level, with a few rolling hills. But the mosquitoes are horrible! Once again, Mamma Dottie's bug salve is something we are grateful to have!

We aren't stationed in barracks. As soon as we arrived, they put us to setting up a tent encampment, and that is where we sleep and store whatever gear we have, which isn't much. But for the time being, it is home. I think I forgot to mention I am part of Company B, 117th Infantry, under Sergeant William Bowden. He's a tough one; he doesn't put up with slacking or much silliness. Johnny has had to learn to curb some of his jokes and silly comebacks.

We are now working with other regiments. The 120th Infantry has been combined with the 30th for training purposes, at least for now. This camp is big, with a lot of interdivision field maneuvers and even mock battles in a simulated Nazi town. The fellas are really enjoying it, and I have been given the rank of corporal. That makes me assistant squad leader of a twelve-man rifle squad. Even though it's not my primary job, I am also being trained as a rifleman with a Browning Automatic Rifle with two assistants. It's always good to be able to assume more than one job.

There are six different practice ranges that I know of. There are at least two Machine Gun Ranges designed for target practice at various distances. Some have pop-up targets to simulate realistic combat situations. The Spencer Artillery Range, fifty miles away, is for heavy artillery training. And the Motlow Range, closer to Camp Forrest, has several different training grounds: light artillery and mortars; small arm ranges for rifle and grenade practice; an anti-tank range; and anti-aircraft ranges. Plus, there are maneuver areas used for infantry maneuvers and tactical training. With so much space and so many different training grounds, you would think it would feel a bit more isolated, but there are several thousand men here.

Our first sergeant is a pretty tough one as I said, but I feel like he is solid and can be depended on. He has earned the trust and respect of the fellas. Even though he is tough and won't allow slacking, he is fair. George was trying to run the other day even though he was sick, and he must have looked sick too, because Sarge sent him to the infirmary and told him to spend the rest of the day in bed.

Tell your friend Rachel that she has made a very happy soldier boy out of George. You would think he had known her all his life by the way he talks about her all the time. "Rachel said this," and "Rachel said that!" Tell her Johnny and I thank her!

I love to hear about your growing business. I knew from the moment you spoke up that day on the porch that you would make a fine businesswoman! You have a good business sense and a willingness to give it a hundred and ten percent. Well done, Mags! By the time us fellas make it back to Deep Gap, you will be the egg queen of North Carolina! Ma wrote that your Daddy had placed a really big lumber order last month, so I'm assuming by now that another chicken house is going up. How are you placing them?

Any word about how Jamie is doing with his driving training? I can see him driving a Sherman tank! I imagine he loves it. And I can only imagine how you are feeling about Gerry. He must be graduating soon and will be off. Is it for sure that he will be going through Fort Jackson like I did?

Maggie, I was wondering if you would do me a favor. I realized the other day that I don't have a single picture of any of my loved ones from home. Not knowing if, or when, I might suddenly be sent to Europe, I wanted to have a few pictures to look at while I am away. Would you either send me a photo you already have, or have one made to send me? If you would rather not, I understand, but I would love to have at least one.

Being away from home this last year has made me realize how much everyone means to me. Ma and Papa have become even more dear to my heart than I ever realized. Oh, of course I knew I loved them very much, but the old saying *absence makes the heart grow fonder* is so true. At least for me it is. And Maggie girl, I miss you something awful. Sometimes I think about and relive our goodbye on your porch last May, and I feel like my heart actually aches with wishing I could see you again. I miss our talks and how easy it is to be myself when I am with you. I miss seeing the enthusiasm in your eyes when you talk, and I long to hear you sing again. That song, Maggie. I have listened to you sing that song over and over again inside my head, and I can hear its haunting melody. I miss seeing the sun set your copper-colored hair aflame with light. Did you know that it actually shimmers?

I'm asking you if you would be my girl, Maggie; I should have asked you a long time ago. Looking back, of course I realize that I should never have started keeping company with Tillie. I was just a very young, and very stupid, young man.

Do I sound silly to you, Mags? Am I overstepping? I hope not. Of course, you may have found someone since I've been away, and if so, please forgive my boldness. But I'm hoping, and praying, that maybe you miss me as I miss you? I always saw you as my little sister that was my sidekick and shadow. And then Tillie and I just happened, and as I said in a previous letter, she kind of became a habit. And then as I grew older, I couldn't count the times I would rather have had you in the seat beside me. But it seemed so ungentlemanly to tell Tillie that my heart yearned for someone else. So, you see, she did me a big favor by being the one to end what wasn't really a relationship at all.

I hope I'm not laying an unwelcome burden on you, dear Maggie. Hoping against hope that you might feel as I do. Sure, we have always been close, and I know you have always cared, but I'm praying and hoping you might be able to care more than just a friend or brother. Write to me and put me out of my misery!

All my love,

Robbie

Chapter Twenty Three

May 24, 1943,

Deep Gap, North Carolina

Dearest Robbie,

I had to write to you as soon as I received your letter, which came just about thirty minutes ago. I should be out in the chicken houses helping with the work, but Daddy and Rachel both agreed I had important business to take care of!

You said in the closing of your letter that you hoped you were not laying an unwelcomed burden on me with your words, but nothing could be farther from the truth! So many times, especially over the last three years, I have felt like I wore my feelings too openly. That might have been why Tillie was constantly taking shots at me, because then you were her beau.

After the horrid things she said though, I have a hard time believing she cared about your feelings or your happiness. By her own words, she was using you. She knew my feelings for you, and like a wolf smelling prey, she could sense my jealousy and used that to get to me. And it worked, because I spent a lot of time alone with my feelings of despair.

I felt that it was partly my own fault because of all the years I held bitterness and anger in my heart. Not only at Tillie, but at you too. I worried that I had destroyed any hope that you would ever see anything but that skinny, redheaded, woods-tromping sidekick. Do you remember that day I blew up at Tillie when we were making our witches' brew? The reason was, even at ten years old, I knew you were mine! I didn't have grown-up feelings of course, but more the feeling that you had always been mine and should always be mine.

Even then, at twelve years old, Tillie had a talent for making you fellas flock around her; she was very beautiful even then. Me, being so plain and knowing it, my ten-year-old self didn't handle that very well. Hopefully, I got better at controlling myself in later years.

So yes, my dear Robbie, yes! If you are saying you love me and want me to be your girl, the answer is yes! That feels mighty bold of me, because you didn't actually say you loved me, but I feel I can read that between the lines that made my heart sing and dance like it never has before. I have actually always been your girl; we are just getting to it. Nobody knows me as well as you do, as the old saying goes, "warts and all." Even as well as Mamma and Daddy know me, I could never share my innermost thoughts with them as I can with you.

Do you know it was right about three weeks ago that Rachel was trying to encourage me concerning you? She guessed how I felt, and I was all gloom and doom, thinking nothing would ever come of it. She felt then that you would come to feel the same, probably not long before you wrote the letter I received today.

I am enclosing a photo that Rachel took of me at the party last October. It isn't the best, but I am planning to have a photo made at the photography studio in Boone, and I will send it as soon as I can. But you now have to do the same for me! I would dearly love to have a photo of you.

Yes, Gerry has gone to Fort Jackson, and Mamma has been struggling with missing him and fearing for him. He left just three days ago, the day after he graduated from high school. Deep Gap just doesn't feel right without all the handsome young fellas around! The only ones left are those not yet old enough to go, those over the age of going, or those with infirmities like Arthel, who cannot go.

Mamma lives in fear that they will start taking those whose ages are on the upper end of the draft, like my Daddy and your Papa.

I guess we'll see where Gerry gets assigned when he's through with basic training. I'm sure he would be too far behind in training to be assigned to your division. Time will tell.

Mabel Jessup told Rachel and me Saturday that she was writing to Johnny, so yes, he's not just pulling your leg! They are writing. She is a quiet girl and doesn't say a whole lot, so I can't really judge right now if she is like Rachel and writing to keep a lonely soldier's spirits up, or if there is something more there. Again, time will tell.

I guess there is no way to know when you will be leaving for overseas. I know that even if you did know, you wouldn't be able to tell us. If I worry about anything, I worry you will be sent, and I won't even know. I also know that once you do go, I will not hear from you very often. How will I know where to send your letters?

You once said you like "newsy" stuff, so I'll just ramble and tell you some of the little things that are going on. Our barn cat Missy had a new batch of kittens, six of them. They are as different from each other as can be! There's a calico, a couple of gray tabbies, a couple of yellow-striped ones, and one that is all black. And as cute as they can be. We have decided to keep them all, because they are needed as mousers in the chicken houses.

Macpherson's store has a brand-new soda machine on the front porch, and it will dispense about eight different sodas, all as cold as ice!

Rachel's daddy, as you know, is the preacher at the Baptist church, and he and our preacher, Brother Reagan, are working together to host a big camp meeting in the field outside of Deep Gap. Those meetings are supposed to start July 10th and last through July 17th. They are having several speakers, some coming in from as far away as Kentucky and Ohio. I'm not sure I will be able to go every night, but I plan to go as often as I can. There's a big "dinner on the ground" planned for after Sunday church service.

Our chick hatchings are going well. We have lost a few chicks, and there have been a few eggs that didn't hatch, but that is to be expected. Right now, we have the third batch in the incubator, and last count there were four hundred and sixty-eight chicks. The third chicken house is close to being finished and will be ready by the time the chicks are old enough for it.

You should see Rachel when she helps Granddad with the grasshoppers! She is such a girly girl, but the grasshoppers don't bother her at all. She will scoop them up barehanded and deal with them. It's funny to watch.

Your Papa drove your old truck over the other day, bringing another load of lumber, and I thought I would bawl seeing your truck without you. He drives it every week or two, so it doesn't just sit and fall apart.

I will seal this up with the photo wrapped inside. Hopefully, it will come through the mail okay. I'm not sure how long it will take to send you a studio photo.

Take very good care of my fella!

All my love,

Maggie

***

June 8, 1943,

Camp Forrest, Tennessee

My Dear Maggie Girl,

You have made me the happiest man in this whole camp! I think Johnny and George are sick to death of hearing me go on and on every time we have a moment we aren't forced to think and talk about military things. Surely you heard my whoops all the way from Camp Forrest! I'm pretty sure too that my boots are going to last forever, because I don't think they are even touching the ground. I am walking in the clouds!

Thank you for the photo, Maggie, it is beautiful. I am keeping it safe, and I need to find something to protect it once we are deployed overseas. Johnny said we can buy a Pliofilm bag in the PX, and we will want to do that before we leave anyway. So, I need to get it done since we will likely not have any warning before we are ordered to pack up and leave.

Maggie, I never knew you compared yourself to Tillie, or anyone else for that matter. There is no comparison! Not that Tillie isn't attractive, she is a pretty person. But you are beautiful in a magnificent way. Tillie is pale and doesn't have much color other than the color she paints on. But you, Maggie, you radiate beauty and are beautiful inside and out. I have always thought so.

Your skin is so smooth, and while not dark, it has a glow to it. Maybe it's what the poets call sun-kissed. And your deep copper-colored hair is something to behold when the sun is behind you and shining on it. It literally shimmers in the light. You have no need to compare yourself to anyone, let alone Tillie. Then there's the matter of the inside. Surely, I don't need to make a comparison there, for the inside of my Maggie girl is pure gold. A man would have to be blind and senseless to not see that you are worth more than a million Tillies.

The book of Proverbs says, *Who can find a virtuous woman? for her price is far above rubies.* And that, my sweet girl, describes you completely.

I guess we both cherish the same memory of our goodbye. Sad, but very bittersweet. I wish I had had the guts to say what I wanted to say then. Next time I hold you in my arms, I will say what's on my mind! I did know you cared about me, but I had convinced myself that you cared about me in the same way you did Jamie, or maybe even Gerry. And I worried that I would look like some sort of philanderer, or a man uncaring about a woman's feelings, if I cast Tillie off. I even hoped she would throw me over while I was gone. Maybe I shouldn't care so much about what everyone thinks, but I do care about the good opinion of people I live among and care about.

This war is like a tug-of-war match. It will seem like one side is winning for a while, then the other. It's likely to go on for some time, and I have no idea how long I will be away. If I get worried or even scared, it's because of the uncertainty. Wondering how long it will be before I see your sweet face again, or my Ma and Papa, and your family who really have been family to me for as long as I can even remember.

It's funny, so many of the men here are looking forward to seeing some of the great cities of Europe. Since we really don't know where we will be sent, they dream of all of them. Rome, Paris, Prague, Strausburg. And it's not that I wouldn't want to see them; if the opportunity comes up, I surely would. But I would be content to live my whole life in the hills and hollows around Deep Gap. Maybe I would feel more eager if you were going to be seeing those sights with me.

Some of the fellas began discussing this war a few nights ago. There were a few who didn't believe we should be going to war with Germany, or even Japan. A congresswoman, Jeannette Rankin, has been campaigning against going to war and even went so far as to accuse the President of provoking the Japanese into attacking us in order to have the support of the American people to go to war. There have been some heated debates over it.

I never gave it much thought before. We were attacked, and we had to defend ourselves. That's how I see it. I do not believe an American President would deliberately bring on the horrible devastation of the Pearl Harbor attack. I don't understand politics, but as slimy as I know some politicians are, I cannot believe it was deliberate.

The thought of killing a man makes me sick, Maggie. Part of me wonders if I can do it, and part of me thinks I can't. I'm struggling with finding a mindset where I can do my duty to my country. I'm patriotic and believe that the Japanese, Hitler, and Stalin must be stopped, or the whole world will be in their sights. I just struggle with doubts that I can point the barrel of my rifle at another man and pull the trigger.

Most of the fellas I have admitted this to think I'm soft or scared of war. I'm not sure what I am, but I don't know if I can pull the trigger on another fellow human being. Does that make me less of a man because I'm hesitant to kill? So many of the men are raring to kill Germans and Japs. I know deep inside it's a necessary evil, but I don't relish it at all.

Training continues, and at times it's so repetitive that I feel like I could do it in my sleep. But then, I guess that's the whole point of it. Do it until it's second nature. It seems to me that while we still run, loaded with packs and gear, and they still push us hard with intense exercise, the focus has turned to military maneuvers and practice with the various firearms.

Some of the training, I think, must be intended to desensitize us. Innards from some of the local butchers are used to hang and string among the rolls of barbed wire we have to crawl through during maneuvers. It's gruesome and disturbing. But oddly, a body does get used to it after a while, which is also disturbing.

The camp meeting sounds exciting. I wish I could go with you. I always loved how the singing would go on sometimes for hours after the preaching was over. Do you think your daddy will go with you all? I hope he can be persuaded to go. I know your Granddad and Granny will be going. I can imagine you all sitting in a row together. Your Granddad can really belt out a song and sings with all his might!

Ever since you sang that song for the chickens, Maggie, I have longed to hear your sweet voice sing again. And that song… it's just so haunting!

Your friend Rachel sounds like a perceptive girl. I only met her, didn't even get to chat for a minute at that party. But I'm so glad you have a good friend that you can spend time with and enjoy her company. I was worried for you after Betty died in the flood. Just one more thing to look forward to after this war: making Rachel's acquaintance.

Maggie, it occurred to me that my truck is just sitting most of the time. If you ever have need of it, feel free to make use of it. I will let Papa know I'm telling you this. Hopefully nothing will go wrong or anything, but I know parts and tires are in short supply. So, if you need it, make use of it.

Enclosed is a photograph of me at Camp Blanding with Johnny and George. I don't have one by myself, so I will have to see about getting one made as soon as possible. I will try to have it by my next letter.

Take care, my sweet Maggie, and may God be with you till we meet again.

All my love,

Robbie

***

Next thing I knew, it was July, and we were preparin' to be away most evenings for a week. I had my doubts I could be away that much and keep up with all the work that needed tended to, but we were going to try. Saturday, July 10th, rolled around, and we spent the day workin' fast to get everything finished because service started at seven. Mamma had supper finished early, and we would do up the dishes when we got home if we didn't have time before we left.

When we pulled into the field just west of Deep Gap, I was really surprised at how many cars and trucks were already parked, and more were waitin' in line to pull in. Word had really made the rounds, because there had to have been at least a hundred cars and trucks.

There was a big white tent pitched in the middle of the field, and four quickly constructed outdoor privies had been built for toilets. Granddad and Granny, Mamma, Charlie and me quickly went inside the tent to find seats. Makeshift benches had been set up usin' raw lumber and pieces of logs cut at about twenty inches, then set on end with the lumber nailed across them. It was pretty rough, but it would work.

As we sat waitin' for the service to begin, I saw there were several gas lamps hangin' on poles here and there that would be lit once it became too dark to see. At seven sharp, a man from the Baptist church got up and welcomed everyone and gave a few announcements, one bein' about the dinner on the grounds planned for tomorrow after church.

He then turned the pulpit over to our song leader who played a guitar as he led the congregation in song. At our church we had a piano and organ, but it just wasn't possible to haul them down here and leave them all week. As we moved from song to song, the enthusiasm began growin', and some folks began raisin' their hands and praisin' the Lord. There was special singin' and a couple of family groups sang, the Watson Family bein' one of them. After about an hour of singin', the designated preacher came to the pulpit and began preachin'. The preacher preached with so much fire and conviction that many folks was cryin' and callin' on the Lord by time the preachin' was over.

I had felt a stirin' inside when the preacher was describin' that God didn't want a body as a fair-weather friend or a Sunday morning Christian. He wanted His followers to be all or nothin'. Completely surrendered to God, and He wanted trust. Even when the Lord allows things to happen in our lives we don't understand, a real believer will still serve Him. Because God knows the end as well as the beginnin', we can trust His will for our lives.

I was ponderin' on the preacher's words all the next day, thinkin' on how it was much easier said than done. I knew Mamma had been thinkin' on the baby sister we had lost back years ago now. That wasn't easy to accept, still yet, and impossible to understand the why of it. God's ways were truly a mystery, and many good Christian folks are able to believe that sickness, tragedy, floods and disaster were just the way of mankind. These things happened. Babies were born, babies died. People got sick, some got well, others died. God knows best.

I wished I had the comfort of that kind of trust, to be able to accept that God in His wisdom knew better than we simple folk and leave it there. If we knew all things like God did, we'd surely make better choices than we do sometimes. Easier said than done. That was a big part of my trouble, trustin' God not only during good times, but in the bad too.

Sunday was a full day. Daddy was goin' with us today, and everyone was secretly excited. We had to get up extra early to get chores done. Mamma had food to fix and get to the meetin' on time. After service, Daddy and I ran home to check on things and finished a couple chores, then hurried back just in time for dinner on the grounds. What a feast it was! We had sacrificed ten hens that Mamma had turned into fried chicken, and there were tables loaded with country hams, chicken and dumplins', casseroles, vegetables, yeast rolls, biscuits, corn bread and the always present jars of pickles, pickled beets and such.

Neglectin' much of the work on Sunday meant we had more work piled on us Monday, so I decided I wouldn't make the service Monday evening. But Daddy and Rachel worked extra-long on Monday, so I was able to make it the rest of the week. Tuesday and Wednesday services were much like Saturday's had been, and there were different speakers every night. Thursday evening, I nearly didn't make it. We had discovered some sick chicks and had been workin' all day to douse them with medicine and were workin' fast to clear out all the contaminated sawdust and separate all the chicks we could tell were sick. But in the end Daddy shooed me away and said he was more than able to finish up and then set watch over the chicks in case more started showin' symptoms.

Lookin' back, I realize that that ol' booger Satan was a tryin' to work against God's plan. As it was, we were a little late gettin' to service because of all goin' on, and we had a hard time findin' parkin'. When we slipped through the back of the tent, singin' was goin' full force, and we had to split up because it was pert near full. There was enough space for me to squeeze in next to Rachel and her Mamma.

It took me some time for my brain to stop whirlin' and worrin' over my flock at home, but eventually I was able to put my mind on the sermon. The preacher was a young man from northern Kentucky and had a real sincere presence about him. He preached in a style I had never heard a preacher use before. He began tellin' the story of Jesus as though he was narratin' a story to the audience, and the people were spellbound. Here in the mountains, storytellin' is considered a gift. People take great pride in the ability to tell a good story and tell it so well the listener feels they are watchin' it unfold before them. This man had the gift.

He began describin' Jesus from His birth, His relationship with His earthly parents, and life as a carpenter in the town of Nazareth. You could see and feel as though you were there, and he painted a vivid picture of Jesus and His humanity. He told how Jesus was tempted in the wilderness to exchange the comin' sufferin' for a life of ease. How Satan took Jesus way up high and showed Him all the kingdoms of the world and offered them to Him, sayin' they could all belong to Him by just worshipin' Satan. And how Jesus overcome temptation by usin' God's Word against Satan. Jesus overcame the evil one, not as God, but as a man. He took us clear through the Garden of Gethsemane, the cross, and the tomb, to the triumph of the resurrection mornin'.

"And why did Jesus do this?" the preacher asked.

"What did he have to prove? Why did he leave Heaven? He had it all. Angels that stood to attention day and night to attend Him; no pain, no suffering, no heartache. The Bible foretells in Isaiah that after being beaten unmercifully, Jesus wasn't recognizable: *that his visage was marred more than any man.* Why would He take this upon Himself when he didn't have to?"

The preacher paused. Many were weepin' at the vivid story of Jesus' life, death, and resurrection.

"He did it for you."

He pointed to different folks in the audience.

"And you, and you."

Then suddenly he swung around to the other side of the aisle where I sat with Rachel and Mrs. Potts, pointed his finger directly at me and said,

"And for you, young lady. Jesus did it for you that you might have eternal life, healing, peace and deliverance. He paid the price so that you could be changed from what man is naturally, bent toward wickedness, to a new creature in Christ Jesus. One with a pure heart. 2 Corinthians 5:21 says: *God made him who had no sin to be sin for us, so that in him we might become the righteousness of God.*

The righteousness of God! Think of it! Mortal man becoming the very righteousness of Almighty God! Not just a good person doing good deeds, but changed. Made new, born again, and filled with the Spirit of God. Then it's no longer you trying to be a good person, but the very life of God living and displaying the righteousness of God in you."

I had begun to cry. In a flash I could see what Granddad had told me on many occasions, that I needed a changed heart. Until that happened, it would always be Maggie at war not only with others, like Tillie Macpherson, but with the feelin's, the inner war. Not only my anger but also my anxiety, and yes, even anger at God. It was God, after all, who had taken my baby sister, was it not? God who had allowed that horrible, devastatin' flood, that my friend Betty and her Ma and siblings died in?

Next thing I knew, I was standin' at the front, along with a dozen or more others who were weepin' and callin' on the Lord. I felt arms around my waist and hands on my shoulders as people were prayin' with me. I trembled and shook under the force of my emotion. The preacher took hold of the hand I had extended to the Lord as I asked for His forgiveness for my sin and rebellious nature.

"Father in Heaven, you see your daughter, repenting before you, asking forgiveness for her sin. Hear her prayer, dear Lord, purify her heart and soul with the fire of your redeeming love. Lead her to the waters of baptism and fill her with your Holy Spirit."

After some time, I slowly came back to myself and saw that Granddad, Granny, Mamma, and Rachel had all been there prayin' with me. I felt so clean, like my inside had been washed and sanitized. I felt light, and the oppression that always seemed to linger around the edges was gone. The anger, gone. With the realizin' of just what the Lord had done for me came a fresh wave of tears. But they were tears of joy.

I was baptized that very same night in Gap Creek, where I had swam and played as a child. Baptized in the name of the Lord Jesus Christ, and I was never the same. Not to say I never had times I didn't need to seek forgiveness for, because that's just part of bein' human. But now I had peace. And even Tillie Macpherson looked better to me, and I felt great pity for her.

Chapter Twenty Four

Summer passed into fall, and we were approchin' another Thanksgiving without the presence of our extended family. Sadly, Uncle Albert had passed away from a lingerin' sickness, and Granddad thought the days of the Virginia kin folks comin' for the holiday were probably over. Auntie Mae was getting too old for travel, and the others wouldn't likely come without her. Times were definitely changin', and I didn't like this kind of change. I knew the families would no doubt drift apart, and within a generation or two, wouldn't even know each other.

Gerry had finished his basic trainin' last month and had been assigned to the U.S. 3rd Infantry Division out of Fort Benning, Georgia. He was bein' trained with the amphibious assault team and seemed to be enjoyin' his role on a mortar squad as a mortar man. He had been given the rank of Sergeant and commanded the mortar team. They were makin' NCOs out of any young man showin' signs of leadership and skill right out of basic trainin' by this time.

Jamie's 745th Tank Battalion had sailed for England in luxury on the R.M.S. *Queen Elizabeth* in August. They arrived in Greenock, Scotland, and then traveled to Wiltshire, England for additional training.

Our troubles back in July with the sickness that had hit our chicks was a big concern. We wound up havin' to hatch more chicks than we had originally planned, to make up for our losses. It was a run of bad luck that all farmers contend with from time to time. What we learned from the whole thing was you can't always keep disasters from happenin', but instead of getting all discouraged, you just dealt with it as best as possible and kept goin'. We wound up hatchin' out a total of six incubator loads which should have been fifteen hundred chicks, but after the Coccidiosis outbreak we had lost over four hundred chicks. But like I said, we just counted ourselves blessed that we caught it early and didn't lose them all. Better yet, it didn't spread to the adult layin' hens.

Two days before Thanksgiving, I received a letter from Robbie. He liked knowin' I would sometimes take his letter up to my favorite spot in the world and read his letters, and sometimes write my own to him from my perch overlookin' my mountains to the east.

It was a fine fall day and, knowin' I wouldn't be able to make the climb very often until spring, I scrambled up the old Indian Trail and settled onto the rocky ledge that jutted out over the valley below. Pullin' Robbie's precious letter from the envelope, I read:

***

November 13, 1943,

Camp Atterbury, Indiana

My Dear Maggie,

Once again you can see from my postmark that we have been relocated to Camp Atterbury, Indiana. I feel certain that we are in the final stages of our training and will no doubt be sent to Europe soon. I doubt that we will be told when we will be sent or where we will be going, but given the nature of our training, we are strongly suspecting that it will be Europe. I wouldn't be surprised if we were sent to England for a time. I found out that they have started sending a lot of other military units there. The 101st Airborne Division was sent back in September. I think it's likely there will be one more camp we will be moved to before our deployment overseas. I guess where they actually plan on sending us will determine which camp

288

we will leave the United States from, so our next location might be a pretty good indication of where we will be going.

One of the things I notice here at Camp Atterbury is they are pulling our whole division together as a unit. Instead of training with just our squad or platoon, we are training maneuvers with the whole division, planning and coordinating different strategies on a much larger scale than before.

Thank you for the photograph! My lord, Maggie girl, you have grown into a beautiful woman! It's so hard to believe that I haven't seen you for over a year and a half. I look at the photo and marvel that you are my girl! The fellas and I had our photographs taken at a photo studio in Edinburgh, Indiana, and I will get that mailed to you as soon as I get them. Ma wanted one too, so I may just mail them together since they will need special packaging.

I can't express to you how happy I was to hear your account of surrendering your heart and soul to the Lord. I had no doubt you would come to that place, Maggie girl. I know how it feels for the heavy burden to be lifted from your spirit. There's no peace like the peace the Lord gives. Even as I prepare for war, and I still fight with uncertainty about my performance as a soldier in the United States Army, I am at peace with my soul. About a week ago, I lay in my cot praying, and I felt the Lord gave me the assurance that when the time came, the Lord would lead me and help me in whatever situation I find myself in, so I quit worrying about it.

I'm glad too that you have peace in your heart now and know that the Lord will be with you and help you in whatever you face. It's comforting to know that He hears us call to Him the instant we do. The Lord is so very good.

Indiana is not much to write home about! If it weren't for the miles and miles of farmland, I wouldn't have much to say about it. I'm sure before it was plowed and it was prairie there was no doubt much more to like. As it is, it's very flat with miles of fields of corn, soybeans, wheat and oats. Pig farming is big too, and it smells like it! I can tell you, Maggie, keeping a few pigs like most farmers do at home isn't the same as a huge pig farm. You can smell them for miles! But man, it's a lot of bacon and sausage on the hoof!

Mags, when I come home (because I believe I will) I hope to settle in and work, marry, and raise a family. My dreams are simple; some might think I had no ambition. I don't yearn to be well known or even do great things. I want only to serve God, love my wife and children and live at peace among the people of Deep Gap. I don't even know yet what work I will do, how I will earn a living, for I'm sure working at Macpherson's store will no longer be an option, even if I wanted to. Maybe I shouldn't be looking that far in the future since I'm about to go to war, but I am. I've been praying and asking the Lord to guide me; I have no doubt He has my life, our lives planned already. But when I envision my life, every time in my mind's eye when I try to see myself with a family, it's always you I see by my side. I see us sitting at the supper table with a couple youngsters of our own laughing and making the same mischief we used to make.

I see us sitting on our own porch, snapping beans and shucking corn, or laughing with family and friends. I see our youngsters playing with their cousins and friends in the yard on a summer evening, and us watching from the porch as they chase fireflies in the cool night. I see us gathered on Sundays and Thanksgiving and Christmas with both sides of our families there, and your Granddad telling his tales and stories to our children.

I guess what I'm saying is I want to marry you, Maggie girl. I want to know that you will live by my side and ride through the good days and the bad with me. I want my children to have your copper red hair and your fierce love and determination. I know we haven't been a couple all that long, but it's not like we need to get to know each other. I don't even remember not knowing you! And like you said in an earlier letter, we know each other, warts and all.

So, will you marry me when I come home, Maggie? Walk with me through life, for better, for worse? I probably shouldn't even ask until I come home safely from the war and have a job and a house. But I want to go knowing I have something real to come home to. Johnny thinks I'm crazy to not wait to ask you until the war is over and I'm home. He says I will be "shootin' myself in the foot," that I will miss out on enjoying the company of the ladies of Paris. I told him that my red rose is worth more than Paris and all its "ladies."

You know the poem put to song by the Scottish poet Robbie Burns? When I first read it years ago in school, I thought of you. With your shining red hair, I always thought you were like a red rose. I never was a big one to like poetry, but I did like this. Probably because I associated it with you. This is how I read it:

O my Maggie is like a red, red rose

That's newly sprung in June.

O my Luve is like the melody

That's sweetly played in tune.

So fair art thou, my bonnie lass,

So deep in luve am I;

And I will luve thee still, my dear,

Till a' the seas gang dry.

Till a' the seas gang dry, my dear,

And the rocks melt wi' the sun;

I will love thee still, my dear,

While the sands o' life shall run.

And fare thee weel, my only luve!
And fare thee weel awhile!
And I will come again, my luve,
Though it were ten thousand mile.

It's as though Rabbie lad had access to my heart and mind when he wrote this, as though he pulled it right out of my heart. I think Mr. Burns knew I would be unable to compose such words myself, so he took the feelings I would have and did it for me.

Put me out of my misery, Maggie girl. Tell me if you will consent to not only be "my girl" but the other half of me, the half that will, along with the Lord, make me a complete man. Tell me yes, and I will buy your wedding ring in Europe and bring it home to you. If you say yes, I will write to your Daddy and ask his permission to marry you.

All my love,

Robbie

***

November 25, 1944,

Deep Gap, North Carolina

My Dearest Robbie,

If I had taken paper and pen with me, I would have answered your letter from the peaks, sitting in my spot. But I was in a rush to read your letter and hurried off without thinking about paper and pen. I wanted to be able to answer without being rushed, so I waited until after Thanksgiving to do it. Yesterday being Thanksgiving, I'm now sitting in my room at my table under the window in the eaves.

The weather turned blustery yesterday; otherwise I might have gone back to my spot to write my reply to your letter. So, I'm sitting here, looking over the tractor barn and harvested fields to my right and the chicken houses to my left. I can see Daddy as he is giving the big tractor some maintenance, greasing the wheels and giving it a good cleaning before parking it for the winter. We now have a smaller tractor we use year-round for hauling the sawdust and chicken manure to the fields, and for small jobs around the farm.

You might wonder why I'm rambling on about everyday things as usual. It's because I have to keep checking to make sure I'm not in a dream, that life is still going on. My sweet Robbie, my darling, my one and only of course I will marry you! It's what I have always wanted, whether I showed it or not!

Did you ever know that when I was really little, seven or eight, me and some of the other little girls at school would play "getting married" during recess? We would role-play for each other. One little girl would be the minister, another the bride, another the groom. When it was my turn to "get married," I wouldn't play if my groom wasn't Robbie Bruce. This didn't always go down well because I wasn't the only one who wanted to marry Robbie Bruce. But you know full well how stubborn I was back then, and I always married Robbie Bruce!

I also feel that we know each other well, probably better than many couples who have been married a long time. We have always said what we thought to each other and talked about serious things as well as everyday things. I know in my heart that we are two halves of a whole that has always been in God's mind.

You fill my thoughts all the time. When I'm working, my heart is often in conversation with you. I'll say something, and you answer back in my mind. I often relive our goodbye on the porch over and over, and it's precious to me. Sometimes I shut my eyes and remember how it felt to feel your arms wrapped around me, holding me close. Do you know, in spite of the fact that you were leaving, and I had no idea when I would see you again, I felt at home and happy in that moment? I felt more at home, more secure than anywhere else. Ever.

I cannot tell you how happy it makes me to know that I don't have to conceal anything from you ever again!

I love that poem by Robert Burns! I never associated it with myself of course, but there's something so achingly tender about it, and I will love it even more now. There's something about it coming from Scotland that makes it even more special, don't you think? I'll read it over and over every time I am missing you more than I can bear.

I love the idea of my ring being chosen by you no matter where you get it, but a ring from Europe will be special. But I have one request, my darling. I'm a working girl, always will be. I don't want to have to take it off and put it away while working. So please, nothing real fancy, with stones sticking out. I want to be able to wear it all the time, so a nice plain band is fine.

Oh, and by the way, tell Johnny he'll have to find out about the ladies of Paris by himself. I would just as soon prefer that you remain ignorant of those women!

I'm so glad you liked the studio photograph. I think the pose is a bit fancy for me, but all in all it's not bad. I'm looking forward to having a good photo of you to sigh and dream over. If you want to mail mine in with your Ma's that's fine. We see them at least once or twice throughout the week, and they always have Sunday dinner with us.

Funny how you see our children as having my red hair. I see them with your golden-brown wavy hair. Lord knows I wouldn't wish my stick-straight hair on my poor young'uns! Maybe we will have some of each to make us both happy.

Now about the down-to-earth everyday things. You mentioned that maybe you should wait to ask me to marry you until you are home, with a job and house. This is a suggestion, and not a demand or assumption. What would you think of working with Daddy and me here at Deep Gap Egg and Poultry?

It's not high-class work for sure, but it's good honest work, and a family business. If you are going to marry me, you're marrying a business as well. Not that you have to work at it, but I hope you can see what I'm saying. I believe a husband and wife share everything. What a husband owns also belongs to his wife, and whatever a wife owns also belongs to her husband. It's all owned mutually.

I guess it's things like this that we don't really know where each other stands and have to be talked about. Even if you choose not to work here at the business, you will still be a co-owner with me. That's how I see it. Just as your truck will be partly mine. (Can you see me smiling?)

That was a very welcome suggestion by the way; we are going to have our truck in Bert Farmer's Auto Shop in the next week or so, having new shock absorbers put on. Daddy will use your truck for deliveries that week. And I'm not trying to twist your arm or talk you into something you don't want to do, but we could sure use another man working the business!

There have been times when Daddy has made deliveries when he didn't feel well, and while I'm driving now, none of us think it's a good idea for me to make the deliveries alone. Any number of things could go wrong that I would have a hard time taking care of. And you wouldn't be just a laborer, but we would want your ideas and have equal say in the business decisions. Just think on it. It's not even something you have to decide right now.

Catching you up on the Gerry news: he was assigned to the U.S. 3rd Infantry Division out of Fort Benning, Ga. He is being trained with the amphibious assault team and has been given the rank of Sergeant and is commanding a mortar team. He too has no idea how soon his unit will be sent but also suspects it must surely be soon.

Jamie, as you know, is in Wiltshire, England with the 745th Tank Battalion. Like you, he believes the men are being trained for something big. He likes England and says the rolling hills of Wiltshire are beautiful and green.

Evening chores need doing, and Rachel has put in a long day, so I need to end this letter and help pull my weight around this place.

But before I sign off, let me tell you how much I love you and miss you. Remember when you were little and you told your Ma you loved her bigger than the old red bull out in the field? It makes me laugh every time I think of it. But to a little boy, that was really big!

I have another rendition: I love you bigger than the mountains, bigger than the sea, and bigger than the biggest sky at night so full of stars. I love you a bushel and a peck and a hug around the neck. And from the beginning of time through eternity. I can say that because I believe that we were together even then in the thoughts of God.

Yours forever and ever,

Maggie

***

Winter seemed mild in comparison to last year. Here it is January 10, 1944, and we have only had one snow that was little more than flurries. There's no rhyme or reason to weather; it does as it pleases, and we take what we get!

I had a letter from Robbie just a couple of days ago tellin' me they were about to once again be moved to another camp. It wasn't clear where, but they were told to pack and be ready at a moment's notice, and he felt like this would be their last stop before deployment. It makes me a ball of nerves knowin' he is about to be sent to war without me holdin' him and tellin' him goodbye. Mamma Claire is tearful nearly every time I see her, understandably afraid for her only son.

One good bit of news is we were due to renegotiate our government contracts and were able to negotiate a five-cent per dozen increase, and they would contract for a total of fifteen hundred dozen eggs every week. That was a big deal for us and went a long way toward getting us up to our goals. We had already had grocery store chains Piggly Wiggly and A&P contact us about contracting eggs with them. We were tryin' to get the size of our flock up to speed so we could do that. We knew the government contracts would only hold out as long as the war did, and we needed to be sortin' out our future.

January 15, 1944. Johnny and Claire Bruce came over today to hand off the news they had just received. Mamma Claire's eyes looked too large in her pale face, and I could see she had been cryin'. Robbie's entire unit had moved from Camp Atterbury, Indiana, to Camp Myles Standish near Boston, Massachusetts. This was certainly the last leg of his trainin' in the United States.

Chapter Twenty Five

January 21, 1944,

Camp Myles Standish, Massachusetts

Dearest Maggie Girl,

I know Ma and Papa relayed the message of our departure from Camp Atterbury to Camp Myles Standish. We were expecting it, so it came as no surprise to us when we were told to report for departure in one hour. So here we are about thirty miles from Boston Harbor, where I'm sure now we will depart the United States from.

Boston itself is a very interesting old town. Johnny, George and I, along with a few other fellas, were given a weekend pass last weekend, and we decided to see some of the sites around town. There was a bit of tug of war over where we would go as a group. Johnny and some of the other fellas wanted to go to some of the clubs around the waterfront that cater to the soldier crowd, but George and I, along with a very small few, wanted to see some of the historical places around Boston. So, we parted ways and had a good time separately.

If by chance we are sent to England, maybe I can look Jamie up. The whole country is about the same square miles as Alabama; that puts things into perspective when you think of going somewhere while there. It isn't very big. If we are able to get any leave time, I will try to do that. Sounds as though Gerry's busy with training as well. It's odd to think we will all three be in the fighting very soon.

We are now being much more closely censored as to what we can say in our letters. We cannot say where we are going (when we know), and we cannot say when, only that it will be very soon. We are also going to be the work crew loading the ship for departure, so we are going to be very busy right up until we leave. This may be my last letter for a while.

Another thing, Maggie girl; once deployed and in the field, I may not always have much time for anything more than a quick note. If that is what you get, please remember that I love you more than life and will write a nice long newsy, and yes, mushy letter as soon as I can. (Can you see me smiling now?)

I got your Daddy's reply to my letter to him, and I cried. Yes, me, a grown man, crying because of the wonderful things your Daddy said to me in his letter. I'm sending it home to stay with you because I want it to be kept clean and not get lost or muddied up or anything. You are welcome to read it if you want to. He has given his permission, and we are officially engaged. I think every time I say to someone, "my girl back home; my fiancée," my chest must expand a size. I couldn't feel prouder and more humbled at the same time that you have consented to be my wife, and your Daddy has agreed to it.

Maggie, when this war is over and we are married, I would love to bring you here to the East Coast to see places like Boston, and maybe other places like Washington, D.C. I know you say you aren't big on traveling, but I think you would love seeing some of the places that were so important to the Revolutionary War, the War of 1812, and even the American Civil War. We both share an interest in history, whether it's our country or the history of Scotland, the country of our ancestors.

And then there's the ocean. Maggie, the ocean's expanse is mind-boggling and immense, even mysterious. I stood there looking out as far as the eye can see to the horizon, watching the waves roll and lap against the shore while water birds of different sizes and kinds run back and forth before the waves, gobbling up crabs, bugs and shellfish the water uncovered. I don't know if I have ever heard a more soothing sound. George actually went to sleep while we were stretched out on the sand soaking up what little warmth the sun gave us. I imagine it's really something on a summer evening. It would be a wonderful place for a honeymoon…

I like the idea of working the family business with you and your Daddy, and the rest of the Spencers that will one day work there. That was one of the nice things he said in his letter to me. His words were, "As a son in the family, we would be honored if you would consider working with us to build Deep Gap Egg and Poultry into a business that will grow and endure beyond the war."

You will have to teach me the ropes from the ground up, and I'm not too stupid to learn! It does make me feel better knowing I have work waiting when I return. And I promise I will hit the ground running! Another nice thing your Daddy said to me was, "And Robbie, you can call me Dad."

So, my red rose, I will close this letter telling you I love you so much. Sometimes it unnerves me a little bit knowing how completely my heart is in your pretty, strong hands. When I get up in the morning, I think of you and wonder what you are doing at that moment and wish I could see you and tell you that I love you. At random moments throughout the day, something will make me think of you Maggie would like that, or that reminds me of Maggie, or even boy, Maggie would hate that! And I wish I could just smile at you and say, I love you, Maggie girl.

When I sit down to an evening meal with the loud noises of hungry men all around me, I sometimes shut my eyes and imagine you sitting across from me at our supper table. My mind's eye sees you with the evening sun shining through our window and spilling over you and setting your beautiful hair aflame with light. And I wish I could reach across that table, take your hands in mine and thank the good Lord for blessing me with my wonderful wife. And then smile at you and say, I love you, Maggie girl.

As the old song says, God be with you till we meet again.

All my love,

Robbie

***

March 12, 1944,

Berkhamsted, England

My Sweet Maggie,

Well, as you know, we left Boston on February 11th and arrived in Liverpool, England, on February 22nd. I was right to suspect that we were going to England, and I have cause to believe that the rumors I heard as far back as a year ago at Camp Forrest are true. There is no way to know for certain, but given the size of the forces being brought together and the kind of training we are receiving, I know deep inside it is true, and it likely will happen within a few months. That's all I can say on that subject.

Guess what. I found out I am a wimp when it comes to ocean travel; I was seasick for the whole eleven days. After disembarking, we traveled by train to Berkhamsted, where we have been since. I can't imagine how sick I would have been if we had sailed through an Atlantic winter storm; just the Atlantic in the winter about did me in!

By the way, you will have noticed that my letter is not the handwritten version I wrote myself, but a photograph of it. Any letters sent from now on will be what is called V-mail, or victory mail. They photograph the letter, send the negative to the U.S. where it is reprinted on this thin paper. It cuts way down on the space needed to ship what is hundreds of thousands of letters. If I send pictures, or anything enclosed, then it will have to be sent by regular mail and will take much longer, even as long as two months.

Berkhamsted is what is called a Market Town. It's smaller than a city like Raleigh but much larger than Boone. It has some of the oldest buildings you wouldn't believe! The oldest inhabited building in Berkhamsted was built between 1277 and 1297. I have never seen anything like these old buildings here, and there is a castle ruin not far away from where we are camped. It is incredible to see! The age and history of this place is something you can actually feel.

The countryside is beautiful with lightly rolling green hills and flatlands. There is a canal called the Grand Union Canal that runs through the town and has a lot of old houses built right up close to the canal edge. It gives the town such a tranquil feeling, and yet we are only twenty-six miles from London.

England is a cold, wet place, at least that's the case in March. I don't know if I have ever seen so much rain. Not torrential hard rain like we get in our mountains, but here it seems to just have a grey drizzle so much of the time. Some of the locals told me summer is much better, with a bit of sunshine in between the drizzle.

Our mountains will soon be turning green, and the rhododendron will put out their little hard knobs that will become blooms in June. The snow melt will fill the mountain streams with icy water, and the bear will come out of hibernation with little cubs scrambling behind their mammas to keep up. Songbirds will return and build their nests, and the wood ducks will have little fluffy babies jumping out of their nests in the trees. I am homesick for you and our mountains, Maggie. Sometimes I do okay, but this evening, I am homesick.

I am told the town hosts a lot of social events to help the locals and the U.S. servicemen exist on friendly terms. I am sure it's been hard for many of the local people to put up with us Yanks. That is what they call us, Yanks. Every southern boy I know has their back up over it! To them, we are all Yankees. Johnny has tried to get me to go to some of the dances, but I'm just not inclined to go. My heart is firmly in Deep Gap, and I have no need to prance around a dance floor in Berkhamsted. Funny how two fellas from the same part of the world can be completely opposite from each other. I wouldn't mind a nice country party like we have at home, but these affairs are a whole different thing.

I checked into the possibility of finding Jamie and meeting up with him. I just don't know if it will work. He is only a little over a hundred miles away, but the bus links aren't direct, and with England at war, their public transportation isn't all that reliable. Sometimes scheduled bus lines get cancelled or redirected. If that happened and caused me to be late getting back to camp, I could be considered AWOL (absent without leave). You can get into a lot of trouble, especially during wartime. If there is time before we leave here, maybe I could write Jamie and see about us meeting up halfway or something like that.

My sweet Maggie girl, I have been haunted by that song you sang nearly two years ago to your chickens that day we said goodbye. It hardly seems possible that it has been that long since we last saw each other. And it makes my heart ache so bad, for I have no idea how long it will be before I see you again. I want to find out how your hair feels under the touch of my hand. My eyes and imagination tell me that it is soft and would slip through my fingers like red silk.

I never even got to hold your sweet hand. And again, my imagination tells me that even though it no doubt shows signs of the work you do, and I know you, Maggie girl, you work hard. But my imagination tells me that your touch is soft, and I long to hold it in mine.

I will close this letter with the verse to the song that I sing over and over in my head:

Roses love sunshine, violets love dew
Angels in heaven know I love you

Know I love you dear know I love you
Angels in heaven know I love you.
All my love, and forever yours,
Robbie

***

April 1, 1944,

Deep Gap, North Carolina

Dearest Robbie,

I can't tell you how relieved I was to get your letter at last! I knew it would be some time before I heard from you, but what I didn't realize was how hard the wait would be. I hate it that you were so sick for the voyage to England. Maybe on the journey home you could request something to help with the sickness. Surely there is something that would help. I guess this would mean that we won't be taking a sea voyage for our honeymoon! (Yes, it is mean, but yes, I am laughing.) Don't worry, sweetheart, I won't drag you onto the high seas!

The V-mail is a great idea, and faster too, so I'm all for it. I will be able to send my letters through V-mail too. I found out I don't even have to pay for the form; the post office will give everyone two free forms a day. So, I'm good!

Your homesickness for home and spring about broke my heart! I sat on my bed and cried reading it. I believe in that moment I could have shot Hitler, Stalin, Mussolini, and Emperor Hirohito myself! I know you would want to hear this, so I will describe what I see outside my window. Of course, there are not a lot of blooms yet, but the Sarvis tree is just starting to push out its delicate white blooms, giving the tree a frothy look. The redbuds are blooming with their purple blossoms, and when they bloom in and with the Sarvis, it is so very pretty.

The Red Maples too are blooming, and their red blooms with the delicate little spikes are attracting the honeybees like nobody's business! And I can't see them from my window, but down along the creek just below the barn, the trillium are blooming their dainty white, pink, and purplish red, tri-cornered blooms, all nestled in their home of dark green leaves. And my favorite, our Wild Mountain Columbines. There's not a prettier flower on God's green earth, and they grow all over our mountain in reds, blues, pinks, and purples.

I saw a mamma bear coming out of a thicket of mountain laurel the other day, and she had three little cubs toddling after her. They were so tiny, I knew they were just out of hibernation. Remember the time we saw that poor little yearling bear that had been sprayed in the face by a skunk? Goodness, I still feel sorry for it, but I'd be willing to bet he never bothered another skunk!

I'm so glad to know that my husband will also be my coworker! And if you happen to worry about having to be around me all day every day, you needn't. With work to do in so many areas, we are often working alone. Sometimes it is a two-man job, but not always.

England sounds very interesting, and it would be something to see real castles. Do you think you will get the chance to see any? I cannot imagine a building in use that was built in 1277. It boggles my mind. That was long before America was discovered by white people, nearly two hundred years before Christopher Columbus was even born! How did they build buildings that are still standing after so long? I would love to see pictures of it.

I'm glad you aren't hankering to prance around a dance floor in Berkhamsted (can you hear me laughing?). My daring you made me laugh out loud. I wouldn't want to keep you from enjoying some company, and even from making friends among the English young men, but I'm very glad to know you won't be prancing with the English women! As you know, we aren't prancing here either. My goodness, when would I have the time anyhow? And rationing has its death grip on everyone, and we don't drive anywhere if it's not necessary.

Even going to church on Sundays, we all squeeze into one truck. Mamma and Granny ride in front while I drive, and Daddy, Granddad, and Charlie ride in the back.

Do you know Rachel told me that there is a huge black-market trade in stolen gasoline going on? Heavens! I knew that people were selling their ration coupons illegally, but stolen gasoline practically under our noses! But then, my goodness, why would it be illegal for Joe to sell Bill a gasoline ration coupon if Bill needed the gasoline, and Joe needed the money? Same amount of gasoline used. Oh well, the Government never asked for my opinion.

Well, I won't spend much time on this next bit of news, but Tillie and Harry have announced their engagement. Harry is going to college, his father says to receive a degree in business so he is "better equipped" to run their tobacco business. Everyone knows it's so he doesn't have to serve in the military. Besides, anyone in any farming industry is exempted from military service anyway. Not that I would wish it on anyone, but it hardly seems fair that a tobacco baron is exempt from military service when so many of our boys are being pulled away from their homes and families. Anyway, they are getting married in August. I did wish Tillie well and will be giving her a nice gift at the wedding. (Yes, I realize I sound petty.)

If you get to see Jamie, please give him our love. I don't write to him nearly like I should. I think I only wrote to him three times last year, and so far, have only written once this year. Gerry was deployed to join the 3rd Infantry Division's replacements. As of yet, I don't believe he has seen combat, but they were in such need of replacements to cover their losses that he and his group didn't get the same amount of training you received. Pray for him.

Now for the part of my letter where I get to tell you how much I love you. You can't know how it made me feel to know how you long to hold my hand and touch my hair. The feeling is mutual, my handsome husband-to-be.

I guess I've never said it, but I have always loved the golden-brown waves of your hair and have wondered many times how it would feel for me to run my fingers through it. I love the firm squareness of your jaw, and even the little scar on the bottom of it is precious to me. I love how you walk and how you tilt your head to the side when you laugh at something. I miss hearing your laugh!

I could hear you laughing in a group of a hundred men and pick your laugh out of them. The sound of it makes me happy, and I have even woken up from a dream of you laughing, and I could swear that I could still hear the echo of it.

And even though I have never held your hand, I have studied them and admired the strong and firm look of them. I have seen the callouses and know they are from work. I'm also looking forward to the day I can hold your hands in mine and feel the strength in them.

There is a song that came out just a few years ago, you've heard it no doubt. The first two stanzas come straight out of my heart:

The other night dear, as I lay sleeping

I dreamed I held you in my arms

But when I woke dear, I was mistaken

And I hung my head and I cried

You are my sunshine, my only sunshine

You make me happy when skies are gray

You'll never know dear, how much I love you

Please don't take my sunshine away

Well, my handsome Rifleman, I look forward to your next letter. May God bless you and keep you and shelter you under His wings.

All my love,

Maggie

Chapter Twenty Six

May was glorious, the spring of 1944, and it was good that there was something positive to remember about it. Somehow, when I forced myself to describe the beauty of spring here in my mountains for Robbie, it shifted my thinkin', and I started payin' more attention to just how beautiful my mountains are. When a body lives somewhere, they get used to what surrounds them. I realized that I had been so caught up in makin' our business that I had stopped lookin' at the stunning beauty all around me.

It's not only the big things, like the heart-stoppin' view from my favorite spot, that are worth noticin'. Often, it's the tiny things that can lift the spirit and bring a body so much joy. I began spendin' time searchin' out the tiny, wee flowers that bloom among the grasses, sometimes in places I would normally have walked through quickly on my way to the chicken houses or barns.

Tiny wild violets, so unbelievably delicate; and when you looked closely, you could see that their surface sparkled ever so slightly and ranged from many shades of purple to nearly white. Bloodroot, with its narrow white petals and gold center of stamens, gets its name from the orange-red sap that colors the roots. The pretty trillium, with its three petals, can be white, red, yellow, pink, or maroon, depending on what type it is. And the trumpet-shaped Virginia bluebells that grow in large patches were always where I would hunt for fairies when I was a little girl. The green patches were overflowin' with the little blue flowers that hung, attached to the stem at one tube-shaped end, and widened out at the bottom like a bell. They grew in the woodlands and loved shady places.

In May, the woods were busy with birds who were tendin' their nests and seein' to their young, and the air was filled with birdsong. The songbirds migrated south in the winter, leavin' the blue jays and cardinals run of the mountains over the winter, but they returned every spring and filled my mountains with their song. I had begun listenin' again to the many different songs, and the remembrance of all the lessons Robbie had given me as a child were comin' back, so I could identify most of what I heard.

I started takin' time to sit and watch for wildlife in the mornings. Takin' a cup of coffee and my Bible out on the porch, I'd read a chapter or two from God's Word and sit for a while, talkin' with the Lord. Early in the mornings or just before dark are the best times to see wildlife. Most every morning, I would see mamma whitetail deer with their spotted fawns step out of the woods and nibble grass at the edge of our clearin'. The graceful mammas would nibble and graze, ever watchful, while the fawns would run and play and sometimes nurse from their mammas.

I would watch the playful gray squirrels as they chased each other in games of tag and hide-and-seek. When alarmed or disturbed, they would sit up on their back legs and chatter loudly like they were givin' me what for. Sometimes I would see the tiny little striped chipmunks as they skittered around the woodpile, jumpin' and playin' like their lives depended on it. Chipmunks are a joy to watch as they played like a bunch of kittens, rollin' around in little mock battles.

Even though the Division of Game and Inland Fisheries claims there are no wolves or panthers in these mountains, the people who live here will tell you another story. Robbie and I saw what we call "painters" when we were youn'uns, while trampin' through the mountains one day. It liked to have scared us to death, because it was the last thing we were expectin' to see. We were climbin' a small bluff below my favorite spot one day when we happened to notice movement below us. We froze still and watched as the tawny-colored painter crossed the trail and disappeared into the laurel thicket below us. We never heard it make one sound. They may be rare but are seen from time to time. I've only seen the one but have heard them scream many times.

We had to spend a considerable amount of time keepin' the possums, coons, and foxes out of the chicken houses. These animals will pillage a chicken house and sometimes kill more than they will eat. I recall Granddad tellin' a tale about his mother, Great-Grandmother Mary Anne Spencer, who passed on when I was too little to recall her. She heard a racket comin' from her henhouse one night and ran out in her nightie to see what was causin' the fuss. Her husband, Great-Granddad Malcolm Spencer, was away with the wagon and team, sellin' their honey and was not there.

When she threw open the door to the henhouse, she saw a possum had taken one of her hens and killed it. The possum was eatin' its kill right there in the henhouse, and Great-Grandmother Mary Anne was so furious that, without thinkin', she grabbed the possum by the tail, toted it over to a tree, and swung it around, proceedin' to bash its brains out against the tree. We Spencer women will take things into our own hands if need be.

We didn't want to stand guard all the time, so we had taken precautions by buryin' fencin' wire all along the perimeter of each chicken house, sinkin' it into the ground a good two feet. That discouraged especially the foxes, who would dig under the walls, tryin' to get inside. We were constantly fillin' in holes where some varmint had tried to get to our chickens.

The sides of our chicken houses were designed so that sections on hinges could be raised and propped open to allow airflow and sunshine to get inside. Those open sections were covered with heavy fencin' wire too, to keep the chickens inside and the varmints out. So part of our daily chores was to go around each chicken house daily, raisin' or lowerin' the sections, as well as inspectin' for signs of diggin'.

On one such day, I was workin', raisin' the sections on chicken house number three when I saw something over at the edge of the field near the back woods. When I turned to take a closer look, whatever I saw just melted into the woods, leavin' me unsure about what I had seen. Was it a bear or a man? I wasn't sure.

When I finished my chores, I found Daddy, who was loadin' his truck with crates of eggs for his weekly delivery to Fort Butner, and told him about what I had seen. He stopped for a minute and stretched his back before answerin'.

"Could have been a bear," he said slowly. "They're definitely out and about now."

I nodded. "Could have been. But I didn't think it moved much like a bear," I said thoughtfully.

Daddy knew that I wasn't prone to wild imaginings and that I knew my wildlife.

"You think it was a man?" he asked.

"I'm thinkin' it did move more man-like," I said.

I would rather it was a bear. A bear would be much easier to deal with than a man. Why would a man be sneakin' around the place to begin with?

"Keep an eye out today but be careful. Don't go back behind the chicken houses closin' them up. I'll close up when I get back."

It made me feel uneasy to think someone was sneakin' about.

"I think I'll get Granddad to come over and spend the day here until I get back," Daddy spoke again. "If it's a man hangin' around, he'll think twice about nonsense if there's a man about."

Again, I nodded, feelin' relieved. Rachel and I would work inside the chicken houses today and worry about outside work tomorrow.

The day went by without anyone seein' anything more, but we were all thinkin' about it. Monday mornin', while I was sittin' on the porch with my coffee and Bible, a strange man came walkin' up the driveway. He walked a bit off-kilter, like his left leg wasn't right. As soon as I saw him, I knew he was what I had seen on Friday. I called for Daddy to come, and he came out on the porch right away.

"Mornin'," the stranger called out.

"Mornin'," Daddy responded.

"My name is Harvey Murray," the man said. "I'm from over near Mountain City, Tennessee. Been livin' in Boone for about six months now."

Daddy extended his hand to the man, sayin', "My name is Ed Spencer."

The man took Daddy's hand and gave it a good firm shake.

"I don't care much about livin' in town," Harvey said. "I prefer livin' out in the countryside and workin' with my hands. Are you hirin'?"

Daddy paused a moment, then asked him directly, "Was you out hangin' around the place Friday?"

Harvey looked Daddy square in the eye and said, "Yes sir, I was. Didn't mean no harm, but was just a watchin' to see if it looked like a good place to work. Sorry about that, I guess it looked suspicious."

Daddy nodded. "Yes, it did. Maggie here saw you and told me about seein' you. It kinda had us all on edge for a bit. Sure do wish you had just approached us like this on Friday."

"Yes sir, I do too," Harvey said, and was about to turn to go.

"What kind of work experience do you have, Harvey?" Daddy stopped him with a question.

"Well, I've done quite a few different things," said Harvey as he turned back to Daddy. "I've done loggin' and truck drivin', and I've been workin' at the newspaper office in Boone the last six months, but I'm not one for bein' stuck indoors all day. That's why I'm lookin' for work."

"Never worked with livestock before?" Daddy asked him.

"No sir, I haven't, but I'm willin' to learn," Harvey said, lookin' very hopeful.

Daddy looked over at me. I had just been sittin', holdin' my cup of coffee durin' the whole exchange between them.

"What do you think, Maggie?" Daddy asked me.

I sat for a moment, tryin' to make a judgment call as to whether or not I thought Harvey Murray looked to be a good choice or not. I liked the way he looked Daddy in the eye, his firm handshake, and I liked it that he admitted he had been snoopin' around without tryin' to cover it up. We needed some help, and that was a fact.

Rachel worked three days a week and couldn't, and didn't want, more time. She helped her daddy around their church on other days. With Gerry gone, it was nearly all we could do to take care of things as they were, and we were plannin' on expandin' again. In fact, we were about to fire up the incubator again.

I looked over at Daddy and said, "We could use him."

I went about my business while Daddy talked with Harvey a while and settled on a wage and hours he would work. He was going to be renting the little cabin behind the post office from Mr. Mitchell. Old man Mitchell, who had played the bagpipes that guided us to safety so long ago, had lived in it and had sadly passed on a couple of years ago.

Daddy gave Harvey a tour of our place, explainin' the work and everything that needed doin'. The biggest part of Harvey's work was going to be shovelin' out the chicken houses and haulin' it to the big compost heap for curin' before it was spread on the fields, then replacin' it with fresh sawdust. The work could keep one man busy pretty much all week, and it would take a big load off of me and Rachel, so we would be able to put our minds to hatchin' chicks and carin' for the hens.

***

May 30, 1944, Berkhamsted, England

Dearest Maggie Girl,

I've sure been enjoying your letters. They are filled with so many things that I miss. Your description of spring was just what my aching, homesick heart needed; I could see it all in my mind's eye. It will be summer soon, and you will have to describe that for me when the time comes. Spring here in Berkhamsted is very soggy, but I am enjoying it anyway. At least it is warmer.

Maggie, I can't say too much about it, as you know. But this will be the last letter I will be writing for a while. What I have been expecting will be taking place, and very soon. You understand? I cannot give any more details than that. Enclosed is the address where mail will find us. It will take longer to send and receive mail while on the front, but it will find us eventually. It feels like another goodbye, for I don't know what our future holds.

Like Stonewall Jackson, I do believe I am as safe wherever the war takes me as I am at home in Deep Gap, in my bed. But I know that pertains to the soul, not so much the body. I know that many of us will fall and not go back home. I'm trying to find that middle of the road with my thoughts. I think a man is not being honest if he claims he's not afraid at all. It's part of being human to fear the unknown, and this is certainly one of those "unknowns." Training can only take you so far, and all the practice and desensitizing of our psyche can only prepare you to a point. Some of the fellas don't seem to realize that we will not all survive this war. They act like they are going to a baseball game and will hit only home runs.

I hope I don't sound like I'm defeated before I've started. I don't feel defeated, but unknowing. Once we are there and actually in the fight, maybe some of this unsettling feeling will settle down. But will you pray for me, Maggie? I'm not wringing my hands in fear, but it's more of a feeling you get when you're trying to feel your way in the dark, blind and unseeing. If I know you are praying for me in this, it will mean so much.

I was promoted to Sergeant a couple of weeks ago. I've heard they are advancing men quickly out of need; so many have been lost, and there is a large number of troops moving into the fight. It's odd to my ears to hear myself called "Sarge." That makes me responsible for the squad, and I have a corporal and twelve men in my command. It's a heavy responsibility. My decisions and ability to act could mean life or death, not only for myself but also for the men under me. I can only imagine how the Brigadier General or Colonel of an entire brigade must feel. No wonder some generals seem to feel like a god.

We had the funniest thing happen the other day. Here in England, there are a lot of women who are farm workers. England is cut off from the rest of the world and isn't able to get the imported goods they did before the war. So, the entire country is basically enlisted into producing as much food as possible. A lot of these women are from London and some of the big cities, and they had never even seen a farm before, let alone worked on one. They're called Land Girls.

Anyway, a few of these Land Girls were moving a small herd of pigs from one farm to another. When passing the encampment we are living in, the pigs bolted and headed into our camp. They squealed and screamed until you couldn't hear anything else, and those poor girls were running behind them, screaming too. Some farm boy in the regiment grabbed a pail of scrap food from the kitchen and finally got the girls to see that the pigs could be led instead of driven. It was quite a ruckus.

I need to go; there's so much to do to get ready for what is coming. Remember, if you haven't heard from me for a while, don't worry too much. I'm told that sometimes it's a month or more before you can get word to family. I will write just as soon as I can. And if the worst happens, just remember that nothing can happen that the good Lord doesn't know about. This is not meant to scare you, just to tell you that if it does, I want you to move on in life. Don't spend years grieving and yearning for the past. God doesn't want His people to live in the past, but in the present and the future. Don't be glum. I'm just covering my bases in case, not expecting the worst but being prepared for it.

Until I see you again, I'll dream of bright copper hair around your beautiful face, and your sweet smile and playful jabs. I like your teasing. I heard someone say once that you only tease the ones you love, and I think that is true.

Until I see you again, I'll dream about the day you are my wife, and I can hold you in my arms and never have to say goodbye again. I dream of the day I can kiss you and know you are mine.

God be with you till we meet again;

Loving counsels guide, uphold you,

May the Shepherd's care enfold you;

God be with you till we meet again.

Till we meet, till we meet,

Till we meet at Jesus' feet.

Till we meet, till we meet,

God be with you till we meet again.

All my love, my sweet Maggie Girl,

Robbie

***

June 15, 1944, Deep Gap, North Carolina

Dearest Robie,

I received your letter today. We now know that you have been part of the big event you knew was coming. Daddy bought a radio so that we could keep up with what was happening. President Roosevelt addressed the nation on the evening of June 6th and announced that the Normandy Invasion was underway. We have been praying hard for all of our brave men in this fight. We also know that Jamie's 745th Tank Battalion was part of the invasion.

There has been no news of either of you since, so we are taking no news as good news.

My darling, it is all I can do sometimes to keep myself calm and not let my mind dwell on what could be happening to you. I'm sure by now you have been in combat, and I pray for you in all earnestness. I know from your letters that you have wondered if you could "do your duty," as you called it, to your country. I admire you, my love, that you are not eager to take life. God is the giver of life, and it's His job to decide when a life is over. But remember, even David in the Old Testament had to fight invading armies and protect his nation. I don't see this as any different. The United States was pulled into the war, and as a nation, we could not stand by and do nothing after the Japanese attacked our base at Pearl Harbor.

Like you, though knowing less of politics and such, I do not believe that our President deliberately provoked that attack just to get us into the war. I'm sure I know very little about what took place, but I don't think it was intentional on the President's part.

One of the things I ask the Lord for is that the things you endure and see in this war will not harden or change you. I love that part of you that is tender and not eager to kill your enemy. I am sure that the fellas who thought they were so eager for the fight probably feel differently by now. You just had the maturity and character to realize it from the beginning. I know you and Johnny and George went to see the film *Sergeant York* in the theater, just like Mamma, Daddy, Charlie, and I did. He felt much as you do, and when he sought the Lord for answers, the Lord pointed him to scripture to give him peace, and he was used in a great way to bring victory in battle.

I know so little about what is actually happening there in Normandy, and I don't even know if you all are still there. We know the Allied armies are moving across France toward Belgium, with the goal of taking down Adolf Hitler and the Nazi government. General Eisenhower reported that the invasion was carried out in good order, though we know that casualties were heavy. Reports are that the beaches were taken and the troops are advancing, but there is very little news about what is actually happening. I know that when you write, you probably will have little time to fill in all the blanks, but maybe you can give some details of your journey. Actually, keeping a journal might be a good idea and help you recall events later when this is over. I can send you a bound journal if you would like me to.

We have a new employee here at Deep Gap Egg and Poultry. His name is Harvey Murray, and he has been a Godsend! I didn't realize how overworked we all were before he came. I knew we worked too hard but didn't see how bad it was until some of that burden was lifted. He is a willing worker and has taken on all the work of cleaning out the chicken houses. He loves driving the tractors and treats his work like great fun. He has come up with a better system for cleaning out the chicken houses and shows signs of having a good mind for solving problems. He's jolly and pleasant to work with, and I am so grateful he's here. He was injured as a child and has a pretty bad limp, and because of that, he was classified as F-4, unfit for military service. It sure hasn't hindered his work around here though, and we are very grateful to have him. You will like his jolly nature, and I know you will get along with him like a house on fire.

We have begun another year of hatching chicks. In spite of the one setback last year, we did well hatching our own, and it was much cheaper than ordering the chicks. We are on the third batch, so currently we have around seven hundred and fifty so far. Daddy, Granddad, and Harvey are working on chicken house number four, and your Papa is over every other day or so with a new load of lumber. Daddy said he's soon going to be an expert on chicken houses; each one gets a little better with new ideas and improvements. This time they won't be going back and adding the lift sides for ventilation, but they will be built in as they go. I think the outbreak of last year might have been prevented had we been better ventilated.

Since Harvey's arrival, I have had a little more time to breathe. So, I climbed the old Indian Trail up to my spot a couple of days ago. It gave me a bit of time to relax and think of you, my love. I was remembering those long-ago days when we roamed these ridges and hills as children, and I had the thought that I can't wait to make new memories with you here in my favorite place in the world. One of the first things I'd like to do is come with you here as my sweetheart and make new memories. Read between the lines if you like! Childhood memories of you are sweet, but I am eager to know you as your wife and sweetheart.

I look at your photograph you sent me, and my heart skips a beat every time. I run my finger along your cheek and jawline and wish it were you and not paper I was touching. I love how it looks as though you are looking straight into my eyes when I sit holding your photograph. Every night before I turn out the light, I kiss your photograph and tell you goodnight.

So, goodnight, Sweetheart. I hope and pray you are well. I can't tell you how many times every day I bring you before our Lord in prayer and ask Him to send His angels to shelter you and protect you. So, if you hear the sound of wings, just know it's heavenly hosts sent to protect you.

All my very best love,

Your Maggie Girl

Chapter Twenty Seven

We held our breaths as we waited to hear from Robbie. Mamma Claire was a nervous wreck, which didn't help my own frazzled nerves. After the initial radio broadcast of President Roosevelt announcin' the invasion of Normandy, Mamma Claire came by to visit and stayed, helping Mamma and Granny Spencer with the farm's produce stand. She said that she couldn't bear to be at home by herself, with Papa Johnny workin' at the sawmill and tire shop all day. I hugged her up tight, and we cried together for a bit before wipin' our eyes and settin' to work.

The waitin' was so hard, but we figured if Robbie had been killed or wounded, we would surely get that dreaded telegram from the War Department. So far, there had just been the oppressive silence. I kept tellin' myself that it could take many weeks for his letter to find its way home, and it all depended on how soon after landing in Normandy he could even write.

So, we filled our time with the usual business, mingled with many whispered prayers throughout the long days. There were nights when I jerked out of a deep sleep, with Robbie heavy on my mind, so I would lie awake sometimes, praying and asking the Lord for His protection to envelop my Robbie and keep him safe.

It was nearly the end of July, and I was startin' to ravel at the seams, so to speak. I became jumpy, and had a hard time keepin' my mind on my work, and began droppin' things. Rachel was helpin' me in the equipment room one day, and we were cleanin' and sanitizin' all the hens' feeders and waterin' tanks, when I dropped the same feeder for the third time. When I dropped it that third time, I just stopped, dropped my head, and began sobbin' helplessly. My hands were shakin' so badly I just couldn't hang on to the feeder.

My friend didn't say a word, but dried her hands and came over to where I stood crying. She wrapped her arms around me and just held me until I had cried myself out. I cried for some time before I was spent and finally could get a hold of myself. I pulled a hankie out of my coverall pocket and blew my nose hard.

"Okay?" was all she said.

I nodded my head but kept it down. I didn't often break down like that.

"You're entitled to a cry, Maggie," Rachel said comfortingly. "You've been keepin' your chin up and puttin' on a brave face, but it's okay to cry sometimes. You're worried about Robbie?"

Again, I just nodded.

"Well, you're bound to hear something soon. If the invasion was the first week of June, I'm sure a letter is en route, and you'll hear from him soon."

We finished up our work, and the cry had helped release some of the tension that had been buildin' up in me. And sure enough, a letter finally came on July 29th. I grabbed it and ran to my room, wanting to read it in private before reading it to my family. I tore open the envelope and began to read:

July 20, 1944, Saint-Lô, France

My Dearest Maggie,

I am writing to you from our position just outside Saint-Lô following our victory yesterday. We were not part of the initial June 6th invasion, but were held back for a second assault on Omaha Beach on June 11th. We landed on an already battle-scarred beach and were facing strong German defenses, despite the initial assault five days prior to our landing. We encountered heavy fire from the Germans' already fortified positions, and behind obstacles on the shore and the high bluffs overlooking the beach. We had our work cut out to secure the beachhead and the Vire-et-Taute Canal, and we had to get a foothold so advancement was possible.

We were part of the Allied offensive codenamed Operation Cobra, which was to free the town of Saint-Lô from German occupation. We were fighting inch by inch, it seemed, and much of the fighting was among the hedgerows and fields around the town before we were finally able to take it. The Germans had the advantage of being dug in with trenches and embankments among the thorny hedgerows, and they were nearly impossible to take.

Our bombers had bombed the town of Saint-Lô heavily on June 6th and 7th, which pretty much destroyed the city, but the Germans were entrenched around the town and had a fortified position. After a week of heavy fighting, we finally captured Saint-Lô yesterday. Today we are taking a breather but remain on high alert. Maggie, we lost a lot of men in this past week of fighting. One of them, our commander, Captain Friday, was wounded, and Lieutenant Sullivan assumed command of Company B.

The things I've seen will never leave me. When we landed on Omaha Beach on June 11th, the beaches were littered with the debris of war. Exploded military vehicles and landing crafts that had been shelled and disabled, and there were still many bodies strewn about the beach and inland.

I don't have much time, but I wanted to give you an account of what we have done so far. Johnny and George are also okay. I think George was having a rough time at first, but he seems to be doing better now; at least he's come to terms with what we are facing.

I love you, Maggie. Especially now, with us in the thick of things, I yearn to see you and hold you tight. You have become my lifeline. When we have a bit of quiet at night, and I have thanked the good Lord for His presence around us, I turn my thoughts to you and imagine I am holding you once again.

Forgive me that this isn't as long as my letters usually are, but it's getting too dark to see, and we need to get rest while we can. I'm sure we will be moving eastward soon, as we move toward Germany. I will write more when I can.

All my love,

Robbie

***

He was safe. I could read between the lines that he had seen more than his words let on, but he was not wounded, and he was alive. Furthermore, so were George and Johnny.

"Thank you, Lord," I breathed this prayer over and over. Tears of thankfulness seepin' out of my eyes and runnin' down my cheeks. That evenin' I read my letter to Mamma, Daddy and Charlie; all except a line or two.

July 30, 1944, Deep Gap, North Carolina

My Dearest Robbie,

You cannot know the joy and relief your letter brought to us all. I have to admit that I had begun to fear and had allowed worry to creep in and torment me. Thank God you are safe, and George and Johnny too.

I climbed the old Indian Trail again to write you from my spot. It's the end of July, so summer is at its peak and has been very warm. The sky is a deep blue today and is filled with large, fluffy clouds that are traveling slowly across the sky, casting shadows on the valley below me. It's peaceful, and I can hear crickets and cicadas chirping in the grass behind me and in the trees above me. Once in a while, the breeze blows and cools me, making it pleasant. I can see birds dipping and soaring in the spaces both above and below me, and they are singing and calling to each other as they fly. I believe the large bird I see soaring high in the distance is an eagle, though it's too high to really tell.

I know that you are enduring things that you or I never thought you would go through. I pray for you constantly that our Lord will give you strength and protection, to help you command and care for your men as He would have you do. If many prayers can keep you safe, you will be wrapped in feathers!

I often think of Granddad's prayer when we were scared and huddled in our living room during the Great Flood of 1940. When the danger was over, he quoted this Scripture: *Psalms 91:4 He shall cover thee with his feathers, and under his wings shalt thou trust: his truth shall be thy shield and buckler.* My darling, I pray every day that He will cover you with His feathery wings of mercy and protection.

Aunt Eunice and Uncle James heard from Jamie; he too is safe and well. I don't have much news, but apparently, the 745th Tank Battalion was part of the June 6th Normandy invasion. They had to wait until early the next morning, the 7th, before they could land because the engineers were detonating mines and clearing routes for the troops. I'll give you updates as I can.

Gerry is with the 3rd Infantry Division in Italy. In early June, the division was involved in the advance on Rome, which was liberated by Allied forces on June 4th. He said they were preparing for something else but, of course, was not able to give details about that in his letter. But he sounded well. Gerry has dreamed of being a soldier since he was a little fella. I have no doubt he is a good one.

I am grateful for the comfort I have in being close to the Lord now. Before I gave my heart over to the Lord at the camp meeting, I was pretty much a Sunday morning Christian. It wasn't that I didn't believe in the Lord, but He was more or less my last resort if I ran into something I couldn't handle. Now, I find myself chatting with Him in a running conversation throughout the day. If I'm about to start something, I'll say something like, "Lord, how should I do this?" and the answer always comes. It's a marvel to me that the Lord of Heaven will walk so close to His children here on earth and cares about everyday things.

When I start fretting and worrying, I quote *Psalm 56:3-4*: *What time I am afraid, I will trust in thee. In God I will praise his word, in God I have put my trust.* God's Word brings me peace in the midst of this storm.

Mamma, Daddy, and Charlie have all asked me to say hello for them and give you their love. They are praying for you too. Yes, Daddy too! He has given his heart over to the Lord, and while he was always a good man, there's something changed about him. He has always been a good daddy and husband, but now he is so tender, especially toward Mamma. And in the night after going to bed, I can sometimes hear him as he prays. It's one of the most comforting things I've ever heard, listening to my Daddy in prayer.

It's getting toward late afternoon, and the sun will start setting soon. I've watched it so many times I can tell you what it will look like. As the sun sets to the west, the skies above the western slopes east of me will catch the orangey hues of the setting sun, and the mountains will fade into the distance row upon row, in lightening shades of blue, then purple in the farthest distance. Evening birds will begin to sing, and then as night falls, the whippoorwills and bobwhites will start calling.

So, I need to wrap up this letter and be on my way. It will take me a good thirty minutes to get home. Remember, I love you so much. I long for the day when there will be no need to agonize and fret, waiting for letters to arrive and fears set to rest. When I can reach out and touch your face and hold you in my arms whenever I please. I pray the war ends soon and you are released to come back home to those who love you best.

Take very good care of yourself, my love.

Forever yours,

Maggie

***

August was a swelterin' hot month, and everyone, includin' the chickens, suffered with the heat. It's a good thing we had made the changes to the chicken houses, because if we hadn't improved the ventilation, I don't think the hens would have survived it. Seems like there's very little middle of the road when it comes to weather. As it was, the heat had caused a fall in the hens' egg production, and we were going to have a hard time fillin' our contract with the military if it didn't let up soon.

On August 18th, we were goin' about our lives as usual, and it was a Friday, so Daddy had taken the delivery of eggs to Fort Butner. Mamma and Granny were cannin' green beans and tomatoes in our kitchen. Granddad and Harvey were in the chicken houses removin' the dirty sawdust, and Rachel and I were tendin' chicks in the broodin' nursery. Everyone was about their work. I stepped out into the drive just in time to see a vehicle and driver pull in that I didn't recognize. Probably somebody from Boone wantin' to buy fresh eggs; we got quite a bit of that.

I started to walk toward them when Mamma stepped out on the porch, dryin' her wet hands on her apron. She saw that I was already headed toward the stranger and nodded for me to carry on. When I reached him, I saw he looked uneasy, as though he didn't quite know what to do. So, I smiled to set him at ease and said, "Howdy!"

"Howdy," the strange man said uneasily. "Are you the lady of the house?"

"I'm the daughter of the house," I said, still smilin', "What can I help you with?"

"I'm with Western Union, Ma'am. I have a telegram for Edward Spencer," the man said gravely.

I came to a halt and froze. I just stood starin' at the man, unable to move.

"Is Edward Spencer about?" the man asked.

I was rooted in one place and felt like somethin' held me there, and I couldn't respond.

Mamma stood on the porch, and with eyes that looked like saucers she said, "I am Mrs. Edward Spencer. Ed... Edward is away for the day."

"If you are Mrs. Edward Spencer, I am authorized to leave this telegram with you, Ma'am, if that is okay." He had turned toward Mamma and began walkin' her way, and she met him at the bottom of the stairs.

The Western Union man handed Mamma the envelope and said, "I'm very sorry, Ma'am," then got back in his truck and left.

It wasn't until he had pulled out of the driveway that I was able to move, and I did so in a rush, running up the steps to Mamma, who had turned white as a piece of paper as she stood holdin' that envelope. We knew it was not a good telegram, but we didn't know if it meant that Gerry had been wounded or killed.

"Should we open it or save it till Daddy gets home?" I asked through stiff lips that felt like they were stretched over my teeth.

Mamma just stood there runnin' a hand back and forth across the envelope and starin at it. "I don't know," she said faintly.

I hollered for Granny, who came out onto the porch right away.

"We have a telegram for Daddy. Would you stay here on the porch with Mamma while I go get Granddad?"

"Of course, sugar, run get Granddad," said Granny as she led Mamma to a rockin' chair and set her in it.

I jumped off the porch and took off runnin' for the chicken houses as hard as I could go. When I burst through the doorway, Rachel looked up with a question, saw the look on my face, and knew something was serious. Something was badly wrong.

"Granddad! I need Granddad!" I was panting from the run.

Rachel pointed and said, "Chicken house three, I think, Maggie." Rachel knew when not to waste words.

I found Granddad, who was herdin' chickens into one end of the chicken house so Harvey could clean the other end. He looked up when he saw me runnin' toward him and knew right away something was wrong. He latched the gate we used as a temporary holdin' pen for the hens and turned back toward me.

"What's wrong, Maggie?" Granddad said lookin' apprehensive.

"A man from Western Union just delivered a telegram," I gasped, winded from the run. "It's addressed to Daddy, and since he's not here, we didn't know what to do."

Granddad looked at me for a minute, then put an arm around me and said, "Let's go together. We'll discuss it."

Granddad and I walked back to the house after I stopped to let Rachel know what had happened. "I'll be prayin'," she whispered.

We climbed the porch steps and all sat for a moment. Nobody said a word for a few heartbeats. Then Granddad said, "What does everyone feel they want to do? Dottie, it's really your call. You are Ed's wife, and in the event that the husband isn't present, the wife can legally open the telegram."

"I don't know," Mamma said softly. "I can't think," she said.

Granddad looked at me with a question in his eyes, so I said, "Daddy isn't going to be home for hours yet. I think not knowin'..."

Granddad and Granny both nodded. "Dorothy?" Granddad said her name as a question, prompting her gently to make the call either way.

Mamma nodded, but her eyes looked scared as she handed Granddad the envelope and said, "Will you read it, Alistaire? I... I... can't."

Granddad took it from Mamma gently, patted her hand, and said quietly, "Yes, I will, honey."

I slid my chair over next to Mamma's rockin' chair and took her cold hand in mine, and we sat graspin each other's hands as Granddad slit the envelope with his pocketknife, took out the single piece of paper, and looked it over briefly. Without lookin' up or givin' anything away in his eyes, he began to read.

The Secretary of War desires me to express his deepest regret that your son, Sergeant Gerry Spencer, was killed in action on the fifteenth of August in France, in the performance of his duty to his country. The Army Council desires to offer you their sincere sympathy.

***

The shock of the telegram never went away. My poor Mamma lived with it for the rest of her life. Gerry, her red-headed charmer, so like Daddy that it had been as though he'd been copied.

Daddy held Mamma in his arms while she cried that whole first night after we received news of Gerry's death. Charlie was near inconsolable, and we held each other as we both cried. Charlie was fourteen now, no longer the little chubby-faced baby, but broken-hearted at the loss of the older brother he looked up to.

Our wonderful Deep Gap community family, friends, and neighbors circled us in their neighborly love and made sure Mamma didn't have to lift a finger for days as she tried to cope with losin' her firstborn son. Uncle James and Aunt Eunice shouldered much of the work besides their own. Uncle James and Daddy, bein' brothers, had always been close. Now it was almost as though their grief bound them even closer. And Aunt Eunice was there for Mamma. She had always been one of Mamma's dearest friends as well as her sister-in-law. Johnny and Claire were at the house daily, and as men are wont to be, Daddy and Johnny didn't talk a lot, but Johnny was there for Daddy all the same.

Claire often paused in all the flurry of work, visitors, and all, to give me little touches and brief hugs. I could tell her mind was travelin' down the same rutted path mine had been spinnin' in... It could have been Robbie. Could still be Robbie.

And my dear friend Rachel worked longer than normal hours and even enlisted the help of some of our friends in the community so that I could be with Mamma, Daddy, and Charlie and grieve with them. Then there was Harvey. The good Lord had sent us an angel in overalls and boots, who shouldered more work than he normally did and took on Daddy's deliveries over the next month to give Daddy time.

Mamma and Daddy received a letter on fancy paper about a month later from Gerry's commanding officer.

September 21, 1944

To the Next of Kin of Sergeant Gerry Spencer

Dear Sir or Madam,

It is with the deepest regret and sorrow that I must inform you of the death of your son, Sergeant Gerry Spencer, serial number 20472893, of the 3rd Infantry, who was killed in action on the 15th of August, 1944.

His death occurred during fierce fighting as the 3rd Infantry Division advanced through the Rhone Valley and into the region of southern France.

Please accept my heartfelt condolences and deepest sympathies for your tragic loss. We are deeply grateful for Sergeant Spencer's courageous service and sacrifice to our country.

You are not alone in your grief. We are thinking of you and all those who loved him during this time of loss and bereavement.

Sincerely,

Major General John W. O'Daniel

Chapter Twenty Eight

The next few months are hard to recall with clarity. We were ravaged by grief for our Gerry. Death is one of those things that you know comes to all men at some time, but it is harder to accept in one who was only nineteen years old. A body that has lived a full life, or an old person plagued with sickness passin' on, is much easier to be at peace with. But when war takes a young man so full of life and the joy of it, it takes a heap of the grace of God to live with it.

Sometimes I would be goin' along with my day when suddenly, out of nowhere, a memory of Gerry's laughin' face would jar me and bring fresh tears and waves of sorrow. Mamma too would often have days when she could hardly bring herself to get out of bed. Daddy didn't say a whole lot, but the sorrow in his eyes was hard to look into sometimes. When he would get that faraway look, I knew he was thinkin' of his boy and rememberin'.

Charlie would hole up in his room across the upstairs landing from my bedroom and sometimes would bolt his door, not wanting anyone to see him cry. During one of these times, he told Daddy that a fourteen-year-old was too old to be a cryin'. And Daddy had taken

Charlie in his arms and said, "The Lord cried too, Charlie. Standin' before the tomb of His beloved friend Lazarus. He knew that He would call Lazarus from the tomb, but His flesh was human, just like yours, and He was grief-stricken by the death of His friend. Tears are the washcloth God uses to wash the hurt, anger, and bitterness from us. It's cleansin' to cry son."

***

Word from Robbie was scarce. I had only had the one letter from him, and he had written to Claire and Johnny not long after. Since then, there had been nothing. We heard the news comin' out of Europe and knew the fightin' was fierce. Everyone was on edge, and worry had become a part of our lives.

The Bible says, *Cast all your cares on Him, for He cares for you*; and I was doing my best to cast my worry off to the Lord. Many times a day, I called Robbie's name in prayer, and Jamie's too. Sometimes, when I was prayin', a thought would knock at the back of my mind, *You prayed for Gerry too.* And it was a battle to keep fear from takin' over and getting the better of me. I was fightin' my own war with fear.

I began writin' down scripture verses and posting them in every area of our house and workplaces to help us all fight the fear and worry.

Isaiah 41:10 — Fear thou not; for I am with thee: be not dismayed; for I am thy God: I will strengthen thee; yea, I will help thee; yea, I will uphold thee with the right hand of my righteousness.

First Peter 5:7 — Casting all your care upon Him; for He careth for you.

Psalm 56:3 — What time I am afraid, I will trust in thee.

And my favorite, *Philippians 4:6–7 — Be careful for nothing; but in everything by prayer and supplication, with thanksgiving, let your requests be made known unto God. And the peace of God, which passeth all understanding, shall keep your hearts and minds through Christ Jesus.*

Mid-October, a letter finally came. Mamma hollered from the porch for me to come quick, and thinkin' something was wrong, I ran as hard as I could. As I came closer, I saw she was smilin' and wavin' an envelope in her hand. I snatched it and collapsed into the closest rockin' chair, tearing the envelope open as I did.

September 30, 1944, Holland

My Dearest Maggie,

I am so sorry that I have not been able to write before now. It has been difficult, but I know you understand. Right now, I am writing you from our position in the Netherlands. I cannot tell you where we are going but am able to tell you where we have been.

First, let me assure you that I am doing well. We are all tired but holding up well in spite of the many engagements we have been in. When we left Omaha Beach, we headed south, then east across France, being engaged June 15th through July 7th in the assault on the Vire-et-Taute Canal, where we lost nearly three hundred men. From there, we headed south, and we didn't see as much fighting for a few days, which was a blessed relief.

When I wrote you last, we had taken the town of Saint-Lô, France, from German control, in a battle that lasted from July 25th to the 30th. On the 24th, the 120th suffered heavy losses from what is called friendly fire. Because of poor visibility, many of the bombers targeted friendly troops. Then it happened again a couple of days later. It's surprising how many are lost to friendly fire. We had a hard time taking Saint-Lô; the Germans, with their Panzers, really put up a hard fight. I heard Jamie's 745th Tank Battalion had a part in the taking of Saint-Lô, but I never saw him.

On the morning of August 1st, Company B was given the job of liberating the town of Tessy-sur-Vire. A German Panzer division held the high ground, and it was a mean fight, but we were successful, and that's what counts. A week later, the Germans launched an SS Panzer division against the 120th Regiment that had just taken up residence in Mortain. The Battle for Mortain lasted a week, from August 7th to 12th, and was a bloody business. Between the dead, wounded, and missing, there were over 1,800 casualties. It would take too long to tell you about the heroism I witnessed, Maggie. That will be something for me to tell you all when I get home.

We got a bit of rest after that, and you would not believe who came out to the front lines and gave a performance for the men.

Dinah Shore sang in a USO show from a wagon that had been rigged up as a stage. They had pulled it in front of a chateau, and the men whooped and clapped. She sure had some guts to travel to the front lines just to cheer us fellas up. And she's a Tennessee girl to boot!

After that, we crossed the Seine River, about twenty-five miles west of Paris, and bypassed that city altogether. Some of the fellas had hoped to see Paris, but we angled north of it. The Germans had superior positions from ridges that were on opposite banks of the Seine, giving them optimal observation points. It took two days of fighting to make a clear breakthrough of the enemy position, and by the 30th of August, the First Battalion, along with the rest of the regiment, was moving just about as fast as their legs would carry them.

There was a shortage of trucks, and they had a hard time keeping enough gasoline coming through the supply line. My 117th Regiment stayed behind due to the shortage of trucks, then had to travel 128 miles in one day to catch up to our advancing army. Our advancement has been hindered since because they just cannot keep enough gasoline coming up the supply line.

On September 8th, the regiment began hiking and marched 27 miles the first day, 22 miles the second day, and 15 miles the third, then wound up pitching camp near St. Simeon, Belgium. We then spent a day nursing our feet, which were not in good shape after hiking 64 miles in three days, loaded down with our gear.

On September 12th, we crossed the Albert Canal and the Meuse River just south of Visé, Belgium, then moved north toward Holland. Very little resistance was received until we reached the Holland border. Here, the Germans had set up a defense. We were able to overcome their opposition, and the city of Maastricht was liberated. After a few days of light fighting, we entered Heerlen, where we were welcomed in a very stoic manner. The Hollanders lined the streets and waved gravely at us. We were accustomed to the hysterical joy of the French and the enthusiastic welcoming of the Belgians. As it turned out, the serious Hollanders were as happy as anyone to see us but just weren't as emotional as the French and Belgians.

We have been in reserve for a few days and are encamped along the Wurm River. The rest is very welcome. I know we will be pushing forward, but do not know what our next move will be. It has been so much more intense than I even imagined, but I keep going, knowing I am being held up in prayer by all my loved ones back home. There have been times when I didn't think I was going to survive the day, but God has seen fit to bring me through it so far.

I am hoping it won't be so long before I am able to write again. It's been a hard push across France, Belgium, and Holland, and I'm sure Germany won't be any easier, probably harder. But I know you will continue to pray for us, and that keeps me going.

Hey, a spark of good news… I was told that Jamie's 745th Tank Battalion is heading in the same direction we are. Since I know that, it might be easier to locate him. Even if it's just for a few minutes, it sure would be nice to see him.

George and Johnny are both doing fine, and Johnny has turned out to be a renowned sniper in our regiment. George is a steady and dependable soldier, and I can't imagine having anyone else by my side. If George has my back, I'm not worried. Tell Mamma Dottie that her famous bug salve has been appreciated even here in Europe. The mosquitoes, black flies, and midges here in Holland have been ferocious.

My sweet girl, you cannot begin to know how much I long to see you. On nights like tonight, I'm writing by the light of a campfire, and many men around me are doing the same. You've never seen so many young men with tired faces, looking at pictures of wives and sweethearts. Many times, we show off the photographs to one another, just so someone can see what we'll be going home to.

I have no idea how long this war will go on. Sometimes we seem to be making fast progress and gaining ground rapidly. Then something happens, supply lines get interrupted, or bad weather slows us down. But I'm praying that the Allied Forces can bring this to an end as soon as possible. I miss my sweetheart and want to come home.

I can't wait to see your sweet smile and flaming red copper hair. I can't wait to hold you tight, and I don't think I'll be able to let you go but just hold you forever. For now, I'll just shut my eyes, tune out everything else, and imagine you.

All my love,

Robbie

***

I was overcome with relief. I knew from the news we had heard over the radio and in the newspapers that Robbie had downplayed the extent of the horrors he had seen. The radio had reported that the Battle for Mortain had lasted seven days, and at one point the First Battalion had been under continuous, murderous shelling for more than fifteen hours.

October 1, 1944 Deep Gap, North Carolina

Dear Robbie,

I was overcome with tears of joy when I received your letter. My darling, I have been thanking God continuously since it came. I'm so sorry for all the hardships you are going through and for the horrors I can only try to imagine that you have seen. I pray our merciful Lord protects your mind as well as your body.

I can only guess, since there was no mention of the news in your letter, that you did not receive my short letter last month with the terrible news of Gerry's death. He was killed in action in Northern France on August 15. We are, of course, devastated, and it does not seem to be real, as though the terrible telegram was part of a really bad dream. I'm sure that losing Gerry will feel much more real when everyone else comes home and he does not. How many young men will have to die, on both sides, of this terrible war before evil men are stopped? I am sure there are many German mothers and sweethearts who mourn the loss of their boys just as much as we do. I pray this comes to an end soon.

Whatever makes men like Adolf Hitler desire to grab power and take hold of other countries? And why did it take the leaders of Europe so long to actually stand up to him? It seems like a war of this magnitude could have been avoided had the bully been put in his place much sooner.

The hardships being faced here on the home front are nothing compared to what you boys at the front lines of this war are enduring, but for the sake of news, here's what is going on at home. Rationing is still the number one thing that makes life hard, especially for city folks. Here on the farm, of course, the only thing that really affects us is the gasoline, tires, and automobile rationing. Sugar is rationed, but since we make our own cane sugar, we don't notice it like others do. And there's always Daddy's honey. Meat is rationed at twenty-eight ounces per person a week, and cheese is four ounces. Thankfully, we raise our own meat and have all the eggs we could ever use.

Tillie and Harry were married the end of August, and I can't believe I am saying this, but she was a radiant bride. It gave me hope that maybe she actually cares for him. For his sake, I sure hope so. Mamma and I gave them a nice set of embroidered table linens that we had made. She thanked us and acted as though she liked them. She is living in Raleigh now, and we aren't likely to see much of them here in Deep Gap.

Rachel has told me she looks forward to George's letters and has relayed some of the same information you did. I'm not sure, but it seems like there's a bit more there than meets the eye. She does talk quite a bit about George and his letters.

Your Papa's tire recapping shop has been a good business for him. It keeps him much busier than just the sawmill. I've seen his parking lot filled with men dropping off and picking up tires on a Saturday. Your Ma comes and spends a lot of time here at Spencer Farm; she just can't stand being alone all day, every day. With Janet living away, she gets very lonely. She says she's able to keep a lid on her worry if she's with us a few days a week. Mamma welcomes her company; it's good for her since we lost Gerry. I worried about Mamma right after we got word of it. She just didn't have any life in her, and I was afraid she would just rather die. She still grieves, as we all do, but at least she is taking part in things and household chores now. At first, she could hardly get out of bed. So having Claire here has been a real blessing.

When you get home, you will not recognize Spencer Farm. I have to confess, I miss the smaller place that was nothing more than a farm and produce stand. Deep Gap Egg and Poultry has grown and now includes four chicken houses. I think this is the size it is likely to remain for a while. Any larger, and it will require more employees, and with the war on, I can't see us getting another Harvey to come walking out of the woods.

Granddad Spencer has had an idea, and he wants me to see what you think of it. Granddad wants to build a small one-bedroom cabin near Mamma and Daddy and let you and me have their house. It is the original homestead on the farm and a little smaller than Mamma and Daddy's farmhouse, but if we need to, we can build onto it in the future. I think it's a good idea but wanted to see if you would be in agreement. We wouldn't be booting Granny and Granddad out. Granny said she would welcome having less house to clean. They will begin building it as soon as we hear from you if you agree.

Normally, this time of year, the community would be bustling with harvest parties and dances, but with the war on, there haven't been any parties. I am sure we will have the party of all parties when you return home. Knowing Granddad, it will be a huge shindig.

I miss you so badly; at times it is a physical ache in my chest. You have been away from us going on three years now. Part of me knows that this war had to be fought, more so than the Great War or any war before it. But knowing that does nothing for my missing you. Knowing that won't bring Gerry back, nor any of the other young men and women who will never return home. I wish it were over, that you were on your way home, and we were planning our future lives together. I want to climb the old Indian Trail with you once again, but this time as your sweetheart. I want to look out over our mountains with you by my side instead of in my heart and mind's eye, sit on the ledge that juts out over the valley, hold your hand, and talk of our future. And kiss your lips.

I saw a bit of a poem quoted in the newspaper and thought it was so fitting for us. For our lips have never met, but through our correspondence, I feel our souls, already bound by friendship, have blended into one soul.

Sir, more than kisses, letters mingle souls,

For thus, friends absent speak. This ease controls

The tediousness of my life; but for these.

Goodnight for now, my darling. May the Lord bless you and keep you safe, hidden under His great wings.

All my love,

Maggie

Chapter Twenty Nine

Radio reports of another big military move into Germany were alarmin' to say the least. We didn't hear anything from any of our fellas for a time, and the only news we had was from the radio and newspapers. We knew that Robbie's Infantry Division and Jamie's Tank Battalion were both involved in the assault on Germany's Siegfried Line and were attempting to take a city called Aachen on the border of Germany and Belgium.

All through October, reports of heavy fighting came through, and no one had any word from our local boys. The beginning of November had come when Claire came over one day, as she often did, with a happy smile all over her face. She had received a very short letter from Robbie and had brought it to share with us. Claire handed it to me to read aloud to everyone there.

October 15, 1944, Alsdorf, Germany

Dear Ma and Papa,

This will be a short note because I don't have much time, but I wanted to let everyone know that I am safe. The fighting has been brutal and heavy as we are attempting to advance into Germany. We expected resistance to be stronger once we crossed over into Germany, and we weren't wrong. Tell everyone I love them and am unharmed, though very tired. Johnny Bailey and George send their love as well. If you will, let their folks know they are safe. Give my Maggie my love.

Love always,

Robbie

It wasn't much, but it was a relief to know that as of the time Robbie had written it, he was alive and well. It was enough to give a boost to my spirit, which had been feelin' downcast. Life had taken on a monotony, each day like the one before it. The only break in our work routine was church on Sunday, and it was like pourin' rain on a sun-parched flower. I soaked up the singing and comin' together with our neighbors to worship in one accord, as the Good Book instructed us to do.

It was one of the few things that brought a measure of peace and calm during the stress and anxiety of that fall and winter. So much was happenin' with the war, both in the European and the Pacific fronts.

I received a brief note from Robbie, informing me that he was well, a few weeks after Claire had received her message. It was pretty much the same, along with post-scripted hugs and kisses. But finally, in the second week of December, I received a nice long letter givin' an account of his division's advancement through Germany.

November 23, 1944, Near Aachen, Germany

Dearest Maggie Girl,

We have been pulled back to a rear position near Aachen for a much-needed rest. We arrived last night, and it felt strange to try to sleep without the sounds of war around me. In fact, it was hard to go to sleep. I guess the mind grows accustomed to being on high alert, and when you are taken out of danger, your mind has a difficult time adjusting to it.

I enjoyed your letter and have read it so many times, with your photograph propped up in front of me, that I think I could recite it word for word. Your letters are my tie to sanity!

Maggie, I felt like someone had hit me right between the eyes with a ball bat when I read your news of Gerry. I did not get your previous letter telling me of it. I am so sorry, my love. How I wish I could be there for you, hold you in my arms, and comfort you as best I could. Gerry was a fine young man, and from all accounts, a good soldier to have been advanced so quickly to sergeant. I know there are no words that can make it better, but I have prayed earnestly for you and your family since I received your letter. Tell Mamma Dottie I am praying for her, as I know she would pray for my Ma if something happened to me. Nothing but the Lord and time will ease the grief and make it easier to bear. It is hard to imagine Deep Gap without his happy-go-lucky spirit and his pranking ways.

You were talking about how you wanted this war to end and how there must be many German mothers and sweethearts who feel the same. George and I were speaking with a German prisoner we had taken captive a few weeks ago. He was sixteen years old, hardly more than a boy was a boy, really. He was glad to be taken captive, hadn't wanted to fight in the war to begin with, but had no choice, and said all boys were required to join the Hitler Youth at ten years old. He said his mother had already sacrificed three sons to Hitler, and he was her last son. We may have saved his life by taking him captive.

Maggie girl, I will happily live anywhere you want to when we are married. That said, we haven't talked about when we would marry. Since we don't know when the war will end, can I just say, I want to marry you the second I step off the ship. Knowing that isn't happening, can I ask if we can be married very soon after I am released to come home? I don't want to waste time, and I don't think I'll be able to bear parting from you once I am home.

But yes, I am happy to live in the old Spencer homeplace. I think it will suit us fine, and like you said, if need be, we can always add on space. I have spent very little of my pay since being in the army.

I have had the Paymaster deposit my pay into a fund that will be available when I request it. I should have a few thousand dollars by the time I'm home. If you would like, we could make some improvements to the old house maybe give you a new kitchen?

Yes, George is besotted with Rachel. I haven't mentioned it because I didn't want to make him sound odd, being he has never met her in person. But they have seemed to open their hearts and souls to each other. I think a real romance could come of it.

Since I last wrote you, we advanced into Germany, and the fighting has been very fierce. As we expected, German resistance has been much greater. Our division spearheaded the assault against the Siegfried Line and concentrated on taking out the German pillboxes along the Wurm River. On October 2, we secured the towns of Pallenberg and Ubach, in spite of heavy German resistance and counterattacks. The Division was part of the forces that encircled and finally took the city of Aachen, and on October 31, the last German garrison in Aachen surrendered. Our division suffered about three thousand casualties during the campaign. October was a long, hard month. We had a two-week rest, and it was the first long period in which the outfit was out of any contact with the enemy.

Since November 16, we have been involved in a heavy campaign to push through German lines. Our division has now been pulled back near Aachen to rest. They are saying for a month. As heavy as the fighting has been, I have a hard time believing we will have a month of rest, but time will tell. Still, we are grateful for the time we have. I plan to, first of all, get a bath, then sleep as much as possible.

I loved the lines of the poem. The poet must have known what it was like to completely meld with another soul through the writing of letters. I read yours over and over, and they comfort me and tie me to home like nothing else. But they also make me long for the day when I can hold you and kiss you, my darling. I guess it's okay for me to say it. I look at your photograph and sometimes place a kiss on your paper lips as I am laying down to sleep.

If we are here as long as they say, I will send another letter before we are sent out again. Take very good care of yourself, and may the Lord be with you.

All my love,

Robbie

***

We were preparin' for another Christmas that was hard to feel excited about. We were all just ploddin' through the motions of livin', but trying to be as cheerful as we could. Thanksgiving dinner had been a slightly scaled-down version of our normal bountiful table. Turkeys were hard to come by, and that was one bird we didn't produce on the farm.

Granny had been the one to rouse us from our rut and said we were going to have a big Thanksgiving feast, whether it was turkey or something else. That something else was chicken, since it was what was readily available to us and abundant. Granny had butchered five hens and treated them as though they were turkey, stuffing them full of her famous cornbread dressing. While the majority of the nation had shortages of food items like butter and sugar, we had no such shortage.

Our big sideboard was as loaded as ever with other dishes from our usual Thanksgiving fare. Candied sweet potatoes were one of the favorites of nearly everyone and were sittin' beside bowls of green beans seasoned with bacon, creamy mashed potatoes, mixed greens also seasoned with bacon, and the beautiful cut-glass bowl of cranberry sauce. As always, there was a mountain of homemade yeast rolls, straight out of the oven and still warm. Abigail's calf, also called Abigale still produced an abundance of creamy, rich milk, from which we churned butter every week. So, while the poor folks livin' in our nation's cities were doin' without, we had an overabundance of it.

The usual pies were also part of our feast. This year we had apple, pumpkin, and pecan pies. Around our table this year were our family, Granny and Granddad, Mamma, Daddy, Charlie, and me; Uncle James and Aunt Eunice and their twin girls, Maude and Lily; Johnny and Claire Bruce, and Rachel and her parents, Mr. and Mrs. Potts. We had made sure that Harvey knew he was included, but he said he had plans to be elsewhere. I could have sworn Harvey was blushin' when he said it and wouldn't meet Daddy's eye. Somethin' was odd about that, because Harvey loved to eat and had enjoyed many meals with us.

So, we were plannin' on pretty much the same meal for Christmas, but would serve up one of Granddad's flavorful smoked hams instead of chicken. I dearly love ham, and I was lookin' forward to Christmas dinner. We had also decided as a family that there would be no store-bought gifts for our family gift giving. Everything must be handmade by the giver. We had drawn names amongst our family since it would be mighty difficult to handmake nine separate gifts for each family member. I had drawn Lily's name. The twin girls were now eighteen years old, and we had grown very close over the last couple of years. They often joined Rachel and me in our girl talk and just hangin' out with us on Sunday afternoons.

The two girls couldn't have been more different from each other if they had been born years apart. Maude was a talkative, boisterous girl who was always teasin' someone, and Lily was quiet and shy and had to be pulled into a conversation. But both girls were much more girly than I had been growin' up, and I had settled on makin' Lily a handbag from a heavy, natural-colored canvas material Mamma had among her fabric stash. I made a shoulder bag with a snap closure at the top, and since I was a fair hand at paintin' flowers and such, I painted a small portion of a wildflower meadow on the front side of the bag. It turned out to be very pretty.

Mamma and I had also decided to make a batch of scented soap, just to give all the women a small gift of a bar of lavender soap.

Makin' this year's Christmas gifts had boosted our spirits. Everyone was secretive and busy on the side with whatever it was they were making, and it added a much-needed holiday feelin' to our house. A few days before Christmas, Mamma and I went into the woods to cut greenery to hang around the doors and windows and to bedeck the fireplace mantel. We cut loads of different varieties of evergreen boughs and Mountain Laurel branches, and we gathered privet berries and pinecones from among the different species of pines. Not only did the house look like Christmas, but it smelled like Christmas.

Mamma also kept a small pot on top of the wood stove filled with water to which she had added fir needles, cranberries, cinnamon sticks, and oranges, and it produced the most wondrous smell.

I had mailed Robbie's Christmas gift at the beginning of December, hoping it would arrive in time for Christmas. Knowing that one of the hardest things for a soldier was keepin' his feet dry and healthy, I had bought Robbie six pairs of thick wool socks. And feelin' sorry for Johnny and George, I had included two pairs apiece for both of them.

Christmas Day came, and Mamma was bustlin' around, getting the ham into the oven. I helped with peelin' the sweet potatoes and the Kennebec potatoes we grew on our farm. I watched Mamma as she worked busily, and I couldn't help but smile. Christmas preparations had been a tonic for Mamma. Daddy had found a station on the radio that was playin' Christmas music, and we could hear Bing Crosby singin' *White Christmas* from the living room.

Dinner was set for two in the afternoon, and everyone began arrivin' around one-thirty, bringin' more of the warm Christmas spirit with them. We had the same crowd we had for Thanksgiving, minus Rachel and her parents. They were hostin' a Christmas dinner at their own house for some of their church members who had lost sons in the war.

When Granddad and Granny arrived, Granny came through the front door alone, carryin' a basket filled with goodies she had brought for Christmas dinner and for snackin' later in the evening. She didn't say anything but had a twinkle in her eyes as she set her basket down and went about layin' her coat and headscarf on Mamma and Daddy's bed.

"Where's Granddad?" I asked her.

"He'll be in directly," was all she said, but she was smilin'.

I could hear scufflin' in the mudroom you passed through just outside the kitchen door on the back porch. I was about to pull open the door to see who was out there when Mamma said, "Maggie, pull the ham out of the oven, please." I could see her and Granny grinnin' at each other behind my back. Christmas secrets; they had everyone smilin'.

After dinner, we were stuffed as full as one of Granny's Thanksgiving chickens. Most of the men wanted a piece of pie right away, but I always liked to wait until my dinner settled enough to enjoy the pie. By the time we finished up with the dishes, the sun was settin', and I could see through the window that looked out over the front porch that it was snowin' lightly. The driftin' snowflakes added to the warm and cozy feelin's that Christmas with family can produce. The Good Lord knew how to cheer the human spirit.

We began our gift givin' starting with the youngest, which was Charlie. Maude had drawn Charlie's name and wrapped his gift in brown paper tied with red ribbon. He pulled out a gray wool winter hat Maude had made. It had a black corduroy visor that could flip up or down, and the same black corduroy earflaps that could tie under the chin to cover the ears, or tie over the top to pull the earflaps up. Inside the hat was a perfectly made baseball. Maude had made it using a piece of rubber she had salvaged from Johnny Bruce's tire shop, forming it into a round shape. She then wrapped it tightly with yarn until it was the size she wanted. Next, she cut the cover from a scrap of leather from an old saddlebag she had found in the barn. Charlie was happy since his old baseball had come apart last year.

Each family member's gift ideas were thoughtful and made with the recipient in mind. When my turn came, Granddad stood up with a smile and said, "Give me a minute, Maggie girl. Your Daddy and I have to fetch your gift from the mudroom."

They came back into the living room, each holdin' the end of a large rectangular-shaped gift, wrapped in a pretty feed sack and tied up with ribbon. When they set it down, it landed with a solid thunk, and my eyes popped open wide. Whatever it was, it was big!

Granddad smiled at me with a twinkle in his eyes. "I drew your name, Maggie girl."

I knelt before his gift and ran my hands over the top and sides. It was very solid, as well as large, and I could feel four corners through the Christmas print feed sack.

I untied the ribbon, and Granddad and Daddy helped me pull the feed sack off to reveal Granddad's gift to me. I sat stunned, and I'm sure my mouth was wide open as I stared at the most beautiful oak chest I had ever seen. Many of my friends, Rachel included, had a hope chest. Sometimes it was little more than a few boxes in which they stored items they had been collecting for their future homes. I had thought about it from time to time but was generally too busy to do anything about it.

This chest was special, and the wood glowed with a satiny shine. Granddad had stained it with a dark walnut stain after carvin' a mountain scene in the top of the slightly domed lid. When I looked closer, I saw that he had carved my favorite spot up off the old Indian Trail, with the slab of rock jutting over the valley, and the mountains fading into the distance. He had flanked the scene with rhododendron bushes on both sides. I looked up at my Granddad to see the love he bore for me shinin' in his blue eyes.

"Oh, Granddad! It is so beautiful!" My words caught in my throat on a sob of joy.

"Open the lid, Maggie girl," Granddad said.

When I opened the lid, I could see he had used beautiful brass hinges, and the inside of the chest was lined with cedar that gave off its unmistakable scent.

"It's for you to store your quilts and such in when you and Robbie marry," Granddad said.

"Oh my!" I said. "Oh my! It's lovely! Granddad, it's beautiful!" And the next thing I knew, I was wipin' tears off my cheeks. "My spot... you carved my spot!"

I was overwhelmed, but not so much that I couldn't jump up and throw my arms around him. "Thank you, Granddad. I will always cherish it."

"I know." Granddad smiled into my eyes.

The rest of the evenin' passed with lots of laughter as we finished our family's gift givin'. Pie and coffee, hot spiced apple cider, and Granny's rich hot cocoa were enjoyed by us all. Granny had made and brought popcorn balls made from popcorn with caramel sauce poured over and shaped into balls. They were delicious!

We shed tears together as we told funny or special memories we had of Gerry. We missed him, and it seemed we could feel him close to us as we sat together in the living room and the fireplace popped and crackled. It brought healin', more so than sadness.

Chapter Thirty

December 25, 1944, The Ardennes Region of Germany

My Sweet Maggie, it is Christmas night, and we are sitting in about a foot of snow. I am in my foxhole, which I share with George. He is holding a candle while I write this letter. I will then do the same for him, since he wants to write Rachel a letter tonight as well.

My darling, I cannot thank you enough for your thoughtful gift. I could have sold each pair of socks for an unbelievable amount of money, had I been of a mind to. There was nothing I needed more, and my feet will always be grateful. Temperatures have been extremely cold, with nights being well below zero. One of the hardest things a soldier has to contend with is trying to keep his feet somewhat dry and warm. It's nearly impossible. But these socks are the best for this weather that I have ever seen. George has asked me to tell you thank you as well, and I haven't seen Johnny yet to give him his. But I can tell you he will be just as grateful as me and George.

I am sure by now you know that our division is involved in the Ardennes Counteroffensive. The fighting has been the fiercest I have seen yet, and every day we count it a blessing to still be alive. The casualties have been staggering, and we have had several changes in command due to losses.

We have been facing down the German 1st SS Panzer Division, which is Hitler's elite. They already have a reputation for cruelty and a total disregard for the rules and articles of war. They must be stopped at all costs, and thank the Lord, so far, we have been able to hold them, though with a heavy cost of life. We are constantly getting replacements to try to cover the losses. It seems like the replacements are getting younger and younger, but I think that is just because we are feeling so much older.

I was right. We did not get the full four weeks of rest we were supposed to have because of the desperate need to hold this line. But what we did get was very much appreciated. I was finally able to relax enough to get a bit of rest before taking up the position we now hold.

Maggie, seeing so much death and destruction isn't good for anyone. I've been seeing dead men in my sleep and even dreamed of dead Germans marching and driving their tanks. I wake up sometimes freezing cold but drenched with sweat. Pray for me that I can find a way to release these awful dreams and be able to sleep without nightmares. I confess, it's been awful.

I'm sorry this letter is short. I need to hold the candle for George, and we need to try to get some sleep while we can. We never know when the shelling will start, night or day.

But let me just tell you, I love you more than life itself. Thoughts and dreams of you keep me going. When I am so cold I can't feel my feet or hands, I think of you and can find a haven from the pain and discomfort. I'm grateful the Lord has given me such a wonderful woman as yourself. Knowing I can put my complete trust in you gives me peace, and I never doubt that you are praying for me and love me the same as I love you.

With the end of the year approaching, I think of the many times we would all sing *Auld Lang Syne*, and the words bring a tear to my eyes. These words are for you, my sweet Maggie.

Should old acquaintance be forgot,

And never brought to mind?

Should old acquaintance be forgot,

And auld lang syne?

For auld lang syne, my dear,
For auld lang syne,
We'll take a cup of kindness yet,
For auld lang syne.
All my love,
Robbie

***

January 4, 1945, Deep Gap, North Carolina

My Dearest Robbie,

Can you believe it is 1945? It doesn't seem possible that you left Deep Gap to serve your country four long years ago, and yet sometimes it feels like you have been away half of forever, my love. Time is a funny thing how it can feel so slow at times and pass so quickly at others.

We have heard radio reports of the hardships and tremendous fighting that has been going on in Belgium and Germany. I am praying for you, for all of you, several times a day. I fight fear every day and choose to hold to the belief that the Lord has you surrounded, not with Germans, but His mighty angel band. I pray to keep myself from worrying. If I didn't pray, all I would do is worry.

Daddy and Granddad have been working on drawing up the plans for Granddad and Granny's new house. They are building it here on Daddy and Mamma's portion of the farm. That way, as Granny and Granddad get older, they will be that much closer for us to look after them and see to their needs. Right now, Granddad can just about outwork all of us, but there's no getting around the fact that they are getting older.

I like your suggestion that we might do a few things to Granny and Granddad's place to make it a little more up to date with a few modern conveniences. Granny still cooks on a wood range, and I have become used to the gas range Daddy bought for Mamma. So that definitely is one thing I would like to change. But these are all things we can do together once you are home. It won't kill me to cook on a wood stove for a while.

Granddad made me the most beautiful cedar chest you ever saw as my Christmas gift. It is a beautiful oak chest, stained a dark walnut, and lined with cedar. I'm now working along with Mamma and Granny making quilts, sheets, and table linens for our new home together, and will be storing them in Granddad's chest. I have put a set of dishes on layaway at Hunt's Department Store. They are the most beautiful dishes I have ever seen and are Franciscan Apple Ware. My love, even if my food tastes terrible, our dishes will be so beautiful you won't notice!

You said in your November letter that you hoped we could marry as soon as you stepped off the ship. Well, my sweetheart, maybe not as soon as that, but since our ceremony will be simple, we can marry very soon after you get home within a couple of days for sure. I'm not planning a big fancy wedding. Rachel will be my maid of honor, and you can choose a groomsman. If we keep it that simple and small, it won't be a problem to have at a moment's notice. I just want you to come home and make me Mrs. Robert Bruce!

Rachel asked me the funniest question the other day. She asked if I thought a person could fall in love with someone having never met them. What do you make of that?

For mundane news, our egg and poultry business is doing well. There are always going to be obstacles to cross and problems to solve. It's just the nature of things. But all in all, the business is thriving, and we have the two grocery store chains, Winn-Dixie and A&P, pushing us to sign contracts. Our biggest problem is that we have a shortage of labor here. We have put off expanding until it looks like the war will end, which might mean we will have to buy another incubator to hatch out chicks quicker.

I had the most horrible (and selfish) fear two days ago. Harvey approached Daddy and me with a startling announcement. He wants to get married. We were stunned because we didn't even know he was seeing anyone! I thought at first he was going to tell us he would be moving away, but he was only asking for a few days off to take his new bride-to-be on a honeymoon. Do you remember the Young family that lived over near Shady Valley? He's marrying the oldest daughter, Jane sweet, quiet Janie Young. They are being married next Saturday, and I couldn't be happier for them. They will be going by train to the Great Smoky Mountains National Park for a week. Lucky them!

Speaking of honeymoons, is planning the honeymoon your job?

It seems the majority of my letter has been about us getting married and so on, but honestly, apart from praying for your safety, that's all I think about.

To close this letter, I want to tell you again how much I love you, Robbie Bruce. I have never wanted to even look at another man. You fill my mind and my heart, and I think sometimes my family wishes I spent a little more time in the present instead of the future. I promise to always love you and be faithful in mind and body. I promise to work beside you to build a home and a future. I promise to pray with you, as well as for you, in our future life. I promise to serve the Lord beside you and raise our children to serve Him and place their trust in Him. I promise that when we have a disagreement, to not let the sun go down on our wrath and to never lay down beside you with anger between us.

So stay warm and dry, my love. Always know that I am here in Deep Gap, missing you, thinking of you, and loving you.

Love always,

Your Maggie

P.S. I also promise to run slower so you can catch me. (Ha, ha.)

***

The news coming over the radio was so alarmin' that I went days without wanting to hear it. Johnny and Claire had also received a letter from Robbie that contained more war news than he had shared with me. He had written that Company B and the First Battalion were on the offensive to straighten out the bulge in the German line that had been created by the German attack.

On January 14, the First Battalion traveled to an assembly area near Malmedy, then headed south, movin' through Geromont, Baugnez, Ligneuville, Recht, and finally taking Rodt on January 24. The Germans had no organized defense but relied on roadblocks and other delayin' tactics. Company B encountered very little resistance, as the German troops in the area were spread thin. However, heavy snow, eighteen inches and cold weather more than made up for the lack of opposition.

The countryside they traveled through was rough, with very few houses where the soldiers might have rotated for a brief chance to rest and get warm. A foxhole could not be made warm in the snow, and frostbite alone accounted for more than one hundred casualties in the Battalion during this operation.

On January 26, a regiment from the 17th Airborne Division relieved Robbie's 117th Infantry. Two days later, on January 28, the First Battalion boarded trucks and moved through Viel Salm to Grand Hallux. This town, like most others, was battle-scarred, but the soldiers soon made some of the houses habitable for a few days of rest. The men were issued new clothing designed specifically for winter campaigning. Unfortunately, the clothes came a little late, as the snow on the ground had already begun to melt.

They then moved to the vicinity of Aachen, Germany. The First Battalion, 117th Infantry, moved by night and reached Verlautenheide, Germany, early in the morning of February 3. The next morning, the troops found enough basements and rooms partially intact to make reasonably decent livin' quarters. The Battalion then moved to Warden, Germany, a town in the Siegfried Line which they had taken. The Battalion stayed there for about two weeks, training for the next operation: the crossing of the Roer River.

On February 19, the First Battalion was presented the Distinguished Unit Citation by General S. Leland Hobbs, Commanding General of the 30th Infantry Division, for their performance at Mortain. The 30th Infantry Division was also awarded the Belgian Fourragere for its performance in the Ardennes and for its role in the liberation of Belgium, September 4–10, 1944.

I was so proud, knowin' that my Robbie had been part of such heroism and bravery. But it had also come at a heavy cost. Word came that Johnny Bailey had been wounded in battle on January 13, when the 30th launched its own counteroffensive to push back the German forces two weeks after Robbie had written his last letter to me. He had been taken to a field hospital in Belgium and would soon be transferred back to England. As soon as he was able, he would be sent home. Johnny had lost his right leg to a mortar explosion.

Operation Grenade was the next reported operation Robbie's division took part in. The crossin' of the Roer River was originally planned for February 10, 1945, but because of floodwaters caused by the Germans blowing up the dams of the upper Roer River at midnight on February 8, the crossin' was postponed until February 23.

Accordin' to the newspaper, the crossin' began durin' the pre-dawn hours of February 23. The first notice the Germans had of the attack came at 2:45 a.m., when all of the cannoneers along a twenty-five-mile stretch of river began a poundin' that would last forty-five minutes to an hour. The 30th Infantry Division front covered eight thousand yards of German front lines. As part of this offensive, the division crossed the Roer River near Jülich, Germany, on February

23. This river crossin' established a bridgehead into Germany that was later used to stage the crossin' of the Rhine.

***

By March, it was starting to look like the war could be close to coming to an end. Allied forces were advancin' rapidly from both the East and the West, crossing the Rhine in the West and reachin' the Oder River in the East. We were practically holdin' our breath every time we listened to a radio broadcast, expectin' to hear that it was over.

Newspapers reported that German morale was at an all-time low. Despite clear signs of military defeat, decades of Nazi propaganda had convinced many Germans that defeat was impossible, makin' it difficult for them to accept the comin' collapse of Hitler's Nazi Party. Even at the very end, some would not believe that Hitler was dead and that Germany had lost the war.

Spring was comin' to my mountains early that year, and I couldn't help but feel my hope risin' with the faint frostin' of green over the treetops on the mountainsides and ridges. Seein' signs of new life in the vegetation and animal life was a reminder of the resurrection of our Lord and Savior. And I thanked Him many times a day that the war looked to be comin' close to its end. *"Hasten the day, Lord, hasten the day,"* I breathed.

Chapter Thirty One

March 28, 1945, Germany

My Darling Maggie, here we are at the end of March, and things are looking up! While there is no official talk of surrender, the German military is losing strength, and the German people are weary of war and tired of fighting. Hitler is losing their faith, and I believe we will see the collapse of the Nazi government very soon. There have even been reports of failed coups that led to the execution of not only the men planning them but their families as well. It goes to show where a brutal dictatorship will take a nation.

We were doing training exercises, practicing for the Rhine crossing, when on March 11, a boat containing one squad of Company B overturned in the Maas River, where training was taking place. Most members were saved, but three of them drowned in the swift current. Our squad was nearly the one chosen for that particular exercise.

We had begun moving troops, and at about 10 o'clock on the night of March 23, we were taking a break in the movement of the First Battalion to an assembly position near the Rhine. General Eisenhower had come and was observing troops in Company B and the rest of the battalion. He came over to where George and I were standing in formation and started chatting with us. He asked me if I thought we would make it across all right.

"General," I replied, "if Company B can't make it tonight, you can give up hope for the whole Ninth Army."

The General laughed and seemed pleased with my confidence.

The First Battalion was selected as the assault battalion for the crossing of the Rhine. The 117th Infantry carried all storm boats to the river's edge in the dark so that the troops selected for the crossing would be fresh for the assault. At exactly 2:00 a.m., the assault platoon shoved off, and the second wave of storm boats carrying the remainder of the companies moved out.

On the whole, very little resistance was encountered. Company B was the first unit to clear its obstacle, a dike. It reorganized and then moved on to take the town of Ork. One hundred fifty prisoners, most of them cowering in cellars, were captured. The operation was possibly the easiest one we made, but the light resistance made it easy. Afterwards, we chased after the 116th Panzer Division, who were running for it.

Shortly after midnight on March 25, the First Battalion moved on through Stockum to Hunxe. Then, the next morning, March 27, Company B and Company C took control of a German airfield and set up a defense of the area, making use of the German barracks just north of the landing field.

We are in reserve for a few days. We are seeing very light resistance, and the General is calling it "mop up." My love, it is looking as though the German resistance is breaking up, and we are pushing hard for the end of this bloody business.

Have you heard any word on Johnny Bailey? He was in bad shape when I saw him in the field hospital, but the nurses assured me he would live. I haven't heard anything about him but assume he is at least in England by now.

I wouldn't be surprised if George and Rachel have found something more than a pen pal through these last three years of writing. All he talks about is meeting Rachel as soon as he is home. Of course, he already feels like he knows her but dreams of meeting her in person. George had an injury to his left hand last month. He's fine but might end up with some stiff fingers.

I cannot wait to see the household things you are accumulating for our home. I don't know what Franciscan Apple Ware looks like, but it sure sounds nice. Your Granddad loves you very much, Maggie. I've always known that, but his Christmas gift to you is just a physical reminder of his love that you will always have.

We will set about remaking your kitchen as soon as we are married, and I can hardly wait. Have everything you would like picked out, and we will start on it as soon as we can. What about one of those nice double porcelain sinks with the built-in drainboards? They are all the thing and look like they would be nice to have.

I hope to be writing again soon with good news. Of course, you will have already heard it, but I am looking forward to writing it just the same.

So, chin up and keep holding on, my love. It won't be long before I'm holding you tight and never letting go. I love and miss you so much that sometimes it hurts.

All my love,

Robbie.

PS; I heard the funniest joke and had to share it with you so hear goes; in war time Berlin, an SS Officer had a side line going as an amateur clock maker and repairer. A customer walked into his clock repair shop with a mantel clock. The SS Officer said "Vhat can I do for you?" The customer replied. "It's my mantel clock. It's not working properly... if you put your ear to it, you will know what I mean. All it does is Tic-Tic-Tic all the time Tic-Tic-Tic It doesn't Toc. The SS Officer said "Okay, leave it vis me, come back Thursday when it will be ready for you". The customer returned to the clock repair shop on the Thursday and said to the SS Officer "how much do I owe you?" "Ten Deutsche Marks" said the SS Officer. The customer paid him, and started to walk out when he stopped and turned to the SS Officer and said "Out of curiosity, just how did you manage to get it going properly again?" To which the SS Officer replied "Vee have ways of making it TOC!"

***

April was a glorious month. Spring had come early, bringin' not only warmer weather, but hope that budded among the people of the nation, along with the trees and flowers. German resistance was continuing to crumble as the Allied forces plowed their way across Germany. Yet every week, the newspaper in Boone was full of reports of the deaths of our region's young men in battle. In Europe and the Pacific, we had lost too many.

Along with the positive, there was new evidence of Nazi depravity that was starting to unfold. Last year there had been reports of places of unspeakable horrors bein' found. Majdanek, an extermination camp, was discovered on the outskirts of Lublin, Poland, on July 24, 1944, by Soviet forces. The Germans tried to hide the evidence of mass murder, but the fast-movin' Soviet advance prevented them from coverin' their crime completely. Auschwitz was discovered on January 27, 1945, also by the Soviets. Upon arrival, soldiers found about seven thousand sick and starving prisoners after most of the others had been forced on "death marches."

On April 4, U.S. troops discovered Ohrdruf. It was the first Nazi concentration camp discovered by American soldiers in Germany and was seen by General Eisenhower, General Patton, and General Bradley.

Then on April 12, Robbie's own 30th Infantry Division freed the Weferlingen subcamp, where four hundred and twenty-one prisoners had been forced to construct a tunnel for an underground factory. One day later, they stumbled upon a stopped train the crew had abandoned, filled with starvin' and sick prisoners near Farsleben, Germany.

There were roughly twenty-five hundred prisoners, mostly Jewish, crammed into cattle cars with little to no food, water, or sanitation, traveling from one camp to another. The soldiers quickly began pullin' survivors from the cars, givin' them food, water, blankets, and medical care. The train's occupants were taken to the nearby village of Hillersleben, which was converted into a makeshift hospital to care for them.

On April 29, Dachau, just ten miles from Munich, was discovered by U.S. forces, where troops found over thirty railroad cars filled with decomposin' bodies near the camp's entrance.

These reports were met with mixed responses. Some folks refused to believe that even Hitler could undertake such actions. But the American troops and Allied forces who were coming across these horrors grew angrier with each passin' day.

Amid the uproar and events in Europe, the United States suffered a blow. Our President, Franklin D. Roosevelt, died at the Little White House in Warm Springs, Georgia. He had gone to Warm Springs forty-one times since 1924 for relief from the pain he suffered. The President was sitting for a portrait when he complained of a headache. He fainted and never regained consciousness. He died the afternoon of April 12 from a massive brain bleed. The news stunned the nation. That same day, Harry S. Truman, our Vice President, was sworn into office as the nation's 33rd President.

On May 2, Rachel and I were workin' in chicken house number one, havin' just washed and sanitized all the feeders and watering cans. We were in the process of refillin' them and setting them out. Daddy, Granddad, and Harvey were all working together to get all the chicken houses cleaned in one day.

I heard someone runnin' toward the chicken house, their feet a poundin' on the dry North Carolina dirt. Mamma broke through the door at a dead run, and it about scared the liver out of me because it wasn't like Mamma to be tearin' around like that.

"Where's your Daddy?" she panted.

"Why? What's wrong?" I asked, terrified to know.

Mamma could see by my face how scared I was.

"No, honey, it's good news! The best news! Hitler is dead!"

Rachel had come to stand beside me, and we both just looked at her. I couldn't believe what I was hearing.

"There was just a radio report! President Truman just announced that Adolf Hitler is dead!"

We heard the tractor bein' shut down over in the next chicken house, and we all ran to give the men the joyous news. We took a break and went to the house to listen to the radio for further reports, while Harvey ran over to fetch Granny to come and join us.

I wondered if it was right to have such joy and celebrate the fact that a human being was dead, but then reasoned that, in light of all the deaths the man was responsible for, it was merciful that he was dead.

We had lunch and talked excitedly about what surely must come soon. Hitler was the idol that Germany circled around. It only stood to reason that a surrender would come soon.

It came. One week after Hitler ended his life, Thursday, May 7, 1945, General Alfred Jodl, Chief of Staff of the German Armed Forces High Command, signed the unconditional surrender of all German forces to the Allies at General Dwight D. Eisenhower's headquarters in Reims, France.

The next day, Friday, May 8, surrender papers were signed by German Field Marshal Wilhelm Keitel in Berlin because the Soviet Union demanded a separate ceremony. Even though the surrender was officially signed on May 7, the second signing in Berlin on May 8, 1945, became the recognized end of World War II in Europe.

It was called VE Day, victory in Europe. We heard later that people in England, Paris, and New York had taken to the streets in their joy, dancin' and celebratin' the end of the war in Europe.

We wondered what would happen now. All those servicemen in Europe would they come home or be sent to help fight the war in the Pacific? The Japanese had not surrendered, nor did it look like they would.

We later found out that on May 27, Robbie's 117th was moved south to a location in Germany, near the Czechoslovakian border, for occupation. While there, they received news that the 30th Infantry Division would be redeployed to the Pacific to fight the Japanese.

***

May 2, 1945, Deep Gap, North Carolina

Dear Robbie, my darling!

The end must surely be close! We just got word that Adolf Hitler is dead, but we haven't heard what happened. There are different reports on what took place. I hope the Lord doesn't hold it against me, but when the shock of it wore off, I had the wildest joy flood over me. Am I wrong? He was such an evil man, but a man with a soul that will answer to God for millions of lives lost, and men like Johnny, whose bodies were mangled and torn. I would hate to be Adolf Hitler as he stands before God on judgment day.

I am hoping and praying they will send you home to me soon. I am praying now that the war in the Pacific will also come to an end, for I am fearful they will send you there next. We have been hearing the most awful things about the Japanese and the things they have done to their prisoners. How can man be so cruel intentionally? I just don't understand how some men can become so low and cruel.

The fighting on the Japanese island of Okinawa has been terrible, with Japanese pilots deliberately crashing their planes into

American ships and other targets. How do you stop someone if they aren't afraid of dying? There's talk that the Allied Forces are planning an invasion of Japan. I wish they would just do it and get it over with.

Mamma and I have been making plans for a small wedding ceremony for soon after you get back. If it is small and simple, it can happen quickly. I know a lot of women are having very large and fancy weddings, like Tillie and Harry's, but I just want my maid of honor, and you to have a groomsman. Depending on the season, I would love to make my bouquet from the many wildflowers that bloom in our mountains or at least use some of them. I hope these plans are okay with you. Knowing you as I do, I didn't think you would mind a small, simple ceremony. We will have a larger reception and party at the farm sometime afterward.

Daddy was saying the other day that he saw Johnny Bailey's pa at the tire shop, and he was saying that Johnny was in a hospital in Washington, D.C. and Johnny's mother has gone to be with him for a while. I guess we will know more about him when she comes home.

Daddy, Granddad, and Harvey are making a lot of headway with the little cabin being built for Granny and Granddad. Daddy is insisting they put in some modern conveniences for Granny. She put up a fuss at first, but I think she's pleased. She picked out a small gas range for her kitchen, and they are putting linoleum on the kitchen floor that looks like stonework. She got one of those sinks you were talking about in your last letter, and I do like it! It will be so handy for preparing vegetables especially.

I've been thinking I do want a gas range for my kitchen, but I don't want to get rid of Granny's wood cookstove, so I would like to build a small summer kitchen on the back of the house to put it in. It would be handy for all sorts of reasons, but mostly because I can't bear to part with it. And another amazing thing we found out about Harvey is that he can build anything, and he does it well. He built Granny's kitchen cupboards, and they are a work of art! I'm sure we could probably get his help to do ours.

It was just a bit nippy, but I climbed the old Indian Trail last week to think of you and enjoy the spring views. I saw a mamma bear with two cubs pass on the trail below me. You can bet I stayed very quiet and let them pass without noticing me! But those little ones were so cute as they rolled around and played behind her. It would have been so much nicer with you there beside me.

One more thing before I get this ready to send. Mamma and I are also making my wedding dress. I went back and forth about spending the money on a dress I won't wear but once. I almost bought a very pretty blue suit I saw in Hunt's Department Store. They also carry bridal gowns that are so beautiful and very expensive. Mamma found enough ivory-colored rayon that has the prettiest shine to the fabric, and I settled on getting that. We are making my dress exactly how I want it. The fancy dresses were very beautiful, but not really me. So, in the long run, I spent less money and was more pleased with my choice.

So, my darling Robbie, all is nearly ready. All I need is my groom. I pray things will come to an end in Japan, and you can hurry home to me. I have not slacked on praying for you just because the war in Europe is over, and I pray for your safe return to me many times a day. I remember over and over how it felt to be in your arms, and I want nothing more than to be there again.

All my love forever,

Maggie

***

May 15, 1945, Germany

My Dearest Maggie,

I am sure you all are as happy as we are! I've never seen so many happy men. At first, there was stunned disbelief that the war was truly over after so many years of fighting. Especially those poor chaps, our limey friends from England. The war has been much longer for them. Then came the realization that although the war may be over here, it's still going on in the Pacific. We will likely be redeployed to help that effort and will no doubt be either shipped back to England or possibly home to the United States before redeploying us to stations around the Pacific. I will let you know what comes of our redeployment. Hopefully, we will know something soon.

Someone came in to tell us we are moving to another location. I'll have to stow this letter and finish it later when I am able.

May 28

We have been bumped from one location to another for the last two weeks. They are telling us that we will be sent to England and redeployed to the Pacific, but there has been no word about when that will happen. It feels so strange to be sitting around so much. We are still doing field training exercises and PT details, but again, we are right back to waiting for something to happen. It almost feels like it did back in March, waiting for what we knew was coming.

So, for the time being, we will remain here around Bad Elster, Germany, on occupation duty until orders come to move out. Meanwhile, we are getting lots of rest and relaxation, playing games of softball, and joyriding around the area as we keep an eye on things.

Yesterday, a woman from a nearby village hugged us and thanked us for bringing Hitler to his end. "It is goot he is dead. Goot he is no longer Führer. He was not worthy to lead the German people." Even though they could not say it aloud before yesterday, not everyone in Germany agreed with the madman.

The countryside around Bad Elster is pleasant even though it is ravaged by war, and it is a restful place to wait for our orders.

May 29

My goodness, I've never written a more chopped-up letter. But when we get summoned, we have to drop everything and go. I just found out that we will be redeployed to the Pacific through England, and we will be going to England in July. It is taking time to move all these troops, so we'll need to wait our turn. That's fine with me. I'm not overeager to jump back into a fight.

I found out that Johnny has been sent to Walter Reed General Hospital in Washington, D.C. He will be there quite a long time. His leg will have to heal, and the end of his leg must shrink before he can be fitted with an artificial leg. He will then go through a time of therapy and learn how to walk with his new leg. I guess it all depends on how long it takes him to heal, but it could be as long as January before he goes home. I wasn't there when he was hit, so I'm not sure how much of his leg he lost. I'm told things are a lot better if the knee is still there.

They are calling us to assemble outside, so I have to go. I'll try to finish tomorrow.

May 31

I'd better not piddle around if I ever want to get this sent! I got your letter, and it was so good to hear from you. I was a little worried, since they were moving us around every couple of days there for a while, that the mail would have a hard time catching up to us.

Whatever you want, Maggie girl, is just fine by me. Whether it's a small wedding or a great big one, it doesn't matter to me. I just want you as my wife. But that said, the small, simple wedding sounds perfect to me too. I would be proud to have you if you married me in a pair of overalls, but then again, a pretty wedding dress sounds mighty nice.

I like the idea of a summer kitchen on the back of the house. My grandma had one, and they are nice. She did a lot of her canning out there, and that helped keep her main kitchen cleaner and cooler. She loved her summer kitchen.

The Japanese pilots that crash into ships and buildings are called kamikaze pilots, and you are right, they are hard to deal with. One man in a plane can take down a ship. And I don't think you are a bad person to be happy that Hitler is dead. If you are, the majority of the world is in the same boat with you. He may have had a soul, but he sold it to the devil a long time ago through his greedy desire for power. At any rate, he is God's to deal with now. But I can tell you, the jokes are flying now. Here's one I thought would make you laugh.

Hitler went to a fortuneteller and asked her, "On what day will I die?"

To which the fortuneteller replied, "You will die on a Jewish holiday."

"What makes you so sure of that?" Hitler asked.

"Because any day you die will be a Jewish holiday," she replied.

Maggie girl, as soon as we can after I get back home to Deep Gap, if the weather permits, let's go for a tromp through the woods and go up to your spot on the ledge. I have missed doing that with you. I am looking forward to being home again. I'll be hard-pressed to want to leave, but I would like to take you somewhere to the East Coast for our honeymoon. Not quite sure exactly where yet, but I believe you will love the ocean. It is a wonder to watch a pod of dolphins leaping out of the water and to see the seagulls and pelicans soaring around.

So, until I see you and hold you in my arms and smother you with kisses, remember I love you with all my heart.

God be with you till we meet again.

Robbie

Chapter Thirty Two

The 30th Infantry Division was moved to Camp Lucky Strike near Le Havre, France, where it was split up for redeployment. Because he didn't have time to write a letter, Robbie sent a telegram to Johnny and Claire to let them know he was redeploying to England.

On July 31, the 117th, Company B, and the 120th boarded the Liberty Ship *Marine Wolf*, and they arrived in Southampton, England, to wait for the British liner *Queen Mary*. It was to take them to the United States to prepare for the planned invasion of Japan. They were being prepared for Operation Downfall, the planned invasion of the Japanese home islands.

Later, we learned that after a difficult deliberation with his military advisors, President Truman came to the conclusion that an invasion of the Japanese homeland would be too costly. Not only would the monetary cost be immense, but the cost in American lives would be astronomical. If we needed any proof that the Japanese would not be an easy invasion, the kamikaze pilots were proof of the Japanese determination and willingness to die for their emperor.

The difficult decision was carried out first on August 6, 1945, when the American B-29 bomber, *Enola Gay*, dropped the world's first atomic bomb *Little Boy* over the city of Hiroshima. Three days later, on August 9, 1945, after the second atomic bomb *Fat Man* was dropped on Nagasaki, the Japanese finally surrendered.

The *Queen Mary* docked at Ocean Pier in Southampton on August 13. The next day, August 14, the troops started embarking, but before sailing, news of the Japanese surrender was received, and redeployment plans were canceled.

On August 17, the *Queen Mary* pulled away from England to dock at Pier 90 in New York City. Five days later, Company B returned to Fort Jackson, South Carolina. We were wildly happy, thinkin' that Robbie would be home by the end of August, and we began settin' plans in place for our weddin'. But as time dragged on, we were all getting frustrated. September was comin' to an end when Johnny called Fort Jackson after he wrote a letter to Robbie's commandin' officer to try to find out what was holding things up.

It would be four years come January since Robbie had left Deep Gap to serve his country, and now that country, it seemed to us, was holdin' him hostage. The government does all things as slow as frozen molasses, though, and finally, three months after arriving at Fort Jackson, Robbie was deactivated from Federal Service on November 24, 1945.

***

We were up early on the Sunday morning of November 25, 1945, when Johnny and Claire came racin' up the driveway in Johnny's old pickup truck. They both jumped from the cab and ran up through the front door Daddy had opened wide for them. I could tell by their faces it was not bad news they carried. Johnny held out the Western Union telegram to me with a big grin splittin' his face and scrunchin' up his eyes.

Leaving Fort Jackson stop pick me up

Winston Salem train station stop

Arriving 3 this afternoon stop

Robbie

I looked up at Johnny and Claire, my eyes starting to fill with tears. Could it possibly be real? After all the agonizin', waitin', prayin' and hopin', my Robbie was at this very moment on a train and headed home! Claire and I wrapped each other in a big hug, just a holdin' each other and cryin' hard. We finally pulled back, wipin' our eyes, and I was just about to ask them a question when Claire spoke up and said, "Would you like to come with us to Winston Salem to pick Robbie up?"

"Oh yes! Yes! Yes! Please, I want to see him so bad!"

Johnny was also wipin' his eyes but laughing too. "I had a little feelin' you might. We'll be around to pick you up about eleven." He gave me a smile and hooked an arm around my shoulders, givin' me a quick squeeze.

"I'll be ready!" I said, still wipin' tears of joy from my face.

When I turned, Mamma, Daddy, and Charlie were all there, every one of them crying right along with the rest of us. Mamma pulled me into her arms, and our tears started flowin' again. But they were the result of the release of so many fears and the tension of the last few years.

I ran upstairs and took a quick bath, using Mamma's lavender soap and washin' my hair. No time for rag curlers, so stick-straight hair would have to do. I dressed in a blue plaid wool skirt and blue sweater. Mamma helped me dry my hair beside the fireplace, and I pulled the sides back with the pretty barrettes she had given me for Christmas a few years ago.

"You look very pretty, hon." Mamma said reassuringly and kissed my cheek. "Don't forget to give Robbie our love, and I'll have a good supper waiting for everyone when you get back."

Trust Mamma to remember to feed everyone!

Johnny and Claire returned at eleven sharp but were not in Johnny's old pickup. I had been mildly worried about causing the cab of the truck to be overcrowded on the trip home, but the thought of being so close to Robbie for the two-and-a-half-hour trip home was a pleasant thought too. Johnny was drivin' a Ford Standard Coupe instead of the old pickup.

"Mr. Macpherson loaned it to me," Johnny said with a smile. "This is the one he uses to run errands in. Mrs. Macpherson wouldn't be caught dead in it." He laughed.

"Why ever not?" I asked lookin' the car over, expectin' there must be something wrong.

"It's not expensive enough," Johnny said with a wicked gleam in his eye. A lot of the guys liked to poke fun at Mrs. Macpherson's snooty ways.

The ride to Winston Salem took two and a half hours, and we didn't have any problems that took up time, other than a stop for gasoline and a snack. We pulled into the train station ahead of schedule at two o'clock. For the next hour, I either paced the aisle in the waiting room of the train station or sat beside Claire and Johnny, twistin' my hankie between my hands. I was anxious and nervous.

Finally, about ten minutes till three, the stationmaster started lookin' busy, like he was preparin' for something. Within five minutes, I could hear the steam locomotive as it came chuggin' into the station with squealing brakes and blowing clouds of steam.

My heart pounded so hard I was afraid I would pass out. We stood waiting for passengers to start filin' off the train and then began watchin' for Robbie's familiar form. Most of the folks gettin' off the train were GIs headin' home, so it was like huntin' a needle in a haystack. I glanced down the line to the third car just in time to see Robbie as he swung down off the train with a suitcase in one hand and a duffel slung across his back. He had on the same khaki uniform, coat, and hat everyone else did, so I'm not sure exactly what caught my eye from that distance. But I knew it was Robbie.

"There he is!" I cried, pointing down the line so Claire and Johnny could catch a glimpse of him in the crowd.

"Where? I don't see him... where?" Claire was frantically trying to find her son.

About that time, Robbie broke free of the other GIs and grinned, waving his hand high in the air. We surged forward to meet him halfway. Robbie dropped his suitcase and duffel onto the platform, and as we reached him, he reached out both arms and snagged me in one and his Ma in the other, pulling us both in tight and holdin' us for a moment. When he released his two crying women, Johnny stepped forward, and they first grasped each other's extended hands, then pulled each other into a big hug. When they released each other, Robbie smiled at us three and said,

"I'm home! I can't believe I'm home." He shook his head as if he was shaking off a dream.

Claire kept reaching out and touchin' Robbie. Touchin' his face and arm, as though trying to reassure herself he wasn't a ghost but warm flesh.

I was suddenly bashful. I wanted to touch him too, but what would Johnny and Claire think if I butted in and interrupted their reunion?

It was then Robbie turned to me and said softly, "Come here."

I stepped right into his arms. They folded around me and held me very close while I sobbed quietly into the front of his coat. Everyone just faded away. There was no train, no train station; even Johnny and Claire had receded from my awareness. Robbie held me close, and I could feel him nuzzle his face into my hair as he bent over me. We just stood that way for a few minutes before breakin' apart with a little laugh. Only then I saw that Johnny and Claire were cryin' too.

"Let's go home," Robbie said, and picked up his suitcase while Johnny grabbed his duffel.

***

The trip home was ecstatic torture. Johnny and Claire were so happy to have their son back home, not only alive but unharmed as well. Claire chattered happily from the front seat and asked Robbie a lot of questions, while Robbie and I sat close together in the back seat, clasping each other's hands. Johnny kept looking into the rearview mirror and grinned at us. Robbie kept up a conversation with Claire, answering her questions patiently, all the while he would caress my hand and smile into my eyes often.

We were nearly home, and darkness had fallen, when Robbie lifted my right hand to his lips and kissed the knuckles. Leanin' close, he whispered,

"We'll talk more tomorrow."

"Okay," I nodded, feelin' weak in the knees.

The whole family was so happy to see Robbie back home in Deep Gap. We all sat around the table and talked for a long time, but eventually Robbie stood and said, "Guess we need to let you all get to bed. Can I come back tomorrow and see Maggie?"

"Of course!" Mamma and Daddy said together.

Robbie, Johnny, and Claire bundled back up against the cold, and after hugs and goodnights, drove away.

The next day, Robbie was back not long after breakfast and stepped into the living room with a wide smile. Again, he pulled me into his arms, and I slid mine around his waist holdin' him tight. He dropped a kiss on the top of my head and said,

"Ready to go a trompin'?"

"Sure am!" I smiled up into his handsome face. Now, having grown a bit more accustomed to seeing this new version of Robbie, I could see the toll the war had taken on him. Oh, he was still my sweet, kindhearted Robbie, but deep in his eyes he looked older, and I could see that he had seen too much death and destruction. I wondered how much my love had suffered that he had not confided to anyone.

Mamma had packed us a basket with peanut butter and jelly sandwiches, some fried apple pies, and a couple of bottles of Coca-Cola, and hand in hand we took off in the nippy late fall air. I didn't always make this climb this late in the season, but it was a sunshiny day without too much wind, even if it was a bit cold. I knew the climb would get our blood pumpin', and we would feel plenty warm once we got a goin'.

Every now and then, Robbie would pull me to a stop and hold me in his arms for a minute. After two or three times, he said,

"I just need to hold my girl. Need to know this is real."

"I know." I sighed happily.

We reached the slab of rock where we first sat as children when Robbie first brought me here when I was six and he was eight. We had come here so many times years ago, but never as sweethearts. We settled down on the jutting edge of the rock and let our feet dangle into the empty space below us, sitting in silence for a moment to catch our breath and just enjoy the moment.

The air was clear, and without the summer humidity cloudin' the distance, we could see clearly the distant peaks within my Appalachian Mountain range. Robbie just sat for a moment, and I could tell he was soakin' in the peace that lay in the undulating peaks and valleys around us. Neither of us minded the chilly nip in the air, for the sun shone brightly, adding the illusion of warmth.

I looked down at the firm, strong hand I held in my own. It was corded with the lines of tendon and bone showing through his skin, with hard, manly knuckles. Robbie had made the final transformation to a fully grown man while he was away from us.

When he left, there were still traces of boy in the lines of his cheeks, with the bright, innocent look of a sheltered youth in his eyes.

There was nothing boyish about Robbie now. His gray-blue eyes, while not really sorrowful, had a look that told me he had seen too much death. Too much destruction. He had seen too much human suffering; his eyes looked haunted, and it broke my heart. For I knew in that moment, he would likely suffer from the memories the rest of his life.

I leaned my head on his shoulder while he gazed over our mountains and prayed silently for him. *Lord, give my darlin' ease and peace of mind. Help him to accept that he was called to defend his country, as was your servant David of old. He was defendin' his home against evil, and there was no wrong in that.*

Robbie pointed to the north of where we sat. "There's Tompkins Knob."

I nodded.

"And down that way is Mast Knob, and just west of it there is Bentley Knob."

"Sure is," I said softly, letting him name the peaks so familiar to us both, for I sensed he was needin' to reorient himself back into this landscape he had been away from for nearly four years.

"And way in the distance to the south, I can see Mount Mitchell. Can you see it, Maggie? It's faint blue, but I can see it."

"I see it. Mount Mitchell is the granddad of these mountains," I said.

For Mount Mitchell is the tallest peak east of the Rocky Mountains far to the west, and stood about sixty miles south of us.

"Maggie, there's something you need to know before you marry me," Robbie said out of the blue.

"Okay," I said.

"I've been havin' trouble sleepin' sound at night."

Robbie shifted so he could turn toward me and look into my face.

"I've been havin' nightmares... seein' horrible things in my dreams. From the war."

He trailed off, then went quiet. I just waited for him to be able to go on.

"I... I even woke up one-night last week in our barracks and was crouched in the corner of the room thinkin' we were under attack. I had the barracks broom in my hands, thinkin' it was my rifle... I thought the Germans were stormin' the room."

I rubbed his arm soothingly. I wished desperately that I could absorb some of his wounds. My darlin' had come home without a scratch on his body. But as I had suspicioned, he did have wounds, but they were deep in his spirit and mind. And I knew only the Lord and time would help ease them.

"I thought you should know. Maybe you don't want to put up with a man who wakes up in the middle of the night, screamin' or even bawlin' sometimes. I just see such awful, awful things in my dreams..."

I turned so my darlin' and I were facin' each other and took both of his war-hardened hands in mine. I raised them to my lips, kissed each hand, and pressed them against my cheek for a moment before respondin' to him.

"When I agreed to marry you, I was agreein' to the vows we would make on our weddin' day. For better or worse, for richer or poorer, in sickness or in health, 'til death us do part. It would never enter my mind to throw aside those vows, and I wouldn't want to."

Again, I brought both of his hands to my lips and kissed them.

"I love you, Robbie Bruce. Remember when I said to you that you loved me, warts and all? Well, I love you, warts and all too. You love me in spite of my difficult parts, and I love you in spite of this. This isn't something of your choosing; it's a wound, as surely as any wound Johnny Bailey has suffered. It's a wound too. It's a gapin' wound in your spirit, and it needs safety and time to heal."

Robbie's eyes were lookin' down at our clasped hands, and a single tear rolled down each cheek. It tore at my heart like nothin' else ever had.

"When we are married, you will never wake from one of those dreams alone. Ever again. And I will be there to pull you back from the dark places that torment your spirit. And I will always pray for you. Always."

My darlin' looked into my eyes, and the love I saw there filled my heart to overflowin'. We were sittin' on the rock ledge, and when he went to pull me into his arms, we laid back against the slab, holdin' each other tight. Robbie nuzzled my hair, then my cheek, brushin' his lips back and forth across the smoothness of my skin.

"So soft," he breathed in my ear.

My breath caught in my throat, and my heart pounded.

Robbie pulled back with a sigh.

"I wish we could get married tomorrow," he said.

Quick as a blink I said, "Why couldn't we?"

Robbie looked at me, astounded. "Could we?"

"Yes," I said. "There's no waiting period for a marriage license. We could run over to the courthouse today for our license, and get married tomorrow... if you wanted to. My dress is finished. There's nothing really except the reception, which we could have another day."

Robbie leaped to his feet, pullin' me up at the same time, and he was all jubilant happiness. We were back at the house in no time flat, announcin' our intentions.

Granddad and Granny had already moved into their new cabin, and while mostly empty, their old homeplace would make for a very cozy honeymoon tryst.

Mamma laughed excitedly and said, "I half expected this when you two lovebirds set out earlier. You two run on into Boone for your marriage license, and Daddy and I will take care of everything else here. Don't worry about a thing."

And we were off to Boone in a flash, stoppin' by Rachel's to tell her, since she was to be my maid of honor.

"Lord, girl, when you decide to do somethin', you sure don't let the grass grow under your feet, do you?"

"Nope," was all I said as I hurried out the door.

Chapter Thirty Three

November 27th, 1945. I was up early, as usual, to help with chores before my wedding ceremony at two o'clock that afternoon. When I came downstairs in my work clothes, Mamma looked at me, puzzled, and asked, "What are you doin'?"

I looked at her just as puzzled. "Goin' out to see to the hens."

"Oh no, you aren't!" Her voice had risen by a note or two. "You are a bride today, and the men are seein' to your regular chores. Come on in the kitchen, I've made you breakfast."

Holdin' my hands up in surrender and laughin', I said, "Okay, okay! Settle down, Mamma hen. Your chick will do as you say!"

Mamma just laughed, kissin' my cheek as she set about dishin' up my breakfast and pourin' me a steamy cup of her strong coffee.

"I see you did your hair in rag rollers last night. So, you're not wearin' your hair up?"

"No... Robbie's one request was that I wear it down," I said, blushin'.

Mamma smiled and nodded. "Your Daddy likes my hair down too."

Odd. While I knew Mamma and Daddy loved each other and were affectionate, I had never thought of Daddy lookin' at Mamma the same way Robbie had looked at me yesterday. Or of Mamma feelin' like I did when I was in Robbie's arms when Daddy held her.

Rachel came over soon afterwards to help with last-minute preparations, since we were havin' a light early supper after the ceremony. Besides our Spencer family, Johnny and Claire were to be there, along with our preacher, Brother Reagan, and his wife, Harvey and Janie, Mr. and Mrs. Potts, and George, who was to be Robbie's groomsman.

For once, Mamma had enlisted some help with the food preparations, and Mrs. Potts and Mrs. Reagan were preparin' the food and bringin' it to our house after the ceremony. This would allow Mamma to enjoy bein' the Mamma of the bride, and Granny could enjoy just bein' my Granny.

We dressed in my bedroom, and Mamma came in with my beautiful wedding dress that she had sewn. I sighed with happiness when I saw it. We had anticipated a late summer or early fall wedding when we designed it, so it had short, slightly puffed sleeves. That was fine by me; I didn't like long sleeves unless it was pretty cold anyway. At noon, the outside temperature was close to sixty degrees, so it felt fine to me. The Lord had blessed me with a beautiful wedding day! But just in case it was a bit chilly, Mamma had made me a pretty shawl-like short cape. It had a hook-and-eye fastenin' at the throat and was made of ivory velvet. I had never had anything so pretty.

My dress was made of ivory rayon that was so light it was nearly white, and it had a shimmer to it that made it more beautiful than silk or satin, I thought. Silk and satin both were hard to get durin' and since the war and were awful expensive. I liked this better anyway. The fabric was soft, and it hung in beautiful folds around me. The bodice was cut in the popular midriff bodice style that flatters any figure. Above the midriff, it attached to the upper bodice just below my breasts and was lightly gathered on both sides, addin' a little fullness to the otherwise fitted bodice. The upper front of the bodice was split; the halves overlapped in the front, creating a V-neckline, and Mamma had added a sparklin' beaded faux collar on the upper sides of the neckline. The skirt was attached at the waist with no gathers and was cut on the bias to give a flowin' drape to the skirt that was fitted at the top but wide and flowin' at the bottom around my feet, with a short train at the back.

Instead of a full-length veil, I wore a headpiece Mamma made from the same fabric as my dress. It was a very wide bandeau she had padded with quilt batting and covered in the same ivory fabric as my dress. She attached a short veil that just came down to the tip of my nose, called a birdcage veil. On the right side of the bandeau, Mamma had cut the fabric to have extra fullness, which she gathered at a point in the middle right of the bandeau, and attached a beautiful jeweled brooch that Granny had given as a gift.

My shoes were ivory mid-heeled pumps that, though very pretty, I had chosen for comfort because I would wear them many times over the next few years.

After I was completely dressed, Mamma stood back and looked me over to make sure there were no threads stickin' out or any other such flaws. There weren't. Mamma was one of the best seamstresses around.

She smiled at me, a soft, lovin' smile, and words weren't needed. I was wearin' the product of the love shinin' in her eyes. She loved me and was proud of me.

"You are lovely, Maggie," Mamma said, with a shimmer in her eyes.

"You are!" Rachel said brightly. "But my job is to get you to the church on time, so we had better be headin' that direction. The menfolk have gone ahead in the truck, and I have Daddy's car to take us to the church."

All of a sudden, I realized I had no wedding bouquet. Since I had always thought Robbie and I would marry while there were wildflowers in bloom, I hadn't planned for anything else. I was about to say something when Rachel tugged on my arm and Mamma gathered up her pocketbook and turned to go outside. I shrugged and thought, *oh well, too late now anyway*. And off we went.

We arrived at the church with ten minutes to spare, and Daddy and Granddad came over to the car to help me and Mamma out. Outside the car, Mamma was busily straightenin' my dress and makin' sure I was put together right when Granddad came up beside me, pullin' something out from behind him.

Granddad had driven into Boone that mornin' and had the florist make me a bridal bouquet. He handed it to me with a twinkle in his eyes.

"I figured this was one thing you clean forgot about," he laughed.

"I had until about fifteen minutes ago!" I laughed too.

The bouquet was everything I could imagine. Granddad, knowin' me as he does, had the florist use the wildflowers that could still be found bloomin' in our mountains in November: purple asters and ironweed, along with yellow goldenrod, and it had wild ferns tucked in here and there, with trailing arbutus spillin' down the front and sides. My wildflower bouquet.

Granddad harrumphed when I started to thank him, kissed my cheek, patted my back, and said, "Go put that poor boy out of his misery, Maggie."

So I did.

***

Later, after the good supper Mrs. Potts and Mrs. Reagan had made, Mamma told me there were a few gifts in the bedroom they were going to bring out for Robbie and me to open. So, Robbie and I cuddled up on the bench we had always sat on over the years. Robbie kept givin' me a look, with a slight nod toward the door. He was ready to go, but I held back, not wantin' to appear too obvious and invite the teasin' I knew would come later. Sittin' on the bench cuddled under his arm, I started wishin' I had just risked the teasin' and gone away with my love.

But when the gifts were brought out, I was very glad we hadn't. The first gift we unwrapped was from Charlie. He had saved his money and bought me a new KitchenAid stand mixer. Mamma had wanted one for years. It was a beautiful, cheery red, and I loved it.

Next were two laundry baskets filled with bed sheets, towels, washcloths, dish towels, and such. This was a thoughtful gift from my Mamma and Daddy.

Rachel laid a beautifully wrapped package in my lap, from her and her parents, that turned out to be a camera complete with ten rolls of film and a photo album.

Brother Reagan and his wife had already gone home after cleanin' up after supper but had left a card with twenty dollars in it.

The last gift was from Granny and Granddad. When I peeled away the paper from the soft, large package, I gasped. There lay the unbelievably intricate and beautiful double wedding ring quilt Granny had been workin' on for at least two years.

Sittin' there, I smoothed my hand over the surface of that quilt, recognizin' fabrics that had been from dresses and shirts both Mamma and Granny had sewn for me, Gerry, and Charlie over the years. There was the flour sack, white with little blue anchors on it, that had been a shirt Gerry had worn. Little bits of memories, little pieces of the childhood I had been privileged to have. I saw bits of the red print flour sack, scraps left from makin' the dress I had been wearin' the day Robbie had clobbered me upside the head with a rock when we were children. I touched it and looked up at Robbie. He was laughin'. Shared memories. And they were precious. Every one.

I looked up at them all, swallowin' hard to try to hold back the tears threatenin' to burst forth. My emotions were so strong that they spilled over onto everyone else. Without a word, they understood because they felt it too.

"Thank you," I whispered.

***

Robbie and I drove around the corner. The drive to Granny and Granddad's old homeplace almost met up with the entrance to Mamma and Daddy's, but angled away, givin' a little distance between the houses. The driveway, now our driveway, curved around the opposite side of the hill that lay between the two houses, giving each privacy. If you hollered loud enough, you could hear but not see each other. It was perfect.

Robbie hopped out of the truck and ran around to open my door. Until Robbie became sick, he always opened the door for me. He always showed me respect as well as love. And when we got to the door, my handsome soldier husband scooped me up in his strong arms and carried me over the threshold.

Mamma and Granny had made things as nice as possible in the living room. There wasn't much in it yet, but that was okay; we had a lifetime to fix that. Robbie took off his military coat and hung it on the coat tree that stood behind the door, topping it with his hat. I had asked Robbie to wear his dress uniform one more time for our wedding, and he was as handsome as handsome gets.

I suddenly felt shy. Nervous. I was unsure how to be now that we were alone, truly alone. Always before, I was saucy with Robbie, teasin', and a bit flirtatious. Now...

Robbie cupped my face in his large, warm hands, tiltin' my face upward toward his, and kissed me softly. This was very different from the kiss we shared in the church and the four or five pecks he had given me durin' our wedding supper and gift openin'. This was warm and searchin'. He raised his head a bit and looked into my eyes, and I saw in his eyes what every woman wants to see in her man's eyes love, certainly love, but desire too.

He kissed me again, deeper, and pulled me tighter against him. My head swam with the heady feelin' his kisses and nearness gave me. I had never been kissed before today, and Robbie's kisses were like firewater.

Robbie pulled me gently toward the bedroom door that was open on the far side of the living room, and on weak, rubbery legs, I allowed him to guide me through the door. Granny had left her old vintage lamp on the bedside table that, because of the flowers painted on the upper and lower globes, gave off a soft pink light. The bed had been made up with fresh new sheets and topped with a light blanket and a quilt that had all been turned down.

Again, Robbie pulled me in tightly against him, kissin' me deeply, and his hands reached up and slid the bandeau from my head, releasing my hair to fall around my shoulders. He threaded his fingers through my hair and kissed me again. And the rest... is nobody's business!

Chapter Thirty Four

Robbie took me on our honeymoon to the coastal town of Charleston, South Carolina. My goodness, what a pretty town, with such old and beautiful houses. The weather was so much nicer than it had been at home, and we enjoyed a week of walkin' the sandy beaches, the older section of town, and The Battery. Robbie was right, I sure did love the ocean. There is somethin' hypnotic about the waves rollin' ashore, with seagulls trying to steal our snacks. But I wonder if I would have liked it so much if I wasn't seein' it with him.

Robbie and I had a happy life together. Oh, I'm not sayin' that he was perfect. I sure wasn't. But it was a happy life, and a good one. He had a lot of patience with the temper I had back in my younger years. Life lessons the Lord sends you have a way of trimmin' down the parts of your makeup that aren't Christ-like. It took years, but the person I was, who could get so angry and blow up, it's like she is dead. Robbie didn't have as many faults as I did, but the older he got, the more like Jesus he became. There wasn't anyone as kind or understandin' as my Robbie, or as handsome either.

We renovated Granddad and Granny's old homeplace, makin' it truly ours, adding a whole section on one side that was also two stories, giving us a total of five bedrooms and two bathrooms. Robbie made sure I had the kitchen I wanted, and I was proud of my home.

We had four of the most beautiful children you ever saw. Our oldest child was a son. I recall when he was born, I cried and cried, sayin' over and over, "He's so beautiful!" Robbie had looked at me like I had rocks in my head and later confessed he hadn't seen any such beauty. He said Sean was squashed, blue and red, and covered in blood. I was shocked, because I hadn't seen any of that.

Sean is grown, with children and grandchildren of his own, and made from the same solid qualities his father was made of. He has the same love for the outdoors. He's a fine Christian man that I am proud of. Proud to call him my son. Robbie would have been very proud of him too.

Our second born was another son, Brian. Like Robbie, he loves to be out in nature and doesn't like bein' around crowds of people. When he was a little shaver, he used to sit out in the blackberry patch behind the house at night to watch the foxes and owls. One day, after I had been watchin' him as he looked out over the mountains, he came inside, crawled up in my lap, wrapped his little arms around my neck, and said, "Mamma, I love you bigger than the Appalachian Mountains!" I felt very loved. Brian too has grown children, and now grandchildren, and a fine man to make any mamma proud.

My third was a little tiny baby girl. Robbie named her Kimberly, and though she is a grown woman and a grandmother to boot, she is Kimmie to the family. There's no way to describe my Kimmie. She is a tiny little thing, but a very spunky, tiny thing. Always was and always will be. And a redhead to boot. She is one of the most loving and giving persons I know. I'm very proud of my Kimmie. She was her daddy's darlin'.

And then there was our baby, another little girl we named Kristen. I thought we were finished havin' babies when Robbie came in one day with a funny look on his face. He had never been one to offhand say, "The Lord told me" this or that. But on this certain day, Robbie came into the kitchen where I was cookin' supper, with a funny look on his face. Slowly and hesitantly, he said, "The Lord told me it is time to have another little girl." I was stunned. It was so unlike him to say something like that at all. Well, we had that little girl, and she held her daddy's heart in her tiny hands. Still does she just can't see that.

We didn't have much, but we had enough. And enough was plenty. You only get one life, and it goes faster than you think.

We lost Robbie when he was only forty-three years old, after a thirteen-month fight with a brain tumor. I don't guess I will ever know or understand all that until the day I stand before the Lord and He explains all the whys of it. But Robbie didn't question the Lord, and so I have tried not to. God knows all things and knows the end as though it were the beginning. I surely don't have that knowledge, so I have placed my trust in knowin' that He is a good and lovin' God.

Instead of dwellin' on my loss, I think of all I have had. A man I was privileged to grow up with and know from the inside out. He was a man of such integrity and Godliness that I could look to him and trust his leadership in our family. I had many years to be cherished by him and bear his children. He was a quiet man who loved much more fiercely than what showed on the surface. And bein' held in his arms never lost its magic.

I have had the most wondrous experience of bein' the mother of our four children. Outside of bein' first a daughter of the Most High God and the wife of the best man who ever walked the Lord's green earth, the next best thing was bein' my children's mother.

I had the experience of bein' reared in a happy, lovin' home. I had parents who loved me and cared deeply about me. I had Godly grandparents who I was privileged to have well into my adult life.

I had dear friends over the years. I have only mentioned two of them, but there have been many who have made my long life rich. People I have lived among, worked with, gone to church with, and worshiped God beside. They were like the hands who held up Moses' tired arms at the crossin' of the Red Sea after Robbie passed away, and even through the months of his illness.

Oh yes, I have had a blessed life, and the Lord has given me so much more than I even know.

The day we buried Robbie, a piper played the pipes from a hill not far from the cemetery. I never knew who played those pipes that day, for old Mr. Mitchell was long since passed away. But *Amazing Grace* had never sounded sweeter, and it was a fitting tribute to my Robbie.

We worked side by side for many years, buildin' the Deep Gap Egg and Poultry into a well-established family business that employed many in the area over the years it was going. Robbie had the terrifyin' nightmares the rest of his life. They did become more infrequent as time went on, but they never lost their ability to haunt my sweet Robbie and would leave him shaken and drenched with sweat.

Granddad Spencer worked with us until, at eighty-eight, he passed away suddenly of a heart attack. "I want to drop in the harness" was what he always said, and that is exactly what he did. But he had a very full life and lived every day with a passion that rubbed off on others around him.

I was forty-one when he passed, so I had the benefit of having him a good long while. It was his influence and instruction that gave me the foundation for my own Christian walk. His influence didn't end when I was grown but continued until his death, and even beyond.

And his legacy continues through my children. For all the stories he told to his grand-young'uns over the years, I have passed on to mine. And I trust that mine will pass them on to theirs the stories of Scotland, and our ancestors who braved hardship and the unknown to come to a new country and build a life in a new land.

Stories of their struggles not only with their humanity but also with God. About how, in their surrender, they found victory. For there is no greater foe to overcome than oneself. This was Granddad's true legacy.

I'm ninety-two, and I still have my quilts tucked away in the oak and cedar chest he made for me the Christmas of 1944.

Granny, too, lived a long life. She was the livin' example of a godly wife, mother, and Christian woman. She made enough quilts in her long life that every single family member has at least one. Beside the beautiful double wedding ring quilt she made for mine and Robbie's wedding gift, I have three others.

Mamma and Daddy died in a car crash several years back. Daddy's eyesight had gotten bad, but he wouldn't give up drivin' though we begged him to. He crashed into a tree that was close by the edge of the road one night. It was thought that he had missed his turn, and while lookin' in his rearview mirror, swerved, hitting the tree. My Daddy was as solid as they come, a good man who only got better after he gave his life over to the Lord. As hard as it was for me and Charlie, and my children, it was fitting that they went together. For if Mamma had passed before him, I don't know what Daddy would have done without "his little honeypot".

Charlie also married but moved to Charlotte, North Carolina, after he attended college at Appalachian State University in Boone. He married a nice girl he went to school with and had two children and five grandchildren. You never think you will outlive a baby sibling, but Charlie passed away two years ago with the same heart ailment our Granddad had.

Jamie had returned to Deep Gap followin' his discharge from the Army in October, the month before Robbie came home. He was restless and couldn't settle, and the next summer he returned to France, where he wandered from battlefield to battlefield, grievin' over lost friends and comrades. He finally met a young French woman who soothed his injured spirit and wound up marryin' her; and spent the rest of his life in France.

My dearest friend Rachel married George a year after Robbie and I married. George came home besotted with her, and Rachel, fond of him from their letter writtin', fell in love very soon after seeing him in person. As two couples, we remained very close our whole lives, and now our children are friends.

I never did know what became of Tillie Macpherson. After she married Harry Duff and moved to Raleigh, Mrs. Macpherson talked Mr. Macpherson into sellin' the store and movin' to be near Tillie. Granddad actually thought about buyin' the store and running it himself, but Granny changed his mind. Instead, George bought it not long after comin' home, and he and Rachel ran it together, turning it into one of the best stores in the area. Of all the changes they made, they never changed the soda machine on the front porch that served out the coldest drinks there ever was.

I would like to think that Tillie had matured and become a nicer person. I hope that she found the Lord and changed inside, as the Lord had changed me. I'm grateful to the Lord that He created in me a new heart, one that could forgive and love.

Robbie loved to hear me sing. I don't think it was because I was much of a singer, but because he loved me and liked to hear my voice. He would often beg me to sing the song I sang to calm the hens so many long years ago.

Sometimes, sittin' on this porch, I still sing it, and I have to confess, it makes my heart ache. Because even though I am an old, white-headed woman, and my voice cracks and breaks with age, in my heart, I am a young red-headed girl, and I'm singin' to my handsome lad.

Roses love sunshine, violets love dew

Angels in heaven know I love you

Know I love you, dear, know I love you

Angels in heaven know I love you.